*To Dorbert Ogle—a truly special friend.
This one is for you.*

Chapter 1

June 1772

Holding her feathered mask to her face, Portia glanced at the various doors around the ballroom, going over in her mind the plan of the North End mansion. She had paid good money to get the correct layout of the house. She touched the locket she wore about her neck and hoped now that the information was correct.

Portia knew the masquerade ball held at the elegant house on Copp's Hill to honor the King's Birthday was the only opportunity she would have. Admiral Middleton almost never entertained, so when else would she be able to gain access to the grounds? Her mother had been locked away for twenty-four long years, and Portia was determined to free her tonight.

As it was, the guest list included only the most elite members of Boston's Tory society, and even included the governor. Of course, no invitation addressed to any Portia Edwards had arrived at the door of Parson Higgins and his wife's home, where Portia was living, but she had forgiven the Admiral the oversight. She had simply lied to a dear friend and deceived people who considered her part of their family. She didn't have any choice, though. It had to be tonight.

"You are very quiet this evening, my pet."

My pet. My pet. Portia tried to not lose her patience at Captain Turner's condescending expression. She turned to the officer. As before, he was standing stiffly over her and leaning forward as he spoke. The gown she had borrowed from Bella was far too tight, and the corset's whalebone stays were certain to leave permanent marks in her flesh. Portia had caught him staring at her breasts a half-dozen times already, and she lowered her mask to cover the revealing front of the gown. The officer looked into her face, and she pasted on a smile.

Captain Turner, a second cousin to her young friend Bella, had been the means for Portia to get into the mansion. Now, however, she was having some difficulty ridding herself of him.

"I am simply *numb* with excitement." Portia raised the mask again to her face and looked around the paneled ballroom in search of a distraction for her companion. The notes of the minuet rose and fell as the other guests paraded about. There were far fewer women than men, though it appeared that some of Boston's less elite Tory families had also sent their daughters. "I do wish you would not feel obligated to remain at my side, Captain. I should hate to make enemies with all these lovely ladies by keeping you to myself."

"Nonsense, my pet. I would not dare ruin your opinion of me by neglecting you. You know that I have been waiting upon you for months . . . and to no avail, I might add."

"But Captain, I have been in the colonies for little more than eight months."

"And I have been your devoted servant since first seeing you after Reverend Higgins's inaugural sermon. You cannot know how delighted I was at my good fortune when my young cousin was introduced to you the following Sunday."

"The good fortune was mine, but—"

"To be honest," he interrupted, "after we met a month later, and then you refused to answer any of my letters,

I was about ready to give up hope. I do not need to tell you, therefore, how thrilled I was when my lovely cousin sent me word that you had finally agreed to allow me to call upon you. And when you consented to accompany me here . . . ah, what delight! And now you suppose that I would step away from the glow of your loveliness?"

Captain Turner continued to speak, and Portia lowered the mask, glancing with disbelief at the officer, whose eyes were again fixed on her breasts. He was a man in his forties, she judged, and though he had apparently been powerfully built in his youth, his physique was now beginning to decline into the softness of middle age. Still, she had underestimated the captain's ardent interest in her.

"Warm, is it not?" she interrupted. "Would you be kind enough to get me something to drink, Captain?"

Her escort bowed, only to turn as a passing servant appeared carrying a tray filled with cups of punch. Portia silently cursed her luck and, with a weak smile, accepted one. When the captain again started with his lean, she glanced desperately about the room.

"I have never had such an opportunity to see so many distinguished people. The military men look so dashing in their finery."

"I should be happy to introduce you to any of them, along with their wives," Turner offered jovially. "We have some particularly fine men serving His Majesty here in Boston, and their wives would be delighted to meet you, I am sure. Whom specifically would you care to meet?"

She looked about for some guest far from where they were standing. She had no difficulty finding one. Leaning with a haughty air against a column near the door stood a man whose black scowl matched his dark attire.

"That gentleman . . ." She motioned with the mask. "I do not believe I have ever seen him."

"I should be surprised if you had met him, my pet." Turner's nose climbed an inch in the air in obvious dis-

taste. "That is Pierce Pennington, a brother to the Earl of Aytoun. An old family, but a scoundrel of a Scot, to be sure. This past year, since coming to Boston, he has been making a name for himself in finance and shipping."

"Is this not a difficult time to be establishing oneself in such pursuits," Portia asked, "considering the townspeople's refusal to pay the tax for English goods?"

"Not if one lacks a certain . . . well, a certain respect for His Majesty's laws of trade."

"Do you mean he deals with smugglers?"

"I mean no such thing, officially. But we shall soon enough identify the key malefactors who are enriching themselves at the Crown's expense . . . and put an end to that nonsense." Turner's gaze remained fixed on Pennington. "There are many things about that gentleman that I do not understand. But then again, my superiors consider him completely loyal to the king, and safely above assisting these troublesome colonists. In fact, Pennington's younger brother is an officer in the army and has a fine reputation, by all accounts."

"You make Mr. Pennington sound all the more interesting, Captain."

"You cannot be serious, Miss Edwards."

"Indeed I am." The sound of carriages and riders from the courtyard signaled the promised arrival of the governor and his entourage. Portia knew he never traveled anywhere now without an armed military escort. She put on her sweetest smile. "I know I am safe with you, Captain. Would you kindly beg an introduction of the gentleman?"

"Of all the fine persons in the room, my pet, I do not understand why you should be so determined to meet this . . . this Scot."

"If you please," she asked. "You know that Parson Higgins's wife is of Scottish ancestry. I should so like to tell her that you took the pains to introduce me to a distinguished countryman of hers."

"Distinguished!" he scoffed, casting a sour glance at the distance that he would need to walk. "If you must, then why not come with me and—"

"No, I cannot," she said, hiding her face once again behind the mask. "I could never allow the rumor to spring up that I was discontent with spending time in your company, Captain. You are far better acquainted with the rules of society than I, but I should think that if you and Mr. Pennington were to approach me, there could be no reason for gossip."

Giving the captain a gentle push in the direction of the man, Portia waited only a moment. As soon as Turner had moved away into the crowd, she slowly backed up. Floor-length windows stood open behind her, and in an instant she was crossing the flagstones of a terrace and running down steps into the moonlit gardens below.

Portia was thankful to find the gardens still empty of guests. If her information was correct, her mother was being kept in a suite of rooms on the second floor facing the rose gardens. The only way to reach her, without going through the house and being seen, was by way of a low balcony off her bedroom.

Raising the skirts of the gown, Portia ran along welltended paths bordered by boxwood and flower beds and soon found her way into the rose gardens. She immediately spotted the balcony, situated above a small pear tree and flanked by sturdy rose trellises. It was just as it had been described to her, and she quickly climbed a small embankment to the house.

Portia Edwards had spent the entire twenty-four years of her life blithely ignorant of her origins. Raised in an orphanage school in Wrexham in Wales, at the age of sixteen she joined the family of Parson Higgins and his wife. In all her life, she had never doubted the stories of her parentage that Lady Primrose, the most generous benefactor and the founder of the orphanage, had told her since childhood. Her mother had died in childbirth

and her father, a high-ranking Jacobite supporter, had died sometime after Culloden during the long years of exile in France. Though she had often imagined longingly what it would be like to have a family, she had none.

Then, about a month ago, her eyes had been opened and a childhood of wishing for the impossible suddenly appeared within her reach. When Mary, the parson's wife, had come down with a cold, Dr. Deming had paid a visit to the house in the lane off Sudbury Street. The physician, admiring Portia's necklace, had recognized the miniature portrait of the woman inside the locket. From that moment on, Portia had not rested until she had found out everything she could about Helena Middleton.

Portia touched the locket at her throat and started climbing the trellis. The narrow balcony served more for the sake of looks than function, for there was not even room to stand inside the railing. The windows had been closed in spite of the warm evening. Realizing that she still had her mask in one hand, Portia laid it on the railing and tried to peer in. Unable to see, she held on to the trellis tightly with one hand and leaned closer, disappointed to find the curtains drawn, as well.

It was rumored far and wide that Admiral Middleton's daughter Helena was mad and this was the reason why she was held in seclusion. In searching out information about the family, Portia had continually heard praise for the old man's compassion and devoted care of his daughter. Portia guessed at the truth. If her father were a Jacobite, then Helena's affair would have been a tremendous disgrace to a trusted Crown official. But was this reason enough to lock a daughter away for more than two decades?

Portia tapped softly on the window. She understood that she had mere seconds to try to explain all of this to her mother. Their resemblance was hardly perceptible. In fact, it was not beyond reason to imagine that Helena might be completely ignorant of her daughter's survival. She tapped again and felt the worry form like a hot

ember in the pit of her stomach. As challenging as explaining their relationship might be, the more difficult task for Portia would be to convince Helena Middleton to escape this house with her.

The curtains pulled back sharply and the burning ember rose from Portia's stomach into her throat. The woman looked older than she had imagined. Touches of gray streaked her golden, waist-length hair. Her skin was pale and marred with dark shadows beneath the eyes. The resemblance to the miniature portrait, however, was unmistakable.

Helena was holding a candle in one hand. She wore nothing over the thin rail that she must have been sleeping in. As she opened the latch on the window, Portia realized that her mother had not yet seen her.

The rose trellis creaked perilously under her weight, and the young woman took hold of the balcony. She had been dreaming about this moment all her life, and now she could hardly breathe.

The window opened. Helena placed the candle on the windowsill and leaned out.

"Mother?" Portia whispered.

Silence enveloped them, and Portia saw the look of bewilderment turn to terror. Color drained completely from her mother's face. Portia reached out a hand and touched the other woman's arm, and Helena let out a scream loud enough to wake the dead.

Pierce Pennington watched as the royal governor and his entourage entered the ballroom. Following the man's gaze as he swept into the chamber, Pierce noticed how Thomas Hutchinson quickly took note of everyone and everything in the room—very much like a herding dog sniffing the air around his flock for the scent of a wolf.

He returned the governor's nod when the older man looked his way. Hutchinson immediately turned his attention on their host as Admiral Middleton approached to greet him. A small string ensemble began to play a

Handel piece, and Pierce pushed away from the large column against which he had been leaning. He had made his requisite appearance. He started toward the large open doors leading to the gardens.

"Mr. Pennington, you are not leaving us so soon, are you?"

An officer had moved to block his path, and Pierce recognized him at once. A few years older than himself, Captain Turner was not distinguished by his physical presence, and at first glance, the man did not leave much of an impression on either friend or foe. Pierce sensed there was more to the man, though, for he had evidently served the Admiral well for many years. It was well known that the captain had Middleton's complete confidence.

"I was on my way to the gardens for some fresh air. Why do you ask, Captain?"

"A young lady of my acquaintance desires to be introduced, sir."

"To me, Captain? Don't tell me she has already tired of your company?"

"I think not, sir," Turner huffed. "She simply wishes to meet a Scot, and you, I believe, may be the only person here who fits the description."

"A lady of discriminating taste." Pierce glanced over the officer's shoulder at the sea of scarlet and blue coats, gold braid, fresh ruffles, hoop skirts, and feathered masks. High-ranking British military men and their women filled the room. "I see no one waiting on you, Captain."

"Is that so?" Turner looked over his shoulder. "She was right there a moment ago."

Pierce answered another nod from the governor and their host as the two men walked past them.

"Is she beautiful?" He turned his attention back to the officer.

"Quite so," the captain replied vaguely, his eyes scanning the ballroom.

"Young?"

"Indeed."

"Does she have a sense of humor?"

"I did not ask you to woo or court her, sir," Turner said, turning to him in annoyance. "A brief introduction will suffice, if you please."

"Then take me to her, Captain, if you think 'tis safe."

With a stiff bow, the officer led him in the direction of a refreshment table. This distraction was costing Pierce precious time. He cast a glance at the large stone terrace overlooking the gardens. By the courtyard entrance, he knew his groom Jack was waiting with the carriage.

Turner's course began to meander as he searched in vain for his escort. He finally stopped and glanced helplessly about the large ballroom. "I cannot imagine where she went."

"You probably frightened her off, Captain," Pierce replied, keeping his tone light. "Perhaps I shall have the good fortune of meeting this mysterious lady another time."

"As you wish, sir," Turner said, still looking.

As soon as Pierce moved toward the terrace doors, though, Turner was beside him.

"Perhaps she stepped out for air. She was just remarking on how warm it is."

With the officer still at his side, Pierce stopped on the empty terrace. Trying to appear unhurried, he looked out at the spires and rooflines of Charlestown across the moonlit river to the north and at the masts of ships in the harbor to the east.

"Your elusive maiden is not out here," he commented, breathing in the smells of the sea and freshly cut hay that mingled with the scent of roses in bloom. "Perhaps you should take another look in the ballroom."

"Indeed . . . perhaps . . ."

Turner's indecisiveness irked Pierce. " 'Tis best if you go inside and ask a few of the other guests. A young and beautiful woman unescorted in a ballroom draws attention, Captain."

"Indeed, sir. My apologies." Without another word, the officer bowed and disappeared inside.

With a practiced air of leisure, Pierce casually made his way down the stairs and along the brick pathways through a small orchard. Although the guests were eagerly showing off their wit and clothes to their peers and their betters, there was no saying that some of them would not venture out onto the terrace. He did not want anyone to see him leaving.

Beyond a cherry tree, the path led toward the stable yards. He paused to cast a final glance toward the house. No one was on the terrace. All was calm.

Then, as he turned to go, a scream cut through the night.

This was clearly not the time to explain anything. At the sound of her mother's response, Portia nearly lost her grip on the railing.

When Helena staggered back from the window, Portia tried to regain her footing on the trellis. As quickly as she dared, she began her descent. All around her, it sounded as if the household had come alive. The barking of dogs in the kennels followed Helena's scream, and shouts of running servants could be heard through the open window.

Halfway down, Portia's dress caught on some thorns. Trying to disengage it, she felt the trellis begin to come away from the house. She had no choice. Tearing the dress free, she jumped, grabbing at a branch of the pear tree as she fell.

As she dropped onto the soft ground, she was aware of her dress tearing and the laces of the corset snapping. Leaves and branches showered down on her, but she couldn't stop to worry about any of it. Quickly she struggled to her feet and started running from the window and the commotion taking place in the chamber above. Crossing the rose garden, she spied an arched opening leading out and turned her steps toward it. Then, as Por-

tia looked back at the house one last time, she collided with a tall and very solid body suddenly blocking the archway. Stunned, she fell back, but a pair of strong hands grasped her shoulders.

Portia looked up in panic, expecting one of the Admiral's servants. Instead, she was relieved to find her captor was the Scotsman she had sent Captain Turner after. Shouts of "Thief!" and "Housebreaker!" rang out in the darkness.

" 'Tis not what you think!" she exclaimed, already knowing that she could not reveal the truth if she ever wanted to come back here to carry her plans through.

"And what do I think?"

"I am no thief." She tried to move away, but the man's hand wrapped tightly around her wrist. She could hear the loud voices of servants coming across the rose garden. "They are mistaken. I was only walking in the gardens. I . . . I must have frightened a lady looking out her window."

"It must have been an arduous walk."

Portia winced when his free hand touched her cheek. She had scratched herself in the fall. He pulled a twig with leaves still attached to it from her hair.

The pursuers were almost upon them. She tugged on his arm and tried to hide in the shadows of the garden wall. Being caught would prove disastrous, she was sure. Admiral Middleton was vicious enough to lock his own daughter away, and Portia did not want to think of what he would do to her if he guessed the relationship between them.

"I came here as a guest. 'Twas too warm in the ballroom. I needed to come outside for a walk." Panic seized her. If he held her for another instant, she would be lost. "Please, you must help me. It will be impossible to try to explain this to them."

"I agree. You are having difficulty explaining it to me."

"Mr. Pennington," she pleaded, "I beg you to believe

me. I am no thief. Where I was and what I was trying to do is perfectly justifiable and explainable to a rational person . . . but not to a pursuing mob. If you would help me get out of here . . ."

"There!" The shout was nearby. "Someone is *there!*"

Portia glanced over her shoulder and saw men approaching. Several had torches. She shrank against him.

"Please," she whispered against his chest.

He pulled her wrist sharply, forcing her to his side as he called out. "Over here."

Chapter 2

The servants' shouts rang out in the adjoining room and then beneath her in the gardens. Helena shrank back against the heavy curtains at the sound of the latch lifting on her door. She looked toward the balcony. The single candle on the windowsill was just a flickering glow, a dying point of light in the sea of darkness that each day claimed a little more of her vision.

She was losing her mind. The dream world was now taking over her waking hours.

The doctors had warned her. They had lectured her about the delusions that she would experience. No matter that they seemed so material, so real, they were only creations of her disturbed mind. They had told her that the medicines would help her sleep, but she must be steadfast in taking them. Religious.

She didn't trust them. She questioned their motives as well as their quackery. She felt more ill with every dose of their poisonous concoctions. But against her better judgment, and out of desperation, she occasionally submitted to their combined will.

Now, however, Helena did not know if the young woman tonight had been real or if it had simply been her mind playing tricks on her.

Mother, the young voice had said. *Mother.*

But she was not a mother. No living creature had ever called her by that name. Her own poor baby had not

lived long enough. Helena touched her arm where she had felt the woman's fingers. This all had been a deception, an illusion created in her mind.

The door opened. The sound of footsteps came across the room. Blurred shapes carrying candles surrounded her.

"Miss Helena?"

She accepted the wrap a young servant placed around her shoulders. She shivered involuntarily, though, when she heard Mrs. Green's heavy steps in the bedchamber.

"Was someone in here?"

"No," Helena whispered.

"Did someone try to break into your room?"

"No one."

"Then why did you scream?"

"I . . . I had a bad dream." She inched toward the window. The balmy night air was soothing against her skin, like the soft touch of the young woman. *Mother,* she had said.

"Practically everyone in the mansion heard your call, ma'am. You have disrupted the party. The guests are upset and the Admiral is quite displeased. You didn't take the medicine tonight, did you, Miss Helena?"

She turned her back on Mrs. Green's implied reprimand and her question. She certainly did drink the bitter potion. She *was* sleeping when she heard the knock on the window. If her eyes had only allowed her to see a face to go with the voice.

Servants moved about the room. Someone leaned over the balcony and called to the ones below. Mrs. Green continued to upbraid her, though Helena ignored her. She reached along the windowsill until her fingers grasped the candleholder.

"I do not know why you insist on keeping a candle lit at night," the housekeeper said bitterly, taking the light from her and moving toward the mantle. "Just a waste of the Admiral's money."

A young servant pushed something into Helena's hands. "Did you drop this, milady?"

She felt the texture of the item—velvet, feathers, the outline of the eyes and nose. Her fingers told her it was a woman's mask, but Helena didn't dare bring it to her face where she could have a better look.

"Yes, I did," she said softly, hearing Mrs. Green coming back. Without another word, Helena tucked the mask beneath her wrap.

The kick to his shin was vicious and unexpected. Pierce uttered a curse as his grip loosened enough for the minx to slip his hold. In the next second she'd disappeared into the darkness of the trees.

He didn't bother to watch where she was going. He simply wasn't interested in the little she-devil. He certainly couldn't care less why she was running, what she'd been caught doing, or how it was that she knew his name. A vague connection formed in his mind about the young woman that Captain Turner had been looking for earlier. If this were the one, she'd do well to run.

Although Pierce had called to the mob, he had intended to say a few words in her defense, perhaps even serve as her alibi. Time was running short now, though, and he had far more important business at the waterfront.

When a number of servants reached him, Pierce pointed in a different direction from the way the woman had gone. As the group rushed off, he worked his way though the gardens toward the stable yards.

News of a possible burglary was already circulating among the grooms. They huddled in groups among the carriages in the crowded yard. Torches illuminated the faces of the bewigged men in livery as they turned to glance at him. Two carriages that had just dropped late-arriving guests at the front door came down the gravel drive, blocking in the rest. Down the path a bit, Pierce

spied his own chaise where he had instructed that it be
kept waiting. As he started toward it, he saw his man
Jack leave some of the other grooms and break into a
trot to catch up with him.

"Ye did a fine job, sir, starting such a commotion in
there," Jack muttered as he came up.

"I take no credit for it."

Pierce steered the groom into the shadows of some
trees as four army officers riding up the drive toward the
front door of the mansion stopped by a line of apple
trees. The men were loud and obviously drunk.

Pierce spoke quietly. "Did you learn anything
worthwhile . . . before all the ruckus began?"

"Aye, sir. The talk here was mostly about the regi-
ments mustering upon the Common this morn. They've
taken note that there weren't too many of the local folk
coming out to watch. Even the exercise and fire on King
Street near Colonel Marshal's place was hardly attended
at all, they say."

"Their disappointment has hardly stopped the ale from
running freely, from the looks of things. Any talk of
regimental activity?"

As the officers traded lewd barbs, two of them finished
relieving themselves against one of the fruit trees. Laughing loudly, they mounted their horses again and rode up
toward the front door of the mansion.

"Nay." Jack lowered his voice further. "But I hear 'tis
all quiet on the waterfront."

"Good news." Pierce gave a final glance at the disappearing group before starting toward his chaise. "But
we're running late."

"We'll get ye there on time, sir."

She shot out of a line of trees like a flying apparition,
and Pierce stared incredulously as she darted a look at
him before scrambling into his open chaise.

"Not if we are traveling on foot," he growled in disbelief. The white evening gown, dark curls flying around a

pixie's face—it was the same woman who had permanently dented his shin only minutes before.

"By the devil . . . wait!" he shouted just as she snapped the reins. The horses took off like a shot down the drive.

With Jack muttering surprised curses, Pierce ran for the carriage as fast as his legs would take him.

Portia heard the man's angry shouts. It was just her luck that of all the carriages in the courtyard, his would be the one that she came upon first. She glanced over her shoulder. The man was still chasing her on foot, and she pushed the horses to go faster.

As she looked ahead down the torch-lined drive, she saw another carriage coming full-tilt toward her. She stared at the narrow bridge over a gully separating them. They would both reach it about the same time.

"Rein in, woman. Halt, there!"

She ignored the shouts from behind her. The Scotsman had been deaf to her explanations and was ready to hand her over to the Admiral's servants. And that was when she'd merely been *suspected* of some wrongdoing. She was certain that he would kill her now with his bare hands for stealing his chaise.

She was almost to the bridge and so was the oncoming carriage. Urging the horses on, Portia focused on the open gates of the mansion and the burning torches in the distance.

The oncoming driver appeared to be in as much of a rush to arrive as she was to leave. He also appeared to be of no mind to give way to her. Unfortunately, the other carriage managed to make it to the bridge first.

Portia could hear Pennington's shouts behind her, but she had no choice. Yanking the heads of the horses to the right at the last minute, she tried to go down the grassy embankment and pass through the gully. The spir-

ited animals, however, balked at her sudden change of plans and reared up at the edge of the gravel drive.

Portia barely kept her seat as the chaise skidded to an abrupt stop on the edge of the grass. The driver and the groom of the other carriage shouted in triumph as they barreled past. She pulled at the reins, clucking at the horses to move back onto the drive.

The little disaster tonight had not deterred her at all. She had to get herself clear of the grounds, but then she would try to return to the mansion and see her mother again—and again. She had to.

Before she could get the carriage onto the bridge, though, an angry and breathless rogue pounced on her, snatching the reins from her hands as he clambered into the chaise.

Pierce was angry enough to kill her, and he made sure his glare showed it. Instead of running for her life, though, the daft woman simply moved to the farthest end of the seat and sat with her hands entwined in her lap, looking like she was ready to be driven to Sunday services.

As Pierce searched for the words to lambaste her, however, Jack caught up to them and moved to the front of the chaise to calm the agitated horses.

"I do not care what reason you might have for behaving like a bloody lunatic," Pierce finally spit out. "But you will step out of my carriage this minute, madam."

"I am afraid I cannot," she said calmly before sliding across the seat toward him.

Pierce held his tongue when he realized the reason for her action. A red-coated member of the Admiral's staff and several of his grooms—one holding a lantern—ran up to the chaise.

"Anyone hurt, sir?" the man asked, peering at them. "That was a near miss on the bridge."

The woman shrank into Pierce's shadow and with both hands clutched desperately to his arm.

Well aware of the noose that would fit snugly around her pretty neck, Pierce was still sorely tempted to hand her over to Middleton's men. The minx was damned lucky, though, that he was not one easily swayed by temptation.

"No. No one is hurt," he growled.

"I saw ye running after the chaise. Were the horses spooked, sir?"

Pierce refrained from telling him to mind his own bloody business. " 'Twas my companion, if you really must know. The lady was offended that I left her alone in the ballroom for a minute too long. She decided to leave without me."

The young officer chuckled and tried to get a better look at her. Pierce felt the woman move more tightly against him as she attempted to hide her disordered appearance. The darkness worked to her advantage.

"Well, with Governor Hutchinson having just arrived, the night is only starting," the man grinned meaningfully. "Plenty of time to win back her affection."

Pierce placed a hand on the woman's knee and, feeling her entire body tense, he smiled with satisfaction.

"I think not." He pressed his leg against hers intimately. "From experience I know that there is only one way to regain *this* lady's affection, soldier, and privacy is called for, if you get my meaning. So if you'll forgive us, we'll be off."

The man's laughter filled the air as he stepped away from the chaise. Without another word, Pierce started the horses down the drive as Jack swung up into his place behind them.

Pierce thought about the rendezvous that lay ahead of him tonight. The meeting was dependent on the tide. The span of time that his client could wait at the waterfront for him was narrow. Already this woman may have detained him too long.

She slid to the farthest edge of the seat as soon as they passed through the gate. "That was quite ungentlemanly of you, sir, to suggest an improper liaison between us."

"On the contrary, madam. I thought it was quite generous *and* gentlemanly of me not to hand you over to them directly."

"And why didn't you?"

He gave her a narrow stare. Leaves and twigs were tangled in the contraption of combs and pearls that were barely holding up her dark curls. Large intelligent eyes returned his gaze. Pierce looked openly at the dirt-stained and torn white gown, letting his gaze linger on the exposed tops of her breasts. A silver locket nestled in the generous cleavage.

"The punishment for your crimes tonight would not have fallen short of hanging. But looking the way you do, madam, and thinking of the jailors who would be more than happy to make your acquaintance, I can only imagine that your day on the gallows would not come soon enough for your liking."

"You're assuming that I have committed some crime," she replied. "If you were more considerate and gallant, you would have heard my explanation earlier in the garden. Then, sir, you would know that other than falling victim to a series of unfortunate accidents, I am . . . well, almost entirely innocent of everything that took place at that mansion."

"Almost entirely innocent. What curious phrasing! But do you call kicking me hard enough to hobble me permanently an accident?" he challenged. "And does an innocent woman run about in the gardens like some she-devil, stealing carriages?"

"You deserved the first attack because I was forced to protect myself. As for taking your carriage, survival dictated my actions."

Pierce stared incredulously at the stubborn woman. No fear, no remorse, no further explanations. They were passing North Church, and she leaned back against the seat and looked up at the towering steeple.

"There's still time for me to turn around and take you back."

She directed at him a look of disbelief. "We both know that you will do no such thing."

"And why is that?"

A bump in the road jarred her in the seat and she fell against him. She quickly slid back to her side. The contraption holding her hair up on top of her head leaned precariously to one side.

She had no trouble, though, finding her voice. "You were obviously bored at the Admiral's party."

"I warrant we would not be bored if we were to return to the party."

"Perhaps not. My point is, however, that boredom is not reason enough for you to move into the gardens just as the governor arrived."

"I was in need of some fresh air."

"You and your groom were heading for your carriage." She shook her head. "There was a reason why you did not hand me over to the Admiral's man when you overtook me. You were leaving, and you could not afford any further delay."

She started pulling pins and combs out of her hair and removed what looked like a tiny pillow that served as the foundation for the mound of hair. She combed her fingers through the liberated mass of curls.

Pierce was momentarily distracted by the blanket of dark ringlets that tumbled around her shoulders. She smelled of roses and night air.

"How close am I to the truth, sir?"

"I doubt that you and the truth are close at all, madam."

"Admit it, Mr. Pennington. You are late for an important appointment. You will not turn around and take me back."

He reined in the horses, bringing the chaise to a sudden stop. She was thrown forward, but without any assistance she scrambled back into her seat.

"How do you know my name?"

"As I explained before, I was an invited guest at Admiral Middleton's ball."

"And your name is . . . ?"

She hesitated.

"Your name, madam," he snapped, satisfied to see her flinch slightly.

"I am Portia Edwards, but that's all you need to know about me, sir." There was a note of caution in her voice. "And I do sympathize with you and the time constraints you must be facing. 'Twas certainly an imposition for me to expect—"

"What would be your recommendation as to the most expedient way of ridding myself of your company, Miss Edwards?" Pierce knew he was being rude, but he was beyond caring.

"Although I hesitate to recommend it, you might drop me off on the side of the road past Mill Creek, since I am really only in need of a ride out of the North End." She pushed the blanket of loose curls over one shoulder, and he had another view of the gown's tight bodice and low neckline. "There are obvious safety issues with that option, of course. If you're going anywhere near Dock Square, however, then it will save me the trouble of walking in the dark and being exposed to all types of dangers that a young woman—"

"Dock Square 'tis." He abruptly snapped the reins, urging the horses to a trot.

Houses and shops now lined the streets, with arched narrow alleys leading into inner courts. People still gathered on the streets and in the doorways on this holiday night, and children ran and danced around fires that had been built in lots that were clear of buildings. She was jostled when they bumped over a crossing pavement at one intersection, but to Pierce's great disappointment, she did not fall out of the chaise.

"So, Mr. Pennington, are you meeting with one of your smuggling associates tonight?"

He shot her a hard look and then forced out a laugh. "I certainly am not. But what could you possibly know of my associates or my business, madam?"

"Absolutely nothing. What I meant to ask was if you were making an illegal trade of some kind tonight."

Pierce studied her more closely. A stubborn chin, intelligent high forehead, direct gaze. She appeared of sound mind and obviously expected an answer.

"Are you accusing me of being a smuggler?"

"Not I, sir. I am simply repeating a rumor Captain Turner related to me. He suggested that you may be lacking a certain respect for His Majesty's laws of trade." She disengaged a leaf from the lace neckline of the dress and passed it on to the safekeeping of the wind.

"Do I understand that your friend, the captain, accuses me of breaking the law?"

"He did not do so in my presence. Of course, I did not converse with him in detail on that topic at the time, nor did I stay at the ball long enough to pursue it . . . should I have had any desire to." The dark eyes gazed at him intently. "But my question about where you might be going tonight is the product of my own simple reasoning. I mean, what better a night to engage in such activities, what with so many of the officers celebrating the King's Birthday."

"May I inquire what your relation with Captain Turner might be, Miss Edwards?"

"He is a second cousin of a friend."

"And you appear to be his confidante."

She irately tossed her head. "I was surprised to learn tonight that Captain Turner appreciates many things about me, sir, but I am quite certain that making me his confidante is not his primary objective."

Pierce followed the movement of her fingers as she tugged and pulled at another twig stuck in some lace that trimmed the bodice of the dress. The act was no doubt intended to draw his attention to the slim waist, to the

fullness of her breasts. He forced his thoughts away from the woman's physical charms as he focused on the situation.

She was too open with what she'd heard from the Admiral's officer to be much of a spy. If Turner were sly enough to go that route, though, Pierce realized that a damsel in distress—and a seemingly talkative one, at that—might be just the method the captain would use.

His own partner Nathaniel Muir had been warning him lately of Turner's cleverness and his influence within Admiral Middleton's ranks. No doubt the English officer would do anything to unmask the identity of the chief supplier of arms to the Sons of Liberty and the rebellious Bostonians, the elusive MacHeath.

"If I were a smuggler, Miss Edwards, perhaps my best course would be to murder you and throw your body into the Mill Pond or Back Bay." He gestured toward the expanse of black water of the tidal flats to their right.

"I hardly know you, but I believe you are a man who values his own neck enough to know that such an action would lead directly back to you."

"Considering the trouble you have already caused me, this might be worth the risk."

She gave him a look of scoffing disbelief before turning her attention back to the passing scenery. He let the subject drop.

During recent weeks, a number of men involved in shipping had been consulted and asked for their cooperation in discovering MacHeath. Neither Pierce nor Nathaniel had been approached, however, and this was a concern. As a result, he'd been looking for an opportunity to improve his image with the British administration on Boston. The last thing Pierce needed was to be the target of an investigation.

He watched Portia successfully remove the twig. Though women in the colonies followed far different codes of conduct than women in England, her outspokenness and lack of timidity were a clear signal that she

was no innocent. She'd gone to the ball with a seasoned officer, and whether by accident or not, she had climbed into the carriage of a total stranger with no hesitation. He let his gaze wander over her once more. Indeed, she was certainly not difficult to look at.

No, Portia Edwards was simply far too attractive an opportunity to pass on.

Chapter 3

Though Portia had been in Boston only since last fall, she was familiar enough with the city to know the carriage's turn to the left was taking them off the route to Dock Square. She glanced over at her silent companion.

"Is there someplace more convenient for you to drop me, sir, than Dock Square?"

"No, I shall get you there. First, though, I need to stop by a tavern I know—the Black Pearl—and make sure a certain lady friend who was to meet me has not yet arrived."

Portia studied the man with new interest. On the positive side, he was tall with broad shoulders and dark brooding features. She really did not want to look too closely at him, however, for fear of finding him too attractive. On the other hand, with the exception of a few moments when she'd been pressed against his hard body, she'd had to keep her distance from him at the risk of having her head bitten off. She had just assumed his plans tonight revolved around business, not something of a personal nature.

"I do not believe I have ever been to the Black Pearl."

"I should be surprised if you had been there."

"And why is that?"

"The place caters to a certain type of clientele."

"Only men?"

"And only a certain *type* of women."

"But you are meeting a lady friend."

"A woman that I would not take to Admiral Middleton's ball." His gaze traveled down the front of her dress. "The type of woman I hinted you were as we took our leave back there."

She shifted in the seat, suddenly uncomfortable with the image. Parson Higgins and his wife were well known and respected among many families in the city. As their live-in charge and the tutor of their two children, Portia was very aware of her responsibility in maintaining a modest reputation.

"I must ask you, sir, not to bring up that unpleasantness again. Night and darkness played in my favor, and I have no wish for the incident to be made public."

"As you wish, Miss Edwards," he said amiably. "But how are you going to explain your sudden disappearance tonight to Captain Turner?"

She looked out at the passing dark and unknown streets. "I shall think of a proper excuse before we meet again, which should not be anytime soon."

"I disagree," he challenged. "Although I do not consider myself a great admirer of the man, I find it unlikely that he would not be concerned with your whereabouts. He was your escort, after all, and responsible for your welfare. He will definitely seek you out tonight to make sure, at least, that you were delivered safely home."

Portia felt her head start to pound with the thought. He was correct. Perhaps it would be better to go to her friend Bella's house instead of going directly to the parsonage. She could ask a groom to carry a message to the captain at the mansion. But that was too complicated, for Bella's young and inquisitive nature would demand plausible answers to how her dress had been damaged, and Portia was not ready to reveal anything.

Her thoughts came to an abrupt halt when she saw the horses turn into the courtyard of a tavern and inn. She caught only a glimpse of the faded sign on the front

of the building. She was fairly certain she had never been
in this part of Boston, and the area appeared to be less
populated, with run-down buildings and warehouses
across from the courtyard. As the groom tied the horses
to a post, Portia peered through the dark with alarm at
the sordidness of the place.

A stable sat leaning at the far end of the yard, held
up by the scarred and burned remains of an oak tree.
To her right, firelight and noises of revelry streamed
from the open windows of a sprawling wooden building
that had to be the tavern. She could smell the outgoing
tide, and she knew they must be close to the harborside.

The yard was filthy, and battered shutters hung awry
from pitch-black windows above. She noticed the white
cloth of a woman's tattered shift draped over one of the
windowsills. Portia glanced quickly back at the stables
when a moving shadow caught her eye.

"You may wait here if you wish. I shall return in a
few minutes."

Portia nodded and sat perfectly still. She watched Pennington cross the yard. As he disappeared through a
door, a chorus of drunken shrieks and laughter greeted
his arrival. The door closed behind him, leaving her again
in darkness. She wiped her sweaty palms on her skirt,
tucked in a tear at the waistline, and wished she had
retrieved her wrap before going out in search of her
mother.

Tonight she had left too much behind, though it would
be easy enough to explain the wrap, for guests must often
leave behind possessions. But what about the mask? She
remembered leaving it on the railing of the balcony to
Helena's room. During the commotion, it could easily
have fallen off into the rose bushes. That might be a
problem.

Bella's dress, her wrap, and the mask. Portia would
not be able to return most of what she'd borrowed, and
what she would bring back to her friend was in disastrous

condition. She ran her hand over the tight bodice and silently vowed to find a way to repay her friend.

The tavern door opened and light spilled out into the courtyard, along with two drunken tradesmen. A laughing woman stumbled out a step behind. As the door closed, one of the men turned and grabbed the woman, pushing her against the wall. Portia swallowed hard when she saw the wench pull up her skirts and fumble with the front of his pants. The man's face disappeared inside the open neckline of her dress. The other was relieving himself against the building, all the while shouting and demanding his turn.

Portia gathered her skirts tightly around her and shrank down on the seat. This was not the staid and safe Boston she knew. Her only comfort lay in knowing that Pennington's groom was around. She looked at the horses, then leaned quickly out the side of the carriage. The groom had disappeared, and she looked around the courtyard as a cold feeling of panic washed over her.

The woman against the building was making sounds Portia had never heard before, and the tradesman was grunting from the exertion. Unable to see the groom anywhere, Portia suddenly felt extremely vulnerable and looked for something she could use as a weapon, should the need arise. As she leaned over to take the whip from its holder, though, a dirty hand darted from the side of the carriage and clutched at the hem of her skirt.

She let out a small scream and tried to move away. A man's burly face appeared. He had a wide smile, largely lacking in teeth. The two men and the woman against the building didn't spare her a glance.

"Well, now. What 'ave we 'ere?" he murmured, leering at his catch.

"Let go of me," she pleaded, pulling hard at her dress.

Portia fell backward when the man, wearing sailor's garb, let go of her skirt. She was relieved to see Pennington's groom shoving the man away from the carriage.

The two men faced each other for a long moment, and Portia thought they were going to fight. Then the sailor simply turned and headed across the yard toward the street.

"The master says 'tis not safe for ye to stay out here alone," the groom growled, looking up at her. "Ye might want to come inside and wait, mistress."

She didn't need to be asked twice. Climbing quickly from the carriage, Portia ran and walked and ran again to keep up with him as he strode toward the tavern door. As they went past the wench and her two men, Portia kept her eyes averted, trying to think of a church hymn that would block out the rising pitch of the cries.

Inside, the echo was not much of an improvement, and a fiddler in a far corner struck up a lively tune as they went in. She had never been in such a echo before. The moment they entered, the shouts of four drunken sailors at the table nearest to the door made her cringe and want to run out. The stench of tobacco, ale, urine, and other smells that she couldn't identify permeated the hot, smoky air. There was a mutton roasting on a spit in a large open hearth, but the smell did nothing to lessen the feeling of nausea rising in Portia's stomach.

At least two dozen tables, filled with what looked to be sailors, tradesmen, and merchants, crowded the room. Games of cards and dice were going on at every table as four or five women plied the men with ale and food and saucy looks. Portia watched in utter shock at a scantily dressed woman with her breasts exposed hitched up her skirts and danced in the center of the room to the cheers of her audience.

A wiry, hatchet-faced sailor from the table by the door pushed himself to his feet and stumbled toward them, making her an offer to join him and his tar-smeared friends.

"I don't think 'tis safe to wait here, either," she said quickly to the groom.

"I'll take ye to the back room where the master is waiting."

"Thank you," Portia whispered in a small voice, staying close to the man's side as they headed toward a door in the back.

Her nautical admirer, though, was not deterred, and as she moved away, his offers quickly degenerated into lewd taunts. His talk attracted the attention of others, as well. As Portia walked between tables, anger replaced nervousness as men openly ogled her. She slapped away the hand of one who touched her bottom, eliciting laughter from his friends. Just as they reached a door near a set of rickety steps leading to an upper floor, the drunken sailor pursuing them grabbed Portia by the arm.

"Not so fast, ye pretty little . . ."

Instinctively, she kicked at the man's shins as he swung her around. For the second time in one night, the tactic worked. The brute relinquished his grip on her arm and stepped back angrily. They now had the attention of most of the tavern customers. Several cheered her on. More rose to their feet in the man's defense. Portia considered herself to be in very big trouble, however, when she saw the eyes of her attacker focus with murderous intent upon her.

"You wait inside." The voice of Pennington behind her sounded like salvation. Jacketless and with his sleeves rolled up, he moved past her to face the mob and shoved her behind him into the room, closing the door.

The scare left her wobbly and leaning against the door. The noises coming through were muffled, but she heard no sound of furniture crashing or of anyone trying to take down the door. Portia took a few steadying breaths, but the stale smell was strong. She looked around her. The small room had only two tiny, shuttered windows high on one wall and no other door. No means of escape, she thought with concern. A single candle burned on a table near one wall. It took Portia's eyes a few seconds to adjust to the darkness. When they did, she felt no better.

A large bed dominated the room, covered with surprisingly well made bedclothes. At the foot of the bed lay Pennington's jacket. There was the table that held the candle, a pitcher and bowl, and a number of other oddly shaped items. There were no chairs, no other furnishings. The walls were of a dark wainscot and one was decorated with an assortment of whips and shackles. She gaped at them for a moment and then moved hesitantly into the room.

The place had too little light by which to read, too little air for needlework. Anyone coming here could have only one thing in mind—and sleeping did not seem likely.

Portia felt her cheeks grow warm at the thought that Pennington had planned to rendezvous here with a female companion. She quickly pushed away the thought and picked up a long, cylindrical piece of carved ivory sitting on the bedside table. Holding the smooth, strange object in her hands, she found her fingers would not encircle it completely. She tested its strength by striking the knobbed end lightly against the edge of the table. For the life of her, she couldn't discern what anyone would use the thing for, but she thought it could certainly be wielded as a weapon. She put it back on the table and decided that she didn't want to know what the other strange contraption on the table might be.

Portia's mouth fell open when she looked up and saw the large oval-shaped mirror attached to the ceiling above the bed.

Hearing nothing from the taproom, she leaned over the bed and stared up in horror at her own reflection. Her hair was a tangled mess, and the dress was torn and disheveled, the top of the gown barely covering her breasts. She looked like a fallen woman, plain and simple.

She tried to adjust the fit of the corset to lessen the effect, but lost her balance and fell on the bed. Quickly trying to regain her feet, she caught the reflection of the locket around her neck—the only *real* thing about her

tonight. It was her sole possession in this world, and Portia stared at the treasure that had started all of this.

The locket shone against her skin. She didn't have to open it. The image of the beautiful young woman inside of it was branded in her mind. Portia wished they looked more the same. Perhaps Helena would not have been as terrified if she'd stared at her own likeness out her window.

She had gotten close enough to touch her mother tonight. No longer a possibility, no longer a dream. She had no doubt about what was truth or what was a lie. Helena was the woman inside the locket that Portia had carried her entire life. Helena Middleton was her mother.

The challenge now lay in finding a way to go back there. If Portia could just talk to her for five minutes, she would do a better job of convincing her. Then, between the two of them they could correct the circumstances that had forced them apart twenty-four years ago. Portia would simply need to be strong enough to take care of both of them.

Portia's gaze moved from the reflection of the locket to the woman sprawled on the bed. She almost felt that she was seeing herself for the first time. Her skin was too pale, and too much of it was showing. Her breasts, barely confined by the loosened bonds of the corset, were too large. Her mouth was too wide. The nose was straight but long. Her eyes were slanted and large, the only feature she'd inherited from her mother. And what of that head of dark untamed curls? She raised her hands and pushed the ringlets from her face. She was past marrying age as a means of finding a way to take care of both of them. She was hard working and tenacious. But she could not impose two people on Parson Higgins and his wife. There would be other jobs, though. She knew a number of women who owned shops in Boston, in fact—the Cumings sisters, Betsy Murray, and she'd heard that the famous Mrs. Inman herself had made her fortune as a merchant here in Boston.

"What are you thinking?" she said aloud. Admiral Middleton's wrath would not allow them to remain here. They had to go back to England or Scotland. Perhaps they could go to Wales or to Bristol where she and the Higginses had lived for the seven years prior to coming to the colonies.

As Portia was thinking of these things, the door suddenly opened. She scrambled into a sitting position.

"Stay there." Pennington's command, though whispered, was sharp. Seeing at least a dozen pairs of eyes leering in from beyond the door, Portia decided to obey.

The image that Portia presented was exactly what he had described to the rowdy tavern revelers who were having their own celebration—in *spite* of the King's Birthday. The woman was his tonight, he'd told them, and no one else would touch her.

She had been lying on her back when he'd opened the door, her legs dangling over the edge of the bed. She looked ready for him to step in between them. As she sat up, Pierce thought she might just burst out of the bodice of that gown, and desire rushed through him. The tightening of his loins was more potent than he recalled happening in quite some time. Indeed, it took him a few seconds to gather his thoughts enough to remember what his plans were.

There were loud drunken chants in the room behind urging him on. A serving man, wearing a wide grin, hurried in and put a tray with a pitcher of wine and a couple of goblets on the table.

The server backed out of the room, and Pierce slowly walked toward the bed. She was like a doe, frozen in that moment just before flight.

"Lie down again," he whispered. "Like before."

"No."

"You will pretend that we are about to make love, or a half-dozen of those boors out there will be taking you on their laps."

She still hesitated, but her gaze nervously went to the open doorway.

"I shan't do anything to hurt you. This is all for show." He slowly unbuttoned several of the buttons of his shirt.

"I shall kill you if you touch me," she hissed under her breath.

"Lie back. Open your arms as if you want me to come to you."

The sound of clapping, chants, and lewd shouts was growing.

"Dead. Do you hear me?" Her eyes spit fire at him when she lay back stiffly and opened her arms.

Pierce turned to the door. "Sorry lads. I told you. She's all mine tonight."

He slammed the door shut and slid a bar lock in place. "Well, we are stuck here for a while."

She couldn't scramble off the bed fast enough. "I am shocked you would have me do such a thing, sir. Your actions in tricking me into this room, in exposing me to these people, are the most dishonorable thing I have ever heard."

"Cease your complaining, Miss Edwards," he said sharply. "You are in this dilemma because of your own silly actions and no one else's. No one tricked you into stealing my chaise. No one tricked you into following me inside this tavern. And considering the situation and how many drunken men I had to face out there, I'd say you should be grateful for the results, so far."

"Of course! Who wouldn't be grateful for having her reputation ruined in such a manner? If I should ever see any of those faces on the street . . ." She took a couple of steps away from the bed before whirling on him. "A true gentleman would have taken me to my destination first before coming back to . . . to . . . this . . ." She shook her hand irritatingly at the walls, the table, the bed, the ceiling.

"Tavern?" he asked.

"Whatever."

"I would have taken you to your home if you had been entrusted to my care, or if you were in distress due to some unforeseen circumstances, or if you were simply a respectable young lady."

She took a step toward him. "How dare you accuse me of not being respectable!"

Pierce stood face-to-face with her. "Respectable young women do not run around a garden with a torn dress and a troop of servants in full pursuit. Respectable young ladies do not steal carriages, nor do they remain in them after being caught and then ride away into the night with a total stranger."

"I was a guest in that mansion, as you were. You of all people should know how discriminating the Admiral is, with regard to those who are invited to his ball."

"You *claim* you were an invited guest. The same way that you claim that Captain Turner was your escort. Now, how do I know that everything you say is not a lie? How do I know that you were not a thief who climbed over the garden wall in hope of breaking inside the mansion? Or a wench, looking for unsuspecting guests like myself. Perhaps you planned to rob me after a quick tumble beneath the rose arbors?"

Her hand came up fast, and she slapped him hard enough to make his ear ring.

When she tried to hit him a second time, Pierce grabbed her hand and twisted it behind her, pressing her body hard against him.

"*Never* do that again," he drawled threateningly.

"You are a disgrace to your country, sir," she muttered, trying to free herself. "Captain Turner was too generous when he described you as a scoundrel of a Scot. You are far worse. You are a womanizer, a rogue, a devil who—"

He kissed her, stifling her words. Portia started to protest, but his mouth slanted over hers, greedily devouring her lips.

She was wild, beautiful, untamed. His growing desire

to strangle her was overwhelmed by the scorching heat of the very air between them and by the hardening of his body.

Portia's struggle was short-lived. Her free hand that had initially wedged itself between their bodies inched up his chest. Her mouth softened beneath his assault. A small noise escaped her throat. Pierce knew this was madness, but the fire between them had ignited, and he deepened the kiss.

The moment he let go of her wrist, Portia realized she should move away, but she couldn't. Objections springing up in her mind grew immediately vague, immaterial, and evaporated before she could voice them. His fingers threaded into her hair. His parted lips were demanding, his tongue plunging. He was kissing her with a passion that took her breath away. In her twenty-four years of life, she had never known this yearning that was driving her. It was a fire that made her only want to burn hotter. She had no experience with a man's touch, and what she had imagined on other warm spring evenings held no comparison to the fever that was taking control of her now. Portia felt herself guided backward until the backs of her legs pressed against the bed.

"I cannot," she whispered, tearing her mouth away.

"We both want this." His mouth traced a path to her neck, and she felt a sweet tingle spread through her body with every touch of his lips. She forgot her name, never mind her next complaint as his arms brought her close against him. It seemed that every curve of her body had a home against his muscular frame. His knee pressed intimately between her skirts. She couldn't understand the searing heat steadily building within her.

Portia tumbled backward onto the bed, and his body followed. He caught his weight and then slowly lowered himself onto her. She struggled to find within herself some desire to fight, but her body rebelled at any effort to push him away. Men did not behave like this with her. She had resigned herself long ago to a life of spin-

sterhood. It was a respectable life for a woman of no
wealth or family. Parson Higgins's sermons condemned
this kind of behavior in no uncertain terms. She was
beyond this, she thought. The parson's wife, Mary, had
long ago stopped warning her of this, for Portia was past
the age of recklessness. She opened her mouth again to
protest, but his mouth was there, kissing her senseless.

Wantonness it might be, but at this moment Portia
found that she needed to touch and be touched. She
wanted to feel the various textures of this man. His lips
were gentle, his hair was like silk, his body was hard.
Her fingers untied the black ribbon holding his long hair
at the nape of his neck and spread it over his shoulders.

Portia was sure she would burn in hell for eternity for
what she was letting him do to her.

"Look at us," he whispered roughly. "Look how beautiful you are."

His mouth was at her chin, then her throat. The sensation was maddening. Temptation won out over will. Portia
shyly glanced upward at the reflection overhead.

Pennington's dark hair spread over the broad expanse
of white shirt. Portia shivered at the sight of his wide
shoulders, at the long, lithe body and powerfully muscled
legs encased in the black buckskin breeches and silk
stockings.

The woman pinned beneath him was beautiful. The
skin on her face was flushed and vibrant, her eyes flash-
ing. The woman's lips were parted slightly as she worked
to draw unsteady breaths. She seemed to be moving rest-
lessly beneath the man's weight. She wanted more.

"Those people up there are wicked," she whispered.

Pierce shifted his weight to one side and met her gaze
in the mirror. "Not yet," he replied, smiling roguishly.
"But they're getting there."

The breath caught in Portia's throat when she saw his
hand push aside the locket at her neck and boldly take
hold of the neckline of the dress. Without a word, he
pulled at the dress and corset, freeing her breasts. Her

nipples hardened immediately, and she ceased breathing entirely when his mouth closed over her flesh.

The sharp knocking on the door came like a cold slap of reality. Every nerve in Portia's body tensed and thoughts of escape raced through her. Pierce kept one arm possessively across her, though, trapping her where she lay as his head lifted in the direction of the door.

"Who is it?" he called.

"Captain Turner of His Majesty's navy. In the name of the king, I order you to open this door."

Chapter 4

Pierce expected the young woman to show some sign of panic; to make some struggle, some effort to hide, but Portia did not react that way at all. She turned her face away and lay still. He knew her mind was racing, though, and he had no idea what she might do next.

Pierce stared with wonder as the tears began to roll down her flawless cheeks. When he sat up, Portia moved to her side and pulled up her bodice. When he stood, she drew up her knees, hugging them to her chest.

The knock on the door came again.

"In the name of the king, open this door at once."

"One moment, Captain," Pierce called out. He immediately gentled his tone. " 'Tis not as bad as you think, Miss Edwards. We can explain our way out of this. Turner shan't stay angry with you for long."

She shook her head. "I hardly care about Captain Turner's opinion of me."

"Then what?"

"He shall tell everyone else he has found me here. The people I live with, Parson Higgins and his wife Mary, will know. Everyone in their congregation will know. He'll tell them he found me in this tavern with you. That will bring shame on that good family's name. The parson would be compromised. He will surely never speak to me again. Mary will be reminded of her own sister and will never allow me to see the children again. I shall be

cast out as surely as you're standing there. I shall be sent back to Wales. I can hardly bear the thought of the disappointment my benefactor Lady Primrose shall feel. Worst of all, though, in being sent from Boston I shall never see my mother again." The tears came faster, and she buried her face against her knees.

The knock on the door this time was heavy enough to shake the latch. "Open the door *now,* Pennington."

Pierce had a hundred questions for the woman, but they would have to wait.

"I said I'm coming," he shouted loud enough to make Portia cringe. He lowered his voice. "Get beneath the covers."

She turned to him. Her eyes were red-rimmed from the tears. "Thank you, but I am not cold."

He took the edge of the blanket and pulled it over her. "Do not say a word. Do not move from under this. Let me take care of him."

Pierce told himself he should not feel like a cad, but he did nonetheless. With the plans for a very important business transaction ruined, he had intended that Turner find him here with Portia. On a night with half the British occupying forces engaged in the Copp's Hill ballroom, it provided a perfect opportunity to prove to the captain his lack of interest in the colonial cause. Pierce had even sent a stableboy from the tavern back toward the mansion to spread the word that he had come here with a young woman.

Turner had not wasted any time.

Pierce undid the front of his shirt and unfastened the top of his breeches. He snuffed the candle, opened the door, and stepped out. Captain Turner was standing a foot from the door, four armed soldiers accompanying him. The tavern patrons sat silently watching them with open hostility. Pierce spotted his groom Jack by the door.

"Captain Turner, I'm surprised to see you here. The Admiral's party prove too dull for you?"

"Hardly, Mr. Pennington." The man's look was cool,

though he could not completely mask the anger in his voice. "Though I'd like to say that I am surprised to find you here as well. Admiral Middleton will be quite disappointed to hear that you left the elegance of his King's Birthday Ball so early and in such haste for this." Turner glanced with distaste around at the taproom and its occupants before his gaze fixed on the partially open door behind Pierce.

"Well, if the good Admiral were not so selective in his list of guests, and if there were more attractive young ladies in attendance, then I might have been induced to stay around longer." Pierce ordered a serving lass to take another pitcher of wine into the room. "But what brings you here, Captain?"

"I am here, sir, because I was told that my escort, Miss Portia Edwards, was seen leaving the mansion in your carriage."

"The lady you intended to introduce me to?"

"My escort," Turner replied, his face flushing slightly.

"A very beautiful young woman, indeed. One that I would have enjoyed immensely getting to know better. In fact, I would have enjoyed spending more time in her company if she were not feeling so terribly ill."

"Feeling ill?" Turner leaned forward. He looked around him before lowering his voice confidentially. "She was fine when I left her."

"I have nothing to say to that, sir," Pierce whispered, giving him a doubtful look. "Though I believe you may indeed be guilty of not paying close enough attention to your charge. By the time I stumbled upon Miss Edwards in the gardens, she was sick to her stomach and quite feverish. She begged me to arrange for a carriage to take her home."

"You should have sent for me at once," Turner snapped. "You knew how concerned I was at not being able to find her in the ballroom."

"I did not make any connection between you two until I was dropping her off at the parsonage of some Higgins

fellow," he replied haughtily. "The young lady I found at the mansion was far too ill for me to demand explanations. I did what any gentleman would have done. But even if I had been aware that she was your escort, sir, knowing you are a member of the Admiral's staff and in part responsible for the ball itself, I would not have wasted time coming for you."

"I escorted her to the ball. She was my responsibility. 'Twas only right for her to leave with—"

"Captain Turner," Pierce interrupted. "My reputation speaks for itself, and I—scoundrel of a Scot or no—have never yet failed to come to the aid of a young lady in distress."

"Indeed, sir." Turner stared at him for a long moment. "Especially since you were already on your way to this squalid little whorehouse for a sordid rendezvous with one of these disgusting wenches."

Pierce took a step closer to Turner. "Because my companion in this room happens *not* to be of the society with whom you usually associate, Captain, that does not mean that she deserves your disdain. The same holds for the people in this tavern. You think you are above them. Well, I drink their wine and their beer, and I even enjoy their company . . . and that is because I understand that this is not Bath or Bristol or even the pleasure gardens at Vauxhall. Still, sir, these are all honest subjects of the Crown, the last I looked."

The silence in the taproom was deadly, and Turner suddenly sensed it. He turned and looked around him again. Unfriendly faces were glaring at the armed redcoats.

"Of course." He cleared his throat. "My words were the result of my initial error in thinking that Miss Edwards might have been exposed to . . . might have been here with you."

"Here?" Pierce said with surprise. " 'Tis astonishing to me that you would even entertain such a thought. How could you possibly think I would expose your escort

to a place that might be injurious to her reputation? And I must say that you are not giving your companion much credit. As a young woman who assuredly must share your attitudes toward the good people of Boston, do you seriously believe she would step inside a place like this?"

"Uh . . . indeed, sir. I was misled. You must excuse me." He stepped back and addressed everyone else. "Please continue with your celebration of His Majesty's birthday."

Bowing stiffly, Turner then started across the taproom toward the door. Pierce remained where he was until the door closed behind the redcoats.

"Well done, lads," he said jovially to the crowd. "You routed them without so much as a shot fired."

Laughter erupted in the tavern, and he nodded to his groom, who went out, as well. A cheer went up when Pierce ordered a round of drinks for everyone, and the fiddler struck up a lively tune. Going to the broad open hearth, he lit a taper and went back through the door into the room. He latched the door and lit the candle again. The bed was empty, and he turned to find Portia standing in the farthest corner of the room. He quickly dressed himself.

"I am grateful to you for what you just did," she said softly.

"No gratitude is expected, madam."

Moving to one corner, he pushed at a section of the wainscot paneling, which opened into a small hiding space. Peering in, Portia looked stunned to see a ladder leading downward.

"These steps lead to a tunnel that will take you to an outbuilding of the chandlery next door. My groom Jack will meet you there in a few minutes. You tell him where you wish to go, and he will arrange to have you delivered there safely, though I doubt you shall get there before Captain Turner. So you'd better prepare something to tell him."

"I do not know how I shall ever repay you, Mr. Pennington."

"No repayment, if you please, Miss Edwards," he said tensely. "My only wish right now is for you to go home and that our paths never cross again."

It was still early enough on the warm holiday evening and people continued to mill about on Sudbury Street. Portia looked neither left nor right as Jack maneuvered the carriage down the lane. When he reined in to a stop in front of the parsonage, she thanked him and hurried to the front door.

Portia knocked softly, hoping that one of the two servants would come to the door, and not Mary or Parson Higgins himself. The disheveled condition of her hair and clothing might be explainable, but she was terrified that her guilt over the indiscreet behavior in the tavern would give her away.

Luckily, Josiah answered the door, and the old manservant's eyes rounded immediately at the sight of her.

"Heavens, Miss Portia! What ever happened to ye?"

"Harmless mishaps, Josiah, all due to my own foolishness, but I am perfectly well." She touched his arm reassuringly and slipped past him.

"Should I call the mistress? Mrs. Higgins and the parson are in his library."

"No. I do not want to alarm anyone. I shall be down as soon as I change out of this dress." Portia didn't wait for an answer and hurriedly climbed the two stories to her low-raftered bedroom on the top floor.

On nights such as these, as soon as the children were tucked into bed, Mary would sit in the library and tend to her needlework as she told her husband about the brides, babies, and the old folks she had visited in the parish. In turn, Parson Higgins would talk of the ever-changing political climate in Boston and read from one of the many newspapers and pamphlets that constantly

circulated amongst the colonial cities. When Portia would join them there, the minister would usually finish the evening reading from Revelations. And only occasionally, depending on his mood, he would read from Psalms.

Portia hurriedly stepped out of the damaged dress and worked on taking off the layers of undergarments. She doubted she was strong enough tonight to listen to any passages discussing sin and damnation.

The knock on the door was soft, and the young woman pulled a wrap around her before opening it. Little Ann was waiting outside.

"What are you doing out of bed, my cherub?" Portia immediately knelt down and opened her arms to the eight-year-old. The child hugged her hard.

"You didn't come up to tell me a story tonight. I had no good-night kiss."

"I told you that I would be coming back quite late from the party, remember? I kissed you before I left." Portia placed another kiss on the child's round cheek. "Now let's get you back to bed before your mama becomes angry with me for keeping you up so late."

"You didn't keep me up. I did it all by myself. And Walter is awake too, but he was too afraid of Mama catching us on the stairs, so he stayed in bed."

When Portia joined the parson's family, Ann had just been born and Walter was only two. For all the days and weeks and years since then, she had been as much part of the children's lives as their parents. In recent years she had developed other roles, as well—tutoring them with their reading and writing, teaching them the basics of the French she had learned at Lady Primrose's school in Wales, serving as their confidante and friend. Leaving these two children was without doubt the most difficult part of the plans Portia had mapped out for the future.

"I will tell you two stories tomorrow night to make up for tonight." Portia pushed to her feet to take the child downstairs, but the mischievous sprite took advantage of the moment and quickly jumped onto the bed.

" 'Tis too late for playing, Ann." She moved toward the child.

"I want to hear about the grand ball."

"That can wait until tomorrow . . . and you can tell me about what happened here."

Ann rolled to the other side of the bed, out of Portia's reach. "Was your dance card filled?"

"You silly creature. I did not dance at all."

"Why not?" She scurried to the other side of the bed as Portia came around.

"Because I left before the dancing began."

Little Ann strategically placed herself on the pillow by the headboard. "Walter and I watched you through the window when you climbed into the carriage with that officer. I think you must have been the most beautiful girl at the ball."

"No, there were many." She reached and caught hold of a slim ankle. As the little girl giggled, Portia dragged her across the bed. "Truly, I believe I was the least beautiful woman there."

Ann ceased playing and looked up worriedly into Portia's face. "But that cannot be. I think you are beautiful. You are even prettier than Mama."

"Ann Katherine."

The mother's sharp words from the door froze the child in place. The laughter stopped, the playfulness ended abruptly. The reprimanding look alone was enough to start the little girl's lower lip trembling.

"To bed . . . now."

With her chin on her chest, the eight-year-old clutched Portia's hand and started toward the door.

"No. You will tuck yourself, young lady."

There were no protests. Ann let go of Portia's hand and obediently headed for the door. At the doorway, she even stopped and placed a kiss on her mother's proffered cheek before disappearing down the stairs.

A strict disciplinarian, Mary Higgins required that everyone around her adhere to her dictated rules of behav-

ior. Though her control over her household was
impressive to outsiders, there were times when Portia
felt that the parson's wife was somewhat harsh and in-
flexible. In Mary's eyes, there was right and wrong, and
on the path of the righteous, deviation—no matter how
small—could not be tolerated.

When order prevailed in the household, though, another side of the young mother's personality showed itself. As demanding as Mary could be, Portia had many
times seen a warmth and affection that appeared almost
boundless. If nothing else, Mary Higgins was a devoted
mother and an exemplary wife for a young cleric.

"I bribed Ann to say that," Portia said, hoping to see
a smile.

The glower lasted as long as it took the eight-year-old
to disappear down the steps. Mary closed the door.

"You did indeed look beautiful when you left for the
ball, but Josiah told me you now looked as if a team of
horses had trampled you. I can see he was not exaggerat-
ing." With a look of concern on her face, Mary gently
touched the scratch on Portia's cheek. "And you are
back much earlier than we had expected. What happened
to you tonight?"

Portia opened her mouth to speak, but then shook her
head. She moved to the bed and sat on the edge. Mary
followed her, sat down beside her, and took her hand.

"Tell me what went wrong. You were so happy when
you left."

Portia could no longer lie. These people were the closest thing to family that she'd ever had. In return for their
kindness, she at least owed them the truth about her
mother. If she had succeeded in convincing Helena to
escape tonight, she'd been prepared to do a lot of explaining, anyway. This was the only place where she
could have brought her mother. She had been counting
on them to be sympathetic, once they had been told
the truth.

Portia looked up into Mary's patient eyes. The wom-

an's blond hair was smoothed back from her face and bound up in a bun at the back. Though only six years her senior, the parson's wife seemed so superior in wisdom, in accomplishments, in knowing and doing correctly what needed to be done.

"I was not truthful with you about my reason for being so eager to attend Admiral Middleton's ball this evening."

"Do you mean you were not elated about going as Captain Turner's escort?"

Portia felt better, hearing the hint of humor in Mary's voice. "No. And I was not keen, either, about the gown that I borrowed from Bella and ruined."

"We can talk about that later." She squeezed Portia's hand. "Why were you so eager to go?"

"To meet my mother." She said it quietly and then waited for Mary's reaction. The other woman frowned, confusion apparent in her eyes. Portia removed the locket from around her neck and opened it, explaining everything from the beginning. She told Mary about Dr. Deming's observation of the miniature's likeness and about her own effort to find out what she could about Helena Middleton's history.

"But none of that offers any proof." Mary stated in a matter-of-fact tone. "Simply because Miss Middleton looks like the woman in this portrait does not make her your mother."

Portia lifted the locket passionately in one hand. "Lady Primrose told me this belonged to the woman who brought me to this world. And from everything I have been able to gather from people who knew the Admiral's daughter, Helena was not always mad. The illness, or whatever it is they've been calling it, only began shortly after rumors of a disastrous affair that she had with a man—a man whom no one speaks of."

"No family wishes to allow scandal to taint their reputation," Mary whispered roughly.

"True." Portia clutched her friend's hand, knowing

well the scandalous incident involving Mary's youngest sister. But this was so different, she told herself. "I was told that my father had fought at Culloden with Bonnie Prince Charlie. I'm told that Admiral Middleton helped negotiate the treaty that robbed the Stewart king of his French allies. It must have been in France that the affair took place. Could you imagine the Admiral's disgrace if it were known that his daughter had an affair with one of the enemy?"

"This is only your imagination running away with you, Portia." Mary rose from the bed and stood stiffly beside it. "Even if what you have heard about Miss Middleton were the truth, still there is no proof that a child was the result of that affair. 'Tis too far-fetched to think that she might be your mother."

Portia held up the locket. "But I believe she is. Look at what is left of the initials engraved on the back of this. And I saw her tonight. We have the same eyes, the same complexion. If Lady Primrose were in Boston, I know she would confirm this. If I had an opportunity to speak to Helena, I know she would admit it, as well. I just know I have found my mother."

Reluctantly, Mary reached out and took the chain and locket from Portia. Moving closer to the candle by the window, she looked closely at the portrait before studying the faint engraving on the back.

Portia didn't want Mary think she was ungrateful after all the Higgins family had given her over the years. She could never tell Mary about the secret loneliness she'd buried within her all her life, thinking she had no family left in the entire world.

Mary straightened up. "Let us suppose—just for argument—that you are correct in thinking that she is your mother. From the little I have heard of her, she spends all her time in seclusion. She does not attend balls, I would gather. What were you planning to do tonight?"

Portia took the proffered locket. "Free her. Ask her to leave with me."

A look of disbelief spread over the face of the parson's wife. She sat down again beside Portia.

"But you couldn't do that. You cannot." Mary placed a firm hand on Portia's knee. "You have been living with us for eight years now. I love you like a sister. But you know I have always been wary of your tendency toward hastily made decisions."

"This decision was not hastily made . . . not entirely, anyway. And the goal was important enough to warrant it."

Mary shook her head, and her expression hardened. "Following your own reasoning, if the Admiral has been hiding this scandalous secret for so many years, he is not about to allow it to be made known now. And he wouldn't let his daughter go."

"It would not be his decision," Portia argued softly. "And there would be no reason to make a public spectacle out of it. I didn't go there to ruin him. No one, other than his household, would have to know. A woman has the right to be free. He has no right to keep her under lock and key, away from the society and companionship of friends."

"A father has no right to protect an afflicted daughter from the world?" Mary waved off Portia's protest. "Never mind that for now. Just tell me how you were going to accomplish your 'rescue' of Helena Middleton? How were you going to give her everything that she has supposedly been missing all these years? How were you going to live?"

Portia gave her friend an apologetic look. "Well, I was planning to bring her here for a day or two and then find some other living arrangement before taking her back to Wales. I have a little money that I have saved. I thought I might use that to keep us until we could find passage. Once there, I felt certain that—with Lady Primrose's

generosity—my mother and I could both stay at the
school until we could find a place that suits us."

She clutched Mary's hand again as the older woman
shook her head in disagreement.

"You and the parson have been so good to me. I love
the children and I would be heartsick to be away from
them. But my life and my dreams were stolen from me
at birth. I only wish to recapture them now."

Mary pushed to her feet and paced the length of the
room in silence. Portia watched her. She was a beloved
wife, the mother of two beautiful children. She was a
respected member of the community. She had eight
brothers and sisters scattered across England and Scotland. Portia could see in the furrowed brow the young
woman's struggle to understand.

Mary finally came to a stop before her. "Portia, we
cannot live in the past. We cannot change things that
have gone by."

"I agree. I wish to do this as discreetly as possible. I
do not intend to create any unpleasantness for anyone.
At the same time, both my mother and I have been
wronged . . . and I intend to make the future right. In
helping her, I shall forge a new future for both of us."

"You, who know so little of the world, will do this."

"Yes."

"And I am assuming that the admiral's daughter
wishes the same thing for her future as you do."

"How can she not?"

"Because what you will be offering her would not be
a life of comfort and order. You could offer her nothing
like what she is accustomed to. Also, she might have
brought you into this world, but I am certain she knows
nothing of your impulsive nature, of your spirited independence. She could not know anything of the danger
you bring upon yourself every time you rise up determined to change the world."

Portia closed the locket and fastened the chain around

her neck again. "I was not planning to act as thought-lessly as I sound."

"Is that so?" Mary asked, sitting down again with a knowing look on her face.

The young woman blushed. "Well, perhaps I was. I suppose I should have approached her tonight only with the idea of introducing myself." She closed her eyes, her shoulders sagging. "You are right. I did not plan every-thing as clearly as I should have. If Helena had climbed out of her window with me tonight, I had no waiting carriage, nor had I prepared you and William to receive her once we arrived here. I had not gone so far as seeing to the matter of securing a passage back to England. I'm not sure I even have enough money for that."

She rubbed her temples, a feeling of gloom taking con-trol of her. "As always, I only focused on the result I wished to achieve and charged after it with no thought as to the consequences. The sad thing is, though, that this is the only way I know of doing things. And now, because of it, I might not ever have another opportunity to make things right."

Mary's hand gently caressed Portia's tangle of curls. Her voice was kindly when she spoke again. "Tell me what happened at Admiral Middleton's ball."

Reluctantly, Portia told her all that had happened at the mansion, including how she had clambered down the rose trellis and run off with the Admiral's servants in pursuit. In her mention of Pierce Pennington, however, something told her that it would be better to make her initial meeting with him in the garden less antagonistic than it really was.

"Mr. Pennington was really quite understanding," Por-tia quickly finished, pulling the robe tightly around her. "He even arranged for his groom to drive me back to the house."

She knew that in Mary's eyes, scaling mansion walls and being chased by a mob of servants—as bad as that

might be—was not half as deplorable as the other things she had done tonight with the Scotsman.

" 'Tis unbelievable that you were not seriously hurt," Mary whispered with concern.

" 'Tis more astonishing that I was not caught by the Admiral himself," Portia said honestly. "Although, if I was, I had prepared a fairly good story to use in my defense."

Mary let out a breath wearily. "I do not think I should like to hear it. But I also want you to tell me you shan't try anything so reckless again."

A long moment of silence fell in between them. The warm air wafting in from the small windows brought with it the familiar scent of flowers in bloom. She thought of the flowers she had smelled in the Admiral's gardens.

"I am still determined to meet with Helena," Portia said quietly. "I cannot stop now."

"But do you intend to meet with her or abduct her?"

"Only meet her," Portia promised. "I know now that I must have frightened my mother terribly tonight, knocking on her window while she was asleep. Next time, I shall think of a more civil approach."

Mary stood up again and walked to the small window at one end of the room, opening it all the way. With her golden hair pulled tightly back and a frown etched on her intelligent face, she was the very picture of concentration when she turned to Portia.

"The Admiral is a man not well liked by the Sons of •Liberty and the Caucuses. I'm certain that his home is well guarded at all times. I think a more civil approach, as you say, will prove much more successful."

"You are going to help me with this, aren't you?"

"I am going to help you get an answer about whether Helena Middleton is really your mother or not, if such a thing is possible. That, I believe you have a right to know. But as far as the rest of your plans, I want no part in them."

"I should be so grateful for any help, Mary." Portia

was too excited to say anything more. The other woman's interest and participation eliminated all lingering doubts of success.

"Perhaps we might even ask for Dr. Deming's assistance in taking you there."

Portia shook her head. "Without explaining my reasons, I did ask the same thing of him the first time he suggested whose picture was in my locket. He told me then that he could not help, since he rarely goes as far as Copp's Hill. In fact, the only times that he attended to Helena was when the Admiral's personal physician had traveled to Newport for a fortnight."

"This makes it even more difficult than I thought," Mary said, her disappointment showing. "Unfortunately, aside from your friend Bella's father, William has no connections with the Admiral or those close to him."

"Asking Captain Turner is out of question, too." Portia added quickly. "After leaving unannounced the way I did tonight, I doubt he shall be calling on me again anytime soon. Not that I would want him to. Going to the ball with him was more trouble than I imagined. His attentions are rather . . . well, pronounced."

"But you shall *not* be climbing any walls again," Mary stressed.

"I hope that will not be necessary."

"What about the gentleman who arranged for you to get home tonight?"

"Mr. Pennington. I was told he is a Scot," Portia said.

"He is, indeed. He comes from a very influential family from the Borders. His brother is an earl, and they are very wealthy, I understand. Also, they are involved in shipping . . . or rather, he is, I believe. I should think that he must be invited to all the important events." Mary looked at her thoughtfully. "I assume you made a good impression on the gentleman."

Searching for an answer to that, Portia's mind went blank. Somehow, she doubted that Mary would consider

her throwing herself at the man to mean making a good impression.

"You are terribly pale, Portia. Are you unwell?"

"No . . . no. 'Tis the candlelight." She rose quickly to her feet and moved away, pretending to look at the damaged gown. "His groom drove me to the house. Why is it important that I left a good impression with Mr. Pennington?"

Mary smiled. "You must have fallen from that trellis harder than you are admitting. He might be able to help you with your plan."

"How could he help me?"

"Pennington has far more connections than anyone else we might know. In addition, he is a fellow Scot. He was invited to the King's Birthday Ball, which means he could get invited to the Admiral's home again, or perhaps even introduce you there if you sought his assistance." Mary lowered her voice. "Also, if Miss Middleton agreed to go back with you to Wales, Mr. Pennington might be the answer to your dilemma there, as well. Perhaps he could be persuaded to assist you in securing a passage on one of his own ships."

Portia's thoughts turned to the man's departing words. He had no desire to see her ever again. He would never be sympathetic to her cause.

"I would have needed to make an *excellent* impression to ask favors of that magnitude," she whispered, feeling ill.

"Indeed, the fact that you made a very favorable first impression might just open those doors for you."

"Indeed," Portia said weakly.

She had no chance.

Chapter 5

"True, the meeting did not take place," Nathaniel Muir said in a low voice as the two men rode their horses down King Street toward the Long Wharf. "The muskets and powder were not turned over. But three necks—yours included, my friend—may have been saved from the noose as a result."

"What do you mean?" Pierce asked.

"Last night was a trap. Many officers may have been in attendance at Admiral Middleton's ball, but twice that many were lying in wait on the waterfront."

"How do you know this?" Pierce asked. Nathaniel had not yet arrived from Newport by midnight.

"You should rise sooner. That has been the talk of the town all morning."

"If you value that ugly face of yours, Nathaniel, you'll bloody well tell me what you know."

"Very well, my impatient friend. Ebenezer sent me word this morning. A couple of soldiers leaving an alehouse on Queen Street last night were coaxed into a fight by some of the lads. Naturally, they were soon joined by a few apprentices from the ropemaker's. They all raised enough of an uproar that an entire company of redcoats—who just happened to be waiting for smugglers—all came running. After that, all hell broke loose. Our friends say it was pure luck that we didn't have another massacre on our hands."

"Did the lads get away?"

"I believe they did."

"Good," Pierce said as they rode out onto the thirty-foot wide thoroughfare that extended the entire length of Long Wharf.

Pierce gazed out along the busy wharf, the largest in Boston. Jutting out into the inner harbor more than eighteen hundred feet, it served a thousand ships of all sizes that docked there in the course of a year, emptying their holds and loading them up again for the voyage back to England's bustling ports. Even now, with heavy pressure against the trade of British goods being applied by the rebellious Boston political groups, dozens of ships were actively being worked on by hundreds of tidesmen and carters.

The smell of tar and wood smoke mingled with the salty harbor odors, and Pierce breathed in the scents deeply. To his thinking, this was the smell of prosperity, the smell of independence.

The two men stopped at one of the buildings that lined the north side of the broad wharf. Pierce and Nathaniel had set up offices above a group of shops and counting houses and beside a warehouse that they used. Behind the buildings, the masts of two fast sailing vessels rose above the shingled roof. The ships belonged to them, two of six they owned. Another ship, which had made an undocumented stop on its return voyage at the free Dutch port of St. Eustatius, sat at anchor in the harbor—just off the smaller Griffin's Wharf—waiting to take its place here.

As they dismounted, a groom from the stable located beside the nearby warehouse ran up to see to their horses.

"Of course, the most pressing question," Nathaniel asked brightly as they walked to the front door of the building, "is, To whom should I be grateful for saving you last night?"

Pierce said nothing, going in ahead of his partner.

"Come now, Pennington. She must have a name."

"What makes you think there was a woman involved?"

Pierce could hear the scoffing tone in the other man's abrupt laugh.

"Because you are, in many ways, a heartless dog, my friend. But you are also punctual, true to your promises, even occasionally heroic. You watch over and worry about your friends. In short, in the ten years that I have known you—"

"Eleven long years."

"Very well, eleven. In those eleven years, I can count on the fingers of one hand the number of times you have missed an engagement." Nathaniel detained him at the bottom of the stairs. "And in each of those occasions, women were involved."

"A woman," Pierce corrected quietly, starting up the steps. "One woman."

Emma. He remembered each of those occasions, too. Emma and her wild behavior. Emma and her stubbornness. Emma and her mindless determination to have what she should not have. Her tendency to show up unexpectedly where she should not be. Her penchant for arguing when anyone else would wisely choose silence. Emma and her beauty and innocence . . . and his own determination to try to guide her, to protect her from herself. Emma and his infatuation with her. Emma, his brother's wife.

"Indeed," Nathaniel admitted, following him up. "But that woman is dead, and you've told me often enough that I'm not worthy of mentioning her name. So there must be another. Come on, you rogue, out with it."

"You are worse than a fishmonger's wife, Muir," Pierce said, shaking his head. It was true, he had definitely discouraged his friend from discussions regarding Emma. He didn't particularly care to discuss anything about his family with Nathaniel.

It was a topic Pierce simply did not care to think about, never mind talk about. He had, in fact, been ig-

noring the letter he'd received from his brother a month ago. The letter remained unopened on the bookcase in his study at the house by King's Chapel. Of course, the correspondence had to be from Sir Richard Maitland, the family lawyer, rather than from the broken earl Pierce had left at Baronsford in Scotland ten months earlier. He could not destroy the letter, but he had not been able to open it, either. If Lyon was dead from his fall down the same cliff that had claimed Emma's life, Pierce didn't want to hear about his brother's demise.

This morning, though, he had found himself standing before the bookcase, staring at the letter, feeling more tempted than he had in a long time to connect with his family and his past.

And the cause lay with a certain Miss Portia Edwards.

She and Emma had similar personality traits, qualities that set them apart from other women. Pierce was honest enough with himself to recognize that this was the reason that he had been attracted to Portia from the moment she first opened her mouth.

Physically, they were very different. Emma was blond, tall, thin, lithe, and stylish. Portia was smaller in stature, a brunette with enticing curves and a strong kick. They did not look the same, but when it came to their rashness, their sharp tongues, and their wildly impulsive temperaments, one woman was a mirror image of the other.

Of course, he had nearly taken a liberty with Portia that he had never allowed himself with Emma. If it were not for Turner's timely arrival, Pierce would surely have made love to the dark-haired minx. That, perhaps, would have put an end to the comparison between the two women. It might even have settled him a bit.

At the heart of it, Pierce wanted to forget about Emma. He had escaped his family, his homeland, and traveled halfway across the world to be free of the nightmare. Still, regret continued to haunt him.

Last night, after Portia had gone, Pierce had found it difficult to shake the feelings. Drinking in the company

of drunken sailors at the Black Pearl had not helped. No amount of ale could shut out the guilt that still weighed upon him.

"At least admit that it was because of a woman." Nathaniel pressed, at the top of the landing.

"Are you so desperate for an introduction, Muir?"

"I might be."

Pierce shot a narrow look at his friend over his shoulder. "The last time I checked, a number of young wives of absent merchant captains were in stiff competition for your attentions. Since when do you need to pick crumbs off *my* table?" He held open the door to the rooms they used as offices, motioning his partner to enter first.

"There is no reason why you should twist my perfectly idle curiosity into—" Nathaniel halted abruptly, and Pierce stopped beside his friend at the sight of two armed soldiers waiting at the high desk of the office clerk.

At least a dozen possible reasons for the visit rushed through Pierce's mind in an instant. One of them involved Portia Edwards.

"Admiral Middleton sends his regards and this message, Mr. Pennington, Mr. Muir." The taller of the two redcoats offered a sealed message to each of them.

Pierce looked at Sean, his office clerk, as he opened the letter. Sean was clearly feeling flustered at the entire proceeding, darting quick glances at the partially open door of Pierce's office.

"An invitation to come for a cup of tea," Nathaniel announced brightly, waving the correspondence at his partner. "How thoughtful of the Admiral to ask me, since I missed the pleasure of attending his ball last evening."

Pierce glanced down at his own invitation.

"Rather short notice," he commented, realizing it was for today. He looked at his pocket watch. They were expected at the Admiral's mansion at noon.

"Please convey our regards and tell the Admiral we shall both be there today," Nathaniel answered.

As the soldiers bowed stiffly, a shadow moved beyond Pierce's office door. He had only a glimpse of dark gray skirts. He directed an inquiring look at his clerk, and Sean returned a pained nod.

Nathaniel took charge of escorting their visitors out.

"Who else is waiting?" Pierce asked the moment the door had been closed on the men's backs.

"No calling card, sir. But the young lady said she is an acquaintance of yours. She introduced herself as Miss Portia Edwards. She has been waiting for ye at least half an hour, sir."

"I want no interruptions," he muttered, striding into his office.

She was standing before the window, looking out at the busy wharf. He closed the door with a bang.

"Miss Edwards, I thought I made it clear last night—"

"Good morning, Mr. Pennington."

She turned around to face him and for the first few seconds Pierce thought it was a stranger, calling under the same name. The gray dress and plain white shawl presented a very different picture from the woman he had kissed last night. Her hair, drawn back tightly, did little to complement the round face, and the small straw hat, pinned somehow to the front of her head, looked ridiculous. Portia Edwards looked somewhat pale this morning, older and spinsterish. Standing rigidly before him, she looked nothing like the nymph he'd found running through moonlit gardens on Copp's Hill. Nothing like the wild creature in a torn ball gown who had assaulted his shin and then stolen his carriage.

"What happened to you?"

"Pardon me?"

He walked closer, scrutinizing her from several different angles. There was no sign of the silken curls he had touched last night, and even Oliver Cromwell would have approved of her clothing. The unembroidered muslin dress, the high stiff collar, and whatever contraptions she

was wearing beneath it hid completely her generous breasts and beautiful curves. The statuelike posture and indifference she showed at his close, personal inspection was yet another disappointment. As he considered this, Pierce was surprised to realize he had actually been impatient to meet her again.

First, though, he needed to draw out the night-dwelling woman he recalled so vividly.

A faint scratch on Portia's face was the only evidence of the near-disaster she had wrought last night.

"What is the purpose behind this disguise?"

"I have no idea what you're talking about, sir."

"I was told that Miss Portia Edwards was waiting to see me."

"So?"

"So, what have you done with her?" He walked to his desk. "This is not the woman I had the pleasure of meeting last evening."

Her back stiffened further, her chin rose, and her lips thinned. She gave him a cold stare. "This happens to be the real Portia Edwards."

"I'm sorry to hear that."

"I'm not surprised, considering the way you behaved with her," she said casually, though she was not as indifferent as she pretended to be. A gentle blush darkened her cheeks. "That woman, however, was reprimanded for her actions and sent away indefinitely."

"Sent away, you say?" Amused, Pierce sat on the edge of his desk. "Pray tell, how does one do that?"

She twisted the ribbon of a small handbag around her wrist. "Well, one begins by recognizing that one was in the wrong. One recognizes that there is danger to one's person and reputation in engaging in certain actions or in allowing oneself to be in certain situations."

"Do I infer enlightenment from your words, Miss Edwards?"

"And misunderstandings may also be dangerous," she

continued, ignoring his question. "At the same time, if no serious harm has been done, a person might resolve never to expose herself to a situation like that again."

"A worthy resolution, if only she could keep it."

"Please let me finish, Mr. Pennington," Portia asked. "The next step, of course, is to make the appropriate apologies."

Pierce stretched his legs out before him, watching her intently. "So are you here to apologize for Miss Edwards's actions last night, Miss Edwards?"

"I am indeed, Mr. Pennington," she said quietly, looking down at the mangled ribbons in her hand.

Pierce crossed his arms over his chest. "Well, I am sorry to say that I cannot accept your apologies."

Her gaze flitted to his face. "Why not, sir?"

"I do not believe in settling matters through a third party."

"But there is no third party involved."

"Of course there is. 'Twas only moments ago that you spoke of sending Portia away."

She took a step toward him. "You are being difficult."

"Are you trying to impersonate the banished Miss Edwards?"

"I am being myself." He could see in her eyes a flash of fire.

"You shall have to provide some proof, I'm afraid, miss."

It took a moment, but in spite of her efforts a smile pulled at the corner of her lips, greatly softening her expression. "You are jesting with me, Mr. Pennington."

"With you? Never." He rose to his feet and approached her. "You are too serious, too proper. I cannot imagine you finding humor in anything anyone might say . . . especially me." He stopped half a step away and lifted her chin until he was looking into her dark brown eyes. She didn't flinch, didn't reject his touch. The image of the two of them lying on the bed at the tavern rushed back into his mind, and his body immediately responded.

"On the other hand, I could definitely jest with the woman I met last night. She was smart and cunning, as well as being desirable and passionate. And she would know that after everything I have been privileged to learn about her—and what she knows of me—straight talk and an honest approach would be her only chance of getting close to me again."

"You told her that you never wished to see her again."

"Indeed, and I was counting on her to be the type of woman who never follows directions." Pierce touched a few strands of loosened hair above her ear. As they escaped their confines, the silken lock formed a soft curl, caressing his fingers.

"You met me only last night, but seem to know all my flaws."

"You give me too much credit. There is no way I could know all of them." He traced the delicate curve of her ear, and her blush burned a deeper red. Her grip on her reticule tightened. "Why are you here, Portia?"

"I came to correct the impression of me you must have from last night."

Pierce ran a fingertip slowly down the side of her neck. "Are you telling me that you are not regularly pursued down dark garden paths by zealous servants?"

She shook her head. "No, that was a first."

"And I suppose you do not make a habit of stealing carriages from strange men?" Pierce leaned down and let his lips hover a breath away from her mouth.

"That . . . that was a first time, too," she whispered, backing away.

Pierce took hold of her wrist. She didn't put up a struggle. Her gaze slowly moved from the purse in her hand to his chest and lingered on his lips before looking into his eyes.

"What are you doing?"

"I am discussing last night." He took the purse out of her hand and dropped it onto the floor. "What do you think I'm doing?"

"I don't know . . . I never expected you would be . . . we would be . . ."

Pierce wrapped an arm around her waist and brought her body against his. Again, she didn't push him away, but placed both hands against his chest, creating a little barrier. The coyness added another element to her seductiveness. He was entertained, enjoying the game she played. He pulled at the pins of the ridiculous hat and was delighted when she reached up and removed it herself. More of the dark ringlets escaped and tumbled around her face. "Why don't you tell me what else was a first time, last night."

"Going to that tavern was a first."

Pierce found her staring at his mouth again. Without asking, he kissed her moist, parted lips. Her taste was as intoxicating as he remembered. He knew what he wanted. He pushed her hands around his neck and molded her body against his.

She tore her mouth away. "Being alone in a room with a gentleman was a first time, too."

He kissed her lips again, this time delving deeper, drawing out her essence. His hands slid downward over the hollow of her back to her bottom, pressing her tight against his hardening manhood.

She freed her mouth again. "What you and I did in that place . . . and in the mirror . . . first times."

"What we *almost* did," he corrected.

"No, what we *did*."

Portia had been ready to make love with him last night. They had been interrupted, but she had come back wanting the same thing this morning. Pierce backed up to his desk, bringing her with him. He felt no guilt over it. The nuisance of this being the wrong time and place was not going to stop them now.

"I don't know . . . I've never done this." She pressed a hand against his chest.

"Nor I. This has been a place for work, never play." With one sweep of his hand, he impatiently cleared the

top of the desk. A ledger book crashed to the floor. Maps and papers followed. He lifted her onto the edge of the desk.

"I . . . I think we have strayed from what I was hoping—"

With raw passion, Pierce kissed her lips. He took possession of her mouth, delving deeper, tasting, reveling in the feel of her against him. In a moment she was leaning into him, kissing him back with the same ardor. It was all the encouragement he needed. He pushed her knees apart and moved between them. His hardened body pressed against the juncture of her thighs through the layers of clothes. He took hold of her ankle and raised it until it looped around his waist.

There was a faint knock at the door, but he ignored it. Portia, however, tore her mouth away. She was flushed, breathless.

"Somebody is at your door."

"Do not be concerned. He will go away." He slid his hand up along her calf and thigh. Her skin was warm and smooth.

She pushed him away and scrambled off the edge of the desk. She was straightening her skirts when the door opened and Nathaniel poked in his head.

"Sorry to interrupt." He smiled broadly at Portia's tumbled hair and clothing and Pierce's murderous glare. "A Mrs. Higgins, the wife of Reverend William Higgins, is here to see you. I have detained her for as long as I could in my office, but she has now become rather worried about all the noise coming from here . . . especially since Sean accidentally mentioned that her charge, Miss Edwards, was conferring with you."

Chapter 6

"Please show her in," Pierce said calmly.

The man at the door winked at Portia before backing out and closing the door.

"Have you lost your mind?" Portia blurted in sheer panic. She hurriedly picked up the books and papers off the floor and put them on the corner of the desk. She pushed a scrolled map under the table and searched the floor for her hat and reticule. "You could at least have told your friend to give us a moment."

"Nathaniel knows what to do."

Portia found the hat and propped it on top of her head. There were no mirrors in the room. She picked up the small handbag and rushed to the open window. He was beside her as soon as she reached it, and grabbed her arm.

"You are not jumping out of this window."

She looked down at the two-story drop and the busy street. "I would never dream of doing anything so foolish."

"I'm sure." His voice oozed irony.

Portia shot him a hard look before adjusting the window and finding her own reflection. "I shall never make this work in time."

Her hair had tumbled to the side, half of it lying in loose curls on her shoulder, the other half barely staying in place with pins. She placed the hat one way and an-

other on her head. Pierce reached up, grabbed the hat, and threw it out the window.

"How could you?" she cried out. The hat caught in the light breeze, floated downward, and was immediately trampled beneath the wheel of a passing cart. She glanced at the door. Voices could be heard just beyond. "She'll know what we were doing here. I cannot . . ."

As her words trailed off, Pierce took her by the arm and sat her down roughly on a chair between the two open windows. Waves of hair tumbled onto her face. He pulled the rest of the pins out of her hair and dropped them onto her lap.

"You are making things worse." Portia pushed his hands away and tried to smooth her hair, gathering it quickly behind her.

"I should have learned my lesson last night. You are more trouble than you are worth, Miss Edwards."

"Thank you for the kind words, Mr. Pennington."

He moved briskly to his desk and sat behind it just as the door opened. Portia watched as Mary was shown in by Pennington's friend. Pierce stood to greet the parson's wife, but Mary's gaze continued to flit toward her.

Portia rose to her feet but said nothing, keeping her distance from the introductions and forced pleasantries. Nathaniel stayed and joined the talk, but Mary's extremely formal expression and tone told Portia that the older woman suspected what had been going on.

"My apologies, Mr. Pennington, for interrupting your business day," Mary was saying. "I was quite unaware of Miss Edwards's visit, and I stopped by to thank you for coming to the aid of my charge last night and delivering her safely home."

"Would you care to sit down, Mrs. Higgins?" Pierce offered politely.

"That shan't be necessary. I can see Miss Edwards is handling the situation the way she sees fit." She directed a withering glance at Portia. "I must put an end to this visit, though, I fear. Since 'tis such a beautiful day, the

children are eager to have their lessons completed this morn . . . so as to spend the afternoon on an outing with their father.''

Portia was well versed in reading Mary's words. She knew the purpose of concluding this visit was not for the sake of the children's lessons but to give herself time to deliver a lecture . . . no doubt on purity, chastity, propriety, and the crushing effects of sin on one's soul. Before Portia could move, however, Pierce's friend interrupted.

''Excuse my brashness, Pennington, but I do not believe I have been introduced to the young lady.''

Scowling fiercely, Pierce made the introduction, and Nathaniel Muir beamed with delight, bombarding her with a number of general questions. As Portia replied, Mary stood stiffly and silently in the center of the room.

''We are running quite late,'' Mary finally cut in with a meaningful look.

Portia had a last minute thought. ''My apologies for overhearing your conversation with Admiral Middleton's men,'' she said, addressing Muir. ''But I managed to leave behind my wrap and mask at the ball last evening, and since I heard you saying that you were going there today, I was wondering if it might not be too much trouble if I accompanied you there to recover my belongings.''

She saw Pierce open his mouth, no doubt to assert that it would be too much trouble, so she continued on.

''I have heard how cautious the Admiral's gatekeepers are to allow in visitors. If you could take me there, I promise to be quick and wait quietly in your carriage until your business there is concluded. Of course, I could even walk there and await your arrival. Then I could leave as soon as I gather—''

Muir put an end to her rambling. ''I have a much better idea, if it does not interfere greatly with your duties with the children. My friend and I need to be going our separate ways after meeting with the Admiral, so I shall be happy to make use of my friend's chaise to con-

vey you to Copp's Hill. After you have retrieved your things, the driver shall deliver you safely home."

"That is very kind of you," Portia whispered, relieved as Mary nodded sourly.

Muir asked for the address of the parsonage and promised to call for Portia at the house in two hours' time. Pennington remained silent, and she was relieved that neither he nor Mary objected to the arrangements.

Moments later, Portia was following her friend down the steps. Mary waited until they were on the street before starting.

"How foolish of me to think that at the mature age of twenty-four, you would be past such . . . such indecency." Mary charged across Dock Square as Portia kept pace. "I cannot believe that I still need to explain the difference between right and wrong, modesty and licentiousness. What do you think a man like him thinks of a woman who would throw herself—"

"I resent your tone, Mary Higgins," Portia replied shortly. "You are speaking as if I have committed the most hideous of crimes."

"You have, have you not? Did you not go to his place of business without a chaperon?"

"You told me yourself the importance of leaving a good impression. I never had an opportunity to thank the gentleman for what he did last evening. And just as I needed no chaperon to be escorted by Captain Turner to the ball, neither do I need one today to visit Mr. Pennington."

Mary stopped and stared at her in disbelief. "Do you really see no difference in the two situations? Captain Turner's interest and intentions toward you are highly honorable and clear to everyone. He has implied as much to the parson himself. Mr. Pennington, on the other hand, has never been properly introduced to you."

"Captain Turner intended to introduce him to me."

Ignoring Portia's words, Mary took her arm and hurried her along. "And I have learned some other things

about him this morning. Mr. Pennington's wealth and family connections make him one of the most eligible bachelors in Boston. These private meetings with someone of your age and lack of means could only be construed to be for the purpose of immoral relations."

Portia stopped dead, frowning into the older woman's face. "Listen to yourself, my friend. Last night, you told me he is my only salvation. Today, you are acting as if—"

"I was suggesting last evening that you seek the man's aid. My suggestion was to inform him of the tragedy of being fatherless, to appeal to his sense of nationalism and his kindness. I never told you to discard your virtue and act so . . . so unspeakably." Mary shook her head and started off again.

Portia ignored the curious looks of those passing by and ran after the other woman. "Mary, I have harmed no one. There has been no scandal. Will you please calm down and allow me to at least explain myself?"

The parson's wife whirled on her, asking directly, "Very well, tell me what exactly happened between you two in Mr. Pennington's office?"

Portia decided on the truth. "He kissed me."

"He . . . he . . ." Five shades of red crept up into Mary's neck and face. Murder would have caused less consternation in her. "You—"

"Say what you will, but Pierce Pennington is the first man who has ever kissed me . . . and no one was harmed by it," Portia asserted quickly. "I know that it was wrong. 'Twas inappropriate to go there and inappropriate to allow him to kiss me. Mr. Pennington knows it, too. He has said as much, himself. But that is behind us. 'Twas a kiss, unintended and impulsive. But the world does not have to stop because of it. No one else knows, other than you, Mary. There shall be no scandal."

"The Lord knows," Mary hissed. "And before this day is done, I will make certain the parson knows, as well."

"Do as you see fit."

"That I shall. There is nothing innocent about what

you have done. You have been living with us for eight years. You know very well how we lead our lives. You know the example we try to set for the people in our congregation and for others who look upon us. We do not stray from the righteous path. No errors—unintended or impulsive though they might be—can be tolerated in our own conduct. Behavior like this will destroy in a moment what my husband has been trying to establish here for all these months. You are doing the same as my sister Ellie. She brought scandal on the family and destroyed William's chances in England. You will ruin him here."

"I am not Ellie," Portia stated, upset that her blunder served as a reminder of a very difficult time in Mary's life. After working seven years as a curate in Bristol, any hope of advancement for Higgins had been shattered when Mary's youngest sister was named as a correspondent in the divorce proceedings of a young nobleman. The scandal was trumpeted in every newspaper from Bristol to Edinburgh. And that had been only one of that young woman's missteps. "I would never do anything to hurt you or William or the children."

"Very true, " Mary snapped, "because I shall not allow you to. From this moment on, I forbid you to have anything to do with Mr. Pennington, his friend . . . and Helena Middleton. You will put an end to this foolishness right now."

"I cannot do that," Portia said passionately.

"Indeed, you can."

"You are asking me to give up the possibility of saving my own mother."

"I care only about my family," Mary said sternly, "the family you have been part of for eight years."

"I appreciate everything you and William have done for me, but I cannot decide between you and my mother." Her voice grew husky as Portia desperately fought back the tears.

"You must decide. There is no middle ground between

right and wrong. You must decide between the family that you have now and the imaginary one that exists only in your mind," Mary stated matter-of-factly. "There is too much at stake for me to allow you to tread in such dangerous waters. The risks are too high."

"I shall be more careful," Portia argued quietly. "You have every right to be angry with me for going to Pennington's place of business. But that is separate from my mother. I promise never to see him again, if you wish. But Helena Middleton—"

"Stop!" Mary shook her head adamantly. "I spoke to William about that last night. He is certain that Admiral Middleton would retaliate against one and all if his daughter were stolen away without his consent. He believes your entire scheme is total foolishness. He has even suggested that we send you to Nova Scotia to live with his parents for a year or so. He believes you will forget about all of this in time."

"Mary, please listen to me," Portia pleaded. "You cannot send me away."

"That is not your choice. After witnessing what you did this morning, I must stand by my husband's decision."

The two women stood facing each other for a long moment. They weren't hearing each other. Neither understood. Then, Portia heard the bell of Old South ring out the hour. Before her, Long Wharf and the rest of the harbor bustled with activity. A merchant ship was just entering the port, passing the fort at Castle Island. A great unknown world lay beyond.

The noise of the street, the people around them, even Mary's face, all receded in her mind as Portia thought of the dark and frightening road that awaited her. Despite the loneliness, she had never endured much hardship in her life. She had never been in any true danger. From the time she had left Lady Primrose's school in Wales, she had been a member of a household where

she was cared for and appreciated for her efforts. Fear now crept into her heart.

Portia wondered if she had the strength to walk away from all that was secure in her life. If she failed in any step, she would be ruined.

A woman passed them. A child was holding on to her mother's skirt, and the little girl glanced up into Portia's face. That one look gave her the answer.

Portia took a deep breath. "I intend to use the opportunity of going back to the Admiral's mansion this noon to chance another meeting with Helena."

Mary's face hardened, shielding obvious disappointment. "I forbid it."

Portia batted away a tear. "Would you like me to remove my belongings before that appointment or can it wait until I return?"

"I would prefer that you leave my house before you go to the North End." Without another word, Mary turned and walked away.

With the door locked, the maps and ledger books were brought out from the secret compartment within the wall panel and spread out on Pierce's desk. Sean was advised to give them the signal immediately if any other visitors arrived in the outer office. The two men pored over the information that Nathaniel had brought back from Providence. It was critical that the meeting today with Admiral Middleton not jeopardize their plans for the coming fortnight.

The British revenue cutter *Gaspee* had been brought in three months earlier to enforce the revenue laws on Narragansett Bay, an area where virtually the entire colonial population was engaged in smuggling. The *Gaspee*'s presence was decidedly unwelcome to all, and her captain had done his best to provoke the navigators on the bay by the arrogant and high-handed manner in which he carried out his duties.

Over the last two nights, Nathaniel had made the final arrangements in Rhode Island. Next week the notorious MacHeath would help lure the *Gaspee* aground in Narragansett Bay. A group of prominent Providence men were to take over from there. The mission was a critical one and had been in planning for some time.

An hour had passed before Pierce, finally satisfied with all the details, folded the maps. "What do you plan to use as an alibi for last night?"

"I was a guest at the Rhode Island governor's ball."

Pierce raised a questioning brow.

"I celebrated the King's Birthday with the same fervor that you did, no doubt . . . and I stayed longer than you did at the Admiral's, I'll wager." Nathaniel corrected. "The important thing was that Governor Wanton and I had a nice chat about the benefits of fine whisky, a conversation that he will attest to, if the need arises. He was also aware that I was leaving for Boston last night, so my early departure was perfectly explainable."

Pierce placed the maps and the books in the compartments and closed the panel. "I expect Middleton to address the same issues during our visit today that he has discussed with others."

"I have an uneasy feeling about it."

"And why is that?"

"I cannot say exactly. Something about the timing of it. We have a ship sitting in the outer harbor ready to take its place at the wharf. The infamous rascal MacHeath has been more active this past fortnight than all of last year." Nathaniel picked up something from the rug and sat down in a chair, studying the small object closely. "Could simply be my imagination, but I am still somewhat concerned."

"The fact that he has invited both of us to attend is a good thing," Pierce commented. "He is obviously focusing on businesses and not individuals. From what I was told, this is the same approach he used with other shipping men."

"Time will tell, my friend. In the meantime, we need to be careful."

Nathaniel's fascination with the object piqued Pierce's curiosity. He was annoyed, though, when he realized the item was a woman's hat pin.

"This definitely gives me more reason to look forward to the ride to Copp's Hill." Nathaniel glanced at his pocket watch. "Do you think Miss Edwards would mind if I called for her slightly earlier than the appointed time?"

"As a matter of fact, I think she *would* mind." Pierce took the pin out of the other man's hand, poking himself in the process.

Muir was unsuccessful in hiding his smirk.

"But you do not have to bother calling for her," Pierce said shortly. "I will take care of that."

"Really, Pierce. I insist."

"You do not want to get involved there. You do not want to know her. You definitely do not want to know how much trouble she is capable of getting into. And you absolutely do not want to know why she is really going back there today . . . considering the fact that she was chased out by a rather threatening horde of servants last night. I will take care of it."

Nathaniel leaned back in the chair and smiled. "I am fascinated."

"For your own peace of mind, try to curb your fascination." Pierce picked up his jacket where he had discarded it on the back of a chair and headed for the door. "I will meet you at noon in the North End. Be on time."

Chapter 7

Portia had no time to look and consider her options. Besides, she had none. She took the only place she knew of, a room on the third floor of the redbrick apothecary shop at the foot of School Street. Dr. Crease the Younger, as he was called—though he was nearly seventy—had mentioned the room that he was looking to let out when Portia had stopped to get medicine for Mary during her illness. Luckily, the room was still available, and Dr. Crease and his wife were both delighted to take her in as a tenant.

By the time Portia arrived back at the house on the lane off Sudbury Street, she had prepared herself to deal with chaos, anger, tears, and outpourings of emotion. When faced with the silence she found there, however, Portia was not entirely sure how to deal with it. With the exception of Josiah, no one else was at home. The old man seemed genuinely upset.

"Mrs. Higgins had a meeting with the Charity Ladies, and the children were directed to go and—"

"You needn't explain, Josiah. I understand." Portia looked up the steep, narrow stairs. "I shan't be long."

Her feet were heavy as she started her ascent. For the first time, the idea of never again seeing the smiling faces of Walter and Ann, of not belonging to this household, of being totally alone, started gnawing at the edge of her courage. She began to see the wisdom in Mary's words.

She was turning her back on real people she loved for what was quite possibly an illusion.

Still, though, she climbed the steps. In her room, she put a small trunk on the bed and went about packing what was hers. It was not much. Three dresses, a cloak, a handful of undergarments, some books, her writing tablets, and the small assortment of mementos she'd collected during her years with the children. Portia looked at the needlepoint heart that little Ann had made for her, at the shell Walter had picked up by the dock before they left England. Where she was going was unclear, and how she was going to live was a mystery. Until she found what she was searching for, these few precious keepsakes would have to be enough to keep her spirits alive.

At the last minute, she also packed what she had left of the things she had borrowed from her friend Bella. She would need to mend and return them soon.

Portia managed to haul the trunk down the stairs herself. Josiah looked embarrassed when he caught up with her by the door as she prepared to leave.

"I never thought ye would be so quick, miss, or I'd have come to bring this down for ye."

"Better my back than yours."

The old man glanced sadly down at the little she was taking. "Will ye allow me to help ye, miss? I've a wee bit of savings that's of no use to me at my age. I'd be happy to—"

"I'll be fine, Josiah. Thank you," she said gently. "I have managed to put a little away over the years, and you know I'm not afraid of working. I do not expect to be without a position for too long." She gave him the address where she had taken the room. "A gentleman by the name of Mr. Muir is supposed to come for me sometime before noon. I shall try to carry my trunk to the apothecary and be back before then, but if he comes by before I return, please do not mention anything about my change of employment and residence."

"I should never do that, miss," Josiah assured her. The

old servant looked out into Sudbury Street. "I took the liberty of sending for the livery boy to bring a cart around for ye . . . and here's the lad now. Let me help ye load the trunk on the back."

Moments later, as the cart jerked into motion, Portia swung around on the rickety seat and looked back at the parsonage in time to see the old man slowly closing the door.

Pierce sat in the warm midday sun waiting for the two mud-covered boys to herd their half-dozen cows out of the lane where the parsonage was located. His groom Jack tried to hurry them along, but the brassy young fellows just whistled him off and continued toward the Common.

By the time they entered the lane, Portia was helping an ancient serving man put a small trunk in a cart as a livery boy stood by. He halted the chaise immediately. She had not bothered to do anything with her hair. The dark locks were gleaming in the sun, ringlets dancing in the light breeze. For a few moments he found himself staring. Despite his objection that morning, he admired how delicate and pretty she looked in the simple attire. He was surprised out of his reverie, however, when she climbed into the cart beside the boy.

Pierce had done the very thing that he had told Nathaniel not to do. He'd arrived early. But he told himself he had a legitimate reason for doing so. He already knew Portia, and sensing that she was heading into some stormy weather with the parson's wife, Pierce had decided he should make a better impression on the parson and his family.

As he watched the cart turn down Sudbury Street, Pierce reminded himself that he was doing this for himself, too. Against his better judgment, he found he had resigned himself to the fact that his and Portia's paths were going to cross. He could live with that. The woman interested and annoyed him at the same time. But he

was also damned curious to know what the she-devil really wanted at the Admiral's mansion.

With a flick of the reins he set off, following at a distance. There had to be a hundred reasons why she would be leaving the Higgins residence with a trunk in tow, but none he wanted to guess at. He only hoped his foolishness that morning was not the cause of it.

The redbrick building on the corner of School Street where the cart stopped was one that Pierce had passed by dozens of times. He brought his own vehicle to a halt several shops up from the apothecary. There was a considerable amount of foot traffic here, as well as riders and street vendors, and Portia didn't notice him. He watched her thank the driver and drag the trunk herself to a side door of the building. She paid no attention to anyone else on the street, and opened the door without so much as knocking. His groom was already standing by the heads of the pair of horses, and Pierce went after her. She and the trunk had disappeared through the door, however, by the time he had reached it.

He stood there for a few minutes, waiting, uncertain of his next move. He was considering knocking and inquiring about her when the door opened again and Portia reappeared without the trunk.

She was clearly shocked to see him. She hurriedly averted her red-rimmed eyes and wiped tears from her cheeks. She'd been crying.

"What is wrong?"

Portia ignored the question. "What are you doing here, Mr. Pennington?"

"I might ask the same thing of you."

"I . . ." She cleared her throat. "I live here."

He looked up at the building. "But this is not the address you gave to Nathaniel. And this is not the house where my groom delivered you last night."

"People move. Situations change." She continued to avoid his eyes and searched the street instead. "My apologies for sounding rude, sir, but I need to get back to the

parsonage in the next fifteen minutes. As you mentioned yourself, that is the address I erroneously gave your friend." She gave him a polite nod and started up the street.

Pierce fell in step with her. "Was it erroneously or did your living arrangements change since you left my office this morning?"

"I do not think that concerns you."

"I had the impression that Mrs. Higgins was unhappy about finding you in my office. Was that what precipitated the move?"

"I must be going. Now if you'll excuse me . . ."

Pierce motioned for Jack to bring the chaise. "My carriage is here. I will take you where you wish to go."

She hesitated for a second, but Pierce took her by the arm and led her toward the vehicle.

"You have a rather overbearing way of giving commands," she said critically, "rather than making offers out of any sense of courtesy."

"I have never felt inclined toward courtesy when dealing with those who refrain from speaking the truth."

"Are you saying that I've told you untruths?"

" 'Tis not so much what you say, miss, as what you do *not* say."

Portia's manner toward the groom was extremely polite, but the glare was back as soon as she was seated in the chaise and turned her attention once again to Pierce.

"Since you have formed such a poor opinion of me," she said shortly. "I cannot understand your insistence on giving me a ride. I also do not understand why you are following me, as that is the only explanation that I can think of for you to be waiting by that door when I came out."

"Perhaps I was there to purchase drugs of some kind." Pierce flicked the reins and the carriage started down the street.

"Is that so? I do not believe there could possibly exist any medicine that will help cure your ailment."

"My ailment?" He smiled. "Which is?"

She glanced in panic over her shoulder. "You are going the wrong way. You needed to go left at that last intersection to get to Sudbury Street."

"I shall get you to your desired destination," he assured her.

"How about my appointment with your friend?"

"He has been warned," he said casually. "I am here to replace him. Now, about my ailment, Miss Edwards?"

She continued to look about her with uncertainty. "I am no physician, sir."

"Still, I would value your opinion."

"I do not believe you can handle hearing it."

"I am much stronger than you give me credit for." He was glad to see the spark back in her eyes. The breeze pushed the curls in every direction, and she looked wild and very tempting. "This might be the only chance you ever get to slander me in person."

"Very well." Portia slid away from him as far as possible and studied him earnestly for a while. "The problem with you, sir, is your lack of trust."

"That is true, but that quality only surfaces in my dealings with strangers. Frankly, I consider that caution to be a sign of good sense."

"You are also a tyrant."

"Another positive quality. There is no government so efficient as that of a benevolent despot."

"I suppose you have some excuse for your consistently foul temperament."

"As Jack, here, I'm certain will verify, my temperament is only occasionally foul, as you put it." Pierce reached over and pushed a lock of hair from her eyes. Just as he recalled, it was soft as silk, and it took great discipline not to allow his fingers to linger. "And in your case, however, I have certainly been provoked."

She gave him a narrow stare. "And then, of course, your lack of decisiveness."

"And why do you say that?"

"One moment, you say you wish never to see me again. But when we meet again, you act like a long-lost friend. You frown, glower, call me troublesome one moment, and in the very same morning you are at my door and cannot be any more accommodating." Portia leaned toward him and placed a hand on his sleeve. "So which is it, Mr. Pennington? Have you come to some decision about me?"

Pierce considered her carefully. She wasn't as vain or as brazen as the dozen or so very willing women who had been haunting him in Boston since his arrival. She wasn't pretentious or childish like the other couple dozen who were in search of husbands. She wasn't notably beautiful or fashionable in dress. She definitely did not seem to have much interest in belonging to the Boston version of the London beau monde that Emma had lived for.

Portia certainly did not fit into the same mold as the women Pierce had been involved with before. But somehow she warmed his blood. He wanted to touch her, taste her, have her, and his physical reaction to her was baffling as hell.

"What little I have seen of your actions goes against any logic. But in spite of it, I find I am attracted to you," he finally answered. "So at the risk of being indecisive, as you charge, I must answer honestly that I do not know what to make of you . . . yet."

She neither pouted or looked disappointed, and Pierce gave her credit. She didn't appear to gauge her worthiness on his opinion or anybody else's. Shrugging indifferently, Portia turned her attention to the various streets that led to the wharves on the right.

"Are you keen to educate me about another unique section of Boston that I might not have seen?"

"No, I like to save those opportunities for the darkest hours of the night, when you are helpless and I can take full advantage of you."

"I shall never put myself in a situation like last night again." She shifted uneasily in her seat.

He made a mental note that she said "last night" and not "this morning," when he had had his hands all over her and could not get enough of her. It was good to know what she feared and what she did not fear.

"I am taking you back to the North End. Though there is no saying that one of the Admiral's servants will not recognize you as the housebreaker who escaped them last night."

"You are determined to think me a criminal. But if I am as horrible as you say, why should I go back and risk being discovered?"

"Perhaps you didn't find what you were looking for the first time."

"Oh, but I did find her," she whispered under her breath.

Pierce gave her a curious look. "Another woman is the cause of all of this?"

For the first time since he had met her, she was speechless. She turned her head away, and the passing scenery became the focus of her attention.

"Who is this woman?"

"I . . . I should not have said so much. Please disregard it."

The possibilities running through his mind were too wild to deserve consideration. He reined the chaise to a stop on a small rise. The Mill Creek ran along the bottom of the hill to their right. He turned to her. "We are going no further, Miss Edwards, until you tell me what this is all about."

"Then I believe I shall get out."

He took hold of her arm and stopped her. "Why not simply be honest with me?"

She was slow to look at him. "Mary . . . Mrs. Higgins told me last night, after your groom delivered me to the parsonage, that I should tell you the truth and seek your

assistance. That is what I intended to do this morning. Somehow, I managed to botch that completely and lose her trust at the same time."

This time he didn't interrupt and watched her struggle to explain.

"I was running from the mansion last evening," she explained hesitantly, "because I had tried to meet the Admiral's daughter and inadvertently frightened her out of her wits. I am going back today to attempt the same thing—to meet her, I mean, *not* to frighten her. I am hoping to have more success in the daylight."

There were only two things that Pierce knew about Middleton's daughter: She was mad, and she had been held in seclusion for some time.

"Why are you so set on meeting her?"

"Because I suspect she is my mother," Portia whispered.

"That would make you Middleton's granddaughter."

"A relation that he would never admit to." She went on with her explanation. "I was born out of wedlock and under extraordinarily difficult circumstances, I believe. My wish is for him never to know about me. I truly believe if he discovered what I intend to do, he would send me to the end of the earth to hush the scandal."

Pierce listened intently as she told him what she knew of her parentage. She told him about Lady Primrose and about her employment with the Higgins family for the past eight years.

"My relationship with Helena Middleton is all speculation, of course, but I shall never know the truth for certain unless I get a chance to speak to her in person. That is why I accepted Captain Turner's invitation and attended the ball last night. That is also why I came to your office this morning. I hoped to secure your assistance in getting back inside the Admiral's mansion again."

Pierce thought of where this was going, and he didn't like it. This was the kind of attention he could least afford.

To have someone of Middleton's position become an enemy for some such trivial matter could be disastrous.

"Parson Higgins's wife thought I could help you?"

Portia nodded emphatically. "She thought your connections could open any door. And she was right. The invitation for today was more than I could have hoped for. This gives me a way to get back to the mansion immediately."

"So there are no articles of clothing left behind from the ball?"

"Of course there are. I do have a reason to go back. Please, Mr. Pennington," she said softly, laying her hand on his. "What I hope to do shall harm no one. I have no intention of making any claims on anyone. I shall make no scene. I shall upset no one. I am only after the simple truth of my parentage. Would you . . . could you find it in your heart to assist me?"

Pierce looked down at the Mill Creek. The masts of ships were visible in the harbor to the east. Not much farther along was the bridge that led to the North End and the Copp's Hill mansion of Admiral Middleton.

"Definitely not, Miss Edwards."

Chapter 8

The Admiral's marines at the gate were the only guards. There was no battalion of grooms or servants waiting at the mansion to apprehend her. A stableboy had been leading Nathaniel's fine hunter toward the stables as they arrived. Apparently, they were the only guests of the Admiral. It was the perfect opportunity for Portia to pursue her plans, if it weren't for the beast in gentleman's clothing sitting stubbornly beside her.

"This is truly ridiculous, Mr. Pennington. Admiral Middleton must think you are insane to be sitting here in your carriage." She kept her voice calm and reasonable. "I told you that I shall abide by your decision. I shall wait here until Jack returns with my wrap and then allow him to take me home."

There was no response. It was the same reaction he'd given to her pleas of reconsidering his decision as they had driven to the mansion. The only thing Portia had been able to get him to budge on was to at least fetch the borrowed wrap.

The Scot sat there, wearing an annoyed frown and staring at the door where his groom had disappeared a few minutes ago.

"Never mind ridiculous," she pressed, glancing at his clenched jaw. "What you are doing could be construed as rude by your host. It could be damaging to your relationship with a representative of the Crown. Your friend

is probably waiting inside, too, worried sick about you. Indeed, perhaps Mr. Muir does not know that you have arrived but are refusing to go in. You should learn to trust people, Mr. Pennington. I do not understand why you think I would do anything to cause you strife.''

Pennington's scowl was so fierce that Portia shifted uneasily in the seat. His grip on her wrist felt like a steel band, though, and she knew she would never break free.

"Here is Jack," he said abruptly, gesturing with his head.

Looking toward the house, she was disappointed to see Bella's wrap draped over the groom's arm.

"Now I only ask that you show your gratitude by causing no trouble for my servant."

What other option did she have?

"Of course, sir," she said amiably, relieved when he released her and climbed from the carriage. As Jack took his place beside her, Portia thanked the groom for fetching the garment and proceeded to fold the wrap carefully and place it between them.

There were no parting words from Pierce for her, but plenty of instructions for Jack regarding what route to take and where specifically she was to be delivered.

She sent a cheery wave at the man, but he only shook his head darkly in response. And as the carriage pulled away, she looked over her shoulder and saw Pennington rooted to the spot, watching them go down the long drive.

As they went out of sight around a hedge and a grove of trees, Portia turned and stared at the small bridge where she'd lost the race last night. The gates of the mansion grounds were still a good way off.

She still had a chance.

"The activities of the colonists here in Boston and in the immediate vicinity have gone far beyond the limits of lawful protest, Mr. Pennington. The militias at Quincy, Milton, Lexington, Concord, Salem, Cambridge, and a

dozen nearby villages are drilling on the greens, and there is open talk of armed conflict with His Majesty's army."

Pierce pushed his tea away and looked steadily into Middleton's weathered face as the Admiral continued to talk of the threat and the consequences of Boston's rebelliousness. Everything they had been told so far, Pierce knew. In fact, his personal knowledge about the various activities was more specific and comprehensive than the generalities that Middleton was sharing with them.

The room was warm, and the tall windows stood open. A scented breeze wafted in from the rose gardens, and the view of the lush grounds beyond distracted him momentarily. Pierce glanced at Nathaniel, who was looking bored and studying the pattern on the china cup in his hand. Captain Turner sat to the right of the admiral with his back to the windows, silent thus far. Like an obedient dog, the officer nodded his head whenever his superior spared him a glance.

"We know a great deal about the South End Caucus and its North End counterpart. We know about their leaders. They are deluded to think that because they stir up trouble, Governor Hutchinson will simply order the forces at his disposal to stop enforcing Parliament's laws and directives. They think by not buying tea or other British goods, by marching on the greens of a few farm villages, they will force us to bow to their wishes. Well, His Majesty's forces will never turn their backs on the loyal subjects here in Boston. We have sworn to protect the Crown and the British people, and indeed we shall, sir."

Pierce folded his arms over his chest. "Why not just round up these leaders, Admiral, and put an end to it?"

"We shall do just that when the time is right, for we know who they are." Admiral Middleton cleared his voice. "That rogue Samuel Adams and his brother John, James Otis, Warren, Quincy, and the rest of the seditious

Long Room Club. These rogues continue to stir up the rabble. And I swear I'll hang a dog named Ebenezer Mackintosh before I'm through."

"Ebenezer, did you say?" Nathaniel chirped up, suddenly looking interested.

"You know him?" Captain Turner said, speaking for the first time and looking at Pierce's partner carefully.

"Indeed I do. The fellow made these boots for me," Nathaniel said, pushing back from the table and lifting a leg to display the riding boot. "A damn good shoemaker, that one. Makes all my shoes. I care not a rush about those other fellows, Admiral, but do wish you wouldn't hang a good craftsman."

"We have more important issues at hand than your boots, Mr. Muir," the Admiral growled. "And when we have the evidence we need, your bloody cobbler will pay for his treasonous behavior."

"I know nothing about any treason, sir," Nathaniel said. "Those issues interest me very little . . . except where my business is concerned, of course. But I must tell you, 'tis damned difficult finding good shoes in Boston."

"Mr. Muir—"

"As you can see, Admiral," Pierce broke in, "my partner has little interest in politics. But as merchants with shipping interests here in Boston, we both appreciate your efforts to keep the peace. But let us come to the point. Why have you asked us here?"

The Admiral sat forward, placing one fist on the table. "Because of this insidious MacHeath fellow."

"MacHeath?" Nathaniel said. "He is a character in a play, sir."

"Indeed, Mr. Muir. But he's also a flesh-and-blood villain here in Boston. He's a bloody mercenary . . . and a traitor to the Crown."

"What do you mean?"

"Someone who is using the name MacHeath as an alias

is supplying the militias—through the so-called Sons of Liberty—with arms and ammunition. He is smuggling arms to . . ."

Pierce couldn't believe his eyes. She was in the damned gardens, running through the alleys of roses. He casually rose to his feet as his groom Jack strode into the garden, chasing after her and looking as angry as a wet cat.

"Do you have something to say, Mr. Pennington?" Captain Turner asked.

Pierce ignored Turner and met the curious stare of Middleton. "My apologies, sir. An old riding injury. I find I cannot sit in one place for too long. Do you mind?"

"Of course not, sir."

"Pray, continue," Pierce said. He walked to the marble fireplace and leaned against it. From this angle, he had a perfect view of the ridiculous chase going on outside. Jack had no chance. She was hiding behind a rose arbor, and the groom went right by her.

"Do you know this for a fact—all this information about MacHeath?" Nathaniel chimed in. " 'Tis possible that all this MacHeath business is nothing more than a fairy tale made up by these Bostonians as a diversion."

"Nay, sir," the Admiral retorted. "We are dealing with facts. MacHeath has been smuggling arms in for months. We believe the weapons are being brought in from France by way of the Dutch island of St. Eustatius in the Caribbean. They are being distributed to militias all over the countryside."

Pierce saw his groom go off in the wrong direction and out of sight. Portia moved out of her hiding place and ran quickly toward the house.

"But what has this to do with us, Admiral?" Nathaniel asked.

"I have been given the task of finding this MacHeath and stopping the flow of arms to . . . to those who would rebel against legal authority here in Boston."

Pierce caught his friend's stare and reluctantly joined the conversation. "And you want our help?"

"Indeed I do, Mr. Pennington. The impressive military service of your brother speaks of your family's dedication to the Crown. At the same time, your business connections give you a critical edge which we lack." The Admiral's tone turned low and confidential. "I had been planning on seeking your assistance for some time now, but Governor Hutchinson's views were to wait until the final decision had been made regarding your brother."

"My brother?"

"Aye. Captain Pennington."

Pierce had corresponded with his younger brother David this past year no more than he had with Lyon. Still, he was not about to admit to these two strangers that he had no idea on what continent his young brother was located at present.

"Captain Pennington has been transferred from Ireland. He is scheduled to arrive in Boston shortly. With the two of you—and Mr. Muir, of course—collaborating on these sensitive matters, I know we shall soon get to this MacHeath."

Pierce did not want to think of the complications that David's arrival would cause right now.

"I see no need to wait for my brother's arrival, Admiral. What exactly can we do right now?"

"Excellent." Middleton's satisfaction was evident in his tone. "We need to know what you know. We believe the rogue is bringing the arms directly into Boston itself, for we are watching every ship and rowboat from Plymouth to Salem. We need to know how this MacHeath is smuggling these arms in, and how he is delivering them to the countryside. Our guards at the peninsula neck are checking every cart and wagon that leaves Boston. You are men of commerce. You are both involved with the merchants and the tidesmen of the town."

"So your concern is solely this MacHeath phantom," Nathaniel asked feebly, "and no other information that

we might run across—demonstrations that are being planned or rumors of what is happening in Newport or New York."

"Of course, we are interested in whatever you might learn. We are . . ."

As the officer continued, Pierce ran a hand impatiently over his face. He walked away from the fireplace and stood by his chair, looking past the officers toward the window. Feelings of frustration were engulfing him, and it had nothing to do with David's arrival or even Middleton's assumption that he and Nathaniel were low enough to become informers and spies.

Pierce's frustration stemmed from the fact that Portia, the daft woman, was trying to climb a tree in broad daylight.

From a branch of the nearby pear tree, Portia peered into Helena's room. The windows and curtains were open, but she could not see her. Perhaps, she thought, her mother was lying on the bed or perhaps sitting in a chair in the corner. There was also the possibility that she had left the room entirely. It was possible that after the incident last night Helena had been moved to another room. She was not familiar with the entire layout of the house. The draper's assistant she had paid for the information had worked only in this wing of the mansion. Still, she had to get inside somehow and it had to be today. What were the chances of ever coming this close again?

Approaching voices drew Portia's attention to a brick walk leading from another part of the garden. Partially hidden by the leaves and branches of the tree, she searched for Jack. The last thing she wished for was to get him in any trouble with the Admiral's servants. She felt bad enough after the scare she had given him by jumping out of the carriage when he slowed down to go over the bridge. Luckily the groom was nowhere to be

found. Two serving women were walking slowly toward the house.

"Ne'er saw her like this before, knocking down the medicine, giving orders the way she did."

Portia held her breath for fear of rustling any leaves as they passed under the tree.

"That's the way ladies *should* act. Those charlatans pour so much heaven-knows-what into the poor soul, for naught would I blame Miss Middleton for her actions."

"Mrs. Green will scorch us good if she hears we left Miss Helena alone in the garden," the first one said nervously, looking back from where they came.

"Let the dragon do her worst. 'Tis not like her ladyship is going anywhere. If it makes the poor soul happy to be left on her own for a few minutes, then who are we to say different. Mrs. Green is just . . ."

Portia scrambled down the tree as soon as the two women disappeared along the pathway. Her clothes were covered with bark and twigs and her hair was a mess again, but her concern about what her mother would think of her appearance came and went quickly. She hurried down the path.

The sun was shining brightly, and the day was warm and beautiful. When Portia stopped at the entry to the enclosed garden, the scene was exactly as she'd always thought heaven would look.

Like an angel, Helena wore a dress of white with a shawl as blue as the sky thrown over her shoulders. Her golden hair was pulled up, and she sat quietly on a stone bench by a green hedge. Flowers of violet and red and yellow bloomed in the gardens around her. She was not reading or painting or sketching, but looking toward a patch of white cloud that was sauntering along the horizon.

Portia stood frozen where she was. For a moment, she forgot what it was, exactly, that she planned to do. For all her life, she had stared at a miniature portrait in a

locket. Now faced with reality, she didn't know where to start or stop, or how to put the longing of all the years into words, into action.

Helena turned her face toward the garden, and Portia thought she looked more like the woman in the locket now than she had last night. Helena picked something up from her lap, and the young woman was surprised to find that the mask she'd dropped was the object of her mother's interest.

The thought of how little time they had alone forced Portia to step through the arched entry into the garden.

"Good day, madam," she said softly.

Helena started and shrank back a little. The mask fell to the ground by her feet, but this time there was no scream.

"I did not mean to frighten you. My name is Portia Edwards," she managed to say. She didn't know if the name meant anything to the other woman or not. She didn't move any closer.

Helena's hands shook a little as her fingers began to search the stone seat for something. Her eyes appeared to be focused on her, but Portia realized that the older woman could not see her.

"Can I help you?"

"Yes," Helena finally whispered. The hands continued the search. "I have misplaced something important—a mask."

Of all the people with whom she had spoken about Helena, none had mentioned her loss of sight. Even Dr. Deming had made no reference to it, and it took Portia a few seconds to overcome the surprise of it.

Her heart was beating so fast that she thought it would at any minute burst out of her chest. A lump the size of a fist was forming in her throat, and Portia desperately fought the waves of emotion that were about to pull her under.

"Are you part of the household, miss?"

"No . . . milady," she replied, forcing the words out.

"Then what are you doing here?"

"I came in search of something I lost."

The short distance took an eternity to cover. Portia knelt before the bench and picked up the mask, handing it to the older woman. Helena's hand caught her own.

"And were you here last night?"

"I was."

The face drew closer. "Were you the one who climbed to my window?"

Portia's voice came from a deep hollow. "That was I."

"Why would you do such a thing?"

They had the same eyes. They were even the same color. "I needed to meet you."

"For what reason?"

Portia took hold of the locket that was around her neck. She brought the chain forward until the cold metal touched her mother's hand. "I have had this for my entire life. I was told that it belonged to my mother. 'Tis the only clue I have of my parentage."

"Did you say your family name is Edwards?"

"That was the name they gave me."

Helena released her hand and focused on the locket. Portia removed it from around her neck and handed it to her mother. Helena turned the locket in her hand. She felt the engraving, opened the latch, and touched the miniature inside. Through it all, Portia knelt on the greensward, suddenly terrified as the thought struck her that the whole thing might have been a lie. What if she had been wrong about it all along?

"How old are you?"

Portia gave her what she knew of her exact age, including the day and month Lady Primrose had told her that she had been born.

"Where were you raised?"

"In Wales." Quietly, in just a few sentences, Portia related her life history—of her childhood under the protection of Lady Primrose, of her time in the household of Parson Higgins, of coming to Boston last fall. Taking

a deep breath, she went on to tell how she learned about Helena and the events of last night.

Helena finally closed the locket and held out a hand to Portia, drawing her onto the bench next to her. The two women sat in silence for what seemed to Portia to be an eternity. Doubts continued to linger in her head. The thought of all of her dreams being nothing more than assumptions, or coincidences, or lies was too difficult to consider. Then, when Portia thought she could wait no longer, the older woman spoke.

"I lost that locket the same day that my child was taken away. The same day that she was born," Helena whispered. "I was not given a chance to hold her . . . or even name her. I was told she died shortly after the birth."

When she saw the pools of tears in her mother's eyes, Portia could no longer control her own emotions. A sob escaped her, and the older woman turned and drew her into her arms.

"Is there a possibility . . . that all of what I have been searching for . . . was not some foolish dream?" Portia asked brokenly. "Could it be that I was that child?"

Helena touched her face, her hair, her hands again. This close, Portia thought she could see.

"Indeed. I always dreamed of someday holding you in my arms, but I thought it would not be in this life."

Portia couldn't stop the tears. As she wept, Helena touched her face again, as if branding in her memory everything that her eyes could not envision.

"There is so much that I want to tell you, Portia." She hesitated. "My Portia! And you called me 'Mother' at my window last night."

"Mother."

They held each other for another moment, each woman drawing strength from the other—each woman building a new world within her that did not exist before. One now had a mother, the other a daughter.

Helena drew back, suddenly panicked. "But he'll take you away from me again. I cannot let them find you out."

"No one saw me come in. The Admiral does not know who I am. I *must* see you again."

Helena jumped at the sound of women's laughter in the distance. Portia assumed it came from the same two women who had passed under the tree.

"You must come back. but they do not let me leave the mansion grounds." Helena squeezed Portia's hand. "But I will come down here—to this same spot—every day. And you must come and see me."

" 'Twill be difficult. The Admiral does not have many guests. Unless one is invited, his guards at the gate do not allow anyone in. I shall try, but I do not know when it will be."

Helena rose to her feet and pulled Portia with her. "Wait! Do you speak French?"

"Oui."

"Excellent. Then I shall ask for a companion who can read me French poetry. You can apply for the position. I shall do that today." She stuffed the locket into Portia's hands. "Now go. Go quickly . . . before they find you here."

She was reluctant to release her mother's hand, terrified that once she walked away, there would be no coming back. How could Portia say good-bye when she had just found her?

"What happens if they choose someone else?"

"I will make their lives miserable until they choose the person I wish."

Women's voices in the adjacent garden startled them both.

"Go . . . my own Portia."

She gave her mother's hands a final squeeze and then ran down one of the brick paths, escaping the garden a moment before the two serving women arrived to fetch their mistress.

Chapter 9

Getting out of Admiral Middleton's mansion was much simpler than Portia had imagined, for Jack—the gentlemanly groom that he was—sat waiting for her in the carriage on the drive. The man scowled fiercely, but he did not refuse to take her back to School Street. Though she said nothing to the groom about it, she was dreadfully relieved that Pennington was still inside with the Admiral. The ride to the apothecary shop was quick, and she rode in silence, thinking back on the momentous event that had just occurred. She could barely contain herself.

She was now a woman with a mission. To stay close to her mother, Portia would do anything. No connection was too unimportant, and she intended to use the help of anyone who could help her secure that position.

Back in her new room, Portia opened her trunk and immediately went to work mending Bella's dress. An hour later, she was calling at her friend's house. The young woman was both delighted and shocked to see her. Portia quickly found out that Bella had stopped at the parsonage earlier and knew about her change of residence.

"No matter what tactic I used, though, Josiah—that old Cerberus—would not tell me a word other than that you had moved. And I waited as long as I could for the parson or Mrs. Higgins to return, but when neither ar-

rived, I had to leave." Bella led her into the sitting room
and ordered a servant not to tell her mother about Portia's visit—and not to bother with tea or cakes, either.
They did not wish to be disturbed.

The two young women had met when the Higgins family had first arrived in Boston last fall. Bella's father was
a well-known lawyer. Born in Boston and graduated
from Harvard, James Turner was a first cousin of Captain
Turner's father. The two families had not communicated
much, however, until the captain arrived in the city as a
member of Admiral Middleton's staff. The Turners were
parishioners of Reverend Higgins, and that was how the
connection had begun. Though Bella was the only child
of wealthy parents and doted on by them, Portia had
been pleasantly surprised to find her completely lacking
in snobbery. Bella's only flaw was her youthful exuber-
ance. The young woman handed the borrowed clothing
to the departing servant.

"Tell me everything, Portia. What is this all about?"
She forced her friend to sit beside her. "I was hoping
you would come back here last night, but you did no
such thing, you horrible creature. And then, early this
morning that beastly cousin of mine stopped by to see
Father. Naturally, I questioned him thoroughly. You
should have seen him, leaning like an Italian tower and
moaning about the Fates being always against him. He
told me that you had fallen ill and had left the ball early
last night. And at noon, I come to visit you at the parsonage and you are gone. So tell me, before another minute
passes, what happened. The mystery of it all is killing
me. What precisely is going on?"

Because Bella was a month shy of her eighteenth birthday, her parents had not allowed her to attend Admiral
Middleton's ball. Portia had sensed the young woman's
disappointment. As repayment for arranging for her
friend to go, however, Bella had made it clear that she
would want to hear in detail who wore what dress and
who danced with whom and all the other gossip that

interested someone of her age on the verge of coming out.

"I am sorry, Bella, but I have lost the mask you loaned me. And there was some damage to the dress, but I was able to repair the worst of it."

The young woman's expression turned threatening. "I do not care about the dress or the mask or any of it, but I will strangle you if you do not tell me this instant what is happening."

"I left the parsonage and I have taken a room above the apothecary shop of Dr. Crease. I am hoping, also, to secure another position very soon."

"But this makes no sense," Bella blurted out. "The Higgins family regarded you as family, and you thought the same of them. How could one night make such a change? You will tell me everything that there is to tell, Portia Edwards."

Considering the size of the favor Portia was about to ask of the young woman, she had no other choice but to comply with her wishes. "But so much has happened."

"Start from the beginning."

"I went to the ball."

"That much I already know," Bella reminded her, settling back against a cushion. "What was it like?"

"The Admiral's mansion is magnificent. And there were at least two hundred guests—if not more—that had been invited to celebrate the King's Birthday." Portia spent some time talking about the beautiful grounds and the impressive ballroom and the types of food and drinks served. She spoke of the music and the fancy gowns. She told Bella how stunningly dashing the officers looked in their colors. Portia tried to cover all the things that she knew Bella would be curious to know about an event so grand.

After listening attentively with a dreamy smile on her face, the younger woman suddenly grew serious. "How did you become ill?"

"Well . . . I . . . I . . ." Portia knew she could not tell

everything to Bella. "Perhaps 'twas the punch . . . or the food. It may have been the excitement of the evening. Whatever 'twas I was standing in the ballroom one moment, and the next I was running for the gardens . . . for fear of becoming ill."

"Captain Turner said that you found a ride home with someone else." Bella was obviously most interested in this part of the evening. "But he wouldn't tell me who this mysterious gallant was. In fact, he became almost irate when I tried to press for an answer, which tells me your champion must be higher in rank than the captain . . . and more dashing."

When Portia laughed, Bella leaned closer. Her black eyes shone with mischief.

"Who was the gentleman . . . and what did he want in return?"

"Really, Bella! What on earth have you been reading? 'Twas simply good fortune that I ran into him, and the gentleman offered me a ride home out of pure kindness. Nothing more."

"A name. I need a name," Bella pressed.

"He is not in military. I was told he is a Scotsman, involved in shipping."

Bella impatiently tugged on Portia's arm. "A name!"

"His name is Pierce Pennington. He is—"

"Oh . . . him!" The sigh was long and deep, and the young woman sank back dramatically on the pillows of the sofa.

Bella passed a few moments in dreamy silence, and Portia looked at her friend in amusement. She didn't remember a time in her life when she might have acted and felt in such a fashion at the mere mention of a name . . . even if the person was as handsome as this particular gentleman. At the moment, however, she could almost understand Bella's reaction.

"I have seen him thrice," Bella said finally, "though only from a distance. Once when he was pointed out to me as I was riding in a carriage past Christ Church. Two

other times I saw him riding his horse down King Street. Tell me, is he as handsome up close as he is from afar?"

"I'm certain I don't know. Last night was the first time I ever laid eyes on the man."

"But he is handsome."

"He could certainly be called that."

"And tall?"

"Mr. Pennington is no giant, but he is tall."

"And was he a gentleman to you?"

Portia could name a few things that he had done that were far from being gentlemanly. "Of course."

The same dreamy look as before took over the young woman's expression. "I think he is absolutely magnificent. And rich, too. I am told there is not a party given in the colony that does not include him on the guest list. I can tell you for a fact that there is not a girl of marrying age in Boston that does not dream of capturing him."

Portia gave her friend a narrow stare. "How do you know all of this? How is it that I never heard of him until last night?"

Bella laughed. "Because you have not been on the marriage market. And because since you first arrived here, your only female acquaintances, other than Mrs. Higgins, have been Ann—who is eight years old—and me." Her tone became confidential. "If you were to consort more with other women, you would be amazed at some of the stories that you hear about the men of Boston. And I should tell you the gentleman who always leads the topic of discussion is your Mr. Pennington."

Portia was not interested. She was not going to get trapped into this. She could not help herself, though. "What kind of stories?"

"The word is that he is not looking for a wife, and a few who have pressured him have found themselves in rather surprising situations." Bella glanced in the direction of the door, making sure it was closed. She leaned forward and lowered her voice. "And more than one has even admitted to having shared his bed."

"Bella!"

"And told others that they would do it again."

"Really, Bella!"

" 'Twas an experience as near to heaven as—"

Portia stood up. "Bella, your mother would skin you alive if she heard you say such a thing."

"If I remember correctly, 'twas in the company of *her* friends that I overheard it," the young woman said with a giggle. "That is why I asked if he was a gentleman with you. Would it not be an experience to treasure . . . being a spinster as you are?"

"Even spinsters have reputations to preserve, young woman."

"Pooh on reputations."

Portia felt her ears burn from the embarrassment, recalling how close they had come to one of those treasured moments last night. With the mirror over the bed and shackles on the walls of that tavern room, she had been just another willing victim of the womanizing rogue.

She walked to the window for some air. "You do not know what you are saying. But now, at least, I understand why Mary was so upset this morning when she found me in Mr. Pennington's office without a chaperon."

"You went to his place of business?" Bella sprang to her feet, clearly excited.

"I did. To thank him for his kindness and generosity last night," Portia lied. "I never thought being alone for a few minutes with the man would be considered scandalous. Mary was profoundly upset when she found me there."

"What was *she* doing there?"

"To thank him on my behalf, I should think."

"Did *she* bring a chaperon?" Bella asked mischievously.

"No. But there was no need. She is a married woman."

"Portia, you told me yourself that you consider yourself past the age of finding a husband," Bella argued,

joining her at the window. "I believe 'twas no less appropriate for her to go there alone than 'twas for you. But you're not saying she asked you to leave because of that?"

Portia shrugged and walked back to a chair. "It does not matter how it happened or who said what. We have been coming to this for some time. As the parson's name becomes better known in Boston, Mary elevates the level of propriety in the household. My impulsive nature would forever remain a liability to his advancement. 'Twas only fair to the family that I should go my separate way."

"But that is a cowardly way of dealing with things," Bella replied. "True, there is impulsiveness and spontaneity in you, but that is the Portia everyone knows and loves. And Mrs. Higgins's rigidity is also no secret. Despite the difference in your natures, though, you two have been friends—like sisters, almost—for so many years. A family talks things out, sorts out their problems. You cannot allow those bonds to break simply because of some misunderstanding or petty quarrel."

Portia sat down on the chair. She could not tell Bella, but her own true family bonds were at the center of the dispute. "Wrong or right, we are resigned to our decisions. I know Mary will do a wonderful job of tutoring the children herself. If she chooses, she can easily find an excellent replacement for me. I'm certain that Parson Higgins, busy as he is, will hardly notice any change in the household at all."

Bella came over and sat across from her. "I am not talking about positions or responsibilities or tutoring. How shall Walter and Ann manage without you? How will *you* feel about being out in the world alone?"

"I shall miss Walter and Ann terribly. I miss them already. But that is not a choice I have. They have a mother, and that is the most important relationship in the world." Portia shook her head at her friend when

Bella began to interrupt. "I shall do fine. I already have a room, and I hope to have a position soon. I am certain that in time I will be received by the family again, but Mary and I need this separation to change the nature of our relationship. We are only a few years apart. 'Tis time she stopped playing at being my mother, worrying about everything I do, trying to make all my decisions for me. 'Tis time I tried out my own wings. I might fall and bruise myself at first, but that is the way of the world, and I must find my own way."

"But why must everything happen so quickly? Why not take your time, approach this in smaller steps?"

Portia shook her head. "The die is cast."

"I am worried about you," Bella said gently.

"Please don't be." She smiled as confidently as she could. "If I succeed in surviving on my own, I shall gain Mary's respect. This will bring us back together again, but as friends. Things might just work out for the better, anyway."

Portia believed in everything she had just said. From the day she had joined the Higgins household, there had been some confusion over exactly what place Portia occupied. She was not treated like a servant, nor was she truly family. Mary had taken it on herself to look after her, to watch and control her, as if Portia were not able to make sound decisions for herself. This control had thwarted the efforts of the few potential suitors who had shown interest in her years ago. All were honorable working men, but Mary had quickly rejected their advances and run them off. Matters of marriage, matters of the heart, were not to be entrusted in those afflicted by youthful impulses. Though Portia had not been truly interested in any of them, she had been allowed no say in the matter. She didn't regret any of that now, for her loyalty always lay with the family. Obeying Mary's wishes had been ingrained in all of them.

Interestingly, the nearly fatal blow to the Higginses'

security had not been dealt to them by Portia, but by Mary's younger sister Ellie. And the damage was indeed severe.

Still, Portia was not willing to pay for Ellie's mistakes with her own life. There was no real connection between them, and if Mary could not keep them separate in her mind, that was her loss.

All that aside, Portia knew that, in finding Helena, she had found her future.

"Will you at least allow *me* to help you?"

Bella's question drew Portia out of her thoughts.

"Why not come and stay with us? I know Mother and Father would be delighted to—"

"I truly appreciate the offer, but no." Portia shook her head. "The living arrangements above the apothecary suits me perfectly. I have a clean room and the use of a sitting room. I can take my meals with them if I choose, as well. But there *is* something else . . ."

"What? What ? Anything!"

Portia ignored the guilty feeling that struck her for using her friend like this, but she reminded herself she had no other choices. "I have heard rumors that there may be a position available in Admiral Middleton's household, a position for someone fluent in French. A woman . . . possibly a companion for the Admiral's daughter . . . someone who could read poetry to her."

"Do you mean they are looking for someone to sit with Mad Helena? Do you think 'twould be safe?"

Portia forced down the immediate impulse to defend her mother's state of mind. She knew now that nothing was amiss with her. "I should think so. And it might be the perfect position, as I am certain it would not require the commitment of long hours. At the same time, it should pay my expenses."

"And you know that Mary would approve of it."

Portia nodded. "Of course, the position might be simply a rumor. I could be building up my hopes for nothing."

"There is one way to find out." Bella patted her on the knee. "I shall send a message to Captain Turner and tell him to inquire about it the next time that he goes to Copp's Hill, which I am sure will be today or tomorrow. I believe his duties require him to go there almost every day."

A devilish smile bloomed on the young woman's face.

"What are you thinking?" Portia asked.

"I'm thinking my cousin would be thrilled if there is such a position available. Just think of the situation. He goes there every day. He can accompany you there, and then he can stop and visit with you at the mansion any time he desires. And then, he could also escort you back."

"Oh, my heavens." The prospect was frightening enough to give Portia second thoughts about seeking Captain Turner's assistance.

"Just leave it to me," Bella assured her, taking hold of Portia's hands. "Even if what you heard is nothing more than a rumor, 'tis quite possible that Captain Turner's interest in you could open the door to *some* position there."

Chapter 10

MacHeath had been waiting for an hour when the burly red-haired man arrived at the Anchor Tavern. It was just after ten. Entering, the newcomer took a quick look about him and then walked directly to the dark corner table where MacHeath sat alone. The place was busy for so late an hour, and one of the tar-covered seamen was leading the dozen or so customers in a rousing chantey. Soon, though, the tradesmen and apprentices would go home to their beds. Then only the seamen and tidesmen would remain to carouse for another hour or two.

MacHeath was wearing clothing like that of a wharf worker. The wide brim of his battered hat was pulled low, shadowing his face. When a server approached to put a tankard of ale before the red-haired man, Mac-Heath looked out the small window beside him at the cobbled street leading from Griffin's Wharf. The harbor was dark, the moon hidden by a bank of clouds.

"How did it go?" he asked when the server moved away.

"The cargo is clear o' the ship. The lads are taking it across to the Back Bay now. They've plenty o' time before the tide runs out. We'll have the shipment out o' Boston by the mornin'."

"Pass on my regrets for having it a day late, Ebenezer."

"A day or two late makes no difference, so long as

we get them. The lads in the countryside are ready for them." The burly man leaned on an elbow. "With them customs gits watchin' close along the Charles and searchin' of every new ship in the harbor, ye are aboot the last who dares to smuggle cargo o' this sort to us. Our mutual friend sends his thanks for what yer doing. Says yer money is coming the usual way."

"I'm not worried about that, my friend." MacHeath looked out the window at the moonless street again. A single wagon slowly rolled by, carrying two dark figures. "The next ship is coming from the Caribbean in a week or two. I shall send you word directly when I know what they've brought for you."

Ebenezer Mackintosh, right-hand man to Sam Adams, nodded and downed the tankard. Without another word, he stood and went out of the tavern. MacHeath waited until he was gone before throwing a couple of coins on the table. Tossing a salute to the tavern keeper, he made his way out the back door.

It was pitch-black in the back alley, but MacHeath knew his way and moved quickly through a warren of the vile-smelling lanes and passageways. When he was a half-dozen buildings away from the Anchor, he emerged onto a narrow street coming up from the harbor. At the corner, a carter sat smoking a pipe in his wagon, obviously waiting for someone.

As MacHeath began to cross the road to an alley on the other side, he spotted a small company of soldiers making their way along the harbor's edge. If he was not mistaken, they were heading for the Anchor Tavern itself. Moving swiftly, he took advantage of the darkness to slip across and into the alley. Houses lined the narrow lane that he knew led through to the next street.

Halfway along, though, he turned as the sound of soldiers at the end of the alley took him by surprise. Pushing himself up against a doorway, MacHeath was stunned as the door opened and a woman stepped out, gasping as she collided with him.

His hand immediately covered the woman's mouth and he closed the door, pushing her into the hollow of the doorway. The deep shadow hid them from the two soldiers peering into the alley from the street. He was relieved when, after her initial shock, she did not put up a fight, remaining still until the redcoats moved on.

His heart gave a violent lurch, though, when he finally looked into her face. The thin shawl that she had used to cover her hair had fallen down to her shoulders. Familiar eyes were staring up at him. He immediately let go of her mouth.

"Mr. Pennington," Portia whispered. She looked at his hat and rough attire. "What are you doing here?"

"I might ask the same of you, Miss Edwards."

"I was making an urgent delivery of medicine for Dr. Crease. There is a sick child upstairs. She has high fever and a very bad cough. 'Twas too late for my landlord to send after his own clerk, and he needed someone to explain the way of using the medicine, as well. So he asked me to bring it here."

"Did you come here on foot?" he asked suspiciously.

"Of course not. Dr. Crease hired a cart to bring me here and take me back. The driver is waiting at the end of the block." She motioned back where he'd come from.

Pierce recalled the cart and driver.

"But what about you, sir? Are those soldiers searching for you? What are you doing dressed like this? And where are you going?"

He placed his hand over her mouth again, but this time much more gently. Her lips were soft, and her eyes opened wide as they looked up into his face.

"So many questions. Far more than *I* was allowed to ask after you made my groom chase you through the Admiral's gardens."

She pushed his hand away. "I have a reasonable explanation for that."

"And for climbing trees like a monkey?"

"Of course."

"As I have reasons for being here."

They looked at the end of the alley where soldiers, some carrying torches, were running down the hill toward the harbor . . . and the tavern.

"I am grateful to you for keeping my secret today at the Admiral's house." Portia's voice lowered to a whisper. "You can expect the same from me now. But I believe you should go now, for I have a sick feeling that those soldiers might mistake you for someone else that they're looking for."

His thumb caressed her cheek once, and then he walked away.

Portia stood in the alleyway for a long moment. Her eyes strained as she peered into the darkness after him. Her mind and body were slow to recover from the astonishment of finding him here. Whatever effect Pennington had on her system before, the condition was worsening. This new mystery about the man only added to the allure.

When she reached the corner by the docks, the cart was waiting. There was a great deal of activity, though, by the tavern a few doors up. There had been singing coming from the taproom when they'd passed by it earlier. Portia could just make out an anchor painted on the weathered signboard above the door. She gestured to the driver and then took a few steps toward the commotion. On the cobbled street, soldiers were lined up, bayonets fixed, as angry customers were led out.

Portia pulled her shawl over her head and hurried down the street.

"Miss Edwards."

Captain Turner's voice surprised her just as she climbed up onto the cart. She hid her frown and waited as the officer approached.

"What in heaven's name brings you here?"

In as few words as possible she explained her changed situation and her delivery tonight. "So now, if you will

forgive me, Captain, Dr. and Mrs. Crease will surely be worried if I do not return immediately."

"Of course, of course . . . I know about the problems you face at present. You see, I had dinner with my cousins this evening. I must say, however, that there is much that I do not understand."

"Perhaps this is not the time, Captain," she said, gesturing toward the tavern, where a rather loud tavern keeper was being led out.

"Exactly right, of course. I shall arrange for an escort at once."

"That shouldn't be necessary." She nodded confidently at the older man who was holding the reins. "Mr. Jeremy here did an excellent job of bringing me, and I am certain he will do just as well taking me back."

Ignoring what she said, Turner called to one of the junior officers to take two soldiers and escort the cart back to School Street.

Only to put an end to the discussion, she said nothing more in protest, but watched the activity as she waited for her escort. Whatever or whomever Turner's men were looking for at the Anchor Tavern, they had obviously not found it. Shouted commands sent torch-bearing soldiers off to search the neighboring houses and alleyways.

The image of Pierce dressed in the clothing of a wharf worker would not leave her. She found herself worrying that he was the one that these soldiers were after.

"Some of the local tradesmen making trouble again?" she asked hesitantly.

"Tradesmen? No, indeed, my pet." Turner shouted more orders at one of his officers about taking a few of the men from the tavern to the Castle for questioning. He turned back to her. "But we almost had him. We still might."

The Castle, located on an island in Boston Harbor, was the fortress where the main body of the British garri-

son was quartered. Portia took advantage of Turner as he tried to do two things at the same time.

"Had whom, Captain?"

"MacHeath." He whispered the name like a curse. "We received word that he was here."

Portia's blood ran cold. The stories she had heard for the past year of the mysterious rogue who was said to smuggle everything from cannons to Dutch tea, flaunting his transgressions at red-faced British officials filled her mind. No one knew where he came from or who he was. Those who sided with Mr. Adams and the rebellious citizens regarded him as a hero, a phoenix that had risen from the ashes of their dashed hopes after the Boston Massacre and was fighting for them. But those who believed in the authority of the king and Parliament considered him a pirate, a thief, and cowardly shadow. There was a hefty bounty on his head.

Of course, there were many—like the Higgins family—who preferred to think of the notorious MacHeath simply as a myth. It was easier that way when one did not wish to take a stance about the problems one way or the other.

Having arrived in Boston when she did, Portia could not help but see around her the spirit of unrest. She had attended some of the town meetings. She had heard Sam Adams and James Otis and Mr. Quincy and the other leaders of North and South End Caucuses speak. She had listened to stories of the atrocities being wrought on the colonies by the occupying army. She had come to agree that Bostonians had the right to govern themselves.

Naturally, Portia's opinions on these matters were bound to create problems. Her open expression of her views had even caused an incident with a church elder's wife, and Mary had drawn the line. Because of her husband's position, she had demanded that Portia no longer discuss politics, even within the family.

Pierce's face came into her mind again. It was too far-fetched to think that he could actually be MacHeath.

Two soldiers and the junior officer returned and took their position behind the cart. Captain Turner reached up and took her hand. She tried immediately to pull it free, but his hold was unyielding. He leaned toward her.

" 'Tis a very unfortunate thing that you have been forced to make such a change in your life. Of course, I understand perfectly Mrs. Higgins's concern. The correct thing for you to have done would have been to seek me out when you became ill. If I could not have taken you home, I would certainly have arranged for a proper escort, as I am doing now. And as far as this morning, sending a note to Mr. Pennington would have been sufficient."

Portia entertained thoughts of murdering Bella for telling him every little detail.

"Still, the fault really lies with Pennington himself, both at the ball and this morning. He compromises you at every turn, it seems. Quite unlike a gentleman, in my estimation. And your reputation must not be compromised, my pet."

He squeezed her hand meaningfully, and came close enough that Portia had to move her knees for fear of his face touching them.

"I am thrilled, however, that you thought of me in your moment of need. I assure you I shall sing your praises when I meet with Admiral Middleton tomorrow. If indeed the rumor is true—though I own I know nothing of it—we shall secure you that position, my pet."

"I am so very grateful, Captain," she said in a strained voice.

"I shall bring you the good news personally after my conversation with the Admiral. Carry on, driver," he ordered in a commanding voice as he backed away.

She was certain that the smile on her face must look positively feeble, but Turner bowed as the cart lurched into motion, the escort trailing behind.

* * *

Pierce would have liked to have believed that women were capable of keeping their word and were as innocent as they pretended to be. The truth was, however, that he couldn't trust Portia or her promise of secrecy. His past had taught him that. She was too much like Emma.

Dressed once again in his own clothes, he arrived at his friend's house around midnight.

In addition to being a faithful friend and a financial genius, Nathaniel Muir was resourceful and connected with people of every class, in the colonies and in England. There was not one shred of information that Nathaniel could not obtain. If it was a person one sought, Nate knew how to find him. He was the man who could get answers, and that was exactly what Pierce was after now.

"You do not know how awkward 'tis for me to see you right now, my friend," Nathaniel said crossly, strolling into his study wearing a lounging robe of blue silk.

Pierce looked over his friend's tousled blond hair and glanced down at the white silk stockings and black slippers that he wore beneath the robe. "If your companion has made no more progress in taking off her clothes than you have, then I should say you have nothing to complain about."

"We were assisting her first, if you catch my meaning." He walked to a side table bearing a decanter of wine and poured each of them a glass. " 'Tis bloody difficult work, some of these dresses women wear nowadays."

"With your assistance or without, my guess is she'll be waiting for you in bed when you return. Who is it this time?"

"I have learned well from you. I shall never tell." Nathaniel smiled and gestured toward a chair. " 'Tis after midnight and you are here without an armed guard, so I must assume you experienced no difficulties tonight."

"None that got in the way of what needed to be done." He took the glass from Nathaniel and sat down. "There

was a wee matter, though, that came up after leaving the Anchor. One that I need your help to see my way through."

The other man's expression immediately sobered. He went to the door, opened it, and looked into the hallway before closing it again. He came back in and took the seat across from Pierce. "Someone saw and recognized you."

" 'Tis appalling how easily you read my mind."

"Who was it?"

Pierce took a swallow of wine and leaned back in the chair. "Miss Portia Edwards."

It took several seconds before the name fully registered. "The same one who came into your office this morning?"

Pierce nodded.

"But she was responsible for stopping you last night. And you say she ran into you tonight? Bloody hell, the woman is everywhere."

"My sentiments exactly."

"How foolish of me to think I was going to like her."

"You still might." Pierce put the glass of wine on a table beside the chair. "She definitely recognized me, and yet there were no redcoats waiting to arrest me at my house. And an hour later, coming here, still there was no one jingling shackles behind me."

Nathaniel relaxed a little. "Now that I think of it, I do like her."

"But 'tis still early. She might not have had a chance to contact her friends on Admiral Middleton's staff."

Nathaniel put his glass down, as well, and leaned toward Pierce. "Out with it. Did the woman recognize you as MacHeath? Did she threaten to hand you over? Give me the bloody details, while we still have time to do something about it."

"She saw me wearing a tidesman's clothing. If she did not make the connection at first, I am certain she made it by the time she got back to the cart that was carrying

her. A group of soldiers seized the Anchor a few moments after I left." Pierce was not worried about who
the informers were, for there were many Tories in Boston. The important thing was that both he and Ebenezer
had gotten away. "Portia did tell me she would keep
my secret."

"Your 'secret,' eh?" Nathaniel pondered on that piece
of information for a while. "If she were *my* lover, I would
trust her."

"She is *not* my lover."

"Too bad. But even if she were, Pierce, you and I are
different. I am too trusting, and you don't know the
meaning of the word."

"Well, I'm happy to hear you admit my judgment is
better than yours. But that doesn't help us here. I'm not
certain what to do about her."

A frown darkened Nathaniel's visage. "You are not
considering having some of those Sons of Liberty lads
murder her, are you?"

"If that were their line of work, I just might."

"Bloody hell, Pierce. You cannot just murder the
creature."

Seeing the look on Nathaniel's face, Pierce gave his
friend's chair a kick. "Of course not, you fool. If you
were just a little more sober, you'd know I was only
joking."

"Well, I make no pretense of sobriety tonight, and I
am quite ready to be rid of you," he complained. "I
would very much like to return to my bedchamber before
a certain young woman becomes nervous and leaves my
bed. So if you came here to ask my opinion of Portia
Edwards, I will tell you that, what little I have seen of
her, she does not come across as deceitful. I think you
should trust her."

"And we know how valuable that judgment is."

"What do you want from me, then? Out with it, dog."

"I want you to find out whatever you can about her."

"Find out what I can about her?" Nathaniel grinned.

"Well, it sounds like you are finally getting ready to propose marriage."

He raised both hands, feigning self-defense as Pierce glowered at him.

"Portia has some secrets of her own. Some of them I already know, the rest I want you to ferret out. I should like to meet her on a level battleground."

"I shall get you your answers," Nathaniel promised. "But if you want to subdue her, just remember that she is a woman—and a spinster at that. I suspect that she hasn't the sophistication of a lady of the *ton* nor the wealth, either. So do what you do best, Pierce. Woo her. Bed her. Then she shall remain devoted to you for as long as you need."

Chapter 11

M rs. Green immediately became uneasy at being summoned to the Admiral's library. She knew he had been meeting with his staff since breakfast, and it was very unusual to call on her on occasions such as this. Entering the library, she found that Captain Turner was the only officer remaining. She expected no small talk or pleasantries, and the Admiral started in directly as she curtsied.

"Mrs. Green, do you know anything about the need for a French-speaking companion for my daughter?"

The thin woman clasped her wiry fingers politely before her. "I cannot say, sir."

Captain Turner leaned toward his superior. "With your leave, sir, may I address the issue?"

The older man nodded indifferently and picked up a report or letter from his desk.

"Mrs. Green," the officer said, walking toward her. "Are you certain that Miss Middleton has expressed no interest in finding someone with such qualifications?"

"Miss Middleton expresses an interest in a great many things. Last winter she wished to have an apple tree planted outside her window. This spring, she wished to have a hawk to replace a songbird that died. During this past month alone, she has expressed an interest in such things as being allowed to sleep on a bench in the garden at night and walking barefoot through the mansion." She

looked from Captain Turner, who was leaning over her, back at the Admiral, who was scanning the paper in his hand. "These are only a few of the odd things Miss Middleton continually expresses interest in."

"Surely, though some of your mistress's requests might seem . . . er, extraordinary, do you not think some of these things have value? Surely, keeping her mind engaged with such worthwhile activities as the enjoyment of poetry, albeit French, should be encouraged."

The housekeeper was not intimidated by the officer's presence, leaning over her as he was. "Miss Middleton has been in my charge for several years now, Captain Turner. I happen to know that what she asks for today is generally forgotten tomorrow. Miss Helena has a great many things around her to keep her mind occupied . . . if she wishes it."

"I see I must speak more plainly, ma'am, if I am to receive a straight answer." Mrs. Green flinched as Admiral Middleton swung around and fixed her with his glare. "Has my daughter asked for a French tutor?"

She was familiar enough with the Admiral's volatile temper, and she was not about to court his anger now. "Aye, sir. She said something about it before the servants yesterday morning. I did not pass on the request, however, because one of the dressers speaks a little French. I thought that for the few minutes here and there that Miss Middleton desires it, the girl will do just fine. I decided 'twould be a waste of money to hire someone—"

"*You* decided," the Admiral barked, silencing her. He turned to the officer. "Captain, ask your friend, Miss Edwards, to report here in a couple of days' time. Mrs. Green will take care of whatever other arrangements need to be made."

Flustered and angry at being treated so roughly, she nonetheless curtsied and backed out of the room. *Well,* she thought as she hurried down the corridor, *a week should be sufficient before Her Majesty tires of this little amusement.*

*   *   *

As there were only two servants working full time in
the parsonage, Clara's position there encompassed a variety of tasks. Housekeeping, serving as personal maid to
Mrs. Higgins, looking after the children, even filling in
for Molly the cook whenever Molly's husband was ashore
from his work on the coastal packet that sailed from
Boston to Newport and New York and back. It had
never been Clara's job, though, to look after Miss Portia,
but the middle-aged woman had a soft spot in her heart
for the young tutor from the first time she'd met her.

And it was because of that feeling that she'd sent word
this morning to Portia and brought the children to Wind
Mill Point. The young woman was waiting for them
there, thankful for being given the opportunity to say
farewell to Walter and Ann properly.

The grassy point sat some thirty feet above the gray-
green waters and gave a perfect view of both the wide
sweeping harbor and the town of Boston. Clara knew
this was a place that Portia loved to bring the children
when the weather was agreeable, and today could not
have been more beautiful. She looked from the clusters
of brick houses and shops to the masts of ships swaying
gently on the water. The harbor surrounded the town on
three sides, and from here she could also see the tapering
neck of the peninsula to the south. Clara breathed in the
fresh salty air. This was *her* favorite place to get away,
as well.

The older woman walked leisurely down the slope to
where the three stood on a bluff.

They had been there for an hour and thankfully there
had been no tears so far. Miss Portia, in her great wisdom, had occupied the children with running and playing
games with them. When they rested, she'd been having
Walter and Ann point out Faneuil Hall, and the Old
South Meeting House, and the tall steeple of Old North
Church way off in the distance. Pointing out the ships at
the Long Wharf, she'd kept them entertained by giving

each of them a turn with a long spyglass she had borrowed from Dr. Crease.

Walter's interest lay with the traffic he could see moving through the crooked and narrow streets of the town.
Ann was far more fascinated by the white sails of a ship
leaving the inner harbor. "Will you take us with you
when the time comes to leave Boston?"

Both Clara and Portia turned curiously to the eight-
year-old.

"What makes you think that I will be leaving?" Portia
asked, joining the girl at the edge of the cliff.

Ann shrugged. "Mother would not give any reason
why you left, and our father could not be disturbed. Still,
Walter and I know that you love us too much to leave
for a better position. So I thought you must be planning
to leave Boston on a great ship that has sails like the
wings of a great swan." She looped an arm around Portia's waist, her small voice breaking. "That would be the
only thing that would convince me to leave *you.*"

The wind whipped Portia's dark curls into her face and
she was glad of it, as tears had finally found their way.
She hugged the little girl tight against her side.

"Give me the glass, Ann," Walter demanded quietly.
"I think if I look harder, I can find our house from here."

"I care naught about you finding our house. I'm tired
of you looking at all the silly buildings and streets." Ann
turned her sorrow into anger and poured it on her older
brother. "Tell Portia how much we miss her. Maybe
she'll come back, then. Maybe she would love us again
if she thinks both of us want her back."

Portia crouched down and cradled the young face in
her hands. "Listen to me, my little cherub. Just because
I am living somewhere else, it does not mean that I love
you any less."

"People who love other people do not leave them.
Mama never goes anywhere. Neither does Father. You
must come back." Ann was weeping openly now.

"They are your parents, my love. You and Walter are

their responsibility . . . and they are yours." Portia wiped the little girl's tears. "Still, I could not love you two any more than I do, even if you were mine to begin with. But you need to understand, Ann, even people who love each other, as we do, sometimes need to move on. They need to find their own families, make their own homes. Someday, you and Walter will move out of the parsonage, too."

"I am never getting married," Walter muttered.

Portia batted away a tear from her own cheek and smiled at the ten-year-old who had moved in within arm's reach. She pulled him closer and held on to each of their hands. "When you move away, that doesn't mean that you have lost what you had. You should think of it as a chance to add on to what you have."

Ann squeezed her hand. "We do not have more, Portia, when we don't have you."

"You still have me in your hearts. But I . . . I need to find my own family, too."

"You are marrying Captain Turner," Walter announced with certainty. "I told Ann that is the reason that you moved out."

"No, I am not marrying Captain Turner."

"I'm glad. I don't like him," Ann put in peevishly. "He's always cross and he leans when he talks and he looks like he's stuffed into his fancy coat."

"I do not intend to defend Captain Turner, but he really doesn't have any choice about his uniform."

"I don't care," Ann said, stamping her foot. "I still don't like him."

"Then who are you marrying?" Walter asked.

"No one," Portia said, relieved that their conversation was becoming less emotional. Everything had happened too suddenly, and her greatest fear had materialized. The children were the ones who were most hurt by her leaving the parsonage.

"Walter would marry you if he were old enough," Ann blurted out.

"I would not," the little boy protested.

"I would make you marry her." The young sister leaned toward him fiercely. "If you married Portia, then she would be family and never go away."

"You are leaning like Captain Turner," he protested, shoving her.

"Say that you shall marry her, so she does not take someone else's offer. 'Twould be horrible if she married Captain Turner. All their children would be fat and look down the ends of their noses and lean this way and that." Ann leaned dramatically toward Portia. She raised her delicate chin, mimicking the officer's pose. " 'Tis simply too dreadful even to think of. She would need to dress them all in little coats and listen to them all march up and down the street, shouting orders."

Portia couldn't hold back her laughter. She looked up and shook her head at Clara, who was close enough to overhear everything that was being said. She appeared entertained, too.

"But they could take their looks from Portia, you know, and be quite beautiful, really," said Walter. "Of course, that is, only if she has daughters."

"Ha! You said it," Ann shouted triumphantly, delivering a blow to Walter's arm with the spyglass. "You said she is beautiful. Why not marry her, then?"

Portia and Clara grabbed one of them each before Walter could retaliate or Ann could attack in anticipation of her brother's retaliation.

"If you two urchins make a mess of your clothing, I shall never be able to bring you out here again." Clara's warning had immediate results. The children ceased their struggle and looked up hopefully at the housekeeper.

"We can do this again?" Ann asked.

"Only if we keep it as a secret," Walter warned. "Mama did not know where we were going today, or she might not have let us come."

"I am good at secrets," the eight-year-old chirped up.

Portia crouched down between them. "Today was a

special occasion—a chance for us to see each other and say good-bye properly. But what Clara meant was that if you do not behave, she shan't be bringing you back to Wind Mill Point whether I am here or not." Portia's clarification brought a somber look into children's faces.

"Will you come to see us?" Ann asked hopefully.

"If 'tis acceptable to your mother."

"But why must we ask her?" Ann whined. "You know she never says yes to anything that is fun."

"Give her a chance, cherub. She might surprise you." Portia addressed both of them. "Even though I no longer live in the same house as your parents, I still respect them. And you should, too. Now, telling the truth, and trusting them to make the best decisions for you is part of that respect, too."

Although Portia did not want Mary and her husband to make life decisions for her, she still hoped someday to gain back their trust. Walter and Ann were wonderful children, and that was because of their parents. On this uncertain road that Portia was traveling, the last thing she wanted Mary Higgins and the parson to think was that she was acting as a wedge between them and the children.

"Someday . . . I might come back." She held on to both of them. "We shall not give them reason not to want me. Now let's go down and look at the shells on the shore."

An hour later, Portia stood on the bluffs and tried to smile bravely as the two angels were led down the slope. When they disappeared into the trees beyond the Point, she sat down on the cliff's edge and finally allowed herself to cry.

Everything appeared to be moving in the right direction, and yet she felt that nothing in her world was right. People that she loved were being taken from her. She had independence, but fear had dug a deep hole beside it, and she questioned her own decisions. Her confidence was stealing away, and with good reason. If she made a

wrong step, no longer did she have soft ground to land on. Every mistake meant a bruise, and quite possibly a severe one. She had no security left in her life. And worst of all, she was alone.

What was left of the afternoon was slipping away, and finally she stood up and brushed the sand from her clothes.

Portia picked up the spyglass, looked once more at the harbor, and turned her steps down the slope. In the best of times, and without much nudging, the ups and downs in her moods and emotions were always extreme. Now she had no one like Mary to remind her of this fault, but Portia somehow forced herself out of the melancholy as she reached the path through the woods. She needed to focus on the good things that might lie ahead.

Captain Turner had promised an answer, hopefully today. This meant that she might possibly meet with Helena again this week. The thought of the officer arriving at the apothecary shop quickened her pace, and soon she was hurrying along the narrow, winding streets of Boston. It took her half an hour to reach School Street. Mrs. Crease was standing by a window of the house next door, holding one of her cats in her arms and gossiping with the neighbor as Portia came by.

"I am glad you are here finally, Miss Edwards. Some time ago—it could have been an hour, I'm afraid—a gentleman called, looking for you. He gave me no card. When I did not find you in your room, I asked him to wait in the sitting room up the stairs." The old woman touched her arm apologetically as Portia petted the large gray cat and stepped in. "I fear I know not if he is still there."

"Thank you," Portia said politely. "I shall go up and see straightaway."

"I hope the gentleman was not offended," Mrs. Crease called up the stairs after Portia. "Please pass on my apologies for leaving him so long. A very nice gentleman. Please send my regards if he is still there."

Portia gave her a friendly wave as she turned the corner on the stairs. She knew of only one man who could affect women, even those as old as Mrs. Crease, like that.

"Mr. Pennington," she said pleasantly, walking into the sitting room off the narrow corridor at the top of the stairs.

"Miss Edwards." Pierce came up to his feet.

He was dressed in buff-colored buckskin breeches, high boots, and a short coat—very much looking like a gentleman coming back from a ride in the country and not the businessman of the day before. Or the wharf worker of the previous night. The first thing that crossed Portia's mind was that Pierce Pennington had no right to look so good in everything that he wore, all the time.

"You've been taking some fresh air, I see."

Portia immediately placed the spyglass on the nearest table and tucked a strand of hair behind an ear. She could only imagine how terrible she must look. Upon receiving Clara's message first thing that morning, she had hurried out with little regard to her clothes or her hair.

"Yes. I was meeting a friend at Wind Mill Point."

"A romantic liaison?"

Portia couldn't hold back a smile as she remembered Ann pressuring Walter. "Actually, I did come close to receiving a proposal of marriage. But my eight-year-old friend could not convince her ten-year-old brother to commit. So it was a day lost, after all."

"Foolish lad. He needs a good talking-to about the rewards of wooing older women, especially when they are as beautiful as you, Miss Edwards."

This time Portia did blush, surprised by the gentle caress of his gaze that seemed to leave not an inch of her untouched.

"And to what do I owe the pleasure of this visit, Mr. Pennington?"

"I thought I owed you an apology about last night . . . and an explanation."

"No apology on your part is necessary, sir. I was very much at fault for running into you in that alley." She said politely. "But as far as the reason why you were there, I have no—"

"Miss Edwards?"

Portia froze at the sound of the man's voice at the bottom of the stairs. *Captain Turner.* Panic washed down her spine like March rain.

"Are you up there, Miss Edwards?"

He was coming up the stairs, and Portia had no doubt this would be where Mrs. Crease would send him if he had stopped to ask for her.

"I cannot believe this," she muttered under her breath. "You must help me, Mr. Pennington. Please . . . no questions. But I need to find a place to hide you."

Portia knew her only hope of securing a position at Admiral Middleton's house lay with the officer who was coming to call on her, and she also knew how he felt about Pennington. If he found her here with the Scot, she would never get to see her mother again.

Frantically, she looked around her at the small room. There was no other way out. No closet or dresser large enough to hide his body, even if she cut him up and quartered him. And if he were to go out the door, Turner would surely hear him or see him.

She ran toward the window and pushed it open, looking down the side of the building. "This way."

"I should like to help," he whispered. "But I am not jumping out of any second-story window."

"Well, do something. Please make yourself disappear," she begged him. " 'Tis critical that he not find you here. I will be forever indebted to you."

Turner called from the top of the stairs. She ran back to the door, hoping to divert the officer before he reached it. He arrived there at the same time.

"Miss Edwards, how delightful to see you." He bowed.

She gave a small curtsy but refused to move away from the doorway. Her mind raced with other possibilities of

rooms on that floor where she could take the officer. But unfortunately, Mrs. Crease had the opportunity yesterday to show Portia only this sitting room and the available bedchamber.

"I am very sorry to intrude on your time, my pet, as you seem already to have had a very busy day. I introduced myself to Mrs. Crease, your landlady, who mentioned that you had another gentleman caller not too long ago."

"So I understand," she replied hurriedly. "I just got back from a long walk . . . just moments ago. 'Tis a lovely day, Captain. Perhaps you'd like to take a walk?"

"Do you know who the gentleman was?"

"It could have been anyone, I suppose. Perhaps Parson Higgins thought to drop over, as I did not have a chance to speak to him yesterday before I left. Or perhaps old Josiah found something I had left behind." Portia stepped away from the door, extending a hand toward the steps, hoping to entice him outside. "I have not gone to my room yet to see what was dropped off. But, now that I think of it, I am sure it must have been Josiah calling on me. He dresses very well and is often thought to be a gentleman. Did I mention what a lovely day it is outside?"

"Indeed you did, my pet. But I have very important duties to accomplish, and I cannot take any time for leisure activities today." He moved past her into the sitting room.

Portia cursed silently and followed him in. Pierce was no where to be seen.

Turner turned and looked at her. "Even so, I have some excellent news for you, my dear."

He was not gone. He was standing behind a panel of heavy draperies that covered some storage shelves set into a shallow niche in the far corner. She was horrified to see the tips of his black boots protruding about a mile into the room.

"Your duties are too important for you to be dallying

with trivial matters such as mine, Captain. Perhaps you should go. In fact, 'tis better if you did go. I could never forgive myself for standing in the way of the king's business. Please, I insist."

"My gallant pet." He spared her a gentle smile. "Are you not curious at all to hear the news?"

"Absolutely." The drapery moved. "But you should sit down."

He started for a chair facing the corner.

"No!" she cried out, containing herself immediately. "Not that one. I was told that chair belonged to . . . to Dr. Crease's father, Dr. Crease the Elder. The family frowns on anyone sitting in it." She guided him to a chair facing the door instead.

Turner obeyed her instructions and sat down with his back to the large lump behind the drapery.

Portia sat down across from him.

"Did you not just say the family opposes anyone sitting in that chair?" the officer asked.

Portia realized what she had done. "Did I not say 'men'? They don't like *men* to sit here. But Dr. Crease the Elder was quite fond of women, I understand. 'Tis perfectly acceptable with the family for me to sit here."

Turner looked at her as if she had grown a second head. This was fine with Portia, though.

"You mentioned some good news, Captain?"

"Indeed." He leaned forward in his chair. "I had a very successful meeting with Admiral Middleton this morning."

The man behind the curtain must have moved, for the drapery followed suit. She tried not to look and instead stared at the officer's long nose.

"First of all, Miss Edwards, I must congratulate you on your astuteness in learning of the position. Admiral Middleton was absolutely unaware that his daughter had expressed such an interest. After some questioning of the household staff, however, your information was verified."

One of Mrs. Crease's cats, a yellow striped thing,

dashed into the room, and Portia reached down quickly and grabbed it. She knew the woman kept the two cats to keep down the mouse population, and she placed the animal on her lap.

"The Admiral was most impressed with the fact that you, with your limited connections and means, were able to hear this before his own household had informed him of it."

The large gray cat that Mrs. Crease had been holding on the street now appeared, as well. When Portia tried to reach for it, however, the first one darted off her lap and ran toward the window. She cringed as both of them headed toward Pierce's hiding place.

"Incidentally, Miss Edwards, you never mentioned who 'twas you learned of the position from?"

Portia wanted to kick herself for not preparing an answer to this question. Her mind was too distracted to think of one now. One of the cats meowed loudly and playfully batted at Pierce's boot. The other stood up on its back legs and clawed at something behind the curtain. Portia closed her eyes. A moment later, the cat skidded across the floor into the center of the room. Delighted, the playful animal rushed back, swatting at Captain Turner's boot as it went by. The officer started to turn, but Portia stood up quickly.

"Is it not too warm in here?"

"Actually, 'tis quite pleasant."

"You are too courteous, Captain. But these animals are far too restless. I really think they need to be outside. Don't you agree?"

"My men are waiting on the street. I would much rather spend my time with you, my pet."

All the more reason for haste, Portia thought. Snatching one of the cats off the floor, she came to him.

"Well, I am not really too fond of—"

She deposited the animal into Turner's lap. She picked up the other one who was at that moment trying to climb Pierce's boot. As she did, Portia caught a glimpse of his

face and she was alarmed by the coldness that she saw there. She backed away from the drapery and started for the door.

"Thank you for your assistance with these creatures." She smiled at the officer, who reluctantly stood up. "You still haven't told me when I can start at the Admiral's house, Captain."

Turner held the discontented animal at arm's length and started across the room. "After I mentioned how eager you were about the position, Admiral Middleton decided that you can start as early as the day after tomorrow, if that suits you."

"It does indeed." Portia waited at the door until the officer had joined her and then started for the stairs. "I feel as if I have been waiting a lifetime for this opportunity."

Chapter 12

Nathaniel's connections were indeed impressive, and Pierce had been pleased with what his friend had been able to gather in the span of a few hours about Portia Edwards.

His partner's inquiries supported her claim to have been raised at Wrexham in Wales. Her parentage was questionable, but because the school she had attended was funded by Lady Primrose, a suspected supporter of Bonnie Prince Charlie and the exiled Stewarts, Nathaniel believed that Portia's father had probably been a Jacobite. From the time the young woman joined the Higgins family at the age of sixteen until their arrival in the colonies last fall, there was nothing of any significance that Nathaniel had learned. In the period since, though, he had learned the names of Portia's few friends, and even how she had become acquainted with Captain Turner.

Based on the information Nathaniel had turned up, Pierce's assessment was that Portia was harmless, which settled whatever concern he still had about running into her the night before. Still, he felt there was definitely a need for some kind of explanation and a closure to the incident, and that was the reason for this visit. He resented, however, being forced to hide like some delivery boy caught in the queen's bedchamber.

From the second-story window, Pierce spied Portia talking cheerfully with the pompous redcoat before send-

ing him on his merry way. As he left, she was approached
by Mrs. Crease and another woman, who took her by
the arm and led her toward the door to the apothecary
shop itself. Nothing more happened for ten minutes, and
Pierce found his mood growing more sour by the minute.

If she intended this as a snub, thinking that he would
simply go away, she was mistaken. He was not going
anywhere until they had their little talk. He was indeed
insulted, though.

The gray cat returned shortly after Portia and the two
older women disappeared. Intelligent creature that it
was, however, the cat sensed danger and maintained a
respectable distance from Pierce as he impatiently paced
the length of the small room.

Pierce did not know what might have delayed the
woman. He didn't want to think about it. Finally, he
heard Portia on the stairs. He ceased his pacing and
stared intently at the door.

"Mr. Pennington," she said with surprise, stepping into
the room.

"Miss Edwards," he said sternly.

"You are still here."

"My apologies, miss. You did not inform me that I
was dismissed."

" 'Tis I who must apologize. I meant no disrespect in
leaving you here . . . or any of it." A deep blush crept
into her cheeks. "You were wonderful to keep your presence a secret from Captain Turner. And then Mrs.
Crease detained me with questions about the new position." She bit her lip and then the prettiest of smiles
broke out on her face. "Is it not wonderful, Mr.
Pennington?"

"What is wonderful?" he asked grudgingly, finding
himself not totally unaffected by her charm.

"About the position. Did you not hear?"

"I only heard some veiled discussions about delivering
information to Admiral Middleton," Pierce growled. "It

sounded to me as if you have accepted a position as a spy for the British military establishment here in Boston."

"Oh, no! You could not be further from the truth," Portia blurted, momentarily upset. "This has nothing to do with politics. Yes, I have the opportunity of employment in the Admiral's household, but as a French tutor and a companion to his daughter."

"Your alleged mother."

"Not alleged. She is my true relation." Portia let out a satisfied breath and came toward him. The excitement of it all was clear from the smile on her face. "We finally met yesterday morning and, though the time was brief, we had an opportunity to talk. All my hopes were realized. Helena does not suffer from any infirmity of the mind, as far as I can tell. With the exception of losing her sight, there appears to be nothing physically or mentally wrong with her. Still though, she is held like a prisoner inside those mansion walls. There was so much that we wanted to say, but there was little time. Her servants were coming back. Helena was the one who planned this thing . . . of asking for someone who spoke French fluently and—"

"This all happened on the same morning that you lied to me, tricked my groom, jumped from a moving carriage, and distracted me in my meeting with Admiral Middleton. Oh yes, I could see you making a fool out of Jack and climbing trees in the garden. A very productive morning, indeed."

"You are being quite disagreeable." When he opened his mouth to object, she waved a hand and shook her head. "I admit I did all those things, and I apologize for using you and your groom to attain my goals. But I asked for your cooperation, and you did not give it. So I used the only option that was left to me."

"You steered the course that you are most familiar with. You take first, apologize later, and give no thought to the effect of your actions on others."

"But that is not at all fair." She shook her head. Her tone became soft. "Considering the magnitude of everything that has happened, and how significant the meeting was not only for me but for my mother, too, you must agree that all my blunders were done for a good cause. After all, no harm was done."

"You can hardly be the judge of that," Pierce retorted. "Miss Edwards, I am not certain you have any concept of what is right or wrong. You have no grasp on the correct way to ask for a gentleman's help. And you have the dangerous habit of using everyone, friend or stranger, who crosses your path. And you seem to have no regard for how damaging your actions might be to them."

"I might have done you a disservice, Mr. Pennington, but 'tis hardly fair to say I use everyone."

"This position at Admiral Middleton's that you are so excited about. Did you not use Captain Turner to secure it?" he asked accusingly. "Did you not use your friend, the daughter of James Turner, to introduce you to the captain and later manipulate them so that you might attend the ball? What about Parson Higgins and his wife?"

"That is enough." There was a slight tremble in her voice. She was wringing her hands before her, but she managed to keep her head high and hold the tears at bay. "You have made your point, sir."

"Have I?"

"You have successfully made me realize how horrible and selfish I am." Her chin quivered a little. "Now, if you are finished, I would ask you to leave me, so that I can reflect on the flaws you have so eloquently described."

It would have been best to walk away, but Pierce found he couldn't. Too many strings already attached them—some business and a few personal. She looked genuinely upset, and this was more than he had intended.

Unfortunately, he had let his temper take charge. Equally unfortunately, right now there was nothing he

had liked better than to pull her into his arms and soothe some of the hurt his words had caused.

Portia had a few flaws, but who didn't? He was making her carry the burden of someone else's, as well. Why couldn't he push through the misty presence of Emma's ghost and see only the woman who stood before him.

"So you start at your new position in two days' time," he said in a gentler tone.

She blinked once, as if checking to make sure she was speaking with the same man. A couple of tears escaped and slid down her smooth cheeks.

"You do not intend to spoil that opportunity for me, do you?"

"No."

"Thank you," she whispered. She stood aside, giving him a path to the door.

He walked toward her. "How do you plan to go back and forth to the North End?"

She stared downward at the space between them. "I shall walk, as most people do in this town."

"And on the days when the weather is not agreeable?"

"I shall not melt in any rain, Mr. Pennington."

"No doubt Captain Turner will be eager to provide you with a ride at every opportunity."

Her dark eyes showed surprise and hurt when they looked up. "That would certainly not be my preference. But you should not concern yourself with that, sir. I am perfectly capable of managing my own life."

"You mean, from now on."

"From now on," she agreed.

"And you need nothing more from me."

Portia's face flushed and she looked down. "I do not, Mr. Pennington. And I apologize again for any imposition, any awkward situation that I afflicted you with. I am also sorry for making you hide behind that silly curtain."

Pierce lifted her chin until he could look into her beau-

tiful eyes. "So is this our final farewell? You never wish
to see me again?"

"I believe that is your wish," she replied in a quiet
voice. " 'Tis definitely not mine."

He wiped the dampness from her cheek with his thumb.
"Does that mean you would like to see me again?"

"I believe this is pointless." Her blush turned deeper,
and she looked away. "It seems our time together is
always marred by arguments and unexpected visitors."

"We could both try to do better regarding our dis-
agreements, and I could certainly arrange it so that we
would have no interruption."

Pierce leaned down and tasted the saltiness of the tears
on her face. She was soft and hesitant, but her lips
opened up beneath his when he pulled her into his arms.
This was perhaps the strongest string that attached them.
Plain and simple, he was drawn to her physically. Something told him that until he made love to her, thereby
taking some of the mystery of his attraction, her mere
nearness would continue to plague him. Nathaniel's advice last night came back to him as his hands roamed
over her back, pressing her soft curves against his body.

"I shall send Jack to fetch you tomorrow night at
dusk," he whispered, kissing the soft skin beneath her
earlobe. "We can have dinner at my house on Purchase Street."

She flattened her hands against his chest and looked
up with uncertainty. "I shouldn't think that is such a
good idea. I have enough complications in my life as 'tis,
and—"

"Dinner, with no interruptions, and I promise to remain civil. You can tell me about your plans for sharing
with Miss Middleton the mysteries of French poetry."

"This is the very thing that Mary warned me about.
She suggested that any plans you have for me could
mean my ruin."

He captured her hands and placed a kiss on each palm.
"How is what I want any different from what you want?"

She seemed to struggle in finding an answer. Pierce kissed her upturned lips with enough heat that when he pulled back, she was unsteady on her feet.

"There shall be no ruin of anyone, Portia. Until tomorrow."

Reluctantly, he let go of her and walked out.

William Higgins was proud of his reputation as a reliable man. He knew many men of the cloth who hid behind the contemplative life they had chosen, shirking the responsibilities of the worldly life. He was never one of those. William stood by his promises despite the difficult circumstances that life presented. He shouldered his responsibilities and never forgot those who relied on him. He was proud of the fact that he had always remained true to his convictions, regardless of the passage of years.

That was why he had been struggling with the situation he found himself in since his wife had told him of Portia's leaving their household yesterday morning.

After nearly a dozen years of marriage, he understood perfectly his wife's sometimes unbending temperament. At the same time, he knew Portia well enough to know that the young woman was capable of pushing Mary beyond reasonable action. What he regretted was that neither of the women had sought his advice or given him the opportunity to serve as a peacemaker in their dispute. Now, at the end of the second day, and with no sign of remorse from either party, William could no longer stay out of it. He had his responsibilities, after all.

He lifted his gaze from the psalm that he had been looking at uncomprehendingly for the past quarter hour. Mary's blond head was bent over her needlework. Like him, his wife had been exceptionally quiet this evening.

"I am told that the children saw Portia at Wind Mill Point today."

"Indeed." Mary continued to poke at the stretched fabric on her lap. "Clara informed me when they returned that she took them there to say their farewells. I

had to lecture her severely for not telling me before they left. I also instructed her never to take Walter and Ann anywhere that there is possibility they might *accidentally* encounter Portia."

"Might that not be going a bit too far, my love?" He closed the Bible on his lap. "Portia is no criminal. She carries only the deepest affection in her heart for our children."

Her head came up. "Portia has made her decision, William. I believe 'tis only right that she suffer the consequences of it."

"So you consider this a punishment."

"I certainly hope she considers it punishment."

"But must our children be punished, too? You know as well as I that they are the ones who are suffering." William paused for a moment. "Ann and Walter were both quite eager to tell me about their visit with Portia. I should tell you they both pleaded with me to intercede on their behalf. They begged me to speak to you about permitting them to make future calls on her."

"That decision has already been made. And I must say, if Clara had not taken them today, no one in this family would be suffering now. In fact, we would not even be having this discussion."

"I believe we would," he announced in a tone that he hoped was still reasonable. "We cannot wish that young woman out of our lives after eight years. We cannot pretend that she never existed."

Mary once again turned her attention to the needlepoint on her lap.

"But there is something else. Putting the affection that our family has for her aside, we are still responsible for her." He laid the Bible on the table beside him. "Have you forgotten the promise we gave to Lady Primrose? There were no months or years tied into it. We agreed that for as long as Portia wished, she would find a safe haven in our home."

"For as long as *she* wished," Mary repeated bitterly.

"The emphasis is on *she. She.* Well, I did not ask her to leave. I gave her a choice."

"A choice that she could not live with?"

Temper rushed color onto her fair cheeks. "You make me sound like a heartless viper. If you recall, 'twas you who suggested sending her to Nova Scotia. You wanted to get her clear of this silliness about her parentage more than I."

"I may have been hasty in that." William leaned forward and placed a hand gently on his wife's knee. "But perhaps you were, too, my love. A choice that denies one's deepest hopes is not much of a choice. And you and I both know that an ultimatum has never had any effect on Portia. On the other hand, the voice of reason—when you chose to use it—and a common-sense approach has always worked with her before. It might have worked in this situation."

Mary shook her head stubbornly. "Portia had made up her mind. There was no coaxing her to do otherwise. I have never seen her more passionate and determined about anything as she is in this matter."

He sat back, thinking of how much influence the Tory families had in his parish. If Helena Middleton were to disappear, they would all be outraged on the Admiral's behalf. William also thought of how much he was indebted to Lady Primrose. He recalled his promise. He remembered Ann and Walter's earlier pleas.

There would be other positions, he decided. Other parishes.

"Then we are the ones who should reconsider our position," he said finally. "Lady Primrose was the one who managed to find this parish for me in Boston. She even financed the expense of our move. Now, I cannot help but wonder if perhaps her ladyship knew that Admiral Middleton and his daughter were here. Perhaps what she had in mind all along was to bring Portia closer to her mother."

"You are imagining things. She never mentioned a word of this to us."

"She wouldn't." William pushed to his feet and went to the window. A company of soldiers marched by the end of the lane. "That good lady is a generous benefactor to a great many people, but she has always been one to keep her own counsel about her plans. Look at what she did for us after our disappointment in Bristol. She might have found us a church in England. Instead, she presented us with the opportunity of moving to Boston. She wanted us here. Perhaps Portia is the reason."

He turned back to his wife.

"You think I have done wrong in putting her out," Mary cried out defensively. "I only want to protect my family."

" 'Tis not a matter of doing wrong. You have done what you felt was right for all of us. But I believe we have a responsibility to her that we are bound by. I think 'twould be best if we supported Portia in her pursuit and see what comes of it."

"What I have done cannot be undone." Mary stuffed the needlepoint angrily into a basket on the floor. "There are more problems than you know. There is her behavior, her lack of decorum and propriety. I have already lost my trust in her. I will not allow an incident like . . . like—"

"She is not your sister Ellie. Portia visited a gentleman without an escort once in broad daylight. But you must remember that we are in the colonies. The rules of propriety are different for women here. I have heard you say so yourself," Higgins said solemnly. "You must put what your sister did behind you, Mary. No one will make judgment on us here based on Ellie's scandalous past. You must let go of what happened. We are in a new world here."

Mary rose to her feet and moved away from William when he approached.

"Please, my love. Do not let that past divide our family. Let go of Ellie. Remember, instead, what a good friend Portia has been to all of us."

William watched his wife's slender back. This had been the nature of their relationship for so many years. He couldn't force her to be what she didn't want to be. He couldn't make her do anything that she didn't want to do. Oddly, in so many ways the two of them were equals in their relationship, and William wanted it that way. He respected and trusted his wife, in addition to loving her, and knew that she felt the same. He had said his peace. Now it was up to her to act on it if she agreed with anything he had said.

"Perhaps . . . perhaps I was more harsh with Portia than I should have been." She finally turned around. The room was warm, but her hands ran up and down her arms. "The truth is that I panicked, William. I saw Portia at Mr. Pennington's office, and all the horrible memories of what happened because of Ellie rushed back. I thought of what we had and how much we lost in Bristol. I worried about how much there is to lose here. I did not want to go through that again. I could not see you be robbed of yet another opportunity."

She sat down on a settee, staring into the empty hearth. "Portia went through all of that with us. She saw our disappointment. She was aware of the unhappiness the scandal brought on us and the children and even on your parishioners. This was why I could not see how she would do anything that might jeopardize our position again. I was furious with her for not understanding—for being so selfish."

William went and sat down next to his wife. He took her hand. "For so many years, we have asked Portia to think only of us. She has made *our* family the priority in her life. Now, for the first time, she is trying to think of her own future. She is also thinking of her mother, if what she believes turns out to be the truth. And we are asking her to turn her back on that. Is there not some selfishness in that, as well?"

Mary let out a frustrated breath and leaned back in the settee. "I know I was not considering her. You would

be shocked to know that I have been as upset about this situation as you and Ann and Walter."

"I know that, my love. I know Portia's place in your heart has nothing to do with any promise."

"She has been my best friend—sometimes my only friend." Tears beaded her long eyelashes when Mary turned to him. "You should also know that I have been keeping track of her for these past two days. She has taken a room in a respectable house. And starting in two days, she will serve as her mother's companion, reading French to her, or some such thing. She is doing far better with her plans than she would ever have done if she were still living with us."

"You have pushed her to independence."

"And perhaps into danger. She is heading blindly down the path she's chosen. She knows nothing of the complications or the consequences of the decisions she is making all by herself."

William placed his arm around Mary's shoulder and gathered her against his side. "Now you are talking like a nervous mother."

"I know. I also heard she had two gentlemen calling on her today. This is more than she had during all the years that she could have entertained suitors."

"Surprising, considering that she is so ancient." William hid a smile as she gave him a jab in the ribs. "So when are you going to visit with her and give her a lecture on accepting spinsterhood with dignity?"

"I shall be giving her no more lectures. But do you think she would receive me?"

"If you have set your mind to mending your fences, I do not believe she could stop you."

Pierce didn't remember Nathaniel ever wanting to discuss business this late at night. He didn't recall ever seeing his friend as provoked as he was now. He had arrived at Pierce's house at half past ten with an armful

of documents he'd carried up from the *Thistle*, their recent arrival that was now tied up to the Long Wharf.

"This just proves that my suspicion was correct." Nathaniel announced as soon as they were inside Pierce's study. "That cordial meeting with Middleton and Turner yesterday was arranged for the sole purpose of lowering our guard. They are now prodding into our business."

He dropped the ledger books and documents on the desk.

"What exactly is going on?" Pierce moved behind the desk.

"This afternoon, without waiting to receive our ship master's report, a bloody revenue officer boarded the *Thistle* with two dozen soldiers."

"They've seized the vessel?"

"Not officially. But they took our books," Nathaniel said with some heat. "They are calling it an inspection. They claimed that as of today—this afternoon, in fact— every ship coming into port will be treated the same. But I know that is a pack of lies, for one foul-smelling whaling ship and two other merchant vessels tied up at the Long Wharf an hour after Captain Preston brought the *Thistle* in, and there has been no 'inspection' of those bloody ships."

Pierce had expected the authorities to begin clamping down for some time now. And he was prepared for it.

"Do not fret, Nathaniel. They'll find nothing. After Ebenezer's men finished unloading his cargo last night, the eight empty casks were filled with seawater. Preston assured me that those are well mixed with the other casks that really do contain wine. The books record that portion of the shipment as forty-five pipes of wine. So unless those soldiers decide to tap every barrel, they shall find everything in order aboard the *Thistle*." Pierce put a calming hand on his friend's shoulder. "And even in the extreme case that they do exactly that, the blame can easily be placed on those thieves in Madeira who loaded the shipment."

"All well and good for the *Thistle*, Pierce, but I am not talking about this one shipment." Nathaniel pulled a chair closer to the desk and sat down, opening the first of the ledgers. "I think their plan is not so much to inspect what we have now, but to question every tidesman and sailor who gets their wages by us. They shall ask and ask until somebody says something that does not agree. And then they shall be at our throats."

"Our men have withstood this kind of scrutiny before. They will do just fine."

"Perhaps, but that is not all of it."

Pierce planted both hands on the desk. "What else is going on?"

"I was delivered a letter tonight that stated the customs officials wish to see the books for the *Thistle*'s last four crossings. This takes us back well over a year. They want to see everything from the time that you yourself became fully involved with the business." Nathaniel thumbed back the pages on the ledger to the date. "They also wish to see what we have in our offices for our other five vessels, going back again to the same time period."

"We supplied those books each time a ship came to shore. They should already have all this information."

"They claim that the governor has ordered them to collect the information again. They also claim this is to be standard procedure for everyone involved in trade."

"That is a blasted lie, if ever I heard one." Pierce turned around the book Nathaniel had already opened and looked down at the entries. During each crossing this past year, the *Thistle* and her sister ships carried weapons among their cargoes. But the ledgers showed records of wine and paper from England, molasses and sugar from the Caribbean. "You've been keeping perfect books. They cannot seize any of the ships based on those."

"The vessels are not my concern, Pierce. But you are," Nathaniel said quietly. "There is an open investigation in progress, but there is also a concealed one. All the

men who were arrested and taken to the Castle after your meeting with Ebenezer at the Anchor were asked one thing: to describe MacHeath."

"The Sons of Liberty will never inform on me, and no one else has enough information to put a rope about my neck."

"But I believe there is someone else. You told me yourself that Miss Edwards saw you last night. If she saw you, others might be able to identify you, as well." Nathaniel pushed the books aside. "Pierce, I think you should find some excuse—preferably one having to do with business—and go away for a time."

"What about you?"

"I am known to be just the money man in our partnership. Everyone knows you run the operations of the business. The worst they could do to me is to seize all the ships we have in port. But I have enough friends here and in Parliament that will swear to my loyalty to the Crown . . . and to my lack of interest in colonial politics. I might get slapped on the hand if they catch you, but you are the one they shall hang."

Pierce had no fear of the consequences of being caught. He knew the dangers of becoming involved. When he had come to America, he'd done so to put behind himself the guilt he carried over his brother's life and Emma's death. Settling in Boston, he had formed a partnership with Nathaniel, an old and trusted friend, and had poured his money and his energy into shipping. He had worked ceaselessly to make his fortune. In the meantime, he had found a sense of commonality with the rebellious citizens of his new home. He had witnessed the demonstrations, heard of the injustices, seen people from all walks of life fighting for the right to take charge of their own destinies. And he had found a home in their cause.

What Pierce had gained from his time here was a sense of belonging to a place and its people. Their cause was now his cause, and it was one he believed in.

The most difficult part of all Nathaniel had said tonight was that the time was quickly approaching where Pierce and his younger brother David could soon face off. They each stood on different sides of a line.

Pierce had lost one brother. He wasn't sure if he was prepared to lose the other one.

"You need to go away, Pierce. You might go to the Caribbean. I can spread the word that our business required you to go." Nathaniel pressed. "Stay away until these bastards start to look to someone else."

"I shall think about it," Pierce said finally. "Even if I decide to go, however, it shan't happen before we take the *Gaspee*. And that is only three days away."

Chapter 13

No matter where she ended up in a month or in a year, Portia could not ignore the excitement that surrounded her in Faneuil Hall. Hundreds of people were crowded inside the building. They represented every class of work—there were lawyers and teachers, tradesmen and servants, sailors and laborers. There were even a number of women in attendance. Portia was familiar with many of the faces after attending so many of the town meetings. She had even learned some of the names. They all came with the same purpose: to make their voices heard about their future.

Each time, different proposals were presented, and votes taken on resolutions that had been drafted. The voices were strong. Over the past nine months, she'd had the opportunity to hear many speakers, though Sam Adams was undeniably the most forceful of the leaders. The message was clear, and the crowds always rose to action. These Bostonians were united in their fight against a common enemy.

As always, Portia started out of the hall when she realized that the meeting was about to end. She did not want to get caught in the exchange of insults that regularly took place between the exiting crowds and the British soldiers stationed around Dock Square following these events.

"This is the last place I should have thought to find you on such a beautiful afternoon, Miss Edwards."

Portia's heart skipped a beat when she turned and found Pierce descending the steps behind her.

"Mr. Pennington." She realized she shouldn't have been surprised. Because of his shipping business, his interest in these meetings was only natural.

He lowered his voice. "I was disappointed to receive your note this morning, canceling our appointment tonight."

Portia twisted the ribbon of the small handbag around her wrist. She had sat up for hours last night thinking of the consequences of going to his house alone. This was exactly what Mary had been warning her about. There could be only one thing that would happen between them. This man's attentions were the forbidden fruit. And as much as she was hungering for a taste of what she knew he was offering, she couldn't allow herself to fall. She had written her note of apology first thing this morning and had slipped it beneath the door of his office on Long Wharf, since she didn't know exactly where he lived.

"With my new position, there was no way I could find the time . . . and I did not think it would be appropriate." Her mind went blank. She could not remember what excuse she had finally used in the letter.

"I understand perfectly. In fact, 'twas thoughtless of me to pressure you to come."

"No, you did not pressure me." Portia let out a frustrated breath and told herself to accept the gesture. "Thank you. Thank you for understanding."

"Will you allow me to walk with you now?"

Portia wished that there was a way she could stop the heat from climbing up her cheeks. "Of course. I am honored, sir."

They walked awhile in silence.

"Are you fond of Boston politics, Miss Edwards?"

"I find it intriguing," she answered honestly.

"So 'tis not your first time listening to the local rabble-rousers."

She shook her head, relieved that he was moving on from the subject of his rejected invitation.

"But you left the meeting early."

"I learned my lesson this past winter. After one meeting, I was leaving with everyone else after the speakers had concluded, and I was mistakenly pelted by a snowball intended for one of the redcoats. As a result, I slipped on a patch of ice on the street and had a ghastly bruise for a week."

"That is terrible, but how do you know you were not the intended victim?"

"My twelve-year-old rescuer confessed to it while walking me home." She rubbed the spot of the old injury on her forehead. "The poor child was more troubled by his mistake than I was hurt."

"It serves him right." He placed a hand in the small of her back, directing her to one side, so others in a hurry could pass by. "I am amazed you continued to come back after that."

Portia gave a small shrug. "Slips and bruises are a part of life. They have little effect in knocking me off the path."

His smile lit a fire in her stomach, and she felt Pierce's hand caress her back once before falling to his side. As they continued along the cobblestones of Dock Square, two well-dressed women were coming from the opposite direction, their children and servants trailing after them. As they passed, she became keenly aware of the appreciative glances the women gave the man beside her.

Portia thought, though, that there was so much more than just his handsome features and his height that set him apart. He had charm and personality and, as Bella had told her, was apparently well known to the women of Boston. She tried to put a little distance between

them, but Pierce took her arm, keeping her at his side while pausing to exchange greetings with three men that she knew were members of the South End Caucus.

"So you, too, are a regular attendee," she commented once the three men had moved along the street.

"I enjoy watching progress. I appreciate what these men are trying to do." He looked around at the hustle and bustle of people. He lowered his voice. "And I like the way they are going about it."

"That is a very interesting position, considering their tactics must be costing you money every time Parliament imposes another penalty on Boston and its people."

"There are some things more important than money."

"I agree with you, Mr. Pennington."

"But I must tell you, attending these meetings causes me pain when I consider our defeat in Scotland fighting for the same thing."

"These people have the advantage of still claiming the rights of Englishmen. Not so, with the Scots."

"Very true."

"And I should imagine that your countrymen have found 'tis far more difficult to voice one's discontent living beneath the heavy hand of British military justice."

"I think you are a genuine radical, Miss Edwards." He turned and nodded toward the pairs of redcoats positioned on the corner of every street. "But that heavy hand is attached to a long arm. We shall have to wait and see how Mr. Adams and his friends succeed in their struggle."

She realized they were moving toward the Long Wharf.

"Do you believe they can succeed?" she asked, deciding to walk a little further with him.

"Of course. These men, or their ancestors, all came to this land to start anew. The leaders are impressive for their intelligence. Their rank among the leadership comes naturally from their talent and ambition rather than from heredity or personal status that ultimately

flows from the Crown or Parliament. Many seek freedom and independence that they believe all deserve. And most important of all, they are not financially dependent on England."

"The colonists have no need of English rule, but England needs the colonists' wealth," Portia commented.

Pierce sent her a surprised look. "Beautifully put."

"But no speech can defeat the British army. As much as I personally detest violence, I believe that the colonists' grievances will never be addressed until ordinary people are armed."

There was a hint of suspicion in his glance, but he quickly looked away. As he did, he took her hand and forced Portia to stop, allowing a team of horses to pull a wagon filled with casks past them.

"An interesting observation. But where would you hear this? At the parsonage? Or has Captain Turner shared some of his insights on colonial rule?"

"Neither. The Higgins family makes it a practice never to comment on politics. And Captain Turner and I do not share any level of confidence where he might voice an opinion such as this with me." She looked out at two British battleships that lay at anchor close to Long Wharf. "This is my own personal observation. I do not believe Mr. Adams or Mr. Otis, or even Dr. Franklin himself will have any effect on the king."

"There is no doubt in my mind that you have the blood," he said quietly, leading her across the street.

"The blood?"

"Jacobite blood. The blood of your forefathers," Pierce said appreciatively.

Portia didn't know what to say. She wasn't accustomed to receiving compliments, but this was definitely praise unlike any she had ever heard. She was also surprised that he had remembered what she had told him about her past. He obviously did not consider it trivial. She chose silence as they continued to stroll down the street, meanwhile she became intensely aware of Pierce's hand

continuing to hold hers. For the sake of propriety, she tried to gently free it, but he entwined their fingers instead.

"So tell me Miss Edwards, what other political views have you been secretly storing in that pretty head of yours?"

"When it comes to my own views of politics, I fear I am not very good at being secretive."

"Then let us just hope that you use good judgment in choosing those with whom you discuss politics. I would not recommend sharing those views with Captain Turner or with your new master, Admiral Middleton."

"I am very well aware of that, sir," she said quietly. "I have my opinions, but I am not a fool."

He gently squeezed her hand. "I know that."

His words, his touch, his attentions created a havoc inside her, flustered her. Still, she didn't want this time with him to end too quickly. She enjoyed talking to him. At the same time, she worried about the appropriateness of a woman sharing what she thought with someone outside of the family. She was treading on unfamiliar ground.

A middle-aged couple strolled by, and she noticed the judgmental glare the woman directed toward their joined fingers. Portia quickly withdrew her hand and looked away. They were standing at the end of Long Wharf, and she could see the building that she knew held his shipping offices.

She frantically searched for something to say, fearing he would ask her to go to the offices with him. "I am surprised to hear you express your dissatisfaction about the situation in Scotland. I believe this is the first time that you have mentioned anything about your country."

" 'Tis *our* country, is it not?"

"Yes, I suppose so. At least, that is what I have been told." She looked down the line of shops on the wharf and the various signs hanging above the doors. "There is a distinct difference, though, when one thinks of their

country and can put faces and names to it. In my case, 'tis difficult to claim it as my own when I have no family that I know of there. No connections. No memories. Not at all like what you have been blessed with."

A deep frown etched his brow. "Have you ever been to Scotland?"

"Only once . . . in the company of Mrs. Higgins. She went to visit her family in the Highlands."

"What did you think of it?"

" 'Tis a vast and beautiful land. But I was surprised not to find many people working the land. 'Tis so sad what is happening there."

"You are talking about the clearings."

Portia nodded and made the mistake of looking up again. The way his gaze studied every inch of her face made her heart beat even faster.

"I shouldn't be surprised if you had a view on that, as well."

"I do, but I would very much prefer to save that for another place and a different time. I am certain you do not encounter many women who, with so little knowledge, are as full of opinions as I am. To be perfectly honest, though," she said quietly, "I would not wish to frighten you off with my prattle."

"Frighten me? Never. Intrigue me? That you already have."

"I believe this is your clerk, sir."

Portia gestured along the waterfront. Sean, Pierce's office clerk, was running toward them with a bundle of papers under one arm.

"You are correct. I fear I have some business that requires my attention for a few minutes. If you would care to wait, then perhaps we could take a ride and continue—"

She shook her head, stopping him. "I do appreciate your offer. But I cannot."

"Of course," he said, sounding actually disappointed.

"The same excuses that you offered in your letter apply now. And why is it exactly that you wish to spend no time in my company, if I may ask?"

At that moment the clerk approached them, but Pierce sent him on immediately to the offices.

"You were saying?"

"The letter . . . well . . ." Her words trailed off helplessly.

"I was hoping you would be candid with me. But as you wish." He gave a polite bow. "I hope I am fortunate enough to cross paths with you again at a town meeting. Good day, Miss Edwards."

He strode off down the wharf, and Portia turned and went as quickly as her feet would carry her. She had to put as much distance between them as she could, before her heart got the better of her reason.

When Mary Higgins arrived at the apothecary shop at the foot of School Street, the parson's wife was able to convince Mrs. Crease that it would be perfectly acceptable to Portia if she were to wait in her bedroom and not the sitting room. Going up with her, the old woman was full of praise for her new tenant. Alone inside the small bedchamber, though, Mary felt her guilt weighing her down terribly.

The room was clean. The furniture and the bedding was certainly adequate. The single window was open, and the sounds of the street drifted in.

What troubled Mary was not the physical conditions in which Portia lived, but how little her former charge possessed.

A small trunk sat neatly stored in one corner and a handful of keepsakes, all gifts from Ann and Walter, had been placed on the bedside table. But that was all Portia had to show for her twenty-four years of life. Mary recalled that eight years ago, the young woman had come to them from the school in Wales with more material possessions than she had now.

Portia had never cared about possessions, though. Mary remembered how hungry for affection the young woman had been then, how eager she had been to please her new family. Mary recalled how much she had wanted to be a part of them.

She and William had been too wrapped up in their own lives to recognize that, if there was one person who needed to marry and have children of her own, it was Portia. She needed family. She wanted to create what she had lacked in her life up to that point. And sharing theirs with her was not enough, for inevitably the day would come when she would be left alone—with nothing and no one to comfort her.

And that was exactly the change that Mary had forced on Portia this week.

Perhaps if they had been more conscious of pushing her into society then, of making some introductions, of encouraging potential suitors, Portia would not be attaching all hope for her future on rescuing her mother. That was a dream that Mary still thought was impossible. It was too far-fetched. It could not be the answer to all that the young woman lacked in her life.

Mary went to the window and stared down at the street below. She also felt guilty for constantly comparing Portia to her sister Ellie. That young woman had grown up amid the bustle of a loving family. She had never lacked affection or material possessions, for that matter. And even when it came to her shocking affair, while others had suffered because of her behavior, Ellie herself had lost nothing in the proceedings. After the scandalous divorce was completed, the rogue had married Ellie in spite of it all.

Now her sister was settled and well provided for. But Portia was not.

Mary saw the red uniforms of some officers riding their horses down the street, and she thought of Captain Turner. Perhaps it was still not too late. The man was certainly interested, and Portia's hesitation might lessen

in time. She just needed time to become accustomed to him. Portia was young enough to start a family, and the officer was certainly of an age to settle down. If all of this were to happen, perhaps Portia would also be happy to let her mother remain where she was.

Mary wandered about the room, planning her strategy. Absently, her eyes fell on a small desk in the corner. As she looked at Portia's pen and ink set and paper neatly arranged there, an idea occurred to her. She sat at the desk and picked up the pen.

Being a concerned friend—she wrote to Captain Turner—she was hoping that the officer would assist the family in looking after Portia in her travels back and forth to Copp's Hill. She mentioned Portia's fondness for him and expressed the gratitude of both the parson and herself. After addressing the note, Mary blew gently on it until the ink was dry, folded it, and stood up.

Time. All they needed was more time together. Hearing footsteps on the stairs, Mary slipped the letter into the pocket of her dress. There was no reason why Portia had to know.

Seconds later, the bedroom door opened, and Mary looked into the surprised face of the young woman.

"Mary," Portia gasped. "You *are* here."

The parson's wife took a step toward the door. "I have had some time to think things through. I have also had time to realize how much I miss . . . my friend."

"I have missed you, too." Portia said quietly.

Mary took another step toward her. "I know I have my stubborn beliefs and fears and restrictions, and you are clearly doing well on your own. We each seem to be satisfied with this new arrangement. But that does not mean that we have to end . . . our friendship . . . and your relation with our family, and . . ."

"Thank you," Portia whispered, walking into Mary's outstretched arms.

* * *

The inquisition taking place aboard of the *Thistle* ended with no charges or arrests being made. Pierce, however, was not so foolish as to let his guard down.

The books for the other crossings had been turned over to the customs commissioner this afternoon. They were told that the inquiry could take anywhere from weeks to months. Pierce had another more pressing matter, though. He and Nathaniel were expecting another ship, the *Lothian,* any day. The ship, en route from the Caribbean island of St. Eustatius carried another cargo of muskets hidden among casks of molasses from St. Kitt's.

Pierce could not allow the vessel to come close to Boston. He had no doubt that the British cutters stationed at the mouth of the inner harbor had been instructed to look for it.

He considered taking the *Thistle* out and trying to intercept the vessel, but that was a nearly impossible task, considering the always unpredictable voyage. Besides, if he tried to sail the brig out of the harbor with an empty hold, leaving in the warehouse the casks of rum that were scheduled to ship, Admiral Middleton would immediately send a warship after him. Without a good head start, Pierce knew he couldn't outrun the *Rose* or her fleet mates.

Though the *Lothian* was scheduled to arrive within a fortnight or so, the ship could still be in St. Eustatius, for all anyone could tell. This, Nathaniel pressed, was another reason for Pierce to leave Boston now.

Arriving at his house that night, Pierce went immediately to his study. Without hesitation, he crossed the room and snatched the letter from Scotland that he had been ignoring for over a month. His talk with Portia that morning had set off a need in him. Her comment about him being blessed with family had cut him deeply. Now, he needed to know what exactly was going on with Lyon. He had not seen or talked to his brother since Emma's death.

He took the letter to his desk and stared at Aytoun's seal. The same seal that their father had used as they were growing up in Baronsford.

There had been a time when parting from his family would have been unthinkable. There was a time when Pierce could never have imagined life without Lyon and David and Emma.

They had all grown up together, Emma climbing the same hills and cliffs as they did. Closest in age to David, she spent all her childhood with the three boys. She was a Douglas, and her family had been neighbors to the east of Baronsford. Everyone in the Borders knew that Emma loved Baronsford as much as any of them.

Pierce broke the seal of the letter.

He knew that each of the three brothers had their own distinct relationship with Emma. Lyon was the eldest. He had high expectations of her, and she had complied during the years prior to becoming his countess.

Of all of them, David had always been closest to her. They were the youngest of their merry band. From the time they were little more than bairns, the two of them had played along the cliffs at Baronsford, and the vision of them together was etched in his mind. David and Emma had been inseparable through the years. Pierce believed that his younger brother may have been the only one who truly loved her.

To Pierce himself, she had been like a sister. He worried about her from the time she could walk, watched over her. Pierce had always considered it his responsibility to teach her and guide her. He too had high hopes, but Emma had been willful and impulsive. She had a streak of wildness that could never be tamed.

When it was time, Lyon had gone away to complete his education and take his commission in the army. Emma had gone off to London with her mother and Gwyneth Douglas, her cousin. Then, their father had died, and Emma was waiting when Lyon returned. She turned the full warmth of her gaze on him. They all knew

that Emma's one wish in life was to be Countess Aytoun, mistress of Baronsford. This was her dream.

And Pierce had warned him. He told Lyon that she wanted this marriage not for love of him, but for love of his title.

Despite the warnings, though, Lyon married Emma, and that was when the wedge had been driven between them. David had taken a commission and gone off to serve the Crown.

Becoming mistress of Baronsford—as grand as that might have seemed to her before—was not enough once she had married Lyon. Increasingly, she wanted more. Pierce knew now that he had been blind to so much at the time. He had even allowed her to pit the brothers against each other. She knew how much Pierce cared for her in spite of his warnings to Lyon, so she had used him as a means of riling Aytoun. If anything at all displeased her, she would run to Pierce. Of course, the fault for every problem lay with Lyon.

He unfolded the letter, but could not see the words. The rain and mist of those last days at Baronsford clouded his vision.

Through two years of his brother's marriage, Pierce allowed himself to be manipulated by Emma, and it wasn't until after her death that he recognized his own blindness. She had been a part of their family for too long. He foolishly trusted her and tried to correct Lyon on every occasion when he had no right to do so. He continued when it was obvious that his interference was breaking the marriage even farther apart. There was so much about Emma that was a lie, and he ignored it until it was too late.

Now, he questioned everything about her . . . even her final words to him.

Emma had thrown a great party, supposedly to celebrate the dowager's birthday. Families from both sides were invited. For the first time in what seemed like months, Lyon and Emma were under the same roof. But

that morning, after most of the guests had gone hunting, the two had had a row.

No one at Baronsford was surprised by it. Everyone knew that Lyon and Emma fought when they were together.

When Pierce had run into Emma in the gardens that morning, she was upset. Without his asking, she started telling him about Lyon's poor treatment of her . . . that the real purpose of this party was to announce her pregnancy. But Lyon was being inconsiderate of her condition—of her wishes. She was distraught, at wit's end.

Pierce had been rendered speechless by the news, but when she saw Lyon coming into the garden, she had run off in the direction of the cliffs. Pierce had stopped him, and then railed at his older brother once again about the poor treatment of his wife.

He would never forget the look on Lyon's face when he told him that Emma was with child. He didn't think his brother heard anything else, not one of the accusations Pierce had hurled at him. As if in a daze, Lyon had simply gone off after his wife.

Pierce had paced the garden for only a few moments before panic seized him. As he ran after them, he knew there was something very wrong. The rain and the mist and Lyon's stunned face were a slap of truth. When he arrived at the river moments later, he had discovered Emma's dead body at the bottom of the cliffs, Lyon's broken one beside her.

Pierce had remained at Baronsford until after the funeral. He could not bring himself to look into his brother's face. Lyon was left a broken man—his body crippled, his mind sedated by the drugs to ease the pain. Or was it to forget what had happened?

There were whispered rumors. There were those who claimed that the earl must have pushed his wife off the cliffs. But Pierce didn't listen to any of it. Deep inside, he did not believe Lyon could hurt Emma.

If there was any blame to shoulder, Pierce felt it belonged to him. And that was when he had decided that he could stay there no longer. He'd left for the colonies and tried not to look back.

Pierce tried to focus on the letter in his hand. The handwriting was not that of their lawyer, Sir Richard. He read the first couple of lines over again, and then stopped and began once more, trying to make certain he was not imagining what he had just read.

The tone was definitely his brother's. This was Lyon, as he had been, before his marriage to Emma—strong and direct, to the point of being abrupt.

In the letter, Lyon said that he was married again to a Millicent Gregory. Regarding his health, he had made vast improvements, and he and his wife were dividing their time between Baronsford in Scotland and Millicent's estate, a place called Melbury Hall, which was situated north of St. Albans in Hertfordshire. They were expecting their first child in the fall, though they had taken in an infant girl already that they intended to raise as their own. They'd named her Josephine, and the "wee lass" was a spirited thing.

Pierce blinked and moved the letter closer to the lamp before reading the first section another time. Hundreds of questions ran through his mind. Lyon with children. He shook his head.

The second part of the letter was all praise of his new wife and the variety of projects that she was involved in at both places. This time, Pierce found himself smiling. This was certainly a change from the Lyon he had known.

The last part of the letter was something that he should have taken care of at first but then had put it aside. Weeks after Pierce's departure, he had received a letter from Sir Richard saying that his brother had signed all the lands of Baronsford over to him.

The lawyer had explained that this was Lyon's attempt to salvage their family. In turning over Baronsford, he

could then withdraw and let the hard feelings gradually fade. Pierce could take charge of the family lands and perhaps bring David back to help him administer them. That way, the people of Baronsford could continue to live their lives peacefully and productively, as they once had. Giving away Baronsford had been Lyon's way of determining the future for everyone. Pierce, however, wanted no part of it. He'd considered the papers meaningless. Lyon was the Earl of Aytoun. He was the one responsible for Baronsford. It belonged to him. Pierce had not even bothered to acknowledge the letter.

The last part of Lyon's letter talked of the land clearings in the neighboring estates and about the tenants' fears that Baronsford's farms were next in line to go. He also explained that the lands were still in Pierce's name, and unless he came back in person to put their people's minds at ease, the anxiety would grow.

Pierce knew he could sign the appropriate papers and send them back to Scotland, revoking what he had never agreed to. In fact, this was something he needed to see to right away, for he didn't want any inquiry into his affairs to include Baronsford. He could send the papers off on the next ship bound for England, and perhaps follow with a visit of his own.

Pierce surprised himself for even thinking of it. But then he picked up Lyon's letter and started reading from the beginning about his brother's recovery and marriage. Perhaps there could be a new beginning for everyone.

A knock on his door interrupted his thoughts, and one of his servants informed him that there was a messenger waiting to see him. Pierce closed the letter, put it aside, and followed the man down.

Standing by the front door, dusty from his travels, a young lad of perhaps fifteen or sixteen stood waiting. When he saw Pierce, he removed a pouch from under his shirt and handed it to him. Going to a window, Pierce opened it and found a letter from the captain of his ship, the *Lothian*.

The vessel had met up with an outbound merchantman commanded by a friend as they each were rounding the cape. Receiving word of what was happening aboard the *Thistle,* Captain Cameron had decided to come about and set a course for Newport. The letter informed him that the *Lothian* was anchored just off Newport, and he would await Pierce's instructions.

"How long were you riding, lad?"

"Not e'en six hours, sir. Captain Cameron said to get a fine mount, 'e did."

"Well done. Off to the kitchen with you, lad. You can fill your belly while I consider how to answer your master."

Chapter 14

Portia had not been at the mansion an hour when Mrs. Green, who had been hovering about while Helena finished her breakfast, brought in the Admiral's physician. It soon became apparent that the military physician visited her mother nearly every day to lecture her on the medications that she was supposed to be taking, but often refused to take. Unsettling as this all was, it appeared to be the routine of the household.

What Portia decided she would not allow, however, was Captain Turner's continual visits, which had begun immediately after the physician's departure. After his second appearance in an hour, it became obvious that he was going to supervise her all day.

Portia had been stunned this morning to find the officer waiting for her with a carriage outside her door. Taken off guard, she had not been able to come up with an adequate excuse, and had been forced to ride to the Copp's Hill mansion, grumbling to herself the entire way. He had informed her en route that he would have to leave the mansion for several hours during the afternoon, but that he would return for her by five o'clock and that she was to wait for him. Silently, Portia vowed that she would be long gone by the time Captain Turner came back.

Between Mrs. Green and Captain Turner, the morning was a series of constant interruptions. Not once did Por-

tia have a chance to speak alone with her mother. Around noon, a small repast of tea and bread was served, and Helena asked her to sit and join her, earning Portia a sour look from Mrs. Green. After the servants had cleared the food and dishes away, Helena turned her head toward the open window.

"The day is a fine one, is it not, Miss Edwards?"

" 'Tis indeed, ma'am."

"Then we shall spend some time in the rose garden."

"I think not, Miss Middleton," Mrs. Green immediately objected. "There is a cool breeze coming in off the harbor."

"The garden is protected, and I shall be comfortable enough in my shawl."

"You'll not be going out today, miss," the woman declared. "You've had enough excitement for one day. The doctor has prescribed rest, and 'tis my duty to see that you get it. You shall retire to your bedchamber for the afternoon."

"You'll not tell me what to do, ma'am," Helena retorted.

"Indeed I shall."

As the quarrel between the two women escalated, Portia and four servants looked on silently. If she had any lingering doubts that taking her mother away from this place was the right thing, those doubts now evaporated.

"This young woman has been brought here to read to me," Helena protested strenuously, her voice cracking. "But you have given her no chance to spend any time with me."

Mrs. Green gestured to one of the servants, who tried to help her mistress to her feet. Helena shook off the woman's touch.

"Do not worry about Miss Edwards," Mrs. Green retorted, motioning a second servant to assist the first one. "She is being paid more than enough for coming here."

"I care nothing about payment. I wanted her here for a reason, and you are determined to ruin that for me."

Frustrated, Helena twisted in the chair to get away from the two sets of hands. "I want her here to spend time with me. Just the two of us. I want to hear her read."

"There will be time enough for that tomorrow."

Portia watched the housekeeper go quickly to a side table and pour something into a cup.

"Tomorrow you will say the same thing. And the day after. You do not want her here. Now you are determined not to give me time with her."

"You are becoming hysterical," Mrs. Green said threateningly.

"I am not. I am perfectly well." Helena's gaze searched the room, unable to focus on anything. She stood up unsteadily. "I am ready to go outside now. I believe 'tis a sunny day. I could feel the warmth coming through the window this morning. I know the perfect place in the garden where I should like to sit and hear Miss Edwards read."

"Not today." Cup in hand, the housekeeper approached. " 'Tis time you took your medication. Then you shall rest."

"I do not care to rest. I get plenty of rest." She backed away and stumbled against a chair. The servants' hands reached out to steady her, but she pushed them away. "Do not touch me. None of you. I do not need any of you." She took another step and put a hand on the back of the chair to steady herself.

"Miss Edwards . . . Portia, where are you?"

"Here, Miss Middleton." She moved toward her, ignoring Mrs. Green's severe look.

Helena extended a hand toward her. "Come and help me. I want you to walk me to the garden. I am fond of sun. Bring your book. I want none of you to follow us."

Mrs. Green stepped into Portia's path and pushed the cup she was holding into Helena's hand. "As you wish, milady. I shall let you have your way for today. Just drink this, and you can go out."

Portia had to restrain herself from voicing her objec-

tion when her mother took the cup. There was no need. A second later the cup flew across the room, shattering into a hundred pieces as it hit the marble hearth.

"You ungrateful wretch!" Mrs. Green snapped, taking hold of Helena's arm and motioning for the other servants to restrain her. "How dare you?"

"No! Do not touch me."

"See here, Mrs. Green," Portia cried out, trying to get around her.

"Let me go. Portia . . . please help me."

As Portia reached out for the struggling woman, Mrs. Green grabbed her arm sharply and spun her around. "You interfere here, and I will make certain that this is the last time you ever step foot inside this house again. I care not a whit how influential you think your friends are, Miss Edwards. There is only one person in charge of Miss Middleton. And that is I."

"Portia!" The two women were practically dragging Helena from the room.

"Tomorrow," Portia managed to call out over the uproar. "I shall be back for you tomorrow."

As her mother went out of the room, Mrs. Green whirled on Portia.

"Do not incite her to hysteria again, Miss Edwards."

Portia stared at her, dumbfounded by the accusation.

"You will leave now," the older woman said, turning and following the wailing woman down the corridor.

Leaving Admiral Middleton's mansion on foot, Portia glanced at the stacked muskets by the gate house. The four guards recognized her from this morning, when she had come in with Captain Turner. She exchanged some pleasantries as she passed through, for she needed every advantage she could garner for what she was now planning.

She had not left the house before deciding that she could no longer wait. Portia had been upset enough to go after Mrs. Green, throw her on her scrawny rump,

and run off with Helena. Knowing, however, that a dozen steps was as far as she would get away had stopped her.

Her original plan was again brewing in her mind. Everything had to happen quickly, though. She could not tolerate leisurely rides with Captain Turner every morning and night going back and forth from the mansion. She was not about to sit through any more bullying of her mother, either. And she was terrified of meeting the Admiral face-to-face. The possibility that something about her could trigger some recollection or recognition in him was a risk she did not want to take.

Portia just wanted to take her mother and leave for England. Now. Today. And though he'd probably need a great deal of convincing, there was only one person she knew who could help her.

By the time she arrived at his business offices on Long Wharf, her shoes and clothes were dusty, she had removed her hat, and she knew she must look a fright. But she was past caring. Portia was relieved when the clerk recognized her.

"I am very sorry, Miss Edwards, but Mr. Pennington is not in the office at present."

"Do you expect him later, Sean?" she asked hopefully.

"I don't know, miss," he replied with a shrug. "He was not in at all, this morning, so I cannot tell you when he is planning to come in."

"Do you know anything of his schedules? Perhaps I can catch up with him somewhere?"

"Sorry, miss." The young man shook his head earnestly.

A door behind him opened, and Portia saw Nathaniel Muir step out of his office. "Well, Miss Edwards. You honor our humble offices."

"Mr. Muir," she said. "I do apologize for the intrusion, but I need to speak to Mr. Pennington."

"If I am not being too forward, may I ask what it pertains to?"

" 'Tis . . ." She searched for words, trying to come up

with a logical explanation, with anything that might make sense. She waved her hand, hoping at least to come up with a convincing lie, but nothing came.

"I am afraid I can only say 'tis personal," she finally croaked.

She must have looked even more desolate than she had sounded, for Muir gave her a sympathetic look and opened his office door all the way. "Why not come in. Perhaps I can be of some assistance."

Portia thought of Mary's objections the first time she'd been here, the warning about propriety. All of that was absolutely the last of her concerns now.

Inside, he offered her a seat. She wasn't aware how weary she was until she sat down.

"My apologies to bother you, Mr. Muir, but is there a way you can get a message to your partner that I need to see him?"

"I'm certain he would be rather difficult to get hold of at this moment, but I would certainly be delighted to deliver a message when he returns." He cocked his head slightly. "But is there anything I can help you with?"

Portia hesitated, but then decided to test her luck. "I need to speak with Mr. Pennington about securing passage . . . to England."

"Passage to England?"

"Yes."

A moment of silent scrutiny passed, and Portia tried to sit still. Though partners and apparent friends, Nathaniel Muir did not have his friend's surly disposition. On the other hand, she was not fooled by his quiet approach and boyish features. He appeared to have mastered the gullible look, but there was a shrewdness that lurked just beneath the surface.

"Is this passage for yourself, may I ask?"

"Yes. For me," she replied. "My situation has changed here in Boston. I am no longer in the household of Reverend and Mrs. Higgins."

"This change came about very suddenly."

"Yes, I was able to find a place to live, however. And I found a new position at Admiral Middleton's house." She had told Pierce what the position entailed, and she wondered now if Muir knew, as well. "Unfortunately, that situation will not work out. Whatever I thought I could accomplish working there, I have since learned was a mistake."

"I am sorry to hear that."

Portia let out a weary sigh. "There is simply no way that I can continue on there. That is why I am in desperate need to get back to England, preferably to Wales. You see, I am certain that Lady Primrose, the benefactor of the school I attended, would be willing to hire me as one of her teachers." Portia stared at the weave of the fabric of her skirt, unwilling to look up. "I . . . I have a little money, but due to my present financial situation, I was hoping to make an arrangement where I could pay for the crossing after arriving at Wales. I am certain that Lady Primrose would reimburse all the expenses of the journey. "

Finally, Portia looked in embarrassment at the man across the desk. "I am sorry. I have the terrible tendency of talking too much. I did not mean to burden you with my troubles."

She began to stand, but he waved her back into her chair.

"Please, Miss Edwards. There is no need for apologies." He shook his head understandingly. "I would be happy to explain all of this to my partner. And I am certain we can find some way to accommodate you. But you appear to be in such haste to leave Boston, if I am not mistaken?"

"I am quite . . . well, anxious." Portia said quietly. "Many things are pulling at me. My financial concerns are primary. My savings is small and—"

"We are not so hard-hearted. We can make some arrangement about that."

"No, sir. I cannot accept charity." Portia reddened.

She sounded worse with each passing moment. "But another reason why I should like to leave as quickly as I can is that since Lady Primrose is not expecting me, I need to arrive in Wales by the first part of summer, or she will have left for Scotland. I know from a recent letter from her that she is planning a journey there. If I don't reach England before she leaves, I shall be as helpless there as I am here until she gets back."

"That is quite understandable."

"I do not know how much Mr. Pennington has explained to you about my recent discovery . . . or at least my search . . ."

His expression gave nothing away. Portia decided her best chance at convincing him lay in talking, explaining.

"May I speak to you in confidence, sir?"

"Of course, Miss Edwards."

"Thank you. I . . . I was under the impression that Miss Middleton might be my mother. That was my reason for securing that position. I wished to spend more time with her. Perhaps get to know her. But after today, I know that there is no point in it. The housekeeper who has charge of her is a bully and a tyrant. 'Tis too painful to watch what goes on there." Her voice wavered, and Portia made no attempt to hide her distress. "I much prefer the strong image of her that I had in my mind to the frail spirit that I encountered there."

Portia brushed away a tear and looked up. Nathaniel was leaning forward in his chair. Concern was etched in his handsome feature.

"I am certain we can help you, Miss Edwards. I need to do some checking into the schedules and the space available on our departing ships. Pierce is the one who usually sees to those matters. But I promise to get back to you very soon. Now, if you would just let me know where I can get hold of you, I shall send you a message as soon as I have an answer."

Chapter 15

The evening was steadily encroaching, and light was failing inside the silversmith's shop. The air inside was stifling from the heat of the forge, in spite of the open doors and windows. Trying to ignore it, Pierce busied himself inspecting the shoe buckles he had been handed. In a moment the young apprentice went out the door, however, to deliver a wrapped and crated pitcher to an address on nearby North Square.

The short, stocky silversmith approached him immediately. "What news, sir?"

"My ship, the *Lothian*, is anchored off Newport," Pierce told the man. "Tomorrow night, the tide will be coming in. When 'tis dark enough, they'll make the run past the lighthouse up into the bay. You shall need at least three longboats to take what you need. You can get them out of Bristol. You know our friends there."

"Aye, and we'll have no trouble bringing them up from there. But how are ye going to slip by the arrogant bastard commanding the *Gaspee*, if ye don't mind my asking?"

"We have already planned a distraction for our friend Lieutenant Dudingston."

The silversmith quickly flashed a set of white teeth. "I cannot wait to hear about that."

"You shall, Paul. Everyone shall hear soon enough." Pierce studied the fine workmanship on the buckles.

"Beautiful piece of work. How much do I owe you for them?"

The master craftsman smiled, holding up both hands. "Yer money is no good here, sir. We shall see ye tomorrow night."

Pocketing the buckles, Pierce left the shop and headed directly for Long Wharf. A stiff breeze off the water brought with it the smell of the sea—something that he was going to get plenty of over the next couple of months. He had made up his mind. Once the *Lothian*'s illicit cargo was transferred, they wouldn't be sailing around the cape to Boston. If need be, Nathaniel could use the excuse of not finding any customer for the molasses that the *Lothian* was carrying. Instead, they would set sail for England.

And Pierce was going back on the ship himself.

As he went along the street, passing tradesmen and shopkeepers, coffeehouses and taverns, he drank in the sounds of the street vendors and carters and inhaled the familiar smells of the chop houses and the bakeries. Pierce knew he was going to miss much about his adopted city, but he told himself that he was coming back. This place had become home, and whatever troubles lay ahead, he wanted to be part of it.

Pierce had a fleeting thought of stopping to say goodbye to Portia, but he knew that Nathaniel was waiting for him at their offices. They had seen each other only momentarily when he'd arrived back in Boston a couple of hours ago, and there was much to be done in the office and at his own house before he left for Newport again tonight.

On the Long Wharf, the shops were beginning to close their doors. The day's work was over. Upstairs in their offices, Sean was still at his high desk, hard at work. Pierce shook the hand of the young man, telling him that he knew Sean would do well.

Nathaniel had been hard at work, as well. He already had ready the books that the shipmaster of the *Lothian*

would need to hand over once they arrived in Scotland. The expense of the crossing would be paid for by the arms they were unloading tomorrow. Still, the reports would be needed to account for the less than full hold of the ship. Pierce was not too concerned about the customs officials, however, on that side of the Atlantic.

There were other documents that the two of them had to go through, as well. They had to discuss items having to do with the business, since there were transactions that Pierce had begun but Nathaniel needed to finish.

Ledger books and maps and sheets of paper cluttered Pierce's desk in no time.

"What would you think if I asked you to take a paying passenger back with you aboard the *Lothian*?"

Nathaniel's unexpected question made Pierce look up from his desk and glance curiously at his friend.

"I must correct that," Nathaniel added. "A passenger who shall be making good on the cost of passage upon arrival."

"I would think you've lost your mind. The *Lothian* shall not be entering any port here. We shall not be carrying any passengers."

Nathaniel sat on the edge of the desk. "Even someone who is desperate to go? Someone that I believe you might be slightly partial to?"

There was a slight jump in his pulse. Pierce attributed it to spending more than twelve hours on horseback in the past day and getting less than a couple of hours' sleep. "When was she here?"

"This afternoon."

"What about her position? All that business about spending time with her mother?"

"It took her one day to realize that she cannot do it, apparently. She came here directly from the Admiral's house. She was nearly frantic when you were not here. Using my undeniable charm, I was able to get her tell me what she wanted. She was hoping that you would help her to get back to Wales. She has decided that she

wants to fly back to the snug little nest of Lady Primrose."

Pierce glanced at all the paperwork that he still needed to go through, at everything else that still needed sorting in his office. He was trying to stuff a fortnight of preparations into a few short hours.

"I do not need this distraction now."

"Have no fear. I shall arrange it so that she will be there when you are ready to sail. You do not need to concern yourself with any of the details."

"Nathaniel, the woman is too unpredictable. Knowing her, she will start a mutiny on the ship, and we'll end up in China or Madagascar. She is trouble, I'm telling you."

"But you can handle her. The same way that you have handled her here."

Pierce straightened up and ran a tired hand down his face.

"If you were here and listened to her tale of woe, you would have agreed to take her along. She has no money, but she is desperate to go. At the same time, she was too proud to accept charity." Nathaniel lowered his voice. "And despite the fact that she must have guessed by now at the connection between you and the notorious Captain MacHeath, she made no attempt to use that to her advantage."

"Not yet, anyway."

"More reason to take her then. She cannot hold it over your head if she is not in the colonies."

Pierce looked out the open window. He could smell the smoke from dinner fires mingling with the scent of tar and brine. It would be so much easier to say no, he told himself. The crossing would be quieter . . . and far drearier.

"We're sailing for Scotland. She wants to go to Wales."

"A minor point. She can make her arrangements for the next leg once you are across the Atlantic."

"You were searching into her past. What else did you find?"

"Nothing to make me concerned for your safety. She appears to be as innocent as a babe."

"That is going too far. You forget, I have seen her in action."

"I am talking about her reputation. I know nothing of her private behavior," Nathaniel said meaningfully.

"Nor do I," Pierce growled in return. "Whatever you think is going on between us, you are incorrect. And having her travel on my own ship does not mean that she will be likely to share my berth."

"Of course not. Why should I think such a thing?" Nathaniel smiled as he crossed his arms and stretched his long legs before him. "Now, do you want to send a message giving her the news, or do you want me to handle it?"

Ann and Walter had been only moderately successful in containing their excitement during dinner. Their own Portia was seated in her old chair. And afterward, being allowed to join their parents and guests in the parlor had clearly been a special treat for them. Having the children refer to her as a "guest," though, was somewhat difficult for Portia to bear.

She had been surprised and elated to find her friend waiting for her in her room above the apothecary shop yesterday afternoon. The offer of peace was a dream come true. Of course, Portia had been thrilled to accept Mary's invitation to dine with the family the following night. What she had not known, however, was that Captain Turner was also an invited guest.

Unfortunately, Portia's arrival had coincided with the officer's, so she had no warning. And since then, the man had been relating in endless detail to the parson and Mary every moment that he had spent with her. He seemed happiest when voicing his complaint that she had left Admiral Middleton's mansion before he'd had a chance to come for her at the end of the day. To someone who did not know better, one would think there was

some "understanding" between them. From the way he spoke about her, often as if she were not even present, it was clear that he had more plans for the days to come.

There was no purpose in denying anything. It was not the time to set him in his place. Portia had to remind herself that she was in a vulnerable position at the moment, considering the plans *she* had in the works. She would tolerate all that she could until she received word from Mr. Muir or from Pierce. And until then, she was thankful for the children's presence. If it were not for them, she would have become ill and excused herself long ago.

Unfortunately, she could not put herself out of earshot of the officer's interminable droning.

"Do not the three of them look lovely?" Mary broke in on one of the rare occasions when he paused for breath.

Portia heard her remark and decided not to acknowledge it. Ann, having heard it, turned her back to the adults sitting on the other side of the room and rolled her eyes. Portia and Ann and Walter had been taking turns playing naughts and crosses on a slate since they'd all retired to this room after dinner.

" 'Tis a wholesome sight, indeed," the officer asserted. "It reaffirms in a man a certain faith in the inherent ability in women to develop that maternal—"

"Portia has the perfect disposition for dealing with children. They are always eager to spend time with her."

"I am sure you are correct, ma'am. And I have to admit, she has the same effect on me," Turner announced. "You cannot fathom the extent of my disappointment when I had to leave her bright face this afternoon. But, as always, she showed complete understanding with regard to my responsibilities. I am definitely in awe of the way she willingly sacrifices her own comforts and wishes to make certain I am under no hardship. You should know that this is a rare quality among the young women these days. Most think only of them-

selves and have acquired a disgusting propensity to consider themselves equal to men. 'Tis most unnatural, but I find the attitude in some of the most surprising places."

Portia glanced quickly at Mary. The parson had placed a calming hand on her arm. She struggled to keep a straight face, though, when Ann began to imitate Captain Turner, leaning stiffly in her direction so far as to place her small chin on Portia's shoulder.

"Is it my turn, yet?" she whispered in the captain's drone.

"Not yet." Walter frowned at his sister. "We each play three games. Now behave, you monkey, and keep score."

Portia placed a kiss on Ann's forehead before wiping the slate clean. Walter went first.

"Are you fond of children, Captain Turner?" Mary asked, her tone sounding much more strained than before.

"Indeed, especially well-behaved ones, like yours. I am told I was an exemplary child myself. But I believe it all comes down to the discipline one receives at an early age. A child must be taught the importance of right and wrong at a time and in a manner that one *never* forgets." Turner leaned forward in his chair. "I was a very fortunate child in that my mother was forbidden to have any say in my upbringing. She was far too tenderhearted. My father, however, bless his soul, allowed for no mistakes. When he was home on leave, he expected perfection and carried a riding crop to be sure I performed to his expectations. When he was away with his regiment, he made certain that my masters beat me once a week whether I deserved it or not. Of course, I had choices as I grew older. If I did not like his way, I always had the option of going and becoming a beggar."

Both Walter and Ann had forgotten about the game and were staring at the officer with their mouths open.

"To this day, I thank my father for his beliefs in child-rearing," he said to the children. "I sometimes touch the faint scars that remain on my body and think how fortu-

nate I was to have been born to such a man of strength and character. He made me the man that I am today. It saddens me, of course, that I could not die beside him fighting heroically against the Scotch traitors on Culloden Moor. . . ."

Turner paused, obviously still moved by the memory of his father's death. The silence in the room was total, and Mary was staring at the floor, her face white with anger. The captain did not look at her, and continued.

"But in any event, I cannot wait for the day when I can pass on my father's legacy to the next generation . . . a legacy of strength and character and discipline."

Absolute silence again descended on the room. Of everyone present, Portia knew the most about Turner's hard attitudes. She had heard little bits of information about his family through his cousin Bella. She'd had no idea until tonight, though, just how twisted his views were. Mary appeared at a loss for words.

"I suppose you two will be thanking the good Lord for a few more things tonight," William Higgins said drolly to his two children.

Turner laughed, obviously ignorant of the parson's intended meaning.

Ann jumped to her feet and ran to her father, nestling in his lap. Walter sat back on his heels and continued to stare with some concern at the officer.

A knock on the door brought an end to the uncomfortable silence in the room. Josiah entered, and the old servant's gaze quickly fell on Portia.

"There is someone at the door for ye, miss."

She didn't ask any questions and made a hasty apology before following him out.

In the front entryway, a young messenger waited. He extended a sealed letter toward her. "I went to the apothecary shop and was told you were here for dinner, miss. I was ordered to deliver this in person and wait for an answer."

Portia looked behind her. Other than Josiah, no one

else had followed her out of the room. She broke open the letter and scanned the contents. Certain words leapt off the page at her. *Crossing. Tomorrow.* Her free hand fisted and pressed against her stomach. She could hardly restrain her excitement. She read the letter again.

There was the opportunity to secure passage on a ship departing with the tide from Narragansett Bay sometime after midnight tomorrow night. She needed to be in Bristol before then. There she would meet the people who would arrange for her to get onto the ship.

Scotland! She looked up in excitement. No one would be coming after them once they were there. She could easily arrange to travel to Wales. She looked down again. She was asked to keep the details a secret, as the ship was not coming to port.

Of course she would keep it a secret. Portia glanced down at the initials at the bottom: N. M. There was no signifying mark on the envelope's wax seal; no other clues that would give Nathaniel away if the letter were to be intercepted.

She thought of running upstairs and writing her response, but then she heard voices leaving the parlor.

"Please tell them yes," Portia said in a rush, opening the door for the young messenger. She stuffed the letter into the pocket of her dress and motioned for him to go. "Tell them I shall be there."

"What is this all about?" Turner asked, pushing past Josiah.

The young man slipped out and ran off down the street. Portia quickly closed the door and put her back to it.

"Who was that?"

She knew her face was flushed. Worry knotted her stomach.

"Someone . . . a boy bringing me a private message."

"From whom?"

A variety of emotions churned inside her. More than

anything else, she wanted to lash out at the man for assuming that he had the right to question her regarding private affairs.

"Nothing that is any of your concern, Captain," she said tersely. "I told you 'twas a private matter."

The officer disregarded what she said and took hold of Josiah's arm, shoving him toward the door. "Go call him back. I need to know what he wanted."

The old servant stumbled and would have fallen, but Portia reached out and helped him regain his balance.

"That was entirely uncalled for," she snapped, turning on Turner. "There is no reason to treat this man so callously! And though you are a second cousin to a dear friend of mine, our acquaintance does not give you any right to delve into my affairs. Is that understood, Captain?"

Turner's back stiffened, and the blood drained from the officer's face. He looked down his nose at her imperiously. "Miss Edwards, as a representative of Crown authority in Boston, I do have the right to question whom I want, when I want, and wherever I see fit. And do you think that you, a woman, are in any position to tell me what my duty might be? In fact, I find it quite presumptuous on your part to think that my inquiry concerns *you*. My commission from the king requires me to—"

"Though I am hardly more qualified than Miss Edwards," the parson said evenly, stepping between the two of them, "I cannot believe the king could be overly concerned about a message from Dr. and Mrs. Crease."

Portia had not realized that they had an audience, but now she saw Mary also standing in the hallway and holding the children against her skirts.

"There are better ways of getting information, Captain," the parson continued. "A simple question, for example. You would be amazed at the miracles that can be produced through polite inquiry. And I must agree with Miss Edwards that there are better ways of giving directives in the households of others." He put a hand

on old Josiah's arm. "I would imagine that even your father used some restraint in his treatment of aging servants."

The pallor of the officer's face remained unchanged, but his hostile tone lessened somewhat. He bowed stiffly to his hosts.

"You are, of course, correct. You must understand that there are so many troublemakers running wild in the streets of this foul town that one sometimes forgets who is a friend of the Crown and who is not. Miss Edwards . . ." He turned to her, his gaze enigmatic. "In the future I suggest you offer an explanation immediately, so that all this unpleasantness can be avoided."

Portia had to bite her tongue to keep from replying. *One more day,* she told herself. She had to tolerate him for only one more day.

Chapter 16

It was not until he was several blocks away that Pierce realized who it was that he had passed hurrying down Purchase Street in the dark. Dismounting in front of his house, he handed off the reins to his groom, who appeared immediately and led the horse away. Waving off his doorman, he waited until Portia came breathlessly into view.

"I am so glad . . . so glad to see you, Mr. Pennington," she started, sounding fairly winded. "But I am very sorry . . . to arrive unexpectedly like this. You told me you lived on Purchase Street, but I hadn't any idea which house. I've been walking up and down, hoping for some indication of which is your house, and—"

" 'Tis nearly eleven at night," he scolded, taking her by the arm and starting for his front door. "Tell me you haven't been walking around in the dark since you sent back word from Parson Higgins's house."

"As a matter of fact—"

"But that was three hours ago."

"I am so happy you received my answer." Portia let out a sigh of relief and stepped through the door ahead of him, returning the doorman's greeting. Pierce helped her remove her cloak, took the candle from his man, and sent him on his way.

"I must tell you that leaving the Higgins family was very difficult for me. You know that the children are

very special to me. I could not say good-bye to any of them properly. But then Captain Turner insisted on escorting me home. 'Twas absolutely dreadful.''

She ran a hand down the front of her skirts, smoothing invisible wrinkles out of the simple but handsome dress. Pierce appreciated that she was again wearing something that accentuated her beautiful curves. Wild ringlets danced around her heart-shaped face. She had the same wild look that had bewitched him that first night. He hadn't realized until this moment how much he had missed her, how much he would like to pull her into his arms and feel her body against his now. But he would bide his time.

It actually touched him that she had come looking for him. She didn't know that he was going back to Scotland on the same ship. He and Nathaniel had made the decision to keep his going away a secret until after the *Gaspee* . . . until after he was gone.

"And that was not even the end of my troubles," Portia continued. "I had to remain in my room above the apothecary for what felt like an hour until he finished giving orders to a company of bloody soldiers on the street."

"Such language, Miss Edwards," he teased, leading her to his study. "You should really consider how you refer to members of His Majesty's army."

"My apologies." This time she smiled. "As you can tell, I am quite excited about the voyage . . . and about actually finding you."

"But I believe I found *you*."

"I am the one who came looking, though."

"Indeed you did." Pierce watched color rise into her cheeks. He closed the door.

Portia moved to the middle of the room and then turned around. "It really does not matter who found whom. The important thing is that I got the chance to see you—one last time."

"So you came to say good-bye."

He saw her eyes were glistening in the candlelight, and she dropped her gaze to the floor between them.

"I came . . . I came to say thank you for what you have already done and what you are doing for me now. I also came to apologize for all the trouble I have caused you. I also came to say that . . . that the little time that I have been fortunate enough to spend in your company has been so . . . so exhilarating."

Pierce slowly walked toward her.

Portia looked up. "I—I—"

He came to a stop only when the fine wool of his coat brushed against the fabric of her gown and his breath mingled with hers. "You think our time together has been exhilarating?"

She swallowed and nodded once. "It has been for me."

His fingers gently stroked the line of her jaw. She rose onto her tiptoes, her lips hovering just beneath his. Her eyes were so large and beautiful looking up into his.

"For me, too, Portia," he whispered. "But what we've had has been just a splash in a rain puddle on a summer day. Where I want to take you is into an ocean of passion where we can plunge so deeply into the waves of desire that we will wonder if we can survive."

Her fingers inched up his chest. "I suppose my ignorance has been my salvation. I know not what I have missed since I have never experienced it."

"Then perhaps we should part ways with just a little sample." Pierce's lips brushed hers, and then he drew back. Her lips followed. He forced himself to hold back, to let her try her own wings and follow her own desires. She kissed him, innocently at first. Her arms slid upward, encircling his neck. Her breasts pressed against him, and she placed soft kisses against his chin, on his lips. She ran her fingers through his hair, her mouth moving to his ear, where she bit gently on his earlobe. Her lips moved back to his mouth and she kissed him again, this time using the tip of her tongue, encouraging him to take command.

As much as Pierce wanted Portia to find her own pace, her innocent play set his body on fire. Instantly, all of his good intentions were forgotten, and he delved deeply with his tongue, boldly taking what she offered. He touched her breast through the dress, kneading her firm flesh. She leaned into his touch, a soft moan escaping her. His other hand slid down along her back until he felt the curve of her hip. He moved against her, feeling the heat rising between them. Unconsciously, she answered his silent invitation, moving her body to some rhythm within her.

They were both breathing heavily when he ended the kiss. His lips began feasting on her neck.

"Will you feel it now, Portia?" he asked, threading his fingers into her hair and drawing her head back until the long column of her neck was exposed. He scraped his teeth against her skin. "Let me show you what it feels like to fly."

"I am afraid," she whispered.

"Do not be afraid." His lips moved downward as his hands slid over her bottom, pulling her intimately against his hardening manhood.

Her full lips parted, and she drew a deep breath.

"This will be my first time." She looked into his eyes. "But 'twill also be my last."

He was not going to correct her. Instead, Pierce kissed her lips hungrily and backed toward the small sofa near the hearth.

Portia's fingers were shy at first, but then grew increasingly eager as they moved beneath his jacket, feeling the contours of his chest beneath the fabric of his shirt. He tore his mouth free when they moved slowly down to the front of his pants.

"I have never—"

"We shall wait on that for a moment or two." Pierce roughly turned her, placing her hands against the mantel. "You do not touch me until I have finished touching every inch of your beautiful body."

"Is that a rule of lovemaking?" she asked, surprised.

"Oh, yes. Rule number one."

"Who made these rules?"

"One of the ancients, I should think. Someone who knew how to prolong the act of love."

Quickly, he started to undo the laces on the back of her dress. When it was loose, he slid one hand around her waist, pulling her tightly against him.

"I'm not sure these rules will be fair." She drew in her breath sharply as his hand moved lower, rubbing the fabric of her skirts intimately against the juncture of her thighs.

"You have made me suffer since that first night at the Black Pearl." He parted the dress on the back and pressed his lips against her exposed shoulders. She was wearing no corset, only a chemise of some kind. "You made me suffer again in my office the next day. I have been dreaming of doing this to you ever since. Is that fair?" He pulled down the dress over her arms.

"You have been dreaming of making love to me in your place of work?" There was mirth in her tone.

Her dress pooled around her feet, and she leaned back against him. As he looked down over her shoulder, her full breasts were rising and falling beneath the thin cloth of her chemise. He undid the chain of the locket she wore around her neck and let it drop to the floor.

"Yes, on my desk." He ran the tip of his tongue along the blade of her shoulder, pushing one strap of the undergarment down her arm. "But not just there. On this sofa. And in my bed. And in the room in some inn that has a mirror overhead where you can watch yourself find the meaning of true ecstasy."

"But we have only this place and this time." She stepped out of her soft shoes and turned in his arms. "And what I am feeling already tells me that I must be in heaven." She helped him to remove his jacket.

"Not yet. But we may catch a glimpse of it still."

Pierce wouldn't let her do anything more. He captured her hands and held them both behind her in one of his. He looked hungrily into her glistening eyes and flushed face, at the stretch of ivory skin descending to her full breasts with their dark tips straining against the fabric. He pushed down the thin material and lifted the breast that filled his hand so perfectly. His mouth closed over her nipple, and she cried out softly.

Tasting her, even looking at her was enough to make his control begin to slip. He stripped the rest of her underclothes from her body, and laid her down on the sofa. She was flushed and shivering with anticipation, but he had no intention of hurrying, if he could help it.

As he stood over her, she immediately placed an arm over her breasts, her other hand covering the triangle of dark curls. Pierce slowly removed his shirt. Portia's eyes followed the movement of his hands. She moved slightly on the sofa when his fingers reached to undo the buttons of his breeches. He smiled when Portia closed her eyes as he undid them. He cast them aside with his boots and went to her.

Her body was one of the miracles of creation. She was an image that he wanted etched permanently in his mind. Her skin, her breasts, her waistline curving to her rounded hip, her long legs. He would relish the feel of them wrapped around him, drawing him in.

Pierce knelt before the sofa and kissed her deeply, reveling in the intense heat that flowed between them.

"Watch," he whispered against her lips as he broke off the kiss.

Portia's dark eyes were clouded with passion when they gradually opened. He took her hand off her breast and placed it above her head. His gaze locked with hers, and he forced her to look down as his mouth traveled down to her breasts. He laved, tasted, teased, and gloried in her body's tremors as her excitement rose higher with every touch. He drew back again and took her other hand and placed that over her head, too.

"Keep them there. Both of them," he said with a devilish smile. He gently brushed his fingers over her stomach, moved lower and teased the dark curls. Her knees were slightly raised and pressed together. "I want you to relax, Portia."

Her hips moved slightly. She closed her eyes.

"Don't look away."

Her eyes opened. The blush had spread from her cheeks down her neck and past her collarbone. She looked as if she was burning with fever.

"Open your legs for me."

She was hesitant, but ever so slowly, her knees parted. Pierce took hold of an ankle and gently placed it on the back of the sofa. His fingers trailed a path downward along the curve of the calf, the back of the knee, along the silky skin of her thigh, ending with a fleeting touch of her moist center. She was quivering now, her lips parted slightly. He reached for the other ankle and placed her foot on the floor. Reaching beneath her, he raised her buttocks, lifting her to his mouth.

Portia exploded in a frenzy the moment his mouth came in contact with her. Her back arched, and she cried out loud, thrashing on the sofa. Her hands were threaded into his hair, raking at his back, but Pierce held her in place. Quickly, her hips found the rhythm of love, and he continued to tease and taste her until she was riding the waves of passion into the very center of the storm. Finally, with a desperate cry, she reached for him and brought his mouth to hers.

It was only then that he lifted her from the sofa onto the carpeted floor and entered her, driving deep beyond her mark of innocence. There was no waiting. He had no thought of prolonging their play. Her cries of ecstasy were unchanged in their zeal, and in a moment he heard his own voice join hers as his body exploded within her.

So this was it. This was what was forbidden. Passion so strong that even thought and reason ceased to exist.

Well, she was not sorry that she had come here tonight. She was not sorry about anything.

Portia cherished the feel of Pierce's weight on her. She held him tight as all the sensitive strings of her body gradually slowed their humming. For the first time she understood it, the power of the act of love. It was a miracle. Suddenly, she understood her own origin, why it was that despite the hardship that they knew must await them, her parents had conceived her. There was no thought of the future. There was no thought of consequences. There was only the moment itself, the feeling that overwhelmed a person, the heat and the struggle and the waves of desire and the unbelievable burst of power that came with that incredible release. And she knew that he had felt it, too. It had come to them at almost the same moment.

His back was broad and warm under her hands. She could still feel him within her. They fit together perfectly. It was truly a miracle.

Still, Portia knew this was their last time together. She had come one last time to meet and say farewell. But she had no regret about what they had done. Even now, she was thinking of what the consequences of tonight might be. What could be more beautiful than a child created out of this much passion? And unlike her mother, she was far more prepared to take care of whatever the future held.

Pierce stirred and slowly withdrew from her. For the first time Portia became aware of the tenderness between her legs and the hard floor beneath her.

"Are you . . . did I hurt you?"

She shook her head.

"This was not the most romantic place to experience love for the first time." He nuzzled her neck.

" 'Tis not the place that matters," she whispered against his ear, sadness suddenly edging into her heart. " 'Twas you."

He fleetingly kissed her lips before rolling off her and

sitting up. Portia felt cold and awkward, and all her brave thoughts fled at once. She scurried into a sitting position herself. She was thankful that her chemise and dress were within arm's reach.

He was totally uninhibited by his nakedness. Portia didn't allow her gaze to wander to him. She didn't want to mourn him here. She couldn't allow herself to fall apart in this room—at his house. When he walked across the room to where a decanter of wine and glasses sat near his desk, she quickly used her underclothes to clean herself and then pulled on her dress. She struggled with the laces but managed to tighten them. By the time he turned around with two glasses of wine in his hand, she was putting on her shoes.

Surprise immediately registered on his face. "You are going?"

"I must." Portia rolled the chemise into a ball and held it tightly against her stomach. She reached down quickly and picked up her locket from the floor, putting it in the pocket of her dress. All the while, she avoided looking at him. "I must go to see my mother tomorrow. I cannot leave without doing that."

Portia was ashamed that she could not tell him the truth. She knew he would never understand. He would never allow Helena to come with her. She also knew that he would hate her when he discovered the truth, for he would think she used him.

At that moment she hated herself.

"How do you plan to get to Bristol?"

"Today . . . today Captain Turner offered to take me home in one of the Admiral's carriages, but I refused. Tomorrow, I thought I might accept it. Once we're outside of the gates, I thought I would pay the driver whatever amount he asks to take me to Bristol."

"You think he'll carry you five hours in the Admiral's carriage?" He put one of the glasses of wine on the table.

"I would give him every penny I have, if need be, but I—"

"Your plan is very risky."

He drank down one of the glasses, and she watched him walk back across the room and pull on his breeches. She wasn't sure what he meant by that. Was it possible that he sensed she would be taking Helena with her? Portia felt suddenly panicked.

He turned to her. "I shall have Jack come and get you at four. He will take you back to your house to get what you need and from there will drive you to Bristol."

"I could not ask that of you. That would be too much trouble . . . for you . . . for him." This meant that she would be using his groom a second time. Portia didn't know if she could stand it if he hated her any more.

"I do not want any groom of Middleton's that close to my ship. Also, there is no saying that one of his guards might not be driving the carriage. Or even Turner himself. Your plan has too many potential problems." No shirt, no shoes, but he was very much the businessman. "Four o'clock. Be ready. Jack will be waiting and take care of things from there."

He walked out of the room and called for his servant. Portia's face began to burn with embarrassment. Everyone in Pierce's household knew what they had done. By tomorrow, half of Boston could know about Mr. Pennington's latest conquest.

She reminded herself that none of that mattered anymore. The road that she was taking would be made up of those who hated her—the ones she'd left behind—and those people in her future, who hopefully would give her a chance.

He came back into the room a moment later carrying her cloak. "Jack is bringing the carriage out front. He shall drive you back to School Street."

Portia bit the inside of her lip, telling herself that she would not cry. Pierce's hands gently draped the cloak around her neck.

"You will be careful," he said softly.

She had to look up, and when she did, his handsome face was only a teary blur.

"I shall never forget you," she whispered, brushing her lips against his and running from the room.

Chapter 17

Portia tried, but nothing she did improved her looks. Her eyelids were swollen and red-rimmed from tears she'd shed during the night. Her face was pale, and her voice was hoarse. She'd hardly slept because of the pounding in her head and the knot in her stomach, and her steps were dragging when she left the apothecary.

She supposed it was unavoidable. She had even expected it. Captain Turner was waiting beside one of Admiral Middleton's carriages on School Street. Still, her mood took another tumble downward at the sight of the officer.

"What ever happened to you, Miss Edwards? Are you unwell?"

"I shall be fine," she replied, not wasting any time with polite greetings. She headed straight for the waiting carriage.

"If you are unwell, perhaps you should spend the day in bed. I can make your excuses to Mrs. Green. I could even send someone after Mrs. Higgins, so that she could—"

"No, Captain," she said, seating herself in the carriage. "I was not well during the night, but I am much better this morning. So if you do not mind, I have no wish to make a bad impression by being late on the second day."

"Of course." Turner climbed onto the seat next to her. "But if anything, my pet, you are early this morning."

"Even better. This way, I can be of more use in the Admiral's household."

Portia was relieved when the carriage started down the street. She needed to employ every odd minute that she could today. She needed time alone with Helena. Her plan for today was slightly better than the one she had conjured the night of the ball . . . but only slightly. She still needed to convince her mother that they could successfully escape. And then, she needed to bring it about.

"I am embarrassed, my pet, that I shall not be available to take you home again this afternoon." Turner patted Portia's knee boldly.

She moved discreetly away from him. "I can manage very well myself."

"Indeed, I still find your sense of independence quite charming."

"Still, Captain?"

"Very much so. But my concern still remains that you do not look very well this morning, and the walk from Copp's Hill to School Street is a very long way."

"Mrs. Crease had the same concern when she saw me this morning," Portia said, thinking quickly. "She said she will arrange to have a cart sent for me at the end of the day. I believe you met Mr. Jeremy, who often drives for them."

"Of course. Well . . . indeed. In that case . . ." He looked terribly disappointed, but he did not say anything more.

Portia thought of possible complications that could surface. The biggest one, of course, was if Turner were to see Jack driving Pierce's carriage. It hardly resembled anything that Dr. or Mrs. Crease would hire. She looked out the carriage window at the bustling activity on the streets. Boston's day was well under way.

"I never realized, in seeking a position in Admiral Middleton's household, that I would become such a burden to you, Captain," she said in a gentler tone. "Going

back and forth to Copp's Hill so many times a day for my sake is really not necessary."

"Nonsense. I look forward to it. Besides, the Admiral likes to receive a daily report from me."

"Still though, that is only once a day," she stressed. "The imposition of having to return a second time is really too much."

"But 'tis no imposition, my pet," he said, leaning toward her. "I was delighted when my cousin mentioned your interest in this position to begin with. But that excitement was nothing compared to being asked by Mrs. Higgins to look after you, my dear. Indeed, that was an honor."

Portia hid her surprise at hearing the little revelation. Mary's interfering was unexpected, but she was not about to hold any grudges. She knew Mary did what she thought was best. It was up to Portia not to allow that to ruin her own plans.

"With the exception of an unexpected situation that will require my being away from you until tomorrow, I can promise you, my pet, that I shall be true to my pledge. I shall be available to escort you both ways, day in and day out."

Day in and day out. Well, that would be no concern to her after today, so long as he did not reappear at the Admiral's door this afternoon. She decided on the direct approach. "And where are you going, if I might ask?"

"I will be leading a small company of men to Newport."

Portia started, feeling a stab of worry. She shifted in the seat and glanced casually at the officer. "That is such a very long ride, is it not?"

"Not bad at all at this time of the year. The roads between Boston and Newport are quite good."

"I have never been there," she said casually. "But I hear Rhode Island is not a very large colony."

"You should not let the size of the place fool you. Rhode Islanders are a troublesome bunch. Traitors, most

of them, and braggarts. They have, quite brazenly, proclaimed themselves to be smuggling champions of the British colonies."

Portia remembered a pamphlet she had recently read defending a Rhode Island merchant who was being tried in Boston for smuggling. The writer of the pamphlet argued that Parliament had robbed the colonists of any other way of earning a living.

Rhode Island had no huge tracts of land for farming, as did the other colonies. Wrapped around the Narragansett Bay as it was, the colony had only trade as a means of making a living. With the lawmakers in London placing more and more restrictions on free trade and levying excessive taxes on imports, Rhode Island businessmen had a right to do what they had to do to survive.

The pamphlet had been very persuasive, but Portia kept her thoughts to herself. She doubted that Captain Turner would share her opinion. Besides, she had more important worries; for instance, the fact that Pierce's ship was there . . . and she was going to meet it.

"There must be some grave trouble there for the Admiral to spare an officer as trusted and valuable as you. The matter must be very important indeed, or he certainly would surely have sent a junior officer."

Turner's chest stuck out, and he nodded at her approvingly. "You are correct, my dear. I would not be boasting to say that he is sending me to be sure that the situation is handled properly."

"But what can be so important?" she asked, trying to sound as awestruck as she could manage.

"Well . . ." The man looked out the window of the carriage. They were almost to the gates of the mansion. "This information is highly privileged, so you mustn't breath any of this to a soul."

"Of course not," she whispered.

"We have intercepted some messages circulating in Boston pertaining to some trouble that is brewing in Rhode Island. We know that the villainous jackal they

call Captain MacHeath has a hand in it. And we believe his aim is to disrupt the work of our revenue ships there in the Narragansett Bay."

"You believe something is going to happen today?"

"That is what our information leads us to believe." He waved to the guards at the gate, and the carriage rolled through. "But we are prepared for them. We have been working to force their hand. If we capture MacHeath in our snares, all the better."

"That is so clever of you," she said, with enthusiasm. "Why wait when you can take the fight to their door. Put *them* on the defensive and capture a ringleader at the same time. But how would you do that?"

The carriage stopped by a side entrance, but Portia showed no interest in getting down. Instead, she stared expectantly at the officer.

"We have been harassing the rogues regularly for some time now. We spread the rumor, however, that starting today every ship entering Narragansett Bay will be seized. All cargo will be sent to Boston if there is even the slightest irregularity—and there will indeed be irregularities—and the ship's masters and owners will be jailed until they can be tried."

"You will do that even if everything on the ship is as it should be?" Portia asked, unable to hold back her surprise at the unfairness of the threat.

"We must, I'm afraid. These Rhode Islanders are rogues and rascals. We are putting pressure on them all to flush out the worst. The best way to teach the thieves anything," he said passionately, "is to disrupt their commerce, interrupt their trade. And when we catch MacHeath, we shall hang him in Newport and drag his body back to Boston. That shall be a lesson for these dogs."

She drew in a deep breath. She was going away tonight; now her concern for Pierce was threatening to upset everything. What if he was indeed MacHeath? Tears once again welled up in her eyes, and Portia had to blink them away. There was no purpose in learning

any more about him, she reminded herself. The less she knew the better. Besides, he could take care of himself. Even so, Portia wanted to be sure.

"I still do not see your role in this, Captain. Why must Admiral Middleton deprive Boston of your presence? Does Rhode Island have no one of authority capable of handling this situation?"

"I must go because the officers commanding the vessels in the Narragansett Bay do not report to the colonial governor in Newport but to the Crown authority here in Boston. The decision was made to send a ranking officer to take command of the situation, should MacHeath act tonight, as we think he will."

She was going to Bristol, Portia told herself, not Newport. It was unlikely that her path and Turner's would cross tonight.

"And you said you will be leaving for Newport this morning?" she asked.

"I do not recall mentioning any particular time." He climbed out of the carriage and turned to assist her.

Portia quickly scrambled out herself. She guessed her pail had scraped the bottom of the well with regard to getting any more information out of the officer.

"Have a safe journey, Captain," she said, quickly backing toward the house.

"I shall make arrangements for someone to escort you here tomorrow morning."

Portia was tempted to tell him there was no need. Instead though, she gave him an amiable wave and went inside.

Let him think what he wished. She wanted Turner to go away with his conscience at ease.

Mary had thought she'd left her house early enough to catch Portia before she left for the North End, but Mrs. Crease told her otherwise.

"We're finding that Miss Edwards is an early riser, ma'am," the older woman said. "Both today and yester-

day, she was up and gone before Dr. Crease and I were even awake. And that's saying something."

Mary considered coming back that night, but for the basket of peace offerings she'd put together. A loaf of fresh bread, a bottle of Portia's favorite jam, a cross-stitched handkerchief Mary had finished working on last week, a small framed silhouette of Ann and Walter. They were just a few things, but Mary wanted to shed the feeling of guilt she'd been carrying since last night.

Mary could not recall ever having been more wrong about a person. Hearing Turner's opinions had been appalling. Thinking that she had slyly encouraged the officer to spend time with Portia without the young woman's knowledge was almost unforgivable. She needed to find a way to gently approach Portia about the matter. She needed to explain her blunder to her friend and perhaps, with her help, find a way of putting an end to the officer's attentions.

"Since I am here, may I leave this basket in Miss Edwards's room?"

"Of course, Mrs. Higgins," the landlady said good-naturedly. "You know the way, I believe?"

Moments later, Mary pushed open Portia's door. Inside, however, she looked about in confusion. All of Portia's belongings had been neatly packed and her small trunk was sitting on the floor beside the bed. All of the small mementos she had previously displayed has been packed away as well, and the room had been thoroughly cleaned.

Mary thought back over last night. Portia had said nothing about moving again. But she remembered that the young woman had not had much chance to say anything, thanks to Captain Turner.

Certainly, it would be understandable if Portia were offered a room at Admiral Middleton's. There was also the possibility that she had found a living arrangement closer to the North End. Mary placed her basket on the

small writing table. That was when she spotted the sealed letter, addressed to her.

Without hesitation, she broke it open.

> *Dearest Friend,*
> *By the time you receive this letter, I will have begun the first leg of my journey back to Wales, where—as I mentioned to you before—I intend to petition the good Lady Primrose for aid and a position. My friend, I thank you for all the kindness you and Parson Higgins have shown me over the years. I am so very grateful for your gift in allowing me to be part of your beautiful children's lives.*

Mary looked up from the letter at Portia's trunk. She could not have left yet. She hurriedly read through the young woman's request that Mary make her apologies and pass on her gratitude to Dr. and Mrs. Crease, and to say good-bye for her to Bella, and to Josiah and Clara. She again paused before scanning the rest of the letter. Nowhere did Portia say that she was taking Helena with her. But was she? She also didn't say on what ship she was departing. If she were going alone, though, then what was the reason for all the secrecy? Unless . . . she did have company.

She read the last lines.

> *If anyone else whom I failed to mention speaks of me, remember me to them. No one knew I was leaving, and I have failed to leave myself enough time to write to each one of them. Please hug the little ones at home. Tell them I will always love them. Farewell, my dearest friend.*

Mary held the letter against her chest and remembered the urgent message that had reached Portia at their

house last night. She could still remember Turner's attempted interference and how upset Portia had become.

She was doing it, Mary thought sadly. The reality of it struck her like a January wind. Portia was leaving, and they might never see her again. And for days or months or years to come, Mary would live in regret over a few unpleasant moments, for not meeting her one last time and putting their difficulties behind them. Mary wanted for both of them to cherish only their eight years of joy. She wanted Portia to remember the family who thought of her as one of their own.

She hurried to the door. Perhaps there was still time to see her . . . one last time.

They were not as strict at keeping watch over Helena today, and Portia knew why. Her mother, heavily sedated, drifted in and out of consciousness.

Still, Portia was allowed into the bedchamber. She sat by her mother's bedside and pretended to be content in reading a book to her in French, as two serving women chatted continuously by the window.

Helena's eyes occasionally opened, but they didn't seem to be able to focus. She was floating somewhere, suspended in a land of dreams. Her occasional descent into reality lasted only a few seconds. She was aware of Portia's presence, though, for whenever the young woman stopped reading, she moved around in her bed. So she continued to read, satisfied and relieved that there was some level of awareness there, hopeful that perhaps there would be a chance to draw Helena out of this stupor before all was lost.

About nine o'clock in the morning, Portia was asked to step out as the Admiral's physician paid his visit. As he left, she slipped back into the room and watched as Mrs. Green prepared more of the medication that was to be given to her charge.

"I'd be happy to give it to her," Portia offered as soon as the housekeeper stepped out.

The young serving woman who had been assigned the

task looked at her askance, but seemed less doubtful when Portia told her how she had done this many times for those sick in Parson Higgins's congregation. When she told her that she lived above the apothecary shop of Dr. Crease the Younger and even made deliveries for him, the girl happily turned the duty over her and went back to chatting with her fellow worker by the window. Portia fetched a spoon and over the next hour made a great show of giving the medicine to Helena.

Never once did the drug touch Helena's lips. Each time Portia tended to her, she carefully poured the spoonful onto a linen cloth that was kept by the bedside.

Her mother's recovery from the drugs was slow, though. Portia knew that neither of the two attendants spoke French, so as she read she altered the words on the page. In a low voice, she told her mother of the open sea and the ship that waited to take them to a place where they would be together. She told her how she needed Helena's help to break out of these prison walls. She also told her that they needed to act today.

Mrs. Green returned around midday to check on everything and Portia looked on nervously. Luckily, Helena's restlessness disappeared for the few moments that the housekeeper was looking closely on her. Portia began to hope that her mother had begun to comprehend what she had been saying.

"I believe the reading is keeping her quiet, ma'am," she said to the older woman.

Mrs. Green grunted. "More likely, 'tis the medication."

"Still, I'm grateful that you allow me to read to her."

"That's what you've been brought here to do, young woman, and you shall earn your keep."

"Yes, ma'am," Portia replied, trying to sound dutifully submissive.

"Still, I expect Miss Middleton to sleep for the rest of the day," Mrs. Green told Portia at the end of her inspection. "You can help yourself to some fish ragout and bread from the kitchen before you go on your way."

"Would you mind if I were to stay until this afternoon, ma'am? Captain Turner went to the trouble of arranging a ride home for me before he left for the day. I should hate to disappoint him."

"Suit yourself. But do not expect to be fed supper, as well."

With a curtsy, Portia returned to her seat by the bed and listened to the instructions to the two young serving women. Apparently, the housekeeper had other duties for them to perform in the afternoon. Her hopes soared when she heard that they would not be watching over their mistress the entire time, either.

"Whoever is the last to leave this room is to lock the door from the outside. Is that clear?"

"Aye, mum," the two attendants said in unison.

The housekeeper had just finished issuing her instructions when a young servant came up to the room in search of Portia.

"One of the gatekeepers walked up to say that there is a Mrs. Higgins waiting there to see you, miss. She says 'tis urgent."

Portia's heart sank, thinking that Mary would come all the way to the North End only if something were wrong with the children. No, she would have sent Clara or Josiah. Something else had happened. There was only one way to find out. Portia quickly tucked the book under her arm and started for the door.

"Who is this Mrs. Higgins?"

At the housekeeper's question, Portia paused by the door. "Mrs. Higgins is the wife of Parson William Higgins, whose church is on Sudbury Street. Both she and her husband are the most generous of souls. I have been a member of their family for eight years—before I joined the Admiral's household here. Mrs. Higgins is a dear friend. I was not feeling too well last night, and I can only think that she has walked all the way here to see if I am better."

The thin housekeeper stared suspiciously at Portia for

a moment before turning to the servant who had brought the news. "Tell the gatekeeper to allow her to come to the house." She turned to Portia. "Mrs. Higgins may join you for something to eat, if she so wishes."

"That is very kind and generous of you, Mrs. Green," Portia responded. With another curtsy, she followed the young servant downstairs and waited until the housekeeper's message had been relayed to the guard.

Portia walked down the drive to meet Mary as her friend hurriedly approached the house on foot.

"I am so glad to have found you before you left."

There was no longer any need to ask. She knew what had brought Mary here.

"You should not have gone through my things, and you should not have read the letter," Portia scolded gently.

"But 'twas addressed to me. How could I not read it?"

She took Mary's hand and took her onto a path that led to the garden, away from prying eyes and ears. "You asked me to keep your family out of my plans, Mary. That is what I have been trying to do. So I want you to please pretend that you did not see it, did not read it. I want you to pretend that you know nothing about any of it."

Mary tugged on Portia's hand and turned her around. "Then 'tis true? You are going?"

Portia looked about her cautiously first. There was no one around. "Yes . . . I am," she finally admitted, unable to stop her voice from breaking slightly. Excitement, sadness—so many emotions—all knotted together and lodged in her throat.

"When?"

"You don't want to know."

"Please," Mary pressed. "I do."

Portia shook her head and moved along the garden path. Her friend followed.

"You are not going to tell me," Mary said with feeling. "After all the years we've known each other, you do not

trust me with the truth. You think I have no right to know? Or that I do not deserve a proper good-bye? How could you think that the children have no desire to see you one last time? Or that William does not need to send you off with some sage advice? You might have already forgotten about all of us, but you are quite important to us, Miss Edwards. And—"

"No more, Mary," Portia pleaded, finally turning to her friend. She was fighting to keep the tears back. "I beg of you, please do not make this harder than 'tis."

"I am not trying to," she said, staring solemnly at the tears that finally escaped. She gathered Portia's hands in her own. "I am just worried about you. I do not want to see any hardship befall you."

"All is well. Everything is in hand. The only trouble I can get into now is if my plans were to be known to . . . to people who could ruin everything."

"Such as Captain Turner."

Portia nodded. "I know you meant well. He told me that you asked him to look after me. But the whole thing was a mistake. He—"

"I know. I know." Mary looked down at their joined hands, her face flushed red with embarrassment. "That is why I came to your room today, to apologize for inviting him last night. Imagine that I thought he might be a proper suitor for you! I spent half the night cursing myself for my poor judgment. I had no idea how disgusting a man he really is. I was hoping that, between us, we could devise a way of ridding you of him."

Portia shook her head. "None of that matters now. He was leaving for Rhode Island today. Before he returns, I shall be gone."

"You are leaving *today*?"

As two workers carrying rakes and hoes entered the garden, Portia grabbed Mary by the arm and steered her toward a bench at the farthest end from the house. "I cannot have anyone hear about this."

"So you are not going alone," Mary asserted as soon

as they sat down together. The gardeners went to work on two flower beds well out of earshot. "But have you thought through all the details? Have you secured a passage across? How are you going to take—"

"Do not ask these things," Portia ordered. "You and William cannot afford to know. When this whole thing is made known, I shall be gone, but you cannot avoid being questioned about it. I want you to be as unaware of my actions as . . . as any stranger walking down the street."

Mary took Portia's hand in hers once again. "I promise to act unaware. I am actually quite excellent at looking shocked, too. And betrayed. And whatever else the moment dictates. You forget, I am a parson's wife."

Portia stared at her friend. "You cannot mean what you are saying. I am trying to learn from my recent mistakes, Mary. I have not forgotten the scandal that nearly ruined your family. William's career was seriously damaged once. I cannot allow you to—"

"I do not want to live in the past, and we cannot change what God has planned for our future. At the same time, I do not care to have you bringing up all my threats and warnings from the day after the ball." Mary smiled, holding Portia's hand tightly. "This time, my friend, you appear to have a much better grasp of the situation. It looks as if you have been planning it carefully. I'm proud of you for that. What worries me, though, are the little details. Anything that you might have overlooked. I want you to succeed, Portia. Lord knows, I do not know anyone who is more deserving of happiness, but has been deprived of it for so long as you."

"Now you shall make me miss you even more," Portia said tearfully.

Mary gave her an affectionate hug. "That is as it should be. I am very much worth missing."

She managed to smile. "You are the most strong-willed woman I know."

"That is without a doubt true." Mary looked around them again. The gardeners were bent over their tasks. "Now, about this journey. When are you leaving?" she asked quietly.

"This afternoon."

"On what ship?" Mary immediately shook her head. "Never mind that I asked. That, I do not want to know. Are you taking your mother with you?"

"I plan to." Portia whispered.

"You are not doing something unthinkable like dressing as sailors or trying to stow away, are you? Your passage is paid for?"

"No . . . and yes. I am expected on board the ship we shall be sailing on." There was no need for Mary to know that neither Pierce nor Nathaniel Muir knew anything about Helena going, as well.

"The ship *is* going to England, I hope, and not to one of those horrid islands in the Caribbean."

"The ship is bound for Scotland. I shall travel to Wales by coach from there."

Mary seemed to consider that answer for a while. "The one who is assisting you with all this . . . I assume he is an honorable individual?"

"Very," Portia whispered. The very thought of him made her throat grow tight. She hadn't even gone away, and already she was missing Pierce. She painted on a smile. "I appealed to his sense of nationalism and his kindness, and he responded."

Mary did not look surprised. Portia pushed the thoughts from her mind of what her friend would think of her if she knew about last night. But she reminded herself that she had no regret.

"And how do you plan to get Helena from here to the ship?" Mary asked.

"A carriage is being sent here this afternoon. The driver has been instructed to deliver us there."

"And how do you plan to get your mother past the guards at the gate? They are stopping everyone who tries

to come in. I assume they will at least look at the ones who are leaving."

Portia was more worried about getting Helena up from her bed and out of the room without being noticed. "If I can get her downstairs and into the carriage, then I shall simply say she is one of the servants. I do not believe any of those guards could recognize her, as she never goes anywhere."

"Don't you think they know who works here or who does not?" Mary challenged.

"I shall hide her under a blanket if I must. Or have the driver charge through the gate—"

"No." Mary shook her head. She looked about the grounds. She stood up and peered at the impressive building on the hill. "This might be where I can be of some help to you."

Portia stared in surprise at her friend.

"Your mother's hair. What is the color?"

"The same as yours."

"And are we roughly the same size?"

"Approximately the same," Portia admitted. "But I could not—"

"And does she have a gray dress . . . something similar to this one?"

"I do not know what she has in the way of clothing, but you cannot be suggesting that I take her out in the carriage and let the guards believe she is you?"

"We are thinking the same thing exactly," Mary said happily.

"No, Mary. How would you get out of here then, yourself? And even if you did find a way, everyone would know that you had a hand in it." Portia came up to her feet. "It cannot work."

"It must."

"No!" Portia shook her head adamantly and stepped away. "I *cannot* get you involved."

"You are not giving me the credit I deserve. I am far more resourceful than you think. I can even claim that

I was victimized, if need be." Mary stopped her, turning Portia around. "And that is just what I will do in case anyone should become suspicious of me. I shall say I was hit over the head. Or drugged. Renting a room above the apothecary shop would give you access to such things, would it not?"

"I don't know," Portia said, trying hard to think the matter through.

"Time is running short, my dear." Mary took her by the arm and started toward the house. "They said at the gate that I was invited to go to the house, and I intend to. You are going to take me up to your mother's room and give me the opportunity to be of assistance."

Portia had no option but to keep up with Mary's determined pace.

Chapter 18

The breeze was blowing gently from the north and the sun had almost reached its zenith as the sloop *Hannah* weighed anchor and sailed out of Newport harbor. The shipmaster had already reported the sloop's cargo at the colony's Customs House, a formality which, for months, had been looked on with growing skepticism by the Crown's revenue officers. Those same people, led by Lieutenant William Dudingston, knew that the Rhode Islanders in the Customs House were turning many a blind eye to the irregularities in the cargo manifests of the ships passing through the port.

Passing the rocky shoals off Rose Island, the *Hannah* set a course northward, up the bay toward Providence. No sooner were the lines taut, however, than the call came from aloft that Dudingston's eight-gun schooner, the *Gaspee,* was in pursuit. Pierce looked out over the stern rail. Sure enough, the sleek two-master was rounding Goat Island with her sails flying.

"Let him come close enough to taste it," Pierce told Captain Lindsey, the master of the *Hannah.*

The plan had begun perfectly. One of the sailors rowing the first mate in with the cargo manifest at Newport had followed his instructions. He'd said—in a voice that a nearby revenue officer could hear—something about the trouble they'd had picking up MacHeath just off Brenton's Point.

On Captain Lindsay's command, the *Hannah* lagged slightly until the *Gaspee* moved up enough to tack in for the intercept. From the stern, Pierce could see Dudingston standing on deck, his ensign signaling them to heave to and prepare for boarding.

"Show him your heels, Lindsay."

The order was quickly passed along, and the sailors jumped into action. They all had heard about Lieutenant Dudingston and his ways. None of them looked forward to being pressed into the service of the Royal Navy, a fate that would surely await more than a few of them if they were boarded. As soon as it was clear that the sloop had no intention of dropping anchor, the *Gaspee* fired warning shots from two of its guns. Moments later, however, the smaller merchant ship was out of range, daring the British schooner to pursue.

And pursue, the *Gaspee* did. This race might have seemed to be a spur of the moment decision to the *Hannah*'s crew, but both men standing by the helm of the ship had been planning it for some time. Dudingston had risen for the bait, now it was up to them to land him. For weeks, Pierce had been studying charts and other information Nathaniel had gathered, and now the die was cast. It was do or die, now. Literally. If Dudingston caught them, Lindsay would stand trial, but Pierce himself would surely hang.

For the next two hours, the two ships tacked back and forth against the headwind, steadily working their way northward into the bay. Skillfully, Lindsey kept the *Hannah* out of range of the pursuer's cannons, though he and Pierce both knew that eventually the bay would narrow, and their room for maneuvering would dwindle. Dudingston knew it, too, and continued to herd the sloop northward, cutting off any run to the south and the open sea.

By midafternoon, it was clear that the British commander was losing patience. The tide was beginning to turn, and he had to assume that the *Hannah* would soon

make her run for it. As the two ships raced northward between Bristol's harbor and Prudence Island, Pierce knew that their moment of destiny was at hand. Once they passed Conimicut Point and entered the Providence River, Dudingston would have to be preparing to tack to the west to cut off their last chance of escape.

The tide was running quickly by the time they passed the point, and the *Gaspee* soon cleared the long underwater sandbar behind them. The schooner was closing the distance quickly now, and Captain Lindsay looked at the man he knew only as MacHeath, awaiting his word. Moments dragged on into an eternity. The *Gaspee* was nearly close enough to use their forward guns. Pierce could see the faces of the sailors in the rigging of the pursuing ship.

"Now, Captain," Pierce said in a low voice.

With a word from Lindsay, the *Hannah* turned slightly to the northwest. Behind them, the crew of the *Gaspee* sprang into action. Pierce watched the schooner tack hard to the west, and he knew Dudingston had sealed his own fate.

Everyone aboard the *Hannah* watched. As old hands in the waters of the Narragansett Bay, they knew that before the *Gaspee* could come about, the sandy shallows off Namquid Point would separate the two ships. The hook was in deep now; they knew Dudingston would be unable to shake it loose.

"Bring her about, Captain," Pierce said.

Just as the *Hannah* completed her turn to the east, the British schooner suddenly plowed up onto the underwater sandbar, shuddering and grinding to a halt. Pierce watched sailors thrown from the rigging drop into the water, Dudingston himself bouncing across the deck. Around Pierce and above him, the crew of the *Hannah* broke into a cheer as the *Gaspee* lurched over onto her side, her sails filling with water.

"Well done, Lindsay," Pierce said quietly, clapping the shipmaster on the back.

"That should hold them, sir."

"Indeed it will." Pierce watched the distance between the two vessels widen. "Well, Captain, I believe 'tis time we let our friends in Providence and Bristol know the sad plight of the *Gaspee*. They now have until the flood tide lifts her off that bar. That would be about three tomorrow morning, wouldn't you say?"

"Aye, sir, if she'll even float free then. Dudingston drove her up hard onto it."

"Indeed he did. I'd say he wanted the *Hannah* very badly."

"Or he wanted a certain Captain MacHeath."

"You could be right, Lindsay."

"Well, he's got more to worry about than that now," Lindsay replied with a broad grin. "And the night promises to be dark."

"I do not feel good about this," Portia whispered as the two women arrived at Helena's door. The door was unlocked, and the same two young women were sitting by the window as before. And they gave Mary a curious look when she followed Portia in.

"Since Mrs. Green had no objection," Portia told them, "I asked Mrs. Higgins to come up and keep me company until I must leave."

She glanced toward the bed. The light curtain of gauzy fabric had been lowered, and Helena was apparently sleep. Portia turned back to the women.

"You know, I shall be watching her if you need to be doing something else."

The two young women looked at each other indecisively. Finally, they stood up.

"We do have a great deal to do before dinner," one of them said.

"You need not fear," Portia told her, ushering them toward the door. "I shall send for help if there is any need. My friend and I shall sit right there where you were sitting."

Mary took one of the seats vacated by the attendant as they went out. Closing the door behind them, Portia went directly to Helena's side.

Her mother's eyes opened, and she stared up into the vicinity of where Portia was standing. Neither spoke a word. Portia squeezed Helena's hand, and the older woman returned the gesture before closing her eyes as the door opened again and one of the attendants reappeared. Portia went to meet her.

"The cook sent up some broth for the mistress a few minutes ago, miss." The young woman pointed to the untouched tray on the bedside table. "She was sleeping so peacefully that we didn't want to disturb her."

"I shall see to her food. No worry."

"And Mrs. Green also came around again and mixed another cup of medicine for the mistress. You should give that to her as soon you can get some food into her."

"I shall take care of that, too," Portia assured her, relieved that they had not given Helena more of the drug that appeared to induce sleep. "Thank you for telling me."

As soon as they were alone again, Portia quickly introduced Mary to her mother. Helena was still a bit groggy, but was obviously forcing herself to focus on her daughter's words.

"We haven't much time. But there is a carriage that will come around to take us at four. If I can get you down to it, we shall be sailing for Scotland tonight."

"So I was not dreaming all of this. The whole thing is real. You want me leave here with you."

It was not a question but a statement. But the tone was not one of enthusiasm. Mary shot her a warning look, and Portia sank down on the edge of the bed and took her mother's hand.

"Do you wish to stay here? To live as you are now?"

Helena paused, considering her answer. "I would gladly stay if I did not have this Methuselah, Mrs. Green, constantly telling me what to do. I would stay if there

were no lock on my door. I would be content if I were given none of these medications that they have been plying me with of late." Both of her hands clutched Portia's. "I would stay and be forever happy if you could come and stay here with us. But the Admiral won't allow that."

Portia was relieved that her mother understood. There was no hope for them if they were to stay.

"These people," Helena continued, desperation creeping into her voice. "They are squeezing the very breath out of my body. They are killing me. Sometimes I almost grieve that I am still alive."

"But you do not need to live like this," Portia whispered. "You do not need to put up with all this mistreatment. I can take you so far away that he shall never be able to find us. We can start anew, together."

"But I have nothing." Her voice cracked. "For so long I have been dependent on someone for every drop of water and crust of bread. I no longer know what the world looks like beyond these walls that have become my prison. I have no friends, no kin that we could go to who can help us."

Helena stared at the bed curtains wafting in the light breeze.

"And I cannot see. How can I go anywhere?"

"You have me. I can take care of you. I shall be your eyes," Portia said passionately. "Once again you shall have your freedom. You shall live again. And we shall be together. Is that not enough?"

" 'Tis enough for me," the older woman whispered through her tears. "But you shall do this for me . . . when I was never the mother to you that I should have been?"

"Neither of us is to blame for what is past. All we have now is the future." Portia glanced at the door as voices could be heard passing it. "This is not an opportunity that shall present itself every day. If you are willing to take my hand, to trust me, then we have a chance."

After only a moment's hesitation, Helena took her hand and sat up. Slowly she moved her feet off the edge

of the bed. She had difficulty with her balance as she stood up, and had to sit again. Mary came around the bed and held Helena's other hand. Together, they helped her to a dressing table by the window.

"You cannot get me out of this room without them knowing."

"I shall take care of those details," Portia said reassuringly. "Now Mary, if you would see to my mother's hair, I shall search through that dressing room for something for her to wear. Do you have a gray dress, Mother?"

Mrs. Green finished her afternoon inspection of the household and was going up the stairs to look in on Helena when the shouts of "Fire!" rang out from the kitchen. Immediately, she rushed back down the stairs.

A handful of the Admiral's men were rushing from the servants' hall to the kitchen, and most of the kitchen staff was running out. The smoke was billowing in thick clouds from the doorway, and between the two groups of people, there was a pure chaos in the hall. She found the cook who had managed to push through the bodies into the servants' hall. Sweat was pouring down his round face, and he was swabbing it with a soot-covered cloth.

" 'Tis not so bad as they're making it out to be," the man said over the din. "There is some smoke, but we've already doused the fire."

"What happened?"

"One of the scullery maids saw the new companion bring the mistress's tray down. I'm not saying for sure, but I think she must have placed the thing too close to the baking ovens. I think the napkin on it caught fire, and then the grease cloths caught, and then the—"

"But you say you doused the fire."

"Aye, the bloody thing is out. Does the Admiral . . ."

"The Admiral went to see the governor this morning."

"Thank God," he muttered, turning away.

The cook went to a bench along the wall and plunked his ample frame down. Mrs. Green saw one of the girls

who had been up with Helena helping the others push open the windows.

She took her by the arm. "Who is upstairs with Miss Helena?"

"Miss Edwards and her friend . . . the parson's wife."

An uncomfortable feeling settled in the pit of the housekeeper's stomach. She worked her way to the doorway of the kitchens and she saw what the cook said was true. There was no fire visible. Even the smoke was diminishing. She headed back through the servants' hall and hurried up the steps.

Just as she'd feared, the door to Helena's room was open. The parson's wife was pacing back and forth in the hallway.

"I'm so glad you've come, Mrs. Green," the woman said worriedly, approaching her. "Is the fire spreading? Should the rest of us leave the building?"

Mrs. Green pushed past her and went into the bedchamber. It was empty. "Where is she? Where did she take Miss Middleton?"

"Miss Edwards was rightly frightened about the fire. Your mistress was quite groggy, and could not move very quickly."

"Yes . . . yes!" the housekeeper snapped. "Where are they?"

"They were going to the garden," the woman explained, obviously offended. "She asked me to stay behind and tell you where they went. She did not want you to get worried for nothing. But are you sure the fire is out? I have two small children, you know. Parson Higgins cannot afford to lose me because I came here to do some good deed."

"Which way did she take her down?" The housekeeper asked impatiently. "What stairway did they take?"

"I'll be happy to show you the way," the parson's wife said, starting down the hallway.

*　　*　　*

Helena leaned heavily on Portia as they slowly made their way down the pathway leading to the drive.

"I am so tired. I cannot breathe. 'Tis been so long since I've walked so far . . . so fast . . . I do not know if I can take another step."

"We are almost there," Portia said, relieved to see a carriage waiting just beyond the last line of trees. "When we get to it, please let me do the talking for both of us."

Jack looked curiously at the two of them when they left the line of trees.

"You are the kindest man this side of the heaven," Portia said brightly. "And you brought a carriage."

"Aye, the master thought 'twould be more comfortable for ye for the long ride."

"Quite right, Jack," she said. "And being the angel that you are, would you help my friend here to climb in? She is quite weak after breathing in all the smoke in the kitchen. It appears someone accidentally started a small fire."

"Accidentally?" the groom grumbled under his breath. Still, he lent a hand and Helena was quickly helped into the carriage. Once she was seated inside, though, he turned to Portia. "The master said I would be taking only ye."

"He must have said I'd be the only one you would know. You don't think I would journey to England on a ship filled with sailors and no female attendant?"

"As ye wish, miss. I know nothing of such things," Jack muttered. He helped her into the carriage and climbed up to the driver's seat. "I just hope ye're not putting me in more hot water with the master."

At the gate Helena brought a handkerchief to her mouth in an apparent coughing fit. Portia leaned out of the carriage and casually told the curious guards about the fire in the kitchen.

"I don't know if they've put out the flames yet," she said in parting. "But I shall be bringing my own food to

work tomorrow, just in case . . . and I shall bring extra for you lads."

As they laughed, she waved and Jack flicked the reins at the team of horses. The gate closed behind them, and Portia sank back against the seat.

"So far, so good," she said, taking her mother's hand and thinking that the worst still lay ahead of them.

"I see no one here. Are you sure your friend was taking Miss Middleton this way to the garden?" the housekeeper asked irritably.

Mary looked about her in confusion. "This is my first time at this house, Mrs. Green. Now, they could not have gone too far. You know better than I how weak your mistress must be. Miss Edwards had to practically drag her out in trying to save her life. Now you say the fire was nothing really. Well, perhaps they heard that and turned around. Perhaps they are already upstairs, and Miss Edwards is tucking your mistress back in bed. Perhaps you are worrying about nothing. Perhaps—"

"Mrs. Higgins, you talk too much," the housekeeper cut in angrily, turning back toward the house.

"I am just trying to be of assistance. My children are waiting at home for me. Aside from preparing for supper, I still need to make two more visits to sick members of my husband's congregation. So if you do not appreciate what I am trying to do—"

"I believe 'tis time for you to leave, ma'am," the housekeeper said sharply, facing her. "You have been very helpful, I'm sure. Now you may be on your way, Mrs. Higgins."

"Are you certain?"

"The gate is that way."

"In that case . . ." Mary said with a huff, turning on her heel and striding out of the garden toward the gate.

They had been riding through the darkness for over an hour when they passed through a tiny village that

Jack told her was called Barrington. It was not long after leaving the cluster of homes behind that the carriage pulled off the post road and lurched to a stop behind a thin grove of trees.

Portia had been breathing in the smell of pine for so long that she was surprised to have the scent of the salt-water now pour into the carriage. She peered out the window and found they had halted by a small point of land. It was very dark, but she knew the black water that stretched out beyond had to be the Narragansett Bay.

"We are a wee bit early," Jack said jumping down and stretching his legs.

Helena had slept for the entire ride, but now she stirred and opened her eyes.

"Where are we?" She reached out a hand cautiously.

Portia took it in her own. "Somewhere in Rhode Island. They are sending a boat soon that will carry us out to the ship."

"Do you see any ship?"

"No. The driver says we're early."

Helena nodded and dozed off against the seat again.

Portia heard a noise in the distance across the water. Curious, she climbed out of the carriage and moved to the edge of the cove.

It was the sound of the muffled oars on the water. She wasn't certain where it had come from, but a longboat was passing. The rowers were strangely hushed despite their numbers.

"Who are they?" she whispered when Jack came down to the water next to her. He too stared out at the long-boat that was quietly passing the point.

"I do not think you really want to know, miss, though I'm guessing that one hails from Bristol, just south of here."

Portia didn't press him, but she wondered if MacHeath was on that boat. This afternoon, as Jack drove them back to the apothecary to fetch Portia's trunk, she had been searching every face they passed. She'd been hop-

ing for a glimpse of Pierce one last time. She had not dared to ask Jack, though.

Perhaps Captain Turner was right. Perhaps Pierce—or rather, MacHeath—had come here after she'd left him last night. Portia looked at the boat gliding away from them into the darkness. The quietness, the sense of secrecy made her think they were smugglers. With this realization came worry. She was terrified to think that Turner and his men might be lying in wait in some cove to arrest them.

"Jack," she said, "Admiral Middleton was sending Captain Turner and some men to Rhode Island today. They left this morning. Should we warn anyone about them? They could be anywhere . . . and the captain had some kind of trap planned. He was certain that they would succeed, and . . ."

Her voice trailed off as Jack shook his head.

"If ye wish to leave tonight, then I wouldn't say a thing, miss. Let the people who know their business do what they must."

Portia felt her nervousness rise. "If the choice is for me to leave or save your master from trouble, then I should tell you now that I will forfeit the journey."

Jack smiled. "Ye fret too much. What I was trying to say was that ye are worrying for nothing. The master knows what he's doing."

"But if I can help him—"

"Ye'll help him by staying out of the man's way until he's done, miss."

Suddenly, the crack of a gunshot came from across the water. Portia moved closer to the water's edge, with Jack right beside her. She could not see anything of the longboat. The sound of shouts and fighting grew louder, though, and continued.

"They could be under attack."

"I should say they *are* under attack," the groom said in a matter-of-fact voice.

"Is there no one we could go to for help?" Portia

climbed onto a rock protruding from the water, hoping to see something.

"Nay. We're to stay here and—"

"We cannot just wait—"

"Aye, miss. We can. My instructions—"

Portia slipped off the rock and fell into waist-deep water with a loud splash. She skinned her elbow as she went, and the saltwater stung fiercely.

"Bloody hell," the groom cursed under his breath, wading in to help her out. "Settle down, miss. Aye, there is a ship under attack. But 'tis not what ye think. There are longboats from Providence, as well, and they . . ."

The sounds of riders approaching drew their attention to the road. Just beyond the thin line of the trees, a dozen soldiers on horses were passing. Still standing in the water, she thought of Helena sleeping inside the carriage.

"Get down, miss," Jack whispered, climbing behind the rock. "Do not let them see ye."

He tried to pull her down into the water with him as two riders at the head of the company cut off the road and reined in beside the carriage.

"Helena," Portia whispered.

At that moment, another gunshot came across the water, and the two riders spurred their horses to the water's edge to get a better view.

Portia tried to get down in the water before they saw her, but she was too late.

Astounded, Captain Turner stared at the woman standing in the water. He had to look again and push his horse toward the boulder. He had to make sure he was not mistaken.

"What the devil are you doing here, Miss Edwards?"

"Sir, the men are getting ahead of us."

The captain quickly looked around them. There was the carriage, but no one else that he could see.

"Catch up to them, Reynolds. Continue on to

Providence . . . but send two men back here. We shall follow." As the junior officer rode off, Turner turned again to Portia. "Well, what explanation do you have for this madness?"

"A very reasonable one." She started to walk toward him, but stumbled and fell deeper into the water. "But would you be kind enough to help me out of here first, sir?"

He nudged his horse into the water and extended his riding crop to her. "Whose carriage is that? Who is that inside?"

"I cannot swim, sir." She reached up, but wasn't able to catch hold of the crop. "Please."

"For heaven's sake, woman, this water is not so deep. Just stand up."

"Something is pulling at me. I think it must be quicksand."

"There is no bloody quicksand in this water. Perhaps the tide could—"

Her head went under, and she disappeared. Turner stared for a moment, but she did not surface again. Mild concern added to his growing annoyance. He had no option but to climb down from his horse into the water. He felt around in the shallow pool for her, but could find nothing.

"Where are you?" he shouted. "Miss Edwards?"

"Have they come for us already?"

The woman's voice from the carriage window drew Turner's head in that direction. It took only a moment for him to recognize the voice. He turned in shock and started toward her.

"Miss Middleton?"

"Captain Turner," she gasped, opening the carriage door. "What have you done with my daughter?"

"Daughter?" he returned. "What is the meaning of this? Have you truly lost your mind?"

"Where is Portia?" Helena stretched a hand out.

"I am here, Mother," she replied from directly behind him.

"I believe you both have a great deal of explaining to do. And you, Miss Edwards, I must place under arrest in the name of the ki—"

As he turned around, Turner glanced up in time to see the dripping rock she held above her head, but he was too late to deflect the blow.

Chapter 19

"Did I kill him?" Portia asked, looking over the groom's shoulder at the body spread on the stony shore.

"A mighty blow, miss. But he is still breathing."

Portia didn't want to think about what she had done. She wasn't going to feel sorry for the officer or worry about the consequences of having been recognized. She had no time for that now. She stepped around him and went to Helena, who was trying to climb out of the carriage.

"Please stay where you are, Mother. Turner's soldiers will be back soon. We cannot wait here, or we shall be discovered."

The explosion behind her lit up the western sky. Portia whirled around and gaped across the water. Not a mile away, flames climbed high into the sky. It was a ship, burning like a torch. She could even see the silhouettes of longboats around it.

"Mighty nice of them to burn the bloody thing and create a diversion for us," Jack commented. He stood up and scanned the waters of the bay.

Portia saw the fishing dory about the same time that the groom did. Two men were rowing quietly toward the point. Pierce's groom let out a low whistle, and one of the oarsmen returned the signal.

"They've come for ye, miss." Jack called over his shoulder.

"Let me help you," Portia said, going to her mother and helping her down from the carriage. The groom was beside them in a moment, hauling down the single trunk and taking it to the water's edge.

The waterlogged clothes weighed Portia down terribly. Helena did not seem to notice the wetness, though, as she clutched tightly to her daughter's arm.

"I am afraid," the older woman whispered quietly into her ear. "I see a red sky. The color of blood."

" 'Tis only a far-off fire. It cannot hurt us."

Portia wished she could believe her own words. The sailors did not question the fact that there were two of them and helped Helena into the boat first.

"Will you be able to get out before Turner's men get here?" she asked Jack.

"I'll be fine, miss. Do not fret now."

"You can always say I forced you to drive us here. At gunpoint. Turner didn't see you, so there is no reason why they should suspect—"

"They're waiting for ye, miss." Jack nudged her gently toward the boat. "Now I know ye think ye might have tried my patience on occasion, but I do not want ye thinking such a thing. Fare thee well, miss."

Portia smiled at the man and climbed into the boat. As they were rowed away from the shore, she continued to look back until she saw Jack driving the carriage off to the south. Turner's horse grazed near the trees. She could see the officer's body at the edge of the water.

Out on the bay, they had a clear view of the burning ship and the flames lighting up the far shore. Portia knew that this was the work of MacHeath. But she also pondered whether there ever would come a time when they would meet again.

*   *   *

While the longboats from a number of towns along the bay were attacking the *Gaspee,* the illicit cargo aboard the *Lothian* was unloaded near Bristol. On shore, those who'd come from Boston for the weapons stowed them away in wagons filled with wool and hay and disappeared into the night. By the time the first explosions aboard the British ship resonated across the water, the merchant ship was waiting for its last passenger.

Pierce and the master of *Lothian* were in the captain's quarters when the first mate knocked on the door with the news that that everyone was aboard, and they were ready to weigh anchor. With a nod from the shipowner, Captain Cameron went on deck to see to the start of their journey. Pierce took one more look out the cabin window at the fire still lighting up the sky to the northwest, and then went back to storing his belongings and the messages he was carrying back to England.

Dawn was breaking across the eastern sky when Pierce stepped out on deck. Though he'd tried to sleep, he couldn't, and he'd known the moment they sailed out of the bay into the open sea from the motion of the *Lothian.* He loved the feel of the ocean. He breathed in the air. The stiff sea breeze was refreshing and immediately washed away any vestige of fatigue.

The New England coastline lay off to port. In the graying light he could just make out sections of beach and bluff. The sound of the canvas popping and straining above drew his gaze upward. The sails had been set, and the lookout perched on the topmast trestletree was scanning the horizon fore and aft for British warships and revenue cutters. Standing by the stern rail, Pierce looked forward at the glorious horizon ahead.

He was doing the right thing in going back to Baronsford, he told himself. It was time to mend the past and move on with the future.

The future!

He thought of the woman belowdecks. She had no idea he was on board. He recalled her beautiful dark

eyes brimming with tears when she'd left his house. He also thought of their lovemaking. How dazzled he'd been by the power of it! How her departure so immediately after had stung him!

It was far too early to awaken her. He would let her sleep. Still, Pierce soon found his steps leading him belowdecks to steerage. There, in the dim light of the long narrow passageway, he stood and stared at the doors of the four passenger cabins.

Going back on deck, he moved forward across the waist of the ship—the center section of the ship between the foredeck and the stern deck. On the foredeck, above the forecastle where the sailors slept in shifts, three tars were lashing down a dory more securely. One of the sailors who'd rowed Portia from Nahet Point, above Bristol, was among them.

"Do you know where they put our passenger?" Pierce asked as they finished the task.

"Aye, sir," the sailor replied. "The two of them are sharing the second cabin."

"The two of them?" Pierce asked, perplexed.

"Aye. There's the young miss, like we was told. And there's the older lady that cannot see verra well." The tar must have sensed that something was wrong, so he went on quickly. "They was both with yer man, sir, when we put in to shore. He set 'em both in the dory, and we brought 'em back. Something amiss, sir?"

"No. Did you hear a name for the older lady?"

The man scratched his beard. "The younger one called her . . . wait, she'll come to me . . . I've a good head for names. Helen . . . or something akin to it."

"Helena?"

"Aye, sir. That's it." The man nodded with certainty. "Helena, she called 'er."

The cabin was no larger than a closet with a small hole high in the wall to let in air. Portia had placed her trunk of clothing—which now had to do for both of them—

against the opposite wall, beside the door. A narrow cot provided the only place to sit or sleep. She had no complaints, though. They were on their way.

When she had sailed from England less than a year ago, she had shared a much larger cabin with the entire Higgins family. She and little Ann had shared a berth, as the sailors called it, and they had been snug enough. This would be a different journey, but one just as thrilling for her.

Helena was still clearly suffering from the effects of the medicines and had gratefully accepted Portia's offer of the narrow bed. The floor and couple of blankets would be comfortable enough for herself. Besides, once they were safely out at sea, she planned to take Helena on the deck as much as possible. She had enjoyed the crossing last fall with the Higgins family immensely, and she was determined that her mother enjoy this one.

There was a light tap on the door. Portia removed the blanket she'd been wearing around her shoulder and went to open it. A sailor stood in the steerage passageway. Behind him, the mainmast—looking like the trunk of some huge black tree—rose out of the floor and disappeared through the ceiling. There were rolled piles of canvas sails and huge coils of rope in the passageway, as well as fixtures of painted and rusted iron that she couldn't identify, and the smell was dank and mysterious.

"Ye're wanted in the captain's quarters, miss."

Portia glanced over her shoulder. Helena lay undisturbed. She considered changing out of her wet dress first, but decided against it. She was almost dry, anyway. And she needed to save what she had for her mother, just in case.

She slipped through the door and closed it behind her. "I'd hoped to speak to him when he had a minute to spare."

"I'd say he's ready for ye now," the man replied, going ahead of her up the stairs.

Portia followed him on deck, and for couple of seconds

she just had to lift her face to the morning sun and the wind and breath in the air. The deep blue of the sky, the wave crests of white foam, the spread of the sails above her made her feel like she had sprouted wings. She was ready to open her arms and take flight.

"Are ye coming, miss?"

She nodded to the couple of sailors on deck who had paused in their work and were watching her, and then ran to catch up with her escort.

"What do you call your captain?" she asked, wanting to have an introduction ready.

The sailor went down another steep set of stairs to a narrow passage closer to the stern end of the ship.

"What should I call him?" she asked again in the dim passageway.

"Sir?" he responded with a shrug, knocking on the door.

She turned away slightly, speaking to herself in a low voice.

"Good day to you, sir." She took a breath and tried again. "Good morning to you, sir."

The sailor was openly grinning at her.

"Very kind of you . . . no . . . 'tis truly a pleasure to meet . . . no, too strong." She shook her head.

"Come in."

Her escort opened the door, and then turned and simply disappeared back up the steep stairs. Looking in, Portia was surprised by the size of the cabin. It was quite large and took up the entire width of the ship's stern. She had no time to dwell on the fine details, though, as a body suddenly appeared, effectively blocking the doorway.

Black boots. Buckskin breeches. White shirt. No vest. Only the sun-burnished skin of a broad, muscular chest peeking through.

"Oh, no!" Portia's hand flew to her mouth.

"Miss Edwards," Pierce said evenly. "Someone might think that you are not entirely happy to see me."

Her heart was thudding so hard in her chest that Portia

thought he had to hear it. Everyone on the entire ship had to be able to hear it. She tried to recover herself. "If someone is eavesdropping, then they should be severely reprimanded."

"A ship is a difficult place to keep secrets," he said, gesturing for her to enter.

"I shall take your word for it." She did not move. "But what are you doing on board of this ship? Should you not be in Boston, seeing to your business? Or perhaps continuing to be a thorn in the side of Admiral Middleton and his men?"

Portia fought off the panic that was beginning to grip her. Maybe he didn't know about Helena, she told herself.

"There must be a great many people," she continued, "who need you in Boston."

"But not you, I take it." Pierce grabbed her by the wrist and pulled her into the cabin.

She entered with no struggle. Not that she had any choice. She cringed, however, when he slammed the door behind her. She decided then that he had to know about Helena. Portia didn't dare look around at the spacious quarters or its stylish furnishings. She also chose not to insult him with small talk. She simply braced herself for the storm.

"I, on the other hand, have been very much looking forward to this visit."

She had a hard time believing what he'd just said. "I would have been looking forward to it, too, if I only knew. 'Tis just such a surprise."

Her voice seemed to be coming from the bottom of some empty barrel. She became even more tense when he started pacing before her. His blue eyes never shifted from her face. She didn't dare meet his gaze, however.

"So you left Admiral Middleton's mansion yesterday with no difficulty?" His voice was low and dangerous and made the hair stand up on her neck.

"No difficulty . . . with the exception of having to set the place on fire. But 'twas a very small fire, and they put it out before it spread anywhere. But that turned out to be a perfect distraction. So, with the exception of that, no difficulty at all."

"And I assume there were no complications regarding Jack's delivery of you to my men."

"No. We made very good time, in fact. No complications at all . . . with the exception of having to hit Captain Turner over the head and leave him unconscious and bleeding on the beach."

"You brought Captain Turner with you?"

"No! The captain simply showed up at the wrong place and at the wrong time, and there was no other way of dealing with him. If we hadn't stopped him, he would have stopped us . . . well, stopped me, in any case. But I was able to handle Captain Turner, so there was no problem at all."

He stopped his pacing, but he was too close to allow Portia any sense of comfort. "So, you're telling me that what should have been an easy departure became a nightmare, an obvious escape because . . . ?" He paused, obviously waiting for her to finish his sentence.

"Because I attract troublesome men?" She stole a glance at him and was sorry she did. His expression was as cold as the ice on Long Wharf in February.

"You think this is all a joke, I take it." His voice was rising, and his cheeks were becoming attractively ruddy. "I asked you to come in here so we could share a good laugh. You think this is all just for our entertainment."

"No, I was telling the truth." She couldn't believe it, but he was almost shouting at her. She'd never heard him even raise his voice before. "Everything happened as I said. And though I tend to speak a great deal when I get nervous, everything I just said was the truth. 'Tis surely a miracle that I am here. Of course, that and the dedicated efforts of your groom and the sailors who

rowed us . . . me to the ship. But in the end, I was able to make it here without any harm befalling anyone . . . except Captain Turner, of course."

"I believe there is a certain groom who will be severely rebuked for not following my directions. And the same goes for those two sailors."

"They didn't do anything wrong," she said quickly, defending the men. "All they did was follow your instructions. Whatever else you think they are guilty of . . . well, you should blame me. As you know I can be very persuasive when plans need a bit of adjusting. If there is punishment that is to be meted out—"

"Yes, punishment. As to your punishment, Miss Edwards, I have decided to place you in a dory and let you row back to shore."

Portia tuned to him in shock. "That is rather drastic, don't you think?"

"Not at all. I think I'm being quite generous. My first thought was to throw you and your mother overboard and let you swim back."

"So you know," she said quietly, unconsciously backing toward the door.

"How could I not know? Did you think you could take Helena Middleton all the way to Scotland without anyone on this ship noticing her?"

She nodded. "Jack and those sailors simply thought that she was just my servant. I could have used the same story on the ship's captain if you hadn't been aboard."

"So now 'tis my fault for ruining your plans," Pierce snapped. He walked toward her, and she took another step back. "I am being the villain here for not allowing you to hoodwink more unsuspecting fools. I am an unfeeling rogue for suggesting that you should be punished for using me and my partner to abduct the daughter of an English admiral. I am a heartless beast because I object to your putting my people and my livelihood in dan-

ger since Middleton will most assuredly send half the Royal Navy after us to retrieve his daughter."

Portia's back hit the door. There was no way she could go around him, and there was nowhere else to go.

"You are no villain, Mr. Pennington. And you are neither unfeeling nor heartless. I believe you are a compassionate soul who I was sure must have known what I intended to do when I told you I needed to secure passage."

"Spare me, Portia," he said hotly. "This is your last chance. Tell me *one* thing that I can believe—one thing that would convince me that you are a step above the lying, cheating, and self-serving person you appear to be."

"Believe *this* . . . she is the only person I have in this world." Portia blinked back her tears. "What would *you* do to save the only kin you have left? There is nothing in the world more important than family. Nothing. What I have done . . . what I am trying to do . . . I would do again!"

Portia turned her face when the tears finally spilled down her cheeks. She knew in her heart that he would not set them in a boat and make them row back to shore. She knew him well enough not to fear such threats. That was not what upset her now. He thought of her as a vile thing, vicious and low. That cut her deeply. That would be the scar she would carry forever.

"Return to your cabin, miss," he said, turning away. "I shall send word once I've decided what to do with you."

It was almost impossible not to reach for her, not to take her in his arms and soothe her. And yet Pierce's hands remained fisted at his sides as he watched Portia struggle with the door in her rush to get out.

She was truly a mess. She looked as if they'd made her swim alongside the dory instead of riding in it. Her hair was tangled and wild. Her dress was still wet and

torn and sagging off her body. She could easily have been the victim of all the disasters she'd spoken of, rather than the instigator. Right now, her tears were leaving trails down her dirt-stained cheeks.

When Pierce could stand it no more, he started toward her, but Portia was finally able to yank the door open. He stopped and watched her go out the door. In a moment she had scrambled up the steep steps and disappeared.

He closed the door and leaned against it. In comparison with everything that he himself had been involved with today, how innocent were her actions! All she had done was give her own mother a taste of freedom. And, when one considered it, how similar were their impulses. Was her act of rebellion any less valid than his? Her motive was the right of a daughter to know her mother. Was his motive so noble?

He moved to the table that held a chart, which he stared at with unseeing eyes. What risk had she added to this voyage? If the Royal Navy were to come after them, it wouldn't be for the reason of rescuing Helena Middleton, but rather to capture those responsible for attacking and burning the *Gaspee*.

Pierce knew there would be many inquiries. The act would be considered treason. It was truly an act of war—the first one committed by the colonists. There were so many involved in the final raid on the ship—eight long-boats filled with men. Leading them had been the most prominent· men in the Rhode Island colony. His own arrest, however, would bring the largest reward. They would love to put a rope around the neck of MacHeath.

Pierce knew he might never be able to come back here. His stay in Scotland might even bring its own difficulties. But none of that bothered him. Whatever life had in store, he would face it.

None of that bothered him anywhere near as much as Portia's actions troubled him.

He looked around the paneled captain's quarters—at

the row of windows at the stern of the ship, at the handsome upholstered sofa beneath it, at the finely carved sideboard and chairs. His gaze fell on the bed built into the port side of the chamber. After their intimacy last night, he'd thought of her surprise when she found him here. He'd been impatient about bringing her to this cabin, about rekindling what they'd shared. He wanted to see if it was as real as he'd imagined—if she was as sincere in her affections as she sounded and acted.

He had his answer today. There was no way to tell the truth from the lies . . . whatever the justification. She had not trusted him to understand. She'd used him, just as Emma had.

Chapter 20

⁓

Portia was blind to the sky and the sea and all the beauties of nature that had so arrested her before. She was unaware of the dozen heads that turned toward her as she ran from the captain's quarters in tears. She raced across the deck of the ship and down the ladder to steerage, stumbling the last steps to her cabin door.

Closing the door behind her, she ran a hand quickly down her face to wipe the tears. As her eyes adjusted to the dim light, she found Helena sitting up on the narrow berth.

"Portia?"

"Yes, mother." Saying the word made her choke up again, and she took a couple of steadying breaths to battle her emotions.

"You just missed a very nice man who stopped by. His name was Thomas. He didn't say his last name. He is the cook, apparently . . . and the surgeon, and the carpenter, and whatever else the shipmaster—a Captain Cameron—calls on him to do. A lovely man. He also made a point of telling me he is a *free* man, and that he has family in Philadelphia."

"Did he just come by to say hello, Mother?"

"As a matter of fact, he wanted to know if we would care to have some breakfast brought up from the galley, or if we were going to take our meals with the owner, a Mr. Pennington, in the captain's quarters."

"I shall go and talk to Thomas in a little while. If you don't mind, we might eat right here, or on deck when the weather is agreeable. It looks to be a lovely day."

Helena stifled a yawn and gathered her knees up against her chest. She looked like a little girl. "I should be just as happy to stay here. I want to be with you. If I could only shake off this pounding headache. And I am so drowsy." She rubbed her temples.

"I think I shall go down and get you something to eat. 'Twill be good to have something in your stomach before you fall asleep again."

"Wait." Helena reached out. "I want to talk to you first."

Portia used her damp sleeve to wipe the last of her tears and approached her mother, taking the extended hand in hers.

"You are freezing." Helena's hand moved up and touched the sleeve, the dress. "You are still wet! You must change at once. How are you going to take care of me if you become ill yourself?"

Portia's spirits lifted when she noticed the smile on Helena's face. "I never become ill."

"I am very happy to hear that, for I am rarely well myself, these days. And I shall hold you to that. But I insist that you change first."

Portia obediently took a clean dress and underclothing out of the trunk and started to change in the cramped cabin. Helena's gaze following Portia's movements, though it was obvious that she could not see clearly.

"I was drifting in and out of sleep, but I thought I heard you being invited to go and meet the shipmaster?"

"Actually, 'twas the owner, Mr. Pennington, who wished to see me."

"And how was your visit?"

Portia pulled her wet shift over her head and began to put on a dry one as she searched for an answer. She wanted to be honest with her mother, but she did not want to frighten her about their position on board. Still,

she knew that Helena might be faced with Pierce's hostility at any moment. She wanted her mother to be prepared for that.

" 'Twas due to Mr. Pennington's generosity that I was able to secure this passage for us . . . or for me . . . he thought. He did not know that I was bringing you with me . . . and I could not tell him since I feared he would not agree to it. But he was not supposed to be on this ship, so I thought he might never find out the truth. But he is here . . . and he knows . . . and he is very angry with me."

"Angry enough to send us back?" Helena asked, concern in her voice.

Portia held the clean dress against her chest. " 'Twould be very difficult for him to do that, so I believe he shall tolerate our presence for the journey. I do not believe he will be as friendly to us as your Thomas."

Helena tucked her hands under her chin, and Portia found herself enchanted by the serene image before her. She looked so innocent, so content. Already the lines of tension had disappeared from her brow.

"Is he a handsome man?"

The butterflies stirred and opened their wings in Portia's stomach. "I have heard that many consider him handsome."

"And young?"

"I don't know his exact age, but I believe he might be my age or slightly older."

"Such a young man . . . and he owns this ship. I must assume he is wealthy."

"He comes from an excellent family. His brother is an earl, I understand. And although he was brought up to be a gentleman, I believe he has worked hard to make his own fortune."

"And is he married or contracted to be married?"

"He is not married."

"He must have many mistresses, then."

Portia remembered that first night they met. Images

of the room at the Black Pearl tavern sprang into her mind. He was supposed to meet a woman there. The sharp blade of jealousy cut into her unexpectedly, but she pushed it away.

"That I would not know, mother."

"But how did you two meet?"

Portia stepped into the dress. She sat on the edge of the bunk as she laced up the front. "We met the night of the King's Birthday Ball, right after I terrified you while trying to break into your room. We met while I was trying to escape your father's servants."

"It sounds so romantic." Helena smiled and reached for her hand. "Tell me everything."

Portia realized suddenly that she didn't feel the shyness with her mother that she had felt talking to Mary or Bella. She felt free and unafraid to speak openly. She somehow knew that Helena would understand her, that her mother would not condemn her because of her attraction to Pierce. He was the first man in her life, the only one for whom she had ever developed such strong feelings. Portia had been helpless against his charm . . . and her own treacherous heart still beat for him alone.

So she told Helena what she would never have dared to admit to anyone else. She told her everything, beginning with the Black Pearl tavern that first night and how close she'd come to being discovered by Turner. She told Helena about his respect for her views on things of the world such as the politics of Boston and the colonies. And how he made her feel intelligent and even beautiful in a way that no one else ever had. Hesitating only slightly, Portia even divulged how she had gone to him at his home, to see him one last time and thank him. In as few words as possible, she told her mother of her blunder in giving away her innocence.

"Do you really think you made a mistake, child?" Helena asked in a soft voice. "Do you wish now that you never had gone there?"

There was a long silence as the two sat in the half-light.

"No. 'Twas no mistake." Portia looked down at their joined hands. "If it had happened that first night at the tavern, then I would say, yes, 'twas a mistake, because I did not know him. But now . . . that last night . . ." She shook her head. "It changed me. I had no regret then, I have none now, and . . . and I know I would feel the same if there are consequences that I must deal with because of it."

"Oh *my*!" Helena whispered. "This is far more serious than I could have imagined. You are in love."

Portia immediately bristled defensively. "I did not say that."

"No need to say it, my child."

Helena reached up and touched Portia's cheek. She had not even realized it, but there were tears on her face. Her mother was right, and she knew it, too.

"How does he behave toward you now . . . after what happened?"

"He is angry, though not because of what we did," she replied. "He is angry because of the lies I told to bring the two of us—you and me, I mean—together. And he is right to be. His accusations are completely justified. I was blind to his feelings. I did not think of consequences. I did not pay attention to the hurt that my actions could cause him, considering the relationship that we . . . that we . . ." Portia wiped the tears off her face. "But in spite of all that, I would not undo what I have done. You are here with me, and I did what needed to be done."

In the end, one's name, one's reputation, one's career are all a man has that is worthwhile.

Even as Turner thought this, though, the humiliation continued. His career was on the verge of ruin. His life's work was in tatters. The other members of the Admiral's staff were laughing behind his back. And it seemed that in every officer's mess from here in Boston to New York, some story or other was circulating that involved the name of Captain George Turner.

Some rumored that on the night of the burning of the *Gaspee,* he was dead drunk in some tavern in Providence. Others claimed he was off buggering some nameless ensign in Newport. There were a few who whispered that Turner was afraid to be caught in the midst of any skirmish, so he was hiding while the *Gaspee* was under attack. His stomach churned at the very thought of these lies.

His anger grew but he endured the sly comments and the looks of disdain. Even the enlisted men were looking at him boldly, treating him with less than the respect he deserved. He tried to weather it and keep his head up, even when the jokes among the other officers became more open and more vicious. It soon became clear he was not to be given an opportunity to set the record straight. Perhaps it was better that no one should know of Portia's trickery. If it were known that he had been bested by a wisp of a girl, his treatment would not improve. In any case, he could not speak, could not defend himself, because the truth exposed Admiral Middleton, who ordered him to be silent about the events of that night.

The Admiral had acted immediately. When it was clear that his daughter was gone, he had packed off four serving women who attended to his daughter to Halifax in Nova Scotia on a brig that was sailing with the tide. Mrs. Green was threatened with her job. No one was to know that Miss Middleton was missing. The official story was that the Admiral's daughter had gone to Nova Scotia for her health.

And more important, it seemed, no one could know that there was any connection between Portia Edwards and Helena Middleton.

This was the part that perplexed Turner the more he thought of it. He had been shocked to learn of the connection the night the *Gaspee* burned. And he was not allowed to ask any questions, either. When he had made his report to the Admiral, the blood had drained from

his face. Then he had lashed out at Turner unmercifully, telling him that because he had introduced this imposter into the household, Turner would be held personally responsible for the entire disaster, including the botched operation that left the *Gaspee* a charred hulk on a sandbar in Narragansett Bay.

Turner paced impatiently in the hallway. His head had been pounding incessantly for six days. He was not responsible for any of it. He had been tricked and wounded in action. He knew that in remaining silent, with no chance of recovering his reputation, he was making the biggest sacrifice of his life. And still, Middleton treated him no better than a whipped dog.

Even now, he was being made to wait in the hallway while less competent officers were in a private meeting with the Admiral. It was the same every day. He had been stripped of all responsibilities having to do with the attack on the *Gaspee* and with the activities of the Sons of Liberty. He had been ordered to look into one thing only, and that was finding out where Portia had taken the Admiral's daughter. It was a demeaning, nearly impossible task since he was forbidden to interrogate anyone openly for fear of the truth coming out.

After a week, though, Turner had uncovered information that he determined was reliable, and he was impatient to report it to his superior. It was time to move on to more important things.

Turner stopped pacing and his back stiffened as the Admiral's door finally opened and three young officers walked out. He glared down the end of his nose at the puerile trio, silently challenging them even to smirk. None of them was brave enough to meet his gaze. The last through the door, though, announced that the Admiral was ready for him now.

Inside, Middleton's reception was cool, as it had been since the incident. His eyes never moved from the papers before him. "You have something to report?"

Turner was bothered that his superior no longer acknowledged him either by rank or by name. "Indeed, sir. I have succeeded in gathering the answers you wanted."

The Admiral looked up, his expression doubtful. "Speak up."

"I believe Miss Middleton and Miss Edwards are traveling to Wales, specifically to the home of a Lady Anne Primrose."

"In Wrexham."

"You know Lady Primrose?"

"Of course I know her. She's a treacherous, troublemaking Jacobite whore, but she's always had too much money and too many connections in high places for us to touch her. And she's as cunning as a fox." Middleton looked at him suspiciously. "Why do you say they're going there."

"Miss Edwards spent her childhood there, in a school Lady Primrose funds."

"How do you know this? How do you know the villainess is not hiding my daughter somewhere in Rhode Island? In one of these godforsaken towns or villages that plague us? How do you know she did not return to Boston and is hiding her right under our very noses?"

"To begin, after a week of keeping watch on the residence of Parson Higgins, we know that they are not there, and that there has been no attempt by the family to communicate with Miss Edwards. I know for a fact," Turner said confidently, "they would have made such an attempt if she were anywhere in the vicinity of Boston."

"Of course, being such a trusted and familiar friend of the family, you would know this," the Admiral said, sarcasm evident in his tone.

Turner had no answer to the insinuation. Indeed, he had been a fool to trust that devious young woman, to trust anyone connected with her. He forced himself to continue.

"Another piece of information that adds weight to my

supposition was given to me by the daughter of my cousin, who lives here in Boston. The girl happens to be a good friend of Miss Edwards and—"

"So bad judgment runs rampant in your family." Middleton leaned back in his chair and looked at him with open disdain.

Turner felt his ears redden as his anger burned hotter inside of him. He remained rigidly at attention, though. "If I may continue, sir . . ."

"What was this valuable scrap of information that your cousin provided?"

"My cousin's daughter was visited by Mrs. Higgins, who told her that Portia had to leave Boston unexpectedly, for personal reasons. The parson's wife also told her that the young woman had no immediate plan of returning. In response to my cousin's insistence that Mrs. Higgins provide her with an address to correspond with her friend, the woman claimed to know nothing more." Turner continued before the Admiral had a chance to make some other disparaging comment. "My cousin was apparently aware of Miss Edwards's difficult financial condition, a fact that did not surprise me. In addition, since she has been in Boston less than a year, the young woman lacks friends and connections here. At the same time, my cousin told me that she had heard Miss Edwards speak many times of her benefactor, Lady Primrose. When one considers all this together, it becomes clear that she would take Miss Middleton there, once she was able secure a place on a ship."

"And could she secure passage?"

"Indeed she could, Admiral." Turner felt his superior's confidence returning, albeit guardedly. "As you know, Mr. Pennington has departed for England."

"His partner notified me of that when he wrote to me about the meeting we had arranged that they would not be attending. What of it? I was told Pennington had to leave suddenly due to a family emergency having to do with his brother, the Earl of Aytoun."

"Very convenient, I should think. He left the same day that your daughter was abducted. The same day that the *Gaspee* was attacked and burned."

"What are you saying, Turner?" Middleton asked impatiently.

"I am saying that Mr. Pennington did not depart from Boston. All of his ships that were in port are still here. He also did not leave on any other ship that we know of."

"So how did he go?"

"I have learned that their ship the *Lothian* is expected any day. There is a report, however, that the ship was seen not a day out of Boston, south of the cape, and on a course that would take her close to the Narragansett Bay."

"Where Pennington could meet her."

"Along with Miss Edwards and your daughter," Turner quickly added. "I believe that when I saw them, they were waiting to be picked up in a boat."

Turner definitely had his superior's attention now.

"But that is not all of it, Admiral. During the two consecutive days prior to the *Gaspee*'s destruction, we know that Mr. Pennington left Boston on horseback, passing through the checkpoint at the Neck and then returning. He did this twice, sir, and my belief is that he was traveling back and forth to Rhode Island in preparation for the attack on the *Gaspee*."

"That is a strong accusation," Admiral said thoughtfully.

"If you would allow me to resume my previous duties, I would be happy to bring you the proof. Pennington had to be involved. Why else he would choose that night to depart?" Turner was pleased with his own reasoning. "I have heard the preliminary investigation into the attack has not proven fruitful. I believe the reason for their failure is that those in charge are chasing after nameless and faceless ruffians. If you were to honor me with such a commission, I would find you witnesses who could

identify Pennington as one of the rebel leaders. He is not a Rhode Islander, and I believe the base knaves would gladly give him up to save their own necks."

Admiral Middleton stood up and walked to the carved marble fireplace, stroking his chin as he considered this. Finally he turned to the captain.

"This is all speculation . . . unless you have any specific names of possible witnesses. Is there anything that you have been holding back from those conducting the investigation?"

"I do not have names as yet, sir. But I shall. With your permission, I can—"

"You can finish the task you've been assigned. You can clear up the mess you have created in my life and in my household before you touch anything else. You must first *earn* back your place, Captain. Before you resume any of your previous responsibilities, you will return the daughter you have allowed that young woman to steal from me."

Turner straightened up, stunned by the reprimand and by the hypocrisy of the Admiral's words. In all the years he had served Middleton, the man had given far more attention to his hounds and his horses and his gardens than he ever gave to his daughter. So long as she remained quiet and out of the way, he was satisfied. Now, suddenly, she was the most important thing in the world.

Turner found himself wondering why the sea change. There was no love in the man, of that he was certain. Why did he want her to be back under his thumb? The thought suddenly occurred to Turner that if Portia was indeed the daughter of Helena Middleton, then who was the bloody father?

If this was the reason for the Admiral's uncharacteristic concern for his daughter, then it would begin to make sense. Middleton's own name, his own career, had always been the most important thing to him. He wanted his daughter back so that no old skeleton would rattle in the

family closet. It must be a horrifying skeleton for the Admiral to think it might affect his career.

"Do we have an understanding, Captain?"

Name, reputation, career. The only things that really mattered in the end.

"Indeed we do, sir."

Turner would bring back Helena Middleton, and he would punish Portia Edwards in doing so. She would pay for betraying him.

"I will attach your name to the committee that is going to England to carry the preliminary reports on the *Gaspee* incident. You will sail on the *Beaver*. When you arrive in England, though, you have only one duty, and that is to find Helena. Do you understand?"

"Aye, sir," Turner said obediently.

"I have allowed word to circulate that Helena shall be returning from Halifax sometime early in the fall. 'Tis your job, Captain, to bring her back by then."

"I shall, sir," Turner vowed.

Chapter 21

It had taken six days for Helena to overcome the sleep-inducing effects of the medicines that she had been given for so long. And for the next seven days and nights, Portia spent endless hours at her mother's side while the older woman's stomach heaved with every pitch and roll of the ship.

During those days, Portia saw plenty of Thomas, the ship's cook and surgeon, and the two of them became friends. The wire-thin black man showed up at their door at least three times a day with a meal for Portia and different kinds of brews for Helena. In addition to the food and company he provided, Thomas even succeeded in pushing Portia out of the cabin for a few minutes each day.

She knew it was because of Thomas that the rest of the crew showed no vestige of hostility against Portia, as the owner of the ship did. Pierce refused to talk to her. He didn't bother to acknowledge her presence on board, in even the simplest of gestures, and she cried inside because of it. What she felt for him was the same, and she desperately searched for a way to get him to notice her. During the second week of the journey, a slight hope flickered when Captain Cameron, a fairly young man with pleasantly weathered features, showed up at their cabin door. Quickly, though, Portia realized the shipmaster was there of his own volition. Cameron offered them his cabin—actually the mate's cabin—which he claimed

was somewhat roomier than the one they were staying in. Grateful for the offer, they declined. Both Portia and Helena were happy with their arrangements as they were.

Still, though she never came face-to-face with Pierce, she saw him whenever the crew was asked to assemble on deck for a drill or for some talk, which, quite often, he participated in. Portia found those drills the most exciting part of her days. As her mother began to improve, she even found herself waiting for the sound of the bell, so that she could go on deck to watch.

For these assemblies, the men gathered in the ship's waist, climbing down from above as well as coming up from belowdecks. Whenever she would see him on the lines, she would stare in awe at the way Pierce could move through the intricate weave of the rigging. The speed in which he climbed the mast was breathtaking.

And on the days that he wasn't there, Portia was still amazed by the sight. She loved the feel of the sea—to be on the ship. There was something thrilling about the sight of the sailors, their tar-covered britches and shirts whipping against sun-darkened skin, as they climbed high above the decks. She studied their movements as they hauled on and worked the lines and tackle until the desired sails were shifted and set.

For three days now, Helena had been well enough to leave their cabin and come up on deck with her. It was a grand show, and Portia was delighted that she could now watch it with her mother.

"Tell me what they are doing now."

The question drew Portia's attention back to her mother. The two of them sat on a bench in the ship's waist, out of the way of the working sailors. "The sails are being tended. They are huge and filled with the wind. They look like the wings of a bird against the sky. The wind has shifted to the north east, and they are making the adjustments Captain Cameron has handed down to the mate. Thomas said this morning there was a change

in the wind. He thinks we may be in for what he called a 'stiff blow.' "

Portia continued to explain what she could see happening above them and on the decks. She had begun to learn a little by listening to other sailors. Thomas had answered questions for her, too, about the wind and how they would use the sails and ropes to change direction or to increase the speed or slow the ship. She tried to describe for her mother where each man was and how graceful and sure-handed they were as they scurried up the ratlines and along the spars.

"Truly fascinating. Men have such interesting lives."

Portia laughed. "I agree. I would do anything to be able to climb the ratlines to the top of the mainmast . . ."

. . . *the way Pierce seems to be fond of doing,* she finished silently.

"Would you now?" Helena said, smiling.

"I would. I have always been fond of heights. I love cliffs and vistas. I even climbed to the top of the Monument when Lady Primrose took me with her to London once. You can see half the world from there, I think."

"I have seen it. 'Tis a glorious sight."

"But I am curious to know how different it feels to go so high while the rope sways beneath your feet, while you fight the wind as you climb and the motion of the ship as it rides over the waves." Portia looked wistfully at the men who were trimming the gray-white sails. " 'Tis just one of those things that I probably shall never have the opportunity to do."

"One never knows." Helena squeezed her hand affectionately. "The world is rapidly changing, is it not?"

"Miss, do ye wish to have this bucket here or in yer cabin?"

Portia rose quickly to her feet. Daniel, a young sailor on his first voyage, held out the bucket of water. He was not taller than Portia, and probably weighed no more than her, either.

"Thank you for fetching it for me. I shall need it down

in the cabin for some washing, but I can take it down myself."

" 'Tis no problem, miss. I'll carry it down for ye." He grinned. "I'm on my way to the galley, anyway, and old Thomas will ne'er feed me if he finds out I left it fer ye to carry."

Portia left Helena on deck where she was perfectly content to sit in the sun and the fresh air. Following the young man down to steerage, she chatted with him. It was extremely pleasant to feel the acceptance of those around them. Although she and Helena were the only women on board, Portia had yet to feel awkward because of it. If she could only get Pierce to notice her.

Back in the cabin, Portia attacked with a vengeance the clothes she'd put aside to wash.

The first day that her mother had been well enough to go on deck, Portia had left her for a moment, running down to the cabin for a shawl for her. By the time she returned, she found that Pierce had come over and quite courteously introduced himself to Helena. On the second day, he'd stopped by to ask after her health, only bowing stiffly to Portia without ever looking at her. And yesterday, while Portia had gone down to the galley to bring up their food, Pierce had taken Helena for a short walk around the stern deck.

Her mother was completely taken in by the man's fine manners. And Portia found herself to be sad and frustrated by her helplessness in mending the past. He wasn't even giving her a chance to speak to him. She just didn't know how to get him to forgive her at least, never mind thank him once again for his kindness to them both.

As she scrubbed the clothes, she broke into a sweat in no time, not so much because of the work, but because of her frustration. She hung the dresses and underclothes over a rope she'd strung across the cabin, picked up the bucket of soiled water, and started back up the ladder.

Helena was not where she'd left her. Portia was not surprised to look up and find her mother on the arm of

Pierce as they strolled on the stern deck. She wasn't jealous, she told herself. Her pain didn't come from Pierce's efforts at being pleasant to Helena.

No, Portia suffered because she loved him.

He watched her whenever she wasn't aware of him looking. He questioned his people about what she was doing. He worried about her comfort and her health, but it seemed she thrived despite the difficulties of taking care of her mother and staying in the cramped cabin. She was more than just making do with the little she had brought along. They told him that she never complained. In fact, "the Miss," Thomas told him, "is steady as any foretopman in His Majesty's whole bloody navy."

Pierce saw her appear on deck again with a bucket in hand. He had ordered the men to do all her chores, but they told her that she generally refused their offers. She cleaned their cabin, washed their clothes, and even insisted on going to the galley to get their own food since her mother was again eating. And that was not the end of it. Pierce had noticed that many on his crew vied for her attention. Even the surliest of the old tars seemed softened by her. They were all quite obvious in their attempts to please her.

In mentioning it to the shipmaster, Pierce heard many reasons for that behavior, and none of them the most obvious. Apparently, she had learned the crew's names within days. She asked about their families, those who had any. And he'd watched from the stern rail, surprised at how many of them gathered on the foredeck while Portia read to them as the sun set.

Even from afar, Pierce could tell that the sea agreed with her. She looked vibrant, beautiful, uninhibited, and it pained him to continue keeping his distance.

"Why do you continue to hold a grudge against my daughter, Mr. Pennington?"

Helena's question scraped the scab off his wound. He saw Portia glance up at them briefly before dumping the

water over the side and disappearing again down the stairs to steerage.

"A grudge, ma'am?" he replied, disappointed that she was gone. "I hold no grudge."

For the past three days, he had hoped that finding her mother with him would give Portia a reason to approach, to say anything to him. But she was being as stubborn as he was.

"I think you are not being entirely truthful."

"And what makes you say that?" He looked down at the woman on his arm. Helena had already exceeded what Pierce had expected of Admiral Middleton's daughter. And she continued to surprise him.

"Because I happen to be in my daughter's confidence. She told me everything that she had to do in order to free me from my father's house. She told me how badly she wronged you and how betrayed you feel because of her actions." She stopped, let go of his arm, and faced him. "But why do you two allow this barrier to exist between you?"

Pierce tried to think of a diplomatic way to word his answer. After being united with her daughter for the first time in twenty-four years, Helena certainly did not need to hear him list Portia's flaws.

"I'll tell you something," she continued. "I think you do not wish to dismiss her from your life, for if you did, I do not think you would be treating her mother with such courtesy and attentiveness."

Pierce shook his head.

"Tell me the truth, sir," she said sternly. "What I have lost in vision, I've gained in my other senses. I feel your hesitation. Let me assure you that there is nothing you can tell me that would surprise or disappoint me regarding Portia."

"Miss Middleton, you have known her for less than a month. And she has, no doubt, seemed perfect in all respects during that time. I do not know what she told you, but I am certain that your feelings might be a little

different if you had actually seen the dangers she exposed herself to while she was trying to free you."

"You are telling me that she takes risks to achieve her goals. Now if she were a man, that would be a quality of greatness. I believe the proverb says, 'Fortune favors the brave.' Do you mean to tell me that you criticize the same virtue in her because she is a woman?"

"Yes and no," Pierce said. "Yes, because the consequences of her actions could have been much more severe because she is a woman. And no, because I would have found her actions objectionable even if she were man. She went beyond what is reasonable, into the realm of stubborn recklessness."

"Did she? I wonder. I do not hear great conviction in your voice, Mr. Pennington. Still, is that reason enough to stay angry with her, considering no trouble befell her or you or me?"

Pierce said nothing for a moment.

"Then what else do you have against her?" Helena pressed.

She wanted honesty, so Pierce decided to give it to her. "Portia is entirely too single-minded. Once she focuses on something, the rest of the world must simply stand aside. She see nothing else but her final goal. She becomes blind to others' feelings, insensible of any hardship that she might be inflicting on others. There is no other way but hers—no other path but the one she has chosen. There is no delaying of her plans for the sake of safety. She—"

"And does she do all of these horrible things for her own good?" Helena interrupted. "Is she ambitious? Selfish? Is she after wealth? Is she doing so much damage for her own sake? To improve her place in the world?"

"No," Pierce said through clenched teeth.

This was the difference, right here, revealed and explained to him by a nearly blind woman who had spent most of her life in some kind of seclusion. This was the

difference between Portia and Emma. At the center of Portia's actions lay the desire to do something for someone else, for her mother. In everything Emma had ever tried to do, her only concern had been for herself.

"Please do not misunderstand," Helena said, gentling her tone. She placed a hand on his arm. "I am not excusing my daughter's actions, but I am trying to explain them in the way that I myself understand them. You see, I have been through all of this before. I have been in your position, Mr. Pennington, and I know how difficult 'tis to understand such behavior. 'Tis nearly impossible, sometimes, to make sense out of it. But I needed to do that—as you must—for this quality is what makes them special. 'Tis at the center of who they are. In a way, 'tis one reason that we feel as we do about them. 'Tis the reason why we must make our own sacrifices."

"I do not understand you, Miss Middleton. You have just met her for the first time—"

"Not exactly." She shook her head. "This is so difficult to explain. But Portia . . . the way she is—her impulsiveness, her reckless love of danger, her inability to recognize the restraints that keep most of us from enjoying life to the fullest—these things she comes by quite honestly. This is the same way that her father was, and most likely still is. She cannot help herself. She was born with adventure in her blood. She has to find causes, and then fight them. If 'tis not one thing, sir, then it will be another. On that you can rely."

Pierce looked at her curiously. "Did you say Portia's father is alive?"

Helena reached for the railing and turned her upraised face to the sun. Wisps of golden hair escaped her long braid and danced in the wind. A softness crept into her expression, and he knew she was remembering a different time. For a few long minutes, Pierce remained silent, allowing her to enjoy her memories. Finally, she turned to him.

"I believe he is alive. I have been in seclusion for many years, but news of that importance would have reached me. If he were dead, I would know it."

He tried to put together in his mind a list of people who could have fathered Portia. A Jacobite. Someone significant enough that news of his death would reach the colonies. The list was very short. "Have you told Portia any of this?"

"Of course not."

Pierce came to stand beside her by the railing. "Why are you telling me these things before revealing them to your daughter?"

Helena looked up at him. For the first time her eyes looked as if they could see. "Because I know what has happened between you. And I know she is suffering now, the way a woman suffers when her heart has been trodden upon."

Objections immediately rose in him. She had been the one who'd destroyed what was between them.

Pierce hesitated. But had she? What responsibility was he taking for all that had happened? It was he who had taken her to the Black Pearl. It was he who had not voluntarily helped her when she asked for it. It was he who had made love to her.

And then he had rejected her, hurting himself as much as her in staying away. Perhaps even more.

"But this is still no reason to tell me what Portia should know."

"I think there is. I need you to understand that, despite her apparent circumstances, Portia is no stableman's daughter, if that is what motivates your actions."

"It does not," he said sharply.

"I am glad to hear that, since there is no way that I can think of to reach her father." Taking hold of the railing, she edged away from him, finally turning and following it along the deck.

He stayed beside her. "Considering how important Portia feels 'tis to have a family—how desperate she was

to find you—do you not think she has a right to know the truth?"

"Yes, I do," Helena said softly. "And I will tell her . . . when the time is right."

The storm that Thomas had predicted came on them quickly around sunset, buffeting the ship for several hours before passing. During the night, the sky gradually cleared, and the sea was again calm by the first light of day.

Portia finished mending the sleeve in the spare shirt that Daniel had loaned her. Before she'd washed it, the fabric had been stiff with tar and saltwater, and it was still, to some extent. It had chafed her skin when she'd tried it on, but it was functional, anyway, and that was what mattered. She folded the shirt and put it on top of the gray breeches. The waistline of the breeches was too big, but she thought a piece of rope looped around them would do the trick.

They would have to do. She definitely would need them for where she was planning to go.

"Good morning."

Portia quickly rolled everything up and put it next to their trunk. She turned to her mother. She wondered how long Helena had been awake. "Good morning."

"What are you doing? I have been listening to you. I thought I could hear the sound of thread being pulled."

Her mother might not be able to see very well, but she was becoming more and more independent every day.

"Just mending some clothes that belong to Daniel." She stood up and folded her bedding. "I went up on deck at dawn. It promises to be a beautiful day. Not a cloud in the sky and a light, steady breeze. I was thinking of getting one of the sailors to show me how they make some of the fancy knots with the ropes. What would you care to do?"

It was fascinating to see Helena spreading her wings. Her diminishing sight was obviously not going to slow

her down at all. Every day, she was insisting more and more that Portia not do things for her that she could do herself.

"After breakfast, Captain Cameron offered to take a stroll with me on deck. And in the afternoon, Mr. Pennington has invited all of us for a cup of tea."

Portia told herself she would ask either Daniel or Thomas to escort Helena to the captain's quarters when the time came. She did not want to come even as close as the door of that cabin.

Her mother sat up in the bunk. "Do you have any dresses that might be presentable for the occasion?"

"The gray dress you wore when we left Boston is in the best condition of all of them. You look beautiful in it."

"I do not mean for me. I was talking about you. Is there anything that you have that you can wear?"

Portia's traitorous heart began to race. "But I am not coming."

"You were invited."

"Was I? Or are you only assuming that the invitation included me?"

Helena gracefully swung her feet over the side of the berth. Her blond hair fell to her waist. Portia saw mischief in her mother's face—and it was a look that she hadn't seen before.

"I think, considering the gentleman's generosity, it would be quite ill mannered to ignore the invitation."

"You did not answer my question. Tell me the truth. What did Mr. Pennington say?"

"He said he hoped I would not be offended if he did not send us a formal invitation, but he hoped we would honor him with our presence. He indicated that he would be serving tea in the captain's quarters at three, that Mr. Cameron would be in attendance, and he hoped we would gratify his request."

"You meant *you.*"

"He used the plural *you.*"

"I think not, Mother. I shall not make a fool of myself attending a tea that I am not expected to attend."

Helena leaned forward, arching an eyebrow at her. "I believe you are being obstinate now."

Portia stacked the folded blankets in a corner next to their trunk. "Please understand, Mother. Nothing has changed. I just do not wish to go where I am not wanted."

"Ridiculous."

"What is ridiculous?"

"You and Pennington. Each of you pines for the other, but neither of you takes a step to solve your problem."

"He does not pine for me."

"I say he does, and you should not argue with me."

"Why not?"

"Because you are my mo—" Helena shook her head. "I meant to say, Because I am your mother."

Portia couldn't help but giggle at the slip. "Then as your mother, I am ordering you not to lecture me on these complicated personal matters."

"I am *your* mother." Helena smiled. "And you are stubborn—just as he says. And there really is nothing complicated about this, at all. Now I want you to put an end to this foolishness. Go and apologize to him so I can stop suffering like this."

"Suffering?" Portia crossed her arms and moved close enough that she knew Helena would be able to see her. "How could you possibly be suffering from something that relates only to Pennington and me?"

Helena reached out and took hold of Portia's wrist. She pulled it until the younger woman sat next to her on the bunk. "Do you realize that every time I come back from walking with him, I have to listen to you sigh and moan for the next hour?"

"I do *not* sigh and moan," Portia cried.

"Your mother is speaking. Do not interrupt," Helena scolded lightly. "And Pennington is even worse. When we walk, he wants to know what you did that morning,

or the night before, or with whom you conversed, or
what book you were reading to the crew, or if the floor
of the cabin is too hard on your back, or if you were
warm enough when you—"

"Helena Middleton, you are telling tales. I cannot believe you. You should be ashamed of yourself, making all
of these things up." She put an arm around her mother's
shoulders and hugged her hard, not giving her a chance
to deny the accusation. "And I love you for what you
think you are doing. But no . . . no . . . no. I apologized
to him that first day. The way 'twas left, he said he would
send word when he had decided his feelings."

"So he is a little slow." Helena touched Portia's cheeks
and looked into her eyes. "Do not blame him for being
a man, my love. Three weeks have passed. He is probably just realizing he *has* feelings. He might need a nudge.
Just a little one. If you do not want to apologize again,
then I can understand that. But at least give him a little shake."

Chapter 22

⌒

The skies looked clear ahead, and the winds were fair and steady. If the weather held, they might reach port as much as a week ahead of schedule.

Joseph Cameron continued to explain their good progress, pointing out the route on his charts and talking of weather and crew and other things. Pierce, however, was having a difficult time staying focused on the words of the shipmaster. Restless, excited, even a little nervous, he was determined to put an end to the difficulties between Portia and himself. And he would do it today.

The door of the captain's quarters had been left open, and he heard Helena's voice as soon as she reached the stern deck. Cameron gathered up his charts. Pierce went to greet his guests, but was disappointed at the sight of the young sailor helping the older woman down the steep flight of stairs.

Pierce thought that he did a fairly good job of recovering from his disappointment, and escorted Helena in. The older woman was quite cheerful, chatting openly and obviously enjoying the company of the two men. Finally, when Pierce thought he could bear it no longer, Cameron asked the one question that mattered.

"Will Miss Edwards be joining us later, ma'am?"

"I do not believe so," Helena replied pleasantly. "I think she is otherwise occupied."

"How so?" Pierce had to ask.

"She thinks I know nothing about it. But after all her questions to the crew about knots and sails and rigging—and then borrowing some clothing from one of the sailors—I shouldn't be surprised if she were up to some mischief this afternoon."

Pierce stared worriedly at the open door.

"Miss Middleton and I will be perfectly happy to have a cup of tea without you, Pierce, if you would care to go and find Miss Edwards and see if you can coax her into joining us."

Pierce was out the door in a moment.

She was nowhere to be seen on the ship's waist, or on the foredeck, either. He doubted that on such a beautiful day as this she would be in the galley or anywhere below-deck. Still he decided he would start with her cabin.

Just as Pierce was going to go down the steps that led to steerage, he spotted the handful of rather anxious looking sailors gazing up at the ratlines leading to the top of the mainmast.

Portia climbed slowly, all the while repeating Thomas's advice again and again in her head: *Do not look up or down. Just pay attention to your handholds on the shrouds and feel the ratlines with your feet.*

She had not realized how much distance there was between each rope rung that led upward. Each time she stood on a ratline, she had to pull herself up to get her bare foot on the next one. And the pulling she had to do with her arms was more difficult than the work required of her legs, but she continued to move steadily upward nonetheless. She was glad to be barefoot, for with each successive move farther above the deck she needed to feel the hard rope ratlines with her feet. But her hands were already feeling chafed and tired, and she wasn't up even a score of rungs.

She was not about to give up, though. Not after all the begging she had done to have Thomas arrange this

for her. It had taken her friend a great deal of talking to persuade the other sailors that it would not be unlucky for a woman to don a man's clothes and try her hand going aloft into the rigging. Day in and day out, watching the sailors climbing up and down these ratlines, moving through the rigging, setting sails and reefing them and taking them down, Portia had become almost obsessed by the desire to know what it felt like to be that high in the air. And now she was doing it.

She broke her resolve and looked down at the crew's nervous faces below. She was perhaps as high up as she would be if she were looking down from her third story window at the apothecary. Not much to be nervous about.

Portia shifted her eyes and focused again on where her hands were reaching. She continued to climb. Thomas had made her promise to climb up only as high as the first trestletree. Reaching that, she glanced quickly at the upturned faces below again and then her gaze moved out past the gray and white sails to the calm seas beyond.

The climb this far, though hard work, was uneventful. Knowing she would probably never have this chance again, Portia decided to climb up a few more rungs of the ratlines before returning to the deck below.

There were some calls from the deck, but a breeze was blowing, and she couldn't make out if the shouts were intended for her or not. She didn't really want to know, and she continued upward. Another dozen steps up, Portia stole another glance at the sea. It was so large and flat. It was an endless field of blue-green grain, with flowers of white. It seemed to go on endlessly. Holding tight to one of the stays, she was enjoying the scenery when suddenly the ship dipped and everything around her twisted and tilted down.

Portia felt her stomach climb into her throat. Her heart pounded in her chest, and then, unaccountably, one of her hands lost its grip as the mast swung her outward.

Her body was bending outward, and she thought for a moment that the momentum would tear her from the rigging and cast her into the sea.

As she clung to the shrouds with one hand, she felt her toes trying to grip the rungs. Every muscle in her body suddenly ached, and her head started to spin. Then, when she thought she could hold on no longer, the ship righted itself, and she found herself pressed into the ropes.

Portia hung on, trying to catch her breath and steady her nerves. She knew she had to go down while she still had the strength, but she could not get her feet to move or make her cramping hands release their death grip on the shrouds.

"This is no place to rest. Shall we go up and see more, or are you ready to go down?"

She hadn't seen him come, but there he was on a spar, just a few feet from her. Portia felt like crying and laughing at the same time. She had never been so happy to see Pierce as she was at that moment.

"I think this is as high as I should like to go."

His expression told her that he was relieved. The sleeves of his shirt were rolled up. The muscled forearm reached out toward her.

"Give me your hand on that, will you, mate?"

Without even thinking, she reached out, and Pierce's fingers took her hand in his iron grip. Then, with a smile, he released it and nimbly swung himself out onto the ratline. In a moment he was just below her.

"Could you climb down on your own?"

Portia nodded. Sliding her hands down the shrouds, reaching into space until her foot touched the next ratline, she descended. She could feel Pierce moving down just below her, talking to her the entire way. He was so close that at times she could feel the brush of her feet against his hands. So close that she had no doubt he would catch her if she were to fall.

It seemed like eternity before Portia edged herself by the lowest of the mainsails.

As she emerged beneath it, she was shocked to hear a loud cheer from the deck. She hadn't realized that the entire crew had gathered to watch.

Portia saw Pierce climb down from the railing, and she was touched when he made no move to help her, but waited patiently until she dropped down by herself to the solid wood deck.

The second round of cheers was deafening.

Pierce controlled his emotions, backing away as the men gathered on the deck cheered her and teased her and even offered her a place in the crew. Pierce kept his distance while the wobble disappeared from her legs and the color and a smile returned to her face. He did not approach her as she untied the ribbon and shook her hair loose in the breeze. He even waited until after the crew dispersed, some returning to their duties, some forming an escort to take Portia back to her cabin.

He waited as long as he could, and then he descended to steerage and knocked on her cabin door.

Portia opened it as if she were expecting him.

The moment he saw her, all his control immediately dissipated into thin air and his emotions burst forth. "You will *never*—"

"I shall *never* . . ." she repeated, pulling him into the cabin and closing the door. "I shall never again do anything so foolish as climbing those ratlines alone."

Then, before he could say anything, she was in his arms and placing soft kisses on his face.

"Pierce, I have never been as afraid as I was at that moment. And then you were there. You knew I needed you. As you always do, you were there to help me."

"As I always do, I would like to strangle you."

But he kissed her instead, pouring the frustration of three weeks into the act of gathering Portia against him

and devouring her lips. She was just as he remembered her. Passionate, beautiful, intoxicating.

She held him tight, her mouth responding with demands of her own. Her lips parted, and she gave as much as she took. She needed him as much as he needed her.

"My God, I have missed you."

She leaned her back against the door. "Does this mean that you have decided what to do with me? Have you decided to forgive me?"

"How could I not?"

He threaded his fingers into her wild curly hair. He looked into her beautiful eyes and recalled how his heart had ceased beating when he'd seen her climbing up the mainmast rigging. The fear that she could fall to her death at any moment was numbing. And then he'd moved faster than he'd ever moved before.

"You are a sorceress. You've cast your spell on me, and I have no choice but to dance to your wishes."

Pierce kissed her again, this time slowly, deeply. He tried to enmesh her in that spell with him and make her desire that intimacy that they'd shared once before. He caressed her throat, slid his fingers downward and cupped her breast through the thick, rough fabric of the shirt.

"I never imagined I'd find myself kissing a sailor," he whispered.

As he brushed his lips against the sensitive skin of her throat and then beneath her ear, Portia leaned her head back against the door and closed her eyes. She tasted of the wind and the sea. His thumb rubbed gently across her nipple until he could feel it harden and extend.

"Are you wearing anything under this shirt?"

She shook her head. He groaned, and the sound of his head thumping against the door made her smile.

"Then we had better get out of this room before I forget all my good intentions," he growled. Pierce ran his hands once more down her body before reluctantly pushing away. "Will you change and join us in the cap-

tain's quarters? Your mother has been waiting there for what must be forever."

"But I believe I like the effect my new outfit has on you," she teased. "Perhaps I should wear this for what is left of the journey."

Pierce pressed his hips intimately against hers to make her realize what she was doing to him. "You come to my cabin tonight wearing this—or anything else for that matter—and I promise the effect . . . and the consequence . . . shall be the same. I shall rip them off your body in a matter of seconds."

"Seconds?"

"Are you issuing a challenge, you minx?"

"No, I just cannot wait for tonight." She ducked under his arm quickly and reached around him to open the door.

Pierce wanted to stay. He wanted to lock them both in his quarters for at least a week. It was not only his body that hungered for her, he found his mind was also starved for her company. He didn't know how it happened or when, but she mattered to him now—a great deal.

Portia hugged him one last time and pushed him toward the door. "You need to go so that I can follow you."

He opened the door and stepped into the narrow passageway, then remembered something that had been lingering in the back of his mind.

"What did you mean when you said you should not have climbed those ropes alone? *Alone*? Does that mean you are going to do it again?"

"Not without you," she whispered, closing the door to his face.

The captain's quarters, spacious and well-furnished, was quite a handsome place, in a masculine way. The walls were paneled and covered with several French tapestries. A high bed was built into the port side, and a

desk with a number of charts and books stood beneath a large oil lamp. There was a table and chairs where their tea was served and later, their supper. But as the afternoon slid easily into evening, Joseph Cameron excused himself and went to see to the watch change and other matters of the ship. It was then that Helena moved to the more comfortable sofa that had been placed near the stern, facing the built-in seat beneath the windows that framed a view of a golden sunset.

Portia had stopped worrying about wearing out their welcome hours ago, when Pierce had whispered to her that this was the least he expected of her as a means of apology. She had a great deal to make up for the time they had been apart.

In fact, when Helena offered to tell them about the years that she had spent in her father's house, Portia thought that he was as eager as she was to hear the account. And she didn't mind, at all, that he should know. She wanted him to know everything, and Portia loved the feel of this newfound openness.

She was amused to have him escort her toward the window seat rather than the place beside her mother. With an air of nonchalance, he then sat next to her. From the sly smile on Helena's face, Portia knew her mother understood what was happening.

"Despite what you may have heard," the older woman began, "I was not always kept in seclusion and under the influence of those horrid medicines. That is only since coming to Boston. But I am getting ahead of myself. Let me start from the beginning."

The sun was still warm on Portia's back, and her mother's face glowed in the golden light. She paused, gathering her thoughts, before continuing.

"I was just a dreamy-eyed girl when my first romance left me expecting a child. I was stunned, of course, but I was not sorry. Naturally, my attitude as well as my affair shocked the Admiral. He was always a stern, self-centered man. He had great responsibilities that he car-

ried out for his country, and he would not allow this scandal to damage his career. Once I knew I was with child, a situation which my family feared since they discovered my affair with your father, they decided that I must be separated from society. Of course, they were correct. Such a scandal would have been devastating to the Admiral's ambitions. Realizing that there was no longer any possibility of your father and I having a future together, I became passive, allowing them to do whatever they desired."

A knock on the door interrupted her, and Thomas entered to light the lantern in the cabin. After asking if they'd care for anything else, he retired.

Portia wished she could stop her mother now and ask about the man who had fathered her. But she knew that was only one link of a long chain that comprised Helena's life. Perhaps now that her mother was opening up to them about the past, it would only be a matter of time before that link would reveal itself.

"My mother, Elizabeth Middleton, was still alive then. And as tragic as my life might seem to you now, it could have been a great deal worse if she had not been there to protect both me and you. She brought me immediately back to England." Helena's gaze moved in the direction of Portia. "Although I was told that I lost you right after birth, I believe 'twas because of my mother that you were taken to Lady Primrose and not given to some gypsy or left by the side of some country lane . . . as the Admiral would certainly have done had he not still been in France on the king's business."

Pierce's hand reached over and took Portia's in his own. She entwined their fingers, relieved that there had never been an opportunity for her to formally meet her grandfather. She didn't think she could have ever understood a man like that.

"My mother continued to shield me from my father's wrath after the birth, as well. He was determined to lock my secret away forever. To do that, I needed to be im-

prisoned. If he could have it, I would be put someplace where I could never be spoken to or seen by anyone again. As his only child, I had betrayed him, he said. I'd tried to destroy his life and his career. I needed to be punished.

"Seclusion had no meaning to me. I had no desire for the frivolity of society. I had no chance of marrying, though that was no issue either, for I would never have agreed to any match. So my mother arranged for me to live in a little house in Dublin for six months of the year and the other six in a cottage by Lake Windermere in Cumberland. I had a woman to watch over me and a few servants. I kept my gardens—and my memories— and, to be truthful, I had all the comforts that one could wish for. But it could not last forever. The late roses were just beginning to fade one summer when I received word that my mother had died."

"When did you lose her?" Portia asked softly.

"Seven years ago. She was ill for some time, and when my father was commissioned to come to Boston after the commotion caused by the passage of the Stamp Act, she simply did not survive the sea voyage. I was told that they buried her in the sea a fortnight after they set sail from Bristol."

"And is that when you were brought to the colonies?" Pierce asked.

"The summer after. Once my mother was gone, the Admiral wasted no time. He'd heard reports that I was beginning to live a life less secluded than he wished. Truthfully, I had befriended a schoolmaster's wife in Dublin, but she passed away the winter before my mother. He also knew that I was beginning to have problems with my vision, although at that time 'twas very slight."

Helena spread her fingers on the embroidered material covering the sofa, feeling the texture. "My father did not really need any excuses, but that served as well as any

for bringing me to Boston. As a dutiful father, he wanted only the best for me."

Portia saw a mocking smile form on her mother's lips.

"And that was when 'Mad Helena' was born. Trouble started between my father and me the first moment I arrived. After all those years, I was accustomed to my independence. For so many years I was mistress of my own houses, though they were never more than a couple of rooms. But still, I was not anyone's charge. That situation, of course, was hardly acceptable to the Admiral. He put that witch, Mrs. Green, over me. Pushing me around until I became angry, claiming that my mind was not sound, insisting that I should be visited by doctors and given sedatives that would keep me subdued—that was her way of controlling me."

"But you fought them," Portia said, thinking how miraculous it was that Helena had somehow been able to maintain some of her spirit after so many years.

"I tried. But 'twas getting harder every day. In fact, 'twas becoming nearly impossible . . . until you came, my saving angel."

Portia moved across to the sofa and into her mother's arms. She shut her eyes to hold the tears at bay. These were happy times, she told herself. They were together . . . and it was all because of the man sitting across from them.

She turned and looked at Pierce. The look of tenderness she saw in his face nearly undid her.

"That is enough storytelling for one night." Helena pulled back and quickly dabbed the wetness from her cheek. "Mr. Pennington, would you be kind enough to escort Mad Helena and her unruly apprentice crew member daughter to their cabin?" She stretched out a hand toward him.

" 'Twould be an honor, ma'am." He immediately rose to help her.

Portia had to hang back for a moment to pull herself

together. She had known she was doing the right thing in trying to free Helena from that house, but now she felt Pierce's approval, too. He didn't have to say it. She saw it in his eyes . . . and she loved him for it.

She hurried to catch up with them.

"A lovely night!" Helena took a deep breath. "Any stars?"

"Millions of them," Portia whispered, looking up at the sky before her gaze locked with Pierce's. "Some of them are so far away, and yet some seem miraculously within arm's reach."

"Those are the best ones," he added softly.

They went down the steep stairs, and at their cabin door Portia let her fingers brush against his as Helena disappeared inside.

"I need to help—"

"I understand," he whispered, pressing a finger gently against her lips. "There will be other times for us."

She kissed his fingers and went inside.

Helena had her blanket turned down on the berth and was already stepping out of her dress. She turned and smiled at Portia.

"You see? I need no help. I can manage perfectly fine by myself tonight."

"I am very happy to hear it," the younger woman replied, starting to help her mother. "But I'm not sure I can. I would value your advice."

Helena sat on the edge of the bunk. "I am the wrong person from whom to seek advice."

"You are the *right* person." Portia frowned, hanging her mother's dress on a peg high on the wall. "I feel that I may be following exactly in your footsteps, and I need to know if—"

"If you think that, then you need to learn more about my past. To be honest, I do not believe our situations are alike at all." Helena pulled on Portia's hand and made her sit down next to her. "The relationship I had with your father was doomed before we even met, and

we both knew it. In the height of my romantic notions about the love that I thought was blossoming between us, I knew that we would each be considered the enemy by our respective families and friends. Even so, the few liaisons we had were thrilling, passionate. They were stolen moments filled with danger and intrigue. There was no future for us, but we cared not. When we were together, the world consisted only of the two of us."

Helena sighed, letting down her long blond hair and combing her fingers through it.

"When they tore us apart," she finally continued, "I continued to live in that loving world. I had to. Unlike you, I was not strong enough to fight against that harsh, real world. I could not stand on my own feet. I was not accustomed to work. My whole life I had been taken care of by my family. I expected someone else to look after me for the rest of my life. I expected my handsome knight to ride back and rescue me. Until then, I would wait."

Helena held Portia's hand tightly in her own. Their hands were so similar, their fingers long and tapered.

"As much as I loved him, your father was not Pierce. He too was a romantic dreamer. There were times when he would look off into the distance and see another world. He was made for greatness, and he knew there were sacrifices that needed to be made to achieve that greatness."

"And leaving you was one of those sacrifices?" Portia asked softly.

Helena smiled and her chin momentarily sank onto her chest. A soft blush had crept up her cheeks. She looked like an innocent, young and vulnerable. "I should like to think that. That is what I have been telling myself all these years."

"I think that must be the truth." Portia pushed a gray-streaked strand of golden hair off Helena's brow.

She looked up. "That young man we just left has more to offer a woman than any man I have ever met in my

life." Helena took Portia's face in her hands and looked into her eyes. "He cherishes life and has a great sense of what is real. He is responsible. He is honest. He plans, but will not allow wild dreams to get in the way of his beliefs or his loyalties. And he strikes me as a person who would not let even a kingdom come between him and the woman he loves."

Helena touched a tear that was rolling down her daughter's cheek. "You and Pierce are far different people than your parents, my love. You two are much better—much stronger. Go to him now. There is a great chance of happiness for you. I had no such chance."

Chapter 23

Portia could feel the change in the air the moment she stepped on deck. The ship seemed almost deserted, with only the sound of the wind in the sails and the low steady roar of the sea to keep her company. Standing by the railing, she stared out in the vast wasteland of rolling black water. She could not tell where the sea ended and the sky began, for there was a low mist enshrouding the horizon. She looked up. Far above her, beyond the straining gray canvas, the stars were visible for only a few moments as openings in the clouds scudded past. As she turned her gaze downward at the water rushing along the dark hull, the sound of a hornpipe floated back from the foredeck. It was a lonely tune, one filled with a sense of yearning, and it cut deeply into her soul.

Helena's final words had not eased her fears about the future. They had not given her any relief at all. Her path was not any clearer now than it had been. One thing Portia was sure of—she was not destined to have the happiness that her mother thought she could have with Pierce. The two of them could never be.

True, she loved him. But he had never bargained for all the trouble she had caused him. From the start, she had pushed herself on him, chased after him, tricked him. Even their initial meeting had been the result of her recklessness. Still, she had not even been able to capture

his interest at the Admiral's ball, when she'd looked her best.

And later, it had been she who showed up at his house, throwing herself at him once more. Portia wondered how his feelings about that night—about her—could possibly be any different than his feelings for any of the dozens of women who went willingly to his bed. She still recalled clearly how quiet, how distant he'd been after they'd made love.

Portia didn't want to dash her mother's hopes for her, but the truth was that when it came to their stations in life, she and Pierce were farther apart than Helena and her mysterious lover could possibly have been.

Pierce was the brother of an earl. He was a wealthy shipowner, a young and handsome bachelor with every woman he met vying for his attention.

And she was Portia Edwards, born out of wedlock, happy to have found her only family, her mother. And what did she have to offer? Eighteen pounds and five shillings in her purse, and perhaps a lifetime of running.

It was simple. The two of them had no chance. Still though, Portia knew she was as dreamy-eyed about this relationship as her mother had been twenty five years ago with another man. All she really wanted now was to savor every moment of the time they had left. There was no future for them; there was only now. However harsh the consequences might be, she would face them when the time came.

A passing cloud decided to shed a few tears on her behalf, and Portia lifted her face to it, almost grateful for the sentiment.

"Lie to me if you must, but do not tell me you are thinking of climbing into the rigging tonight."

Portia turned to see Pierce descend from the stern deck. He'd shed his jacket again and had rolled up the sleeves of his shirt. The collar was undone. He'd also forsaken the ribbon he generally used to tie his hair. As he came toward her, she thought he moved with the

smooth confidence of a Mohawk Indian she had once seen at Faneuil Hall in the company of one of the western landowners—dark, confident, noble. As she looked at him now, her breath caught in her chest to think that she was the object of this beautiful man's attention— even if it were only for this moment.

"I did not know you were up here." His gaze traveled down the front of her body, and she felt the fires immediately kindle within. "I did not see you when I first came up."

Leaning against the rail, she fisted one hand around the shroud behind her. He stepped closer, slipping one hand around her waist. When his chest came fully in contact with her breasts, she ceased to breathe completely.

"But you did not answer me, my bonny water monkey." He wrapped a hand around the back of her head, and his lips hovered over hers. "I saw you concentrating so hard. What mischief are you contemplating now? Fomenting mutiny perhaps? Do you plan to conquer or destroy my ship?"

Portia couldn't help herself. His lips were so close, his body so warm. She raised herself slowly on her tiptoes and brushed her lips against his. "What I was thinking had nothing to do with the ship. I was thinking of you."

His blue eyes looked black in the night. Small wrinkles appeared as he smiled. "Conquering me or destroying me?"

"Neither." She shook her head and kissed his chin, brushed her lips fleetingly against his mouth again. Shyly, she bit on his ear. "I was thinking of other things. Like a promise you gave me this afternoon."

She tried to move her hand from the shroud, but Pierce took hold of her hands and trapped them behind her back. His slow smile sent a shiver through her.

"In that case . . ."

He kissed her. Leisurely and with sublime tenderness. It was a long time before he drew back. Portia parted

her lips, starved for more. He sealed their mouths again as they began a seductive dance of lips and tongues. Portia struggled to free her hands, but he held them tighter, the kiss deepening even more. Her excitement built, her body straining against his.

She moaned softly when he pressed a knee intimately between her legs. Her ankle wrapped around his calf. Heat rushed through her body when he rubbed his loins against her middle. He was fully aroused, but he was clearly in no hurry. It seemed that he took pleasure in making her slowly burn.

An unexpected trough caused the ship to heel, and Portia felt them both leaning dangerously over the railing. Pierce freed her hands and she wrapped them tightly around him. He, too, held her tight, gripping the shroud with his other hand.

She laughed a little nervously and pressed her cheek against his heart. "Well, if I am to die, what better way to go than while I'm being made love to by you."

"You can forget about dying, or being hurt, or anything else terrible happening to you." As the vessel righted itself, Pierce lifted her chin until their gazes locked. "I am not going to let any of that happen. Like it or not, you are now mine to protect."

Although both had distinguished military careers in the colonies to their credit, their paths had never crossed until Lieutenant Dudingston was assigned to patrol the Narragansett Bay in March of this year. They met when the ambitious young officer began reporting directly to his new superiors in Boston.

Even before meeting him, Turner had been impressed by Dudingston's reputation. Tolerating no nonsense and treating the troublemaking colonists with a heavy hand— the way they deserved to be treated—the lieutenant and his ship, the *Gaspee,* had been churning up the waters leading to Philadelphia. In four years, he had harassed or seized enough suspected vessels that several colonial

governors had written letters of protest to the Admiralty in London. Turner had considered Dudingston's move to Rhode Island a strong and positive step. It was a sentiment that was obviously not shared with anyone in that filthy little colony.

Turner believed the burning of the *Gaspee* and the wounding of Dudingston proved that strong colonial authority in Rhode Island was simply non-existent. There was clearly no fear of reprisals in the colonists. Even the paltry reward—one hundred pounds—offered by the governor for information about the person who wounded the lieutenant was laughable.

The preliminary report of the incident was appalling. The bullet had passed through Dudingston's left arm, breaking it. The ball had then lodged in his groin, five inches directly below the navel. Bleeding badly and in great pain, the officer had lain on the *Gaspee*'s deck while the attackers had taken control of the ship and removed the crew to the boats. He'd been left there suffering while the raiders had gone through the ship. Finally, the leaders of the attack had forced the bleeding man to beg for his life on his knees before summoning a trained surgeon to help him.

Even after the ordeal was over, Dudingston had feared for his life. When he'd been removed to Newport, the lieutenant had refused to mention names or give any details. He would wait, he said, until his court martial in England for the loss of the *Gaspee.* Turner understood the officer's reasoning.

The captain wished his own reason for silence were so easy to explain. Since their departure together on the *Beaver,* he and Dudingston had spent many hours in each other's company, sitting in the captain's quarters, playing chess and cards. Perhaps because of his injuries, the lieutenant was spending a great deal of time drinking heavily. Turner was beginning to look forward to the end of this journey, for every time the officer was in his cups—which was quite often, of late—the injured man would

begin to goad him about the vagueness of his mission to Wales.

"I overheard one of the mates relate the most improbable story about your assignment today," Dudingston said, reaching unsteadily to move his chess piece.

Turner said nothing. He already knew he was not going to like the explanation.

Dudingston was not deterred. He poured himself another cup of rum. "What I heard about your mission is that there is no mission."

Turner tried to concentrate on his next move on the board.

"This is all over a woman, they tell me. A woman! 'Twould be a fine thing to have one on board right now." He laughed bitterly and then downed the cup. "Although I have no idea why it should."

Turner did not look up.

"I'll tell you a secret," Dudingston said in a low voice. "The bloody surgeon tells me that it might never work again."

"Shall we finish this game tomorrow?" Turner pushed his chair away from the table.

"Unmanned, Captain," he continued, pouring another drink. "Do you think there is a special decoration for that?"

Turner stood up. He didn't care to pursue this discussion at all, and Dudingston was becoming quite drunk.

"I think I shall see Lieutenant Lindsay about our posi—"

"Sit, Captain. I must apologize. This kind of talk is entirely unseemly for two gentlemen such as ourselves." He waved Turner to sit. "Please, Captain."

Reluctantly, Turner sat down and turned his attention back to the game. "I believe 'tis my move."

"Aye." Dudingston took a deep draught of rum and they sat in silence for a moment. "Besides, I want to hear about this woman. They tell me the whore struck you down like a dog and ran off with some filthy Scot.

They say that is why you are after her, to teach her a lesson."

Turner felt his ears catch fire. Fighting down his anger, he kept himself in control. He took Dudingston's bishop.

"I believe your queen is in jeopardy, Lieutenant."

Dudingston's hand hit the table, spilling the rum. With an angry sweep of his unbandaged arm, he knocked the board and pieces off the table.

"Bugger the queen. They were laying odds you never even had her. But I don't care to believe that, Turner. Tell me how many times you stuck the whore. I want to think that the dirty Scot ended up with only a worn, ill-used doxy. Tell me—"

In his rush to leave the cabin, Turner knocked his chair down, but he did not stop to right it. Out on the deck, he leaned over the railing and breathed heavily.

Dudingston was right, he thought. She is a whore! She was the sole cause of his ruin.

He did indeed have a mission, however. He'd bring Helena back to the Admiral. But, by God, he'd make sure Portia paid for all of this first.

Pierce gazed down at the woman tucked into his embrace. He didn't want to take his eyes from her angelic face as she slept. He hadn't thought of how tiring these past weeks must have been on her until she'd fallen asleep soon after they'd finished their lovemaking. She was not only taking care of Helena, but also sleeping on the hard floor of a cramped cabin. He'd offered her no comfort. He hadn't done much of a job of taking care of her. But everything was going to change now.

Portia did strange things to his insides. She made him ache in a way that he'd never felt before. Before meeting her, he'd known many women. He'd experienced passion, the physical power of desire. But Portia managed to awaken so much more in him, and it was liberating to know that he no longer compared her to Emma.

She was her own person. And his hunger to be with

her, to make love to her, to protect her was unmatched by anything he'd ever felt for any other woman.

He thought of how close they were to the end of this journey. He regretted how many weeks he'd wasted keeping his distance from her. Touching a lock of a silken curls on his pillow, Pierce looked down at Portia's beautiful face and knew that he was not ready for their time together to end. She stirred in his arms, and he brushed his lips against her brow. Feeling the way he did now, Pierce didn't think he would ever be ready to let her go.

He watched her eyelids flutter and then open. Her magical eyes gradually focused on his face. "I fell asleep."

She stretched lazily, and his body came to life at the feel of her smooth skin against his, at the tease of her foot rubbing innocently against his leg. She was a master at exciting him, at driving him mad with desire, and she didn't even realize it.

She looked in the direction of the windows. "I should get back to my cabin before Helena awakens."

"Not yet. 'Tis still too early." He brushed her lips with his own. "Besides, I believe I have your mother's blessing to look after you."

"This is certainly some kind of looking-after." She smiled and rolled until her head lay on his arm and she was facing him. He ran his hands over the gentle curves of her back as she nestled her body against him. "Do you know, I never thanked you for everything that you have done for her? You have truly been a gentleman, a saving angel, a—"

"A fool for not realizing how right you were about taking your mother away from that house." He shook his head. "For having been a stubborn, pigheaded—"

"Stop!" She raised her head off his arm and glowered at him. "You will *not* berate yourself like that. *I* am the one who started everything off wrong, and from there it

all simply went downhill. If there is anyone who should be blamed—"

He pressed a finger to her lips. "Very well. I shan't berate myself, but neither shall you. But I do apologize. And you must accept it, or I shall pretend I am you and drag this conversation on until—"

"Accepted." She smiled, dropping her head back on his arm and looking at him with such adoration that Pierce began to feel awkward.

He tried to think of the right words for the question that he'd been contemplating as her fingers caressed the day's growth on his face. He finally decided on the direct approach.

"Will you come to Baronsford with me?"

"I cannot," she said without a moment's consideration.

"Why?"

"Because my mother and I must go to Wales. I need to find Lady Primrose before she goes anywhere for the summer."

"She might already be gone," he reasoned.

"Then we shall wait for her there until her return." She rolled on her back, staring at the ceiling.

"But that might not be safe." He pushed up onto one elbow and looked down at the stubborn set of her mouth. "Think of it, Portia. Whatever the circumstances were surrounding your birth, they were shocking enough to make Admiral Middleton more than uncomfortable for all these years. What makes you think he is going to simply let it go now? He is certain to send someone after you."

"He doesn't know where I am."

"Admiral Middleton has built his entire career on knowing the whereabouts of his enemies." Pierce took hold of her chin and drew her face toward him. "Everyone you knew in Boston has had heard you speak of your benefactor. How long do you think it will be before he decides that you have returned to Lady Primrose?"

"Lady Primrose has great influence. She can find a place for me somewhere, a place where we can hide until we find a more permanent position."

"Is that what you want to do? Find a place to hide? You could be running and hiding for the rest of your life."

"That is my only choice." She pushed herself up onto an elbow, too. "But freeing my mother is worth it. We are both willing to make that choice and live that life if we must. We shall do whatever we need to do to keep her from going back."

Pierce nodded. "Then come to Baronsford with me. You can send Lady Primrose a letter when the ship puts in at Greenock. You can tell her where you're going, and she can send her answer to you there. That way, there is no chance of putting yourself or Helena in unnecessary danger. Think of it as the opportunity to put your plans in order. 'Tis an opportunity to do things right. And in the meantime, we'll be together."

"No," she said, starting to get out of the bed.

He pushed her back down, glowering at her. "You are not being reasonable. Why?"

"That is the time you should have with your family. You do not need me and my mother—"

"But I *do* need you." Pierce pressed a hand against her chest to keep her down when she tried to rise again. "Does that matter to you at all? I do need you with me when I go back to Baronsford."

Pierce shocked himself as much as he did Portia. He hadn't even realized the truth until now.

"I admit that I am somewhat nervous about going back. I left that place . . . well, under some very unpleasant circumstances. My older brother, the Earl of Aytoun, had been very badly injured. In fact, he was in danger of dying. His wife Emma, a woman I knew my entire life, was dead. Our family had been torn apart by the events leading up to the tragedy. I left, vowing never to go back. But now I am, and you are largely responsible

for it. 'Twas because of things you said to me, because of the value you place on family that I finally read Lyon's letter. And that was when I learned of the changes in *his* life. That is when I decided that I must go back . . . and perhaps make peace."

The floodgates of his past were open. Pierce didn't try to stop himself. He went on and told Portia about Emma. About David. About Lyon—the man he had been and the man he appeared to be now. He told her all the news he had learned of the changes that were occurring at Baronsford. She remained silent through it all. Her dark eyes welled up, though, when she heard how he had been the one to find Lyon and Emma at the bottom of a cliff.

"You are the only solid thing in my life right now." Pierce told her finally. "It may sound strange, but you make me whole. And I need all of me . . . there . . . when I go to Baronsford."

Portia rose up and kissed him, tears glistening in her eyes.

"I will come. I will be there for you."

It was still dark in the little cabin when Portia quietly slipped in through the door. Lying there awake, Helena stared at the dim shape that she knew was her daughter. She said nothing until the young woman came close and gently adjusted the blanket on her.

"I am very comfortable, thank you."

"I awakened you. I'm sorry."

"I am awake, but you are not responsible for it. In fact, because I was not subjected to your nightly moaning and groaning, I had a very good night's sleep."

"I am glad to hear it," Portia whispered, reaching down and placing a soft kiss on her cheek.

Helena felt it, the touch of sadness in her daughter's voice. She caught Portia's hand before she could pull away.

"Talk to me, my sweet. What's wrong? What silliness has gotten between you two now?"

Portia sat down on the edge of the bunk. "There is nothing wrong. But I beg you . . ." Her voice wavered. "I beg you, Mother, to not make any comments about Pierce and I being . . . having . . ."

"Being lovers? Being two people clearly made for each other?"

"Pierce and I might be . . . well, lovers," she said shyly. "But that does not mean there is any future for us. And this is why I am begging you not to think that there is more to what I am about to tell you than there is."

"What, child?"

"We have a change of plans. Pierce wants us to go with him to Baronsford, his family's home in Scotland. He thinks if I were to send a letter to Lady Primrose as soon as we reach port, then we might have an answer soon after we arrive at Baronsford. It makes sense, for if she thinks we are safer in Scotland than we would be in England or Wales, even temporarily . . ." Portia shrugged. "It just appears much easier this way."

"He wants to introduce you to his family. I understand."

"Please, Helena," Portia said, her voice cracking slightly. "This is more painful than I thought it would be. You must understand that there can never be any future between Pierce and me."

"And why is that?" The older woman sat up and wrapped an arm around her daughter's shoulder. They sat for a moment in silence. "I understand. This is all about differences in your place in society—about money. Well, I can tell it matters a whit to your young man that you have no dowry."

"But it matters to me," Portia said stubbornly. "Not a dowry, necessarily, but I shall not walk into any relationship where I do not bring something that gives me some . . . some footing."

"Even Mad Helena knows that a woman's social class has little to do with a woman's real value."

"But *I* know that he and I are just too far apart . . .

in everything in life." Portia turned to her. "Please, Mother. Let it be."

Helena wanted to reason with her daughter, but she also understood. Portia might have been raised in a school without the everyday guidance of a real parent. But Helena had an idea that she knew what Lady Primrose probably instilled in this child—all the moral standards and restrictions of their class structure.

"Very well. I should like to send a letter to Lady Primrose, as well," she announced to her daughter.

"I thought you do not know her."

"She took care of you. Raised you. I believe 'tis time I introduced myself."

Portia patted her hand. "I should be honored to serve as your scribe."

"Thank you. But you will not do."

"I fear you are up to mischief now, Helena."

"Nothing you need to worry yourself about." She was glad to hear the laughter in her daughter's voice. "This is just something between two old women. I need to make my requests as to the kind of position Lady Primrose might provide for you. Oh, let me think! Pierce will not do either as my secretary. But that young man—Captain Cameron. He is a kindly Scottish gentleman. I believe I shall ask him. I think he shall do very nicely."

"I think you are becoming fond of Captain Cameron," Portia said, teasing her. "I wonder if this might all be just an excuse to spend time with him."

Helena smiled. Let her think what she might. It was time for secrets to reveal themselves . . . time for lives to change. She was not about to sit back and allow her daughter to suffer any longer.

Chapter 24

The residential school of Berse Drelincourt, near Wrexham in Wales, was located on the grounds of an imposing Georgian manse belonging to Anne Drelincourt, widow of the third Viscount Primrose. An orphanage for girls, the school was a quiet, protected place, and visitors had always been discouraged from calling. Captain Turner did not expect to be treated any differently. Still, he had official business, and he knew she would agree to see him.

He would not be going in unprepared, either. A fortuitous stop for dinner at a tavern in the nearby town of Broughton had given Captain Turner a surprising amount of information. Over the years, the old innkeeper, a former foot soldier in Marlborough's own Welsh Regiment, had heard many rumors about the older woman. One was that Lady Primrose had been actively involved with the Jacobite cause during the 1745 Rising, and that she befriended Flora Macdonald, the Highland woman who had aided Bonnie Prince Charlie in his flight from Scotland after his bloody defeat at Culloden.

It was somewhat surprisingly that this matched what Admiral Middleton had told him, as well as what additional information he himself had obtained when the *Beaver* had put in to Bristol. Indeed, following Flora's imprisonment in England, Turner learned, it had been

Lady Primrose who had secured her release and aided her financially.

There were other rumors of Lady Primrose, too. Lowering his voice, the innkeeper told him that it was said that she regularly corresponded with the exiled Young Pretender himself, arranging secret visits to England and Scotland. Her ladyship was high and mighty, though, and had friends close to King George, himself, according to the innkeeper.

After learning all he could about the elusive woman, Turner had ridden into the village of Wrexham and spent two days drinking with the locals and bribing whoever he thought might provide more incriminating information.

The footmen and the grooms who met him when he rode up to the front door of the stately house had eyed him with suspicion. The steward, however, carried his note in while Turner stood waiting in the foyer under the watchful eyes of two burly doormen.

Lady Primrose received him with polite greetings in her elegant sitting room. He wasn't fooled, however, for there was no welcome in her expression. She was somewhat younger looking than he expected, and conveyed a practiced air of indifference.

"Your note says you have very recently arrived from the colonies on the HMS *Beaver*. If what I have just read in the *Gazette* is true, you must be connected then to the investigation following the burning of that ship. What was its name? The one that was destroyed by those American colonists?"

"The *Gaspee*. Indeed, milady, I am connected with that," Turner lied, satisfied with the momentary look of interest that flickered across the woman's face. "The reason that I have come all the way here, however, has to do with another, more personal matter that involves my commanding officer, Admiral Middleton."

She appeared to consider the name for a few moments, but then she shook her head. "I don't believe I am acquainted with the gentleman."

"But you might be acquainted with his daughter, Helena Middleton."

She considered this name for a few seconds longer, Turner thought, but the end result was the same. "I do not believe I have ever had the pleasure."

"Perhaps Portia Edwards, then?" The words cut through the air with more hostility than he'd intended. The old woman's eyes told him that she'd noticed it, too. Immediately, he tried to recover himself. "You surely must know Miss Edwards. She was a student in your school a few years back."

"How could one ever forget Portia?" Lady Primrose sat straight in her chair, her hands demurely in her lap, her hair perfectly styled and powdered. "But it has been too long since I have seen that lovely young woman. So what is your connection with our Portia, Captain?"

He had no intention of being the receiver of questions. "Miss Edwards was a member of Admiral Middleton's household."

"A servant?" The woman immediately bristled. "That cannot be."

"A companion," he continued. "The young woman read French poetry to Helena Middleton before her disappearance. And that is why I am here, Lady Primrose. I believe . . . Admiral Middleton believes that Miss Edwards may have been coming here."

"Oh, that is so exciting. Very delightful news, indeed," she said jovially, reaching for the bell on the table beside her and ringing it. "We shall prepare her old room. Do you know when she is arriving?"

"She left Boston before I did. She should already be here."

"But she is not. Oh, my, that is bad news." She rang the bell again just as a servant appeared. "Tell me all you know, Captain Turner. She came on what ship? What day? What port? I shall send someone after her at once."

Turner felt his temper about to boil over. He was no

puppet to dance to this old traitor's tune. "Lady Primrose, are you certain that Miss Edwards has not yet arrived, perhaps with a companion?"

"A companion?" She waved at the servant who was waiting obediently by the open door. "Two rooms. Have two rooms prepared for Miss Edwards and a friend." She turned again to Turner when the servant went out. "When, Captain? Please do not keep us in such suspense. You *must* have more information that you are not revealing to me now."

"And *you* must know more than you are admitting to, milady."

"Pardon me, sir?" Ice could have easily formed in the air between them. She leaned forward in her chair, her eyes narrowing. "What is the meaning of this visit? What are you accusing me of? And what have you done with my Miss Edwards?"

Turner had never been intimidated by a woman before—especially not one who surpassed him in age by at least a dozen years. But he found himself feeling strangely uneasy now. This was a woman with steel claws beneath her kid gloves. The thought flitted through his mind that this was a very dangerous woman, and it would be very easy for her to hide the body of an enemy in the deer park surrounding her genteel home.

Suddenly, he couldn't wait to get out of this room— out of her house.

"I want answers, Captain," she said severely. "And while you are at it, you evaded my question as to *why* you are here. Why does your Admiral Middleton wish to find Portia?"

Turner had been prepared to say that Portia had abducted Helena, if it turned out that Lady Primrose refused to give up the two women. He had been certain they would be here, but now he wondered if he had miscalculated.

Indeed, now nothing made sense, and sitting here and being browbeaten by this aging Jacobite would hardly

serve his purposes at all. He should have known that direct tactics were the wrong approach with someone as crafty as Lady Primrose.

"I believe I have overstayed my welcome." He stood up and bowed stiffly. "Please give my regards to Miss Edwards when she arrives. Good day to you, milady."

There was no surprise at his hasty departure, and she made no attempt to delay him. He knew he had overplayed his hand, while Lady Primrose had held all the trumps. She was a very dangerous woman, but he was not through with her yet.

Moments later, Turner rode away from Berse Drelincourt and went directly to the village inn, where he would await his next appointment. The young man he was to meet, a trainer in Lady Primrose's stables, was easily the most talkative of all the potential informants he'd interviewed—and the greediest. He was an Irishman from someplace called Buttevant, north of Cork City. He was a horse trainer of some ability, if he was to be believed, and he'd been serving Lady Primrose for less than a year.

The young man met him as they'd planned, in a small glade beyond the churchyard, and he counted every coin in the bag before answering anything Turner asked.

"Thankee, Captain. Much obliged to be sure." He tucked the purse into his rough wool shirt. "Ye asked about two lady visitors?"

"Did you see them?" Turner asked impatiently.

"Nay, sir. For certain, there be no lady visitors in that house. No new servants, neither. Nothin', Captain, but for a courier that brought some letters for her ladyship. 'Twas not a fortnight ago, but it surely put her ladyship all in a dither."

"Where were the letters from?"

The man shrugged. "I cannot read nor write—not that I'd be able to lay me hands on 'em, in any case. Just saw the courier bring the letters. Her ladyship was in the

stables with her new hunter, sir. A fine steed 'tis, too, sir. Got him from—"

"How do you know your mistress was put in a 'dither,' as you say?"

"Her ladyship went off calling for her steward, sending off letters of her own in every direction, turning the household topsy-turvy. I carried one to Dr. King myself. He be the principal o' St. Mary Hall. My understanding is she only asks him to come see her when something real important is going on."

Turner knew William King was another Jacobite ally of Lady Primrose. He reached inside his purse and passed another coin to the man. "I want those letters."

The trainer put the coin away and then shook his head helplessly. "I dunno about none o' that, Captain. I would not e'en know where to look."

"You told me you had a girl inside the house who would get you anything you asked her," Turner snapped angrily.

"Aye, sir. I would ask and Mary would oblige, to be sure. But now, with her ladyship ready to go away, the lassie is far and away too busy with—"

"Where is Lady Primrose going?"

"Scotland, they say."

"When?"

"Mary says her mistress is waiting for an answer to something first. It should be soon, but none of us knows exactly when."

"Listen to me." Turner leaned toward the man. "You can earn yourself twenty pounds. Do you hear me? Twenty *pounds*," he stressed.

The Irishman whistled softly. "With all that money, sir, I could set myself up in Cork City with a—"

"I care nothing about what you do with the money, but you get nothing unless you do as I say."

"I'm your man, Captain. Just say the word."

"I want that letter when it arrives. I want to know who

that letter is coming from, and I want to know where and when she is supposed to go."

The man frowned, thinking hard.

"Do you understand what I am asking for?"

He finally nodded. "Aye, Captain. For twenty pounds, I'd sell my mother, sir."

In the course of a sennight, every sitting room, salon, and bedchamber in Baronsford had been turned upside down and shaken. Every idle person within five miles of the place had been pressed into service and put to work. Every window had been opened. Every floor had been scrubbed. Fresh-cut flowers had been scattered throughout the rooms, on the great staircase, in the halls, and in the ballroom.

For the day of the arrival, Millicent Pennington, Countess of Aytoun, had directed that every villager and tenant farmer was to come to the castle and to bring their spouses, parents, children, and dogs. Today was to be a celebration like no other.

Indeed, Millicent was determined to present a different view of Baronsford to her brother-in-law than that which had greeted Lyon when they had come home last winter. She had already warned Walter Truscott, who managed the estate, that she wanted the grounds to look like a fair day. She would not allow the formality of any receiving line in evidence when Pierce's carriage rolled up to the front door.

Mrs. MacAlister, the normally stern housekeeper, patrolled the castle like a regimental sergeant-major, directing her mistress's wishes with barely concealed glee. Mr. Campbell, the steward, struggled to keep up with the women. Peter Howitt, the earl's secretary, was not spared from the work either. He was directed to play with little Josephine while the bairn's nursemaid helped with other chores.

It was early in the afternoon when Lyon Pennington,

coming back from the village with Truscott, cornered his wife in the library.

"You are finished working," he announced with finality, directing the housekeeper and the steward to take charge and complete the preparations.

"But there are so many other things that I should like to see to," she protested when he closed the door on the madness outside. "Really, Lyon, I have not told them everything that needs to be done."

"If you have not told them already, then that means you have not thought of it, which means it does not need to be done." He leaned heavily on his cane as he took a step toward a settee by the window. Just as he'd expected, Millicent's reaction was immediate. She hurried toward him, taking his arm.

"You are the one who has been doing too much. I cannot believe you rode to the village this morning instead of taking a carriage."

He kept up the pretense of pain until she had sat down on the settee beside him. He placed an arm around her shoulder and drew her against him. His wife's flushed cheeks and bright eyes were evidence of her excitement. She was glowing from the inside. As it was becoming his habit these days, Lyon laid his hand protectively over Millicent's swelling belly.

"The house is ready for him, my love," he said.

"What about you? Are you ready?"

He nodded and gathered her tightly against him, laying his cheek against her hair. She understood his apprehensiveness. Pierce's ship had arrived on the west coast of Scotland nearly a fortnight ago, but rather than coming directly to Baronsford, he'd sent a messenger first, bringing the signed documents annulling the transfer of lands. His brother's letter had said that he didn't want their visit have anything to do with business. Pierce was back in Scotland to visit with his family.

Lyon wished that he'd just come—that their first meeting

were behind them. This anticipation of what his brother thought, and if indeed that letter was meant to be a peace offering, continued to tug at his heart. But the wait was coming to an end. They should be arriving before dark.

"I wish the dowager were already here," Millicent said wistfully.

"My mother will arrive soon enough." Lyon's mother had taken a liking to Millicent's estate, Melbury Hall, so much that she spent months at a time visiting there. Lyon knew the truth was that the old woman's friendship with Ohenewaa, a black healer that Millicent had freed from slavery, was the main reason that kept his mother there. "Though she's probably badgering Ohenewaa right now about coming with her to Scotland."

Millicent lifted her head off his shoulder. "Were you able to learn anything more about Miss Edwards and her mother, other than what Pierce mentioned in his letter?"

Lyon shook his head. "Nothing."

Pierce had said the two women were traveling with him and that their ultimate destination was Wales. He wrote that he'd succeeded in convincing Portia to delay their plans for what he hoped would be an extended stay at Baronsford.

"But unless I was reading too much into that letter, there was certainly more than a hint of interest in Miss Edwards on the part of Pierce."

"Well, there is nothing like love to help heal wounds. I believe I am going to like Miss Edwards. I only hope that Pierce is not disappointed in me."

Lyon looked into his wife's beautiful eyes. He knew she was talking of a comparison between herself and Emma. Two women a world apart in character and affection.

"He shall not be anything but thrilled. You are my life and my love. Pierce would be a fool not to see that if he wants to make peace, it must be not with me—but with us." He kissed her lips. "And I do not believe my brother is a fool."

*   *   *

As the carriage rolled eastward in silence, Pierce's mind continued to battle the dozens of questions that had been haunting him since the ship had docked at Greenock.

The letter he'd received from Lyon in Boston had been sent early in the spring. The few words were the only communication he'd had from his brother. Now he wondered about the state of Lyon's health. And whether the earl's marriage was still as blissful as he described it in the letter. Was he happy? And did he still want to see Pierce after having his letter left unanswered for months?

There were more practical questions, too. He didn't even know for sure that Lyon and his wife were in Scotland. Pierce had just made the assumption and sent off the correspondence, announcing his arrival on a designated day. Perhaps he should have requested an answer, or at least waited for an invitation. Perhaps he was not even welcome.

Pierce put aside his misgivings when Portia's hand moved onto his knee. She was sitting across from him and leaning forward. She entwined her fingers with his. He looked at her beautiful face and saw the lines of tension in her face, too. Next to her, Helena's head bobbed gently while the older woman slept. Pierce tugged on Portia's arm, and she moved across and sat next to him.

"You are tearing yourself up," she whispered, and reached up with feathery softness to caress his brow, the line of his jaw. She brushed her lips against the corner of his mouth and quickly drew back.

Pierce wrapped a hand around her shoulder. He pressed her head against his chest and kissed her silky curls. She was responsible for his sanity. This fortnight, as they had gone from Greenock to Glasgow to give his letter time to reach Baronsford, he had kept his attention focused solely on Portia.

Whatever hours they could steal had been the only

hours of the day worth living. When she could, Portia had slipped into his room in the middle of the night. He'd even cornered her several times in a secluded corner during the day when they would snatch a few minutes of frenzied lovemaking. Neither seemed to be able to get enough of the other. Pierce was as aware of her every touch as she was of his. Memories of other women who had occupied his time were dashed from his mind. She was the only one that he wanted to remember.

She managed to make him smile in a dozen ways. She had given him no end of trouble when he had tried to order a new wardrobe for her and for Helena in Glasgow. With any other woman, it would have been an easy feat. With Portia, it required the same strategic maneuvering—with enough promises and conditions of reimbursement—as some great international treaty.

He looked outside the window and his mind again turned to thoughts of his brother. Pierce hoped Millicent was everything that Lyon had described her to be. He looked down at the woman in his arms and realized he'd been imagining Millicent to be like Portia—but that was too much to ask.

" 'Tis a beautiful sunny day," she whispered, straightening up and staring out the carriage window. "Certainly unlike the other time I was in Scotland."

"A welcome sign," he said hopefully.

Portia's dark eyes shone with agreement when she turned to him. "Tell me about Baronsford."

" 'Tis a house."

"That is very helpful, Mr. Pennington," she said, checking on her mother. She was still asleep. Portia looked up at Pierce. "Then tell me about the people. Whom I should know? Whom I should be wary of? Where should I go and what should I say or not say?"

"Well, I've told you about Lyon and the very little I know about Millicent. As far as the estate, that is run by Walter Truscott. He is my cousin by the way of my mother's brother. He is younger than David, and he grew up

with the rest of us at Baronsford. Walter is very much like a brother to all of us. Then there is Mrs. MacAlister, the housekeeper. She is a dragon—a tyrant of a woman."

"Like Mrs. Green?" she asked uneasily.

He shook his head. "Not at all. The woman truly has a heart of gold. Still, she brooks no nonsense and likes to order everyone about. Let me see . . . the steward is Martin Campbell. Short, wiry, and old, but has a great deal of energy. As far as the other servants, I really cannot help you for I do not know who is still there."

Considering the cloud of scandal and uncertainty that had hung over Baronsford for so long, it would be amazing if any of the servants had remained.

"But to answer your question about what to say . . ." Pierce looked down into Portia's expectant expression and felt the mischief rise in him. He leaned close to her ear and lowered his voice. "You should tell Mrs. MacAlister that you are my lover. Then, simply insist on having your trunk taken to my bedchamber." He nibbled on her earlobe. "Oh yes, and tell her if she does not like it, she can just go straight to the devil."

"You are incorrigible, Mr. Pennington." She jabbed him in the chest and pushed him away.

He smiled at the pretty blush that had quickly reddened her beautiful cheeks. Selfishly, he enjoyed her denial of what had to be obvious to others around them. But it was not just physical attraction that she held for him; he loved lying together and talking with her. Her quick wit and her idealism made her exceptional in every way. Since that night that she'd run into him in the Admiral's garden, the two of them had grown into something more than lovers. They were friends, companions, even confidantes. He wanted no end to where they had come, to all that they were sharing.

There was only one choice that lay before them. And Pierce was just waiting for the right time to ask her the question.

Helena stirred. Portia immediately went across and sat

next to her mother as the older woman's eyes slowly opened.

"How close are we?" she asked sleepily.

Pierce looked out at the familiar countryside, and his gaze was drawn immediately to the rocky rise and the large castle rearing up arrestingly on top. Baronsford.

"We have arrived."

It was midafternoon when the Irishman showed up at the rooms Turner had taken. Obviously excited and very eager, the man asked twice if the officer's offer of twenty pounds still stood. Turner assured him of it and asked the man to follow him inside.

"A messenger arrived last night, bringing a letter for a Miss Fines. I happened to be up by the front of the house, seeing as my Mary was pickin' flowers for the house. So I stepped up to take the horse for the lad. From his accent, we could tell he was a foreigner. A Frenchman maybe, I'm thinkin'. Now in the time I've been working there, there's been no Miss Fines at Drelincourt. Seeing the fellow come in, though, a maid to Lady Primrose come runnin' quick and takes the letter, ye see. And off she goes with the letter, runnin' up into the house. Have ye anything for a lad to wet his throat, sir?"

A pitcher of ale sat on the sideboard, and the trainer downed a cup in one gulp before continuing.

"Well, sir, I saw her run and I quick sent my Mary in after her. My gal is thinkin' now how all that money— ye *do* have the money, sir?—that money'll set us up. So she follows her in and puts an ear to a door, so she tell me. My Mary heard a fair bit o' the talk between her ladyship and the maid. Near as we could tell, the sender o' the letter agreed with Miss Fines's suggestion, and would meet her at some place called Barrisford . . . or Bearsford . . . or—"

"Baronsford. I know the place," Turner said hotly. "Did they say when they'll meet?"

"Aye, Captain, that they did. On the last Wednesday in July."

This was too good to be true. Everything was being tied neatly to Pennington.

"Aye, sir. Mary said she thinks the place must be in Scotland. After coming out o' the room, Lady Primrose started givin' orders for traveling north."

"Who was the letter from? Give me a name."

The man's face fell. "I've got no names, sir. But I've no doubt this was an answer to the message she sent out before."

"I want the letter."

"Beggin' your pardon, sir, it cannot be done."

Turner leaned over the man. "If you want that twenty pounds, my friend, it must be."

The Irishman scratched his head. To tempt him, Turner held out another small bag of coins to the man. The puzzled expression became a look of determination. "I'll ask my Mary, see what she can do, and bring word to ye."

The trainer let himself out.

Turner was certain that it must be Charles Edward, the infamous Young Pretender himself, going secretly to Baronsford. But he needed proof to support his thinking. To capture a person of such importance, an enemy to the king, he would need at least a regiment of soldiers behind him. And to get them, to convince any regimental commander to give him such support, he needed that letter in his hand.

The carriage had not yet come to a full stop before Pierce found himself pushing the door open and stepping out. It was the same castle, but it could hardly be the same place that he had left. It looked more like a festival was taking place, for hundreds of people had gathered on the drive. There were pipers from the neighboring villages, and the music struck up the moment they arrived. The smell of roasting meat filled the air, and bar-

rels of ale had been set up on makeshift tables. The villagers—many of them he knew well—were all in their finest clothes, and children and dogs were running everywhere. The noise and cheers increased the moment his foot touched the drive, and he could see more crowds approaching from across the fields.

Pierce's throat knotted, and he was back in a time when Baronsford had been a home. A place where he and his brothers ran with other children like mad fools through the grounds, climbing the cliffs and swimming in the river. Those were careless days with no worries. Days when dealing with betrayal was only as complicated as rubbing one's nose into the dirt. Those were days when forgiveness was granted just for the asking.

He tried to focus through an unexpected mist in his eyes, and saw his cousin Walter Truscott coming toward him. Pierce pulled the younger man into his arms and hugged him as soon as he was within reach.

"How is Lyon?" he asked, not quite able to clear the tightness in his throat.

"I am very well, thank you."

Pierce turned, seeing his brother not a half-dozen paces away. Their cousin stepped aside. Pierce looked at the cane in Lyon's hand, and his throat closed even tighter as he recalled the broken man he'd left behind. Then he saw Lyon take a step toward him. His legs supported him. He looked up at the straight back, at the broad shoulders, at the strength and confidence that was once again evident in the man before him. Pierce looked into his brother's face and saw the smile.

"Are you going to stand in that bloody spot all day?" Lyon growled.

Pierce went to him and ignored the extended hand of his brother. To the crowd's delighted surprise, he lifted Lyon off the ground, albeit only a few inches.

"You are much heavier than you were. Gone to fat in your middle age, I see."

"And you've grown shorter and far, far uglier." Lyon

hugged him back once his feet touched the ground. "I had forgotten what a wee frail thing you are."

"I can still knock you to the ground, you old dog." He kept his arm around Lyon, jostling him.

"I should like to see you try. But what the devil is going on with the long hair?" He pulled Pierce's queue.

" 'Tis all the rage in the colonies. We'll pay no taxes for hair or wig powder, you know."

The earl laughed. "We hear you'll not pay taxes for anything."

" 'Tis true. But I was thinking of growing a beard, too. Trying to work on my look of suffering, hoping you'd feel sorry for me and take me back."

The joking stopped, and Lyon's expression sobered. The crowd around them became hushed. The earl's blue eyes were misted over when he stretched a hand toward him.

"Welcome home, brother."

Chapter 25

⁓

The rolling fields of Baronsford spread out like a great tapestry before the eye. She had seen a lushly forested deer park, a lake, beautiful walled gardens, miles of footpaths weaving in and out along cliffs overlooking the river Tweed. Portia knew there was probably much more that she hadn't seen. And on the inside the castle, renovated by the great Robert Adam himself, was grand enough to house a king. It also had enough rooms to house every family in Boston, or so Portia decided as she was led through wing after wing and floor after floor of salons, sitting rooms, formal parlors, libraries, dining rooms, suites, and bedchambers.

There was no doubt in Portia's mind, though, that Baronsford was absolutely the most beautiful place she had ever seen or read about. The magnificent structure and the grounds were that of a fairy-tale castle, and Portia remembered what Pierce had told her about the aspirations of the earl's first wife, Emma. She had always wanted this place for herself, to own and to rule.

Portia could never imagine herself having such dreams. And somehow she doubted the present Countess of Aytoun, who was showing her around, would have ever considered such a thing a priority in life, either.

Millicent, as she'd asked to be called, was warm and welcoming to both Portia and her mother, and had treated them with the same enthusiasm as she had

greeted Pierce from the moment they had descended from the carriage.

And Portia had received the same warm welcome from the earl. Still, for the first few moments it had been unsettling to see the strong resemblance between the two brothers. Lyon, however, was older, and there was a weathered edge to his features that told tales of life's hard experiences and, she knew, suffering, as well. He wore it well, though, and his heart showed none of the scars that his face bore.

Portia had taken an immediate liking to her host and hostess.

"What do you think of it so far?" Millicent asked when they arrived at the second floor of the east wing.

"I find it . . . intimidating," Portia admitted.

Millicent smiled, opening the door to the bedchamber where Portia would be staying. "I was overwhelmed the first time I saw it, too. But I believe 'tis the people who make a place a home. I think you shall soon become accustomed to it, too."

She held her tongue, even though they wouldn't be staying long enough for that.

"Before you arrived, Portia, we had thought to place your mother in the bedchamber adjacent to yours. But now, realizing she has some difficulty with her sight, I was wondering if you thought she might be more comfortable in a room on the ground floor. Or we could easily arrange for a suite that you two could share."

"I think the adjacent rooms will work well," Portia whispered. "Honestly, you are very kind to think of it."

Her trunk had been brought up earlier, and as she circled the huge room, she was surprised to see her handful of new dresses had already been unpacked and laid out. She stopped by the open windows overlooking the gardens and the greenswards leading to the cliffs. Portia leaned out one of them and saw her mother strolling with an attendant along a gravel footpath. Having spent too many hours in the carriage, the older woman had

preferred to walk a little rather than have a tour of the house. The two women appeared to be engaged in some pleasant conversation, for Portia heard Helena's laughter drifting up.

Millicent moved over to her and looked out as well. "That is Bess. She is the sweetest young woman. If you don't mind, I should like to ask her to see to your mother's needs. She will make herself available whenever Helena needs her."

"That is very sweet and kind," Portia said, genuinely touched.

"Oh, please. We are just so delighted that you are here." Millicent turned around. "So what do you think of this room? Will it do?"

Portia turned away from the window and studied the enormous space, the elegance of the furniture, the fine paintings on the walls, the plush oriental carpets on the floor—even the finely embroidered bedcovering made of silk. Beautiful as it all was, it made Portia somewhat uncomfortable. She certainly did not deserve this kind of reception. She was uneasy that Millicent was thinking she was something more than she really was. This room was truly fit for a queen, and she hated the thought that this gentle soul might have been misled regarding Portia's place in society or her worth. She wanted no more misunderstandings or deceptions between her and this family.

"Millicent, this room alone is larger than the entire first floor of Parson and Mrs. Higgins's house in Boston. I was the tutor to their children for eight years prior to leaving them this past month."

"How old were the children?" Millicent asked with no apparent interest in Portia's revelation about her need to earn a living.

"They were eight and ten years old. A girl and a boy."

"Close in age. Did they get along?"

"For the most part, especially when they were younger. Lately though, Ann, the eight-year-old, has been trying to establish an upper hand for herself."

Millicent smiled and touched her swollen belly. "This bairn and our Josephine will be less than a year apart, so hopefully their difference in age shall be too small for either one of them to have the upper hand, as you say."

"Josephine?" Portia asked.

"You shall meet her as soon as she awakens from her nap. In fact, you shall more than likely hear her, first. She is quite fond of her own voice, and sometimes only quiets down when Lyon goes to her." Millicent rubbed her lower back and seated herself on a nearby sofa. "If my husband asks, please be sure to tell him that I took plenty of rest during our walk."

"Of course." Portia smiled and joined Millicent when the countess patted the seat next to her.

"Josephine is our daughter . . . or rather, she became our daughter when her mother died giving birth." A sadness crept into the young woman's face. "I know it sounds odd, but I am not quite resolved about how to speak of her, yet. I should like to take credit for her and say she is ours, but at the same time I do not want to take away from the struggles of the woman who went through the pain and suffering to bring a child so beautiful into this world."

A cloud continued to linger over Millicent's mood. Portia thought of her own life.

"Well, I have a feeling she has much joy ahead of her. Your Josephine shall not grow up in a orphanage, but here in your home among a real family. If I might be so bold as speak from my own experience, I think 'twould be best if she simply considered you and the earl as her real parents. There should never be confusion in the heart of a child as to where her parents are. That is, of course, if her mother and father are dead."

"I was there with her mother when she died. And as far as her father . . ." She shook her head. "I fear some secrets should never be revealed."

Like the secret about her own father, Portia thought again. She looked up at her hostess and yearned to see

the smile back on her face. "So tell me when your bairn is due."

The transformation was immediate. Millicent's bright smile returned, and Portia knew that a friendship was in the making.

Pierce realized the full magnitude of the changes in Baronsford the moment he walked through the grand entryway and looked up at the first landing of the wide, curved stairwell. Emma's portrait was missing. He saw later that it was only a reflection of the changes in his brother's life when he saw the tenderness in Lyon's look when Millicent took Portia to show her around.

Emma's reign had ended. Both Baronsford and Lyon were truly free of her.

In the library, just the two of them sat and talked, and no mention of their last confrontation was made. Pierce realized what this meant. They had both come to terms with the ugliness of their mistakes. Finally, the past was buried for the two of them, and now, together, they could move ahead.

Pierce was enthralled to hear about how Lyon and Millicent had first met. It had been the result of a marriage of convenience arranged by the dowager and their lawyer, Sir Richard Maitland. The ceremony was a hurried affair, for their mother was in the midst of one of her anxiety spells about dying at any moment. He became even more spellbound as his brother told him about Melbury Hall and how, under the care of Millicent and a former slave named Ohenewaa, Lyon had recovered. Listening to him, it was stirring to get a sense of the depth of this man's feelings for his wife. His love clearly knew no bounds, and his enthusiasm about their plans together spoke only of their happiness.

"There is a cloud hanging over us, though," Lyon said. "What we are feeling in our personal life is very different from what is happening around us."

The earl went on to explain about the land clearings and the effect it was having on everyone.

"When you are ready, I should like to ride with you into the village and out to the farms. Perhaps we can even visit some of our neighbors. Our tenants' minds will be much more at ease, now that they have welcomed you home. Not a day goes by, however, when we are not faced with another wave of unfortunates who have lost their homes, forced off the land they have worked and lived on for generations. And 'tis simply greed that drives this tragedy."

It was a small jump from there to the situation in the colonies. Pierce was surprised that his brother knew about the smuggling he and Nathaniel were doing for the Sons of Liberty.

"I suppose this is what I get for hiring Border men on my ships."

"Especially those with kin in the village." Lyon agreed. "But I think your secret is safe here. You know there is no love lost between Baronsford's people and our "Farmer King" and his ministers in London. The *Gazette,* however, ran an interesting story about a notorious smuggler named MacHeath. You wouldn't know anything about this fellow?"

"A respected shipowner like me? How could I know anything about the fellow?"

"I cannot imagine, except that I believe he may be very close to me." Lyon gave his brother a narrow glare. "I expect a full report."

"Before we get to that, however," Pierce said solemnly, "you should know that David is being sent to Boston. I fear that he and I may stand on different sides of the field when it comes to our politics."

"Then I am very glad you are here and not in the colonies."

"But I shall not be here for long. I will need to go back fairly soon, and I do not look forward to confronting him there."

"Well, then we have to think of a solution. It has taken me thirty-four years to come to realize what matters in this life and what does not." Lyon placed a hand on Pierce's shoulder. "Millicent is my life, our children will be what our dreams are made of. This family is the foundation of all of it. We shall do whatever we have to do to keep peace between you and David."

Portia was delighted to add her name to the list of the infant's conquests, though she was at first surprised that the Earl and Countess of Aytoun were so eager to include the baby in the company of so many adults. Even in the Higgins household, where Ann and Walter were valued far more than occurred in many families, they were kept to their own friends and to their studies and to the kitchen, except on special occasions and for prayer. Not so here, and Portia was happily surprised.

Indeed, Josephine was a joy. Loud and messy and beautiful, a bundle of moving hands and feet, she refused to be ignored by anyone, no matter what their excuses might be.

She had won Helena over immediately, waking up while Bess was showing Portia's mother the nursery. When the older woman had held Josephine up to her face, the infant had patted her on the cheeks and suckled the end of her nose. Pierce had turned out to be another easy mark, since the bairn had mistaken him for Lyon and had reached out for him with waving arms, kicking legs, and very loud shrieks. With Portia, the baby had been quite fascinated with her dark curls, taking fistfuls of them and smiling whenever she pretended to cry out in pain. Portia didn't mind the mild torture for the toothless smiles and belly laughs she received in return. In fact, she had a hard time giving up the child when the time had come for the nursemaid to take Josephine away for the night.

After a sumptuous dinner, the three women retired to

the sitting room while Pierce and Lyon and Truscott lingered in the dining room, drinking and discussing politics.

"Now you understand what I was telling you before about that bairn." Millicent said to Portia sometime later. The countess had already explained to Helena what she'd told Portia of the conditions surrounding the infant's birth. "Josephine is truly amazing. Even at her age, she is developing a sense of confidence that is admirable."

"But do you not think that is due to your attentions, as well as to your husband's remarkable fondness for her," Helena asked. "A bairn, as you call her, is not born with such qualities."

"In the years ahead," Portia said earnestly, "if you are ever in need of a tutor for her, I shall make myself available, no matter where I am."

"Tutor? I am already counting on you visiting us in another capacity."

Portia blushed, not wanting to think about what Millicent meant exactly. Her discomfort increased when she looked up and found the men entering the sitting room. Pierce was at the front of the group and, from the look he gave her, she guessed he might have heard Millicent's comment.

"Would you young ladies mind if I were to steal Miss Edwards away for a walk in the gardens?"

Her blush became a burn. Millicent's and Helena's agreeable responses were answered by Truscott's and Lyon's immediate objections.

"I do not believe anyone asked you two." He bowed politely and offered Portia his hand. She had no choice but to take it.

"I know the moon is on the rise, but 'tis still quite dark outside," she whispered, stealing a glance up into his deep blue eyes. His face was very close as he drew her out of her chair.

"My point exactly."

When Portia made some rather unintelligible apologies

to the others, Millicent came to her rescue, asking Helena questions about the weather during their crossing. Pierce looped her arm through his and escorted her through one of the open doors to a terrace. Portia held her tongue, but when they were safely down the steps and on the grassy lawn, she gave him a piece of her mind.

"I have been trying so hard to behave all afternoon. I have been extremely careful of not doing—"

He pulled her into his arms and silenced her with a kiss. As always, she was out of breath and light-headed when he finally drew back.

"I am very happy to hear that you have been struggling to keep your hands off of me, too." He smiled devilishly, pulling her down the hill and through an arched entrance, into an extensive garden enclosed by boxwood.

Portia had to run to keep up, laughing in spite of herself. She took a step away from him, though, as soon as they were hidden by the high green hedges.

"Pierce, I want you to know I have already developed a great deal of respect for your sister-in-law."

"I have, too."

Portia took a step back as he moved toward her. "She is a lovely woman."

"I agree. I have never seen Lyon happier."

She took another step back. "We need to remember, this place is their home, and quite respectable. The last thing I wish for is to have any hint of scandal touch—"

"I agree," he said with a laugh, catching her by the wrist and pulling her against him.

She was helpless when it came to his power of persuasion. Her mouth answered his demands, and her body strained against his as one large hand kneaded her breast and their hips rocked and ground together. She tore her mouth free.

"Everyone must know that we came here for this."

"They'd be dolts not to know."

"You're mad."

"Indeed, my love," he replied, pulling her onto a nearby stone bench. "Mad for you."

He might be out of his mind, but so was she. At this moment, nothing could overcome the power of their passion. She was clumsy in undoing the front of his breeches. He was impatient in pushing up the skirts around her waist. Somehow, though, they succeeded. Kneeling astride him on the bench, Portia lowered herself onto him and gasped for air when he lifted his hips to meet her, embedding himself deep within her.

Pierce held her upright with his strong hands while her body stretched and wrapped even more tightly around him, drawing him in. The need to move, to rock, to bring them to satisfaction surged through her, but Pierce wrapped his arms around her, holding her captive. She heard herself moan, and he took possession of her mouth with his. By the time he broke off the kiss, she was about to lose her mind.

"Do you feel me?" he whispered, his voice husky and raw.

Portia nodded, her body aflame.

He shifted her slightly and lowered her even farther onto him. "How deep do you feel me?"

"In the very center of me," she whispered back.

When he moved again, ever so slightly, she had the sensation of teetering on the edge of a cliff, ready to plunge headfirst into the abyss.

"I feel you all around me. Here." His hand slid down past her buttocks to where their bodies were joined. Excitement jolted through her when his fingers touched her so intimately. In a moment he moved his hand, taking one of her wrists from his shoulder hand and placing her palm against his heart. "But I also feel you here. You, Portia Edwards, have become part of me."

Tears flooded her eyes. How could it be that this beautiful man could feel this way about *her*? Her hands were trembling when they cupped his face. She kissed his lips and tasted her own tears. "I love you, Pierce. God, how I love you."

Portia marveled how in that exact moment he lost his control. His body strained and he lifted her before driving again into her. And again. His hands pulled at the neckline of her dress and his lips suckled mercilessly on her breast. Higher and higher they rose, driving together, losing themselves as they found love's rhythm, until they cried out in unison to the stars, and burst into a heavenly sphere as one.

Pierce waited until their hearts slowed after their wild race and she lifted her head off his shoulder.

She was so stunningly beautiful. She was wild and untamed. She was selfless and giving. She was his, and she would remain his. Then and there, under the stars that shone like diamonds around her, he whispered the words that he'd grown so impatient to say.

"Portia, my love. Will you marry me?"

She stared at him, her face filling with such confusion that he thought for a moment he had spoken in some unknown tongue.

"Will you marry me? Will you become my wife?" he repeated.

Silence was again his answer, and he saw her grow almost frantic searching for words.

Suddenly, she squirmed on top of him, working herself off his lap. He watched her back away from him, clumsily trying to straighten her skirts. He quickly straightened his own clothes as he moved to block her path when he realized she was about to run.

"Do you have no answer for me? Do I not at least deserve *some* word?"

Tears glistened in the moonlight when she looked up. "The answer is no. I cannot marry you."

The fires of his temper flared up, but only momentarily. He knew her so well. Deep within him, he had expected this response from her.

"I want a reason," he demanded, keeping his anger out of his voice.

She brought her hand to her face and turned away. Pierce moved around her until they were face-to-face again.

"I cannot marry you. That should be answer enough for you."

"But 'tis not enough." He took her wrist when she tried to walk away again. "I know you. I know what you are thinking. You cry at this declaration of my love because you feel the same for me. But in your mind, an offer of marriage brings us back to who we are and what we are worth and where in society we rank."

"And what I have to offer you," she cried. "Nothing! Your offer brings us exactly to that. You and I are not . . ." Portia stopped and waved her hand in the direction of the castle. "Look around you at all of this, Pierce. Look at where you come from . . . and then look at me."

"I *am* looking at you. And I am telling you what I see." He lifted her chin, forcing her to look into his eyes. "I see a beautiful and intelligent woman who stirs my blood and challenges my thinking. I see the woman I love. The woman who has become my life. The woman who has captured my dreams and holds them in her fist. The woman who might even be carrying my child."

She became flustered and tried to pull her wrist free. He didn't let her go.

"You cannot run away from the truth, my love. And what if it turns out I am right? Do you wish for this child a life like your own? Do you think your pride is more important than the joy that we could share as a family?"

"Please let me go, Pierce," she pleaded tearfully, pulling away. "Please."

He let her go. He watched Portia run away, knowing that he was not about to give up. She was stubborn, but so was he.

Portia came into the house through a side entryway and ran up to her bedchamber without being discovered

by others. She didn't bother to light any tapers, but threw herself onto the bed.

The tears wouldn't stop. The sadness clutching at her heart wouldn't go away. Pierce's words continued to play again and again in her mind. He loved her. She loved him. So why couldn't that be enough? Why couldn't they just leave things as they were? Why must they marry?

She couldn't get it through his head, and she didn't know how to say it any clearer. How could she enter into a marriage knowing that the scale was so skewed? She could give him nothing. She would bring nothing into that union. Her concerns might seem to be nothing today or tomorrow, but she knew they would create a division in their life soon enough. The tears continued to fall.

Sometime later, there was a soft knock on her bedroom door. Portia didn't know what the hour was. She had been crying in the dark. She sat up on the bed and hoped whoever it was would think she was sleeping and go away. But the knock sounded again.

Resigned, she went to the door and opened it a little. Helena, already changed into her nightdress, was waiting in the hall.

"May I come in?"

"I . . . I was getting ready for bed myself." Portia couldn't fight the choking sensation.

Her mother didn't wait for an invitation and pushed her way into the room. "Well, then I am here to help you."

Portia closed the door, then quickly moved a small table out of her mother's way so she wouldn't stumble over it.

"Really, Mother. I . . . I can manage."

"No, I think not," the older woman stated firmly. She found the bed and sat on the edge. "Come here."

Portia bit her lip when she saw her mother's serious expression. "Helena, I am not in the mood for a lecture."

"Good, since I am horrible at giving them." She patted the bed next to her. "I said come here."

Portia obediently moved to her and sat down. Helena's hands reached up until they touched Portia's tearstained face. "I thought so."

"You thought what?"

"That you two quarreled again."

"We did not."

"You might think you can fool others, but I am not so blind—well, figuratively speaking. Pierce stormed back into the house like a wounded bear. Now, tell me what is wrong."

"Nothing."

"Portia!" she scolded. "The truth."

A moment passed, and then she gave up. She choked on the words, though, as she spoke them. "He told me he loved me."

"Ah, that is horrible." Helena pulled her daughter's head against her chest and caressed her hair. "I always knew he was an unfeeling young man. How could he say such a thing?"

"You are making fun of me." Portia cried and laughed at the same time.

"I am not. But that cannot be the only reason for all these tears."

Portia blew her nose in a kerchief that Helena handed her. "He also asked me . . . asked me to marry him."

"The nerve of the rogue!" she said more dramatically.

Portia sat up straight. "You *are* making fun of me. But I am serious. He is upset because I rejected his offer. I love him, but there is no way I can marry him when we are from worlds so far apart, when there is nothing I could bring to such a match."

"Do you think *you* are not enough?"

Portia shook her head and blew her nose again. "Please, Mother."

"I'm speaking seriously," Helena said more forcefully.

She lifted Portia's cheeks. "*You,* Portia are the one he wants. *You* are what is important to him. The person, who you are, all that is inside of you."

"Mother look around this place, where he was raised, the level of society that he belongs to."

"Now, you are the one who should be looking, and not with your eyes, but with your heart . . . and then add that to your thinking. Forget about the world for a moment, and think about just the two of you. Do you believe Pierce could love you *more* if your family's wealth was equal to his? Do you believe he would treat you differently as his wife even if you were a king's daughter?"

"Of course not," she cried, blurting out her answer.

Helena fell silent, and Portia realized what she had said—what she had admitted.

"If that is so, then everything else," her mother said finally, "the bonds you forge in marriage, your entire future together, rests in your own hands."

Chapter 26

Standing stiffly at the window of the regimental offices of the West Yorkshire 24th Foot, Turner thought it was appallingly undignified that someone of his rank and record of service was being treated with no more respect than some lowly infantryman. He looked at his watch, furious that he had yet to be given an audience with Colonel Kilmaine, the commander of the regiment.

Stationed in the colonies for so many years now, Turner had not realized that a wedge was growing between those serving His Majesty King George here and in America. It was obvious from the talk he had heard in even the few days that he had been back on England's soil that those in the military here felt that the troops in the colonies were not strong enough. They were not using a firm enough hand to quell the troublemakers' growing acts of rebellion.

As if to affirm that, Turner had heard just yesterday that the king had issued a far stronger proclamation than the one Governor Wanton of Rhode Island had delivered regarding the *Gaspee.* The bounty on the head of the person who had shot Lieutenant Dudingston was raised to one thousand pounds, an amount that was probably twice the value of the ship itself.

In some ways, though he had never consciously considered it before, Turner agreed with these views. But he was an exception. He believed that stronger action was

needed against the rabble in Boston and Philadelphia, in particular. Clearly, though, these armchair soldiers had lumped him in with those they considered weak and were treating him that way.

His temper was ready to boil over, and he knew it. Still, he needed to get this Colonel Kilmaine to realize that he was in possession of evidence that would make them both heroes to their nation.

He was only one step away, but it was proving to be an extremely slow step. An hour ago, Turner had reluctantly given the letter—a copy he had written out earlier himself—to a member of Colonel Kilmaine's staff. Since then, waiting in an outer room, he had seen two junior officers called in to speak with the regimental commander. Neither of them had left, yet, and this was at least promising.

A quarter of an hour later, he was ushered into the office.

Colonel Kilmaine was a stocky man of advanced years and a brusque manner. His eyes of watery blue looked Turner over appraisingly, but gave away nothing of his assessment. After a curt introduction, he sat down again behind his desk and gestured to Turner to sit. The two young lieutenants, Cobham and Huske, remained standing on either side of their commander.

"I assume you have the original of this letter, Captain?"

"Of course. Because of its importance, I felt the need to safeguard the document."

"Indeed. Well, we have spent a great deal of time going over the information you have given us, Captain, as well as this letter."

He could hear the tone of indifference in the voice and stared at the copy lying on the colonel's desk. He thought to himself that they had certainly not spent a *great* deal of time, as they'd had it for only an hour.

"Then you understand the urgency and the importance of my request."

"Frankly, there is nothing we see in there that tells us this correspondence is from Bonnie Prince Charlie."

Turner felt his temper again begin to rise. He was clearly dealing with an imbecile.

"Then allow me to explain to you—as I wished to do an hour ago—the context of this letter so that you can understand its importance, Colonel."

As he explained in detail the connection of the Young Pretender to Lady Primrose, the pale blue eyes remained fixed on his face. Turner told him of her importance in the web of Jacobite traitors still operating in England. He impressed upon him the momentous opportunity to crush this movement which threatened their English way of life.

"I know about crushing Jacobites, Captain," the colonel cut in. "I was at Culloden."

"As was my father, sir. He died a hero's death there."

"As did many. Still, I do not see any evidence—"

"Wait." Turner knew his only chance of convincing this man lay in revealing the secret he'd promised to keep for Admiral Middleton. That, and telling what he believed must have occurred, piecing together all the information he'd learned. "There is more, but 'tis information that must not leave this room. Some of what I am about to tell you was spoken to me in confidence by Admiral Middleton himself."

The two young officers exchanged a quick look over the colonel's head. Ignoring them, Turner took a deep breath and began.

"During the year preceding October in 1748, my commander, Admiral Middleton was assigned to the delegation meeting with officials in France. Their negotiations resulted in the Treaty of Aix-la-Chapelle. That pact, as you know, effectively ended French support of Prince Charles Edward and the Stewart court in exile. During that period, many of the members of the delegation brought their families to France, and Admiral Middleton was no different. Somehow, while in France, Middleton's

own daughter Helena commenced to have an affair with the Stewart prince himself. I believe that Lady Primrose herself may have served as liaison between the lovers, though I cannot prove that." Though he was stating as facts things that he could only guess may have been true, Turner knew it was essential that he sound entirely convincing. Looking at his audience, he was pleased to see he now had the three men's undivided attention. "When Middleton learned of his daughter's scandalous behavior, he acted to protect himself from such a politically disastrous secret. He sent the girl home with his wife. But the damage was done. His daughter was in a family way. While he concluded his work in France, a baby girl was born and she was spirited away and grew up in the care of Lady Primrose in Wales. The Admiral's daughter, Helena, has led a reclusive life since then. This is how the situation stood until last month when the daughter and mother were united in Boston and escaped to England."

Turner looked haughtily down at the end of his nose at his audience. It was sheer genius that he had been able to connect the pieces of the puzzle.

"This letter, gentlemen, is the answer to Lady Primrose's request that Charles Edward see his daughter. The two women left the colonies on a ship owned by Pierce Pennington, the brother of the Earl of Aytoun. From my spies, I know that Lady Primrose is going to Baronsford, the family seat of Lord Aytoun in the Borders. From this letter, we know she is going to meet Charles Edward there. We cannot ignore the evidence we have in hand. We cannot let the Stewart Pretender slip through our fingers."

Colonel Kilmaine sat silently, rubbing his chin for few minutes before looking up. "Wait outside, Captain Turner. I need to consider."

Pierce opened the door of his bedchamber and walked directly into Portia, who was hurrying down the corridor.

He immediately reached out a hand to steady her. Her face was wan and her eyes red-rimmed.

"You are unwell," he said, worried.

"No. I am fine." She smiled weakly. "I had this little problem, though. I could not find you. And I could not ask anyone in which room you were staying. So I walked the corridors of the West Wing without any success, and then came back to this floor. I should have guessed you would be near us."

"You were looking for me?" he asked, his hands moving gently up and down her arms.

She nodded.

"For how long?"

"For most of the night," she said shyly.

"You did not sleep at all?"

She shook her head.

Pierce brushed his lips against her brow and wrapped an arm around her shoulder. Turning her, they began to walk toward her own bedchamber.

"So you are no longer angry?" she asked.

"I was never angry. Frustrated? Yes. Disappointed? Very." He pushed her door open and ushered her in. "But determined to change your mind? Absolutely." He closed the door behind them and lifted her chin. Her color was returning. "I am not giving up, my love. I shall do whatever I need to do. I shall play the rogue if I need to and trick you if I must. I shall abduct you, carry you off, keep you tied to my bed—"

Her laughter was the most beautiful sound. He smiled. "Now you are forcing me to reconsider . . . yet again."

"What do you mean 'again'?" He glared at her suspiciously.

Portia threw her arms around his neck and lifted herself on her tiptoes until their faces were an inch apart. "I was searching for you all night to say . . . yes."

"Yes?" He lifted her off the ground. "Yes . . . you will marry me?"

"Yes." She laughed when he whirled her around. "But that was before you talked of tying me to your bed."

"You should know that comes with marrying me anyway. But have no fear, 'tis I who am helpless when it comes to you." He kissed her deeply, and then whirled her again. He could not think of a happier moment in his life.

There was a knock on the door. Pierce put her back on the ground. Portia cast a nervous glance toward it. "I do not think 'twould be proper for anyone to find you here this early in the morning."

Pierce shook his head. They were completely clothed . . . and he didn't particularly give a damn anyway.

"I do not think anyone will give it a second thought, my love, since I plan to let not only this household but the entire countryside know about our engagement this morning."

Holding her hand, he opened the door. It was Lyon's clerk, Peter Howitt.

"Good morning, Miss Edwards," he said politely, turning to Pierce "Excuse me, sir, but his lordship has a matter of great import that he needs to discuss with ye. He awaits in the library, sir."

"Bad news?" he asked, immediately concerned about their mother.

"Nay, sir. Or at least, I do not believe so."

"Do not go anywhere. Get some rest," Pierce whispered into Portia's ear, stealing a kiss before following the man down. "How did you know where to find me?"

"His lordship said to look in your bedchamber first, and if ye were not there, then to knock on Miss Edwards's door."

Pierce was amused that Lyon knew, and he couldn't wait to tell his brother about their news. Last night, after Portia had left him in the garden, he and Lyon had stayed up long into the night talking. He had told his brother everything about her. He'd poured out his heart

about what he felt for her. Curiously, Lyon had been confident that Portia would give in. They just needed to rely on Pierce's stubbornness and a little time. It had been the encouragement he'd needed.

Lyon was alone in his study, and Howitt closed the door, leaving the two men. There was nothing gloomy in the earl's expression, so Pierce decided to make his announcement first.

"Portia has agreed to marry me."

The older brother's blue eyes shone with the excitement as he pushed himself to his feet and came toward him. "That is indeed wonderful news."

"I think so. Would you mind very much, sending someone up to awaken your wife and tell her, as well? She was the first one who hinted at it, I believe, when we decided to join the ladies after dinner."

"Not on your life. I want that pleasure all for myself." Lyon clapped him on the back and shook his hand.

"Of course, I haven't discussed it with Portia yet, but if you think Millicent would be agreeable, I would like to have the wedding here at Baronsford."

"She would be delighted with that, I am quite certain. But before you become too distracted with such things, I believe we should prepare ourselves for another visit." Lyon picked up a letter from his desk and handed it to Pierce. "A messenger arrived with this only a few minutes ago."

Pierce read the letter, reread it, then looked up in shock.

"Have no fear. Baronsford shall be ready to receive him."

Portia couldn't understand what was going on. Only minutes after he'd left, Pierce stormed back into her bedchamber. Taking her by the arm, he led her to Helena's room.

When she responded affirmatively to his knock, they

entered and he handed a letter to her surprised mother. Helena was, luckily, awake and dressed and sitting on a settee by the window with the young attendant Bess.

" 'Tis time you explained this, madam," he said to Helena as soon as the attendant left the room.

"What is this all about?" Portia asked him, trying to go to her mother. "She cannot see to read it."

Pierce held her back. "Would you care to try, madam?"

"Of course," Helena replied.

"Really, Pierce."

"Do not fret so, daughter," Helena said. "Let me see."

Getting up and going to the window, she stood in the bright sunlight and held the paper close to her face. Portia watched in amazement as her mother slowly worked her way through the words on the sheet, and then sat down again on the settee with the prettiest of smiles on her face. When she looked up at Portia, she had tears in her eyes.

"What is in that letter?" Portia asked, now completely confused. She looked from her mother to Pierce. "Who is it from?"

Pierce would not answer, continuing to keep his gaze on the older woman.

Helena stretched a hand toward her, and she took it, sitting down beside her. Her mother laid the letter on her lap and took Portia's cheeks with both hands. "He is coming. He will arrive next week. He wants to meet you."

"Who?" Portia asked.

"My prince, of course. Charles Edward Stewart. The true King of Scotland and England. Your father."

Lieutenant Huske, a company of twenty-five foot soldiers, and four wagons to carry the men and supplies were all that Colonel Kilmaine grudgingly spared to help Turner on his mission at Baronsford. The colonel's instructions were precise. Huske was in charge of the mis-

sion. Turner was only to accompany them as an advisor. It would take several days to prepare to leave, but the company would still be in Scotland before the date the "supposed" Stewart royal was scheduled to arrive. Kilmaine made it clear that he was making his men available only as a gesture to honor Turner's father, not because he was convinced of any Jacobite plots.

Turner accepted with as much decorum as he could muster. He knew he had no time to go anywhere else for troops. These would have to do. In any event, if things went as planned, the final triumph would be his. He would take Helena and Portia, and he would make sure everyone in England knew that he alone was responsible for the capture of Bonnie Prince Charlie.

"The colonel discussed the appropriate strategy for this mission," Huske told Turner as they set up camp alongside the Tweed two days later. They were only a three hour march from Baronsford. "We shall time our arrival at Baronsford for the late afternoon, though I shall have a scout there at dawn. If we go too early, he may see us and our efforts will be in vain anyway."

A mist, thick and ghostly, was rising from the river, and Turner found himself hoping for foul weather—the better for surprising the traitors.

"I must repeat to you that when we arrive, I am in charge. I shall do all the talking that needs to be done and give all orders. Colonel Kilmaine's instructions were clear that we are to treat the Earl of Aytoun and his family with the utmost respect. We have no indication that they are in any way cognizant of any visits. They may not even be in residence at this time. And you will keep in mind, Captain, we are here *only* for your Bonnie Prince and no one else."

Turner nodded curtly and moved off toward the river. He could hear the sarcasm in the pup's voice. Still, he was not about to rebuke Huske for his insolence now. There would be time enough for that later.

Right now, Turner wanted to focus only on tomorrow.

No matter what, he had every intention of taking Helena and Portia into his custody. And he knew in the excitement surrounding the capture of the exiled Pretender, he could do whatever he wished.

She tried, but it was just not the same. Oddly, Portia found she could feel none of the excitement that had taken hold of her upon the discovery of her mother.

She was not naïve enough to think of this as a family reunion. After his defeat at Culloden, the Stewart prince had gone off to France and Italy to live his life in exile. Charles Edward had shown genius as a financier and a campaigner, and many in Scotland and England still held out hope that he would someday return and replace the unpopular Hanover now occupying the throne. After the death of his father, the "Old Pretender," Bonnie Prince Charlie had proclaimed himself king, but he was still only the "King over the Waters" to his most fervent supporters.

As she thought about the reason for his coming, Portia came to the conclusion that this visit must be politically— or financially—motivated. The Earl of Aytoun, in addition to being rich, was well respected by many Scottish leaders. She doubted that her father would make such a dangerous journey just to see her. He was just using her presence there as a way of cultivating the support of another wealthy Scottish family. What surprised her to no end, however, was Lady Primrose's connection with the Stewart prince.

When the day finally arrived, though, Portia realized that all her worries centered on Helena. Charles, past fifty now, had this past March married the nineteen-year-old Princess Louise Emanuella Maximiliane de Stolberg-Guedern, a young woman of German extraction with Scottish blood through the Bruces of Elgin. Apparently, everyone in Scotland knew of the marriage, but Millicent was gentle in breaking the news to Portia.

Portia didn't think her mother was aware of this mar-

riage, either. In fact, she found herself wondering if the letter Helena had sent to Lady Primrose had been for the purpose of arranging to see the man she'd loved her entire life just one more time.

Lady Primrose arrived in a coach midmorning, and after a warm reunion with Portia, told her that Louise was not traveling with Charles, but was waiting for him in France before they returned to Italy.

"I do not wish to see him," Helena announced when Portia came to get her.

"But Mother, Lady Primrose is already here. Everyone is expecting him. He could arrive at any moment."

Helena smiled and shook her head. "I should be delighted to meet with Lady Primrose in private, later, as I owe a great debt to that kind lady for what she has done for you. But . . . as to seeing Charles . . . that is out of the question."

Portia sat down next to her. "But you are still in love with him."

"I am in love with the dashing prince I have kept in my mind and in my heart. I am in love with the man he once was. I always will be. But I want nothing to alter those memories for me." Helena held on to Portia's hands. "I know about his life, my love. I understand his need to marry and produce a male heir that can carry on his dreams. At the same time, I have my own dreams. I have you and Pierce and the beautiful life you two will build together."

"But you asked him to come."

Helena shook her head again. "In the letter I sent to Lady Primrose, I said 'twas time for him to acknowledge you as his daughter. I knew then that it would be important for you to know how noble is the blood in your veins."

"But now I realize how unimportant that is. The fact that he is my true father does not mean to me what you think it does. You are the one that I have come to love and respect as my parent."

"And I love you, too." Helena kissed Portia's cheek. "I have everything I could ever ask for. Now go, give your father a chance to claim the greatest treasure he will ever know."

There were enough physical resemblances between them to make it obvious they were kin. As they stood in the Grand Salon, what Pierce found most charming, though, was that Portia's ways of expressing herself, the regal way she introduced herself, and even her hand gestures resembled her father's. And then, of course, there was the matter of her willfulness and her reckless passion. She was certainly the daughter of Bonnie Prince Charlie, Pierce thought, and it was clear she captured the fancy of the exiled king.

And as he had anticipated, Charles Edward was as interested in him as he was with Portia. When the two of them told him of their engagement, the news was greeted with immediate approval.

The visitor wanted to talk politics, though, and the discussion soon turned to the colonies. Not surprisingly, Charles Edward truly enjoyed the trouble the American colonists were making for "that fat Hanover farmer." He wanted to know what he could do to support such rebellious behavior.

As Pierce answered his questions, he glanced at Portia, concerned that this might not be what she had expected this day to be. Her expression told him, though, that she was content. He even wondered if she weren't a little restless to be rid of their guest.

When she looked into his eyes, he suddenly realized that the Charles Edward had not inquired at all about Helena. For that reason alone, Pierce knew beyond a doubt, the Bonnie Prince would never be more to his daughter than a guest.

Chapter 27

There was no entourage in the courtyard of the monstrous castle. No guards in place. No carriages at all in evidence. Turner was not discouraged, though. He doubted Charles Edward would do anything so stupid as to draw attention to his presence.

The sky was steel gray, and though there had been no rain all day, the mists were already beginning to rise from the lowlands and the river. The scout sent ahead informed them that there was no sign of any visitors yet.

"Do not forget our orders, Captain," Lieutenant Huske reiterated as the two men dismounted from their horses. The rest of the men formed a line in the courtyard, awaiting further instructions. "I will do any speaking that needs to be done."

Turner was becoming extremely tired of the junior officer's impertinence, but they were so close to their quarry now that, for one last time, he let the comment pass.

As they approached the impressive main entrance, the door opened and a short, wiry man stepped past a doorman and introduced himself without any hint of hospitality as the steward.

"We are here to see the Earl of Aytoun on Crown business," the lieutenant announced. "Will you take us to him?"

"Very sorry, sir, but his lordship is not at home at the moment."

Turner stifled an urge to order the soldiers to fan out around the castle to make certain no one fled. Huske, sensing his impatience, shot him a warning look.

"I understand that the Lord Aytoun's brother is here. We would like to see him, then."

"Mr. Pennington is with his lordship, sir. If you wish to speak to anyone, I can see if Lady Aytoun is available."

"Very well." Huske called two of his men to accompany them into the castle and started in behind the steward.

Turner hung back, thinking he take the opportunity to issue some brief orders to the soldiers remaining outside. He knew Pennington and wanted them to be alert to any trickery.

"This way, Captain Turner," Huske snapped.

Ignoring the curious glances of the servants and the steward, Turner entered. It was truly a fine house, obviously well-kept and modern in every convenience. As they were led in, however, Turner refused to be impressed by the lavish furnishings as the lieutenant clearly was.

The traitors were here. He knew it. All of them. Bonnie Prince Charlie, Portia, Helena.

He walked impatiently to a window looking out over the Tweed and pushed it open wide. They were being played for fools at this very moment. While they were waiting on this Lady Aytoun, Pennington and his brother were no doubt spiriting the villains to safety. He scanned the gardens and the fields beyond.

"How can I help you, gentlemen?"

Turner turned and was somewhat taken aback by the pleasant face of a pregnant woman who entered, the steward in tow. Huske, suddenly apologetic and humble, quickly introduced himself and Turner.

"Mr. Campbell here says that you are looking for my husband. I am afraid he and his brother have been out visiting the farms for most of the day, and I don't know

when exactly they shall return. You are welcome to stay, however, and wait for them."

"Actually, milady," Huske replied politely. "You might be able to assist us. We have been sent here to investigate a rumor that you are to entertain a certain . . . well, high-ranking Jacobite here at Baronsford today."

"A high-ranking Jacobite?" she repeated with a smile. "I am very sorry Lieutenant Huske, but in Oxford, where I was raised, we entertain in a very different manner than what you see here. Does it look to you as if we are entertaining today?"

"Well, no, milady."

"But I am curious that you are looking for Jacobites. To be honest, I didn't know there are many of them left. Are there, Lieutenant?"

"I really cannot say, milady. But there are obviously none here."

"Quite right, sir."

"Begging your pardon, milady," Huske said good-naturedly. "You said you are from Oxford? I've spent a great deal of time there, myself, when I was younger."

"What a coincidence! Actually, I went to school there. Mrs. Stockdale's Academy."

"I know exactly where that is. My uncle had a small estate just on the outskirts. There was horse trader just up the lane from St.—"

"Enough of this," Turner cut in brusquely. "Lady Aytoun, we have reason to believe that the Young Pretender himself is here . . . now . . . as we speak."

He crossed the room and leaned toward the woman to impress her with the seriousness of the visit.

"Hold there," the steward growled, coming forward protectively.

"Wait, Mr. Campbell," the countess said, growing pale. "I must know what he means."

"To speak more plainly, milady, you will be convicted of high treason for sheltering and supporting the exiled traitor if you do not cooperate with us immediately. So

enough of this meaningless banter. Take us to where you are hiding him."

The woman stared up at him, a look of horror on her face. "Sir, how can you make such an accusation? What reason do you have to believe such a thing?"

"I must apologize for the captain, milady." Huske said, stepping between them and encouraging her to sit down.

"High treason?" She turned to the young officer. "Lieutenant, I want you to know that my home is open to you and your men. Feel free to search every inch of this castle, as you see fit. I am shocked to find that such a rumor could circulate outside these walls. In fact, I insist that you start this moment and continue searching. We have nothing to hide. I want you to look until you are convinced that we house no Stewart princes."

Turner looked on in disgust as the fool, rather than starting the search, pulled a chair close to the countess and continued to make apologies.

"Milady, I have no doubt that this rumor is false. I do not think that we need to—"

She shook her head. "No, I insist. I will not have you leave this place with any doubt in your mind."

Turner offered to lead the search, but Huske immediately refused, ordering the two soldiers to divide the rest of the company into parties and to make a quick search of the castle.

As he stood in silence by the window, the two continued to talk like old friends.

Not even an hour later, the two soldiers returned. They had found nothing to report. Turner was appalled to find the lieutenant satisfied.

"Again, milady, my sincerest apologies to you and his lordship for any inconvenience. I will make certain that a complete report of this visit is made to my commander, Colonel Kilmaine. I must tell you that he believed from the first that information we received was far from reliable."

With a deep bow, Huske motioned for the captain to follow him out.

Anger churned and rolled through Turner, threatening to explode. They had not even looked. They did not even search the grounds. The information he received could not be wrong. The letter had said the meeting was to take place today. Here. They just had to wait them out.

Outside, in front of the foot soldiers, Huske laid into him. "I warned Colonel Kilmaine of your unreliability, Captain. Anyone who betrays the confidence of his own superior as you did of Admiral Middleton is not a man to be trusted. Your conduct was ungentlemanly and callous to the countess. You, sir . . ."

Turner shut his ears to the man's raving, for in the distance he spotted two women who were walking from the gardens across the fields toward the river. Even through the mist, however, he had no trouble recognizing the wild head of black hair falling in cascades over slim shoulders.

Someone would pay dearly for this, and he had just found the perfect someone.

Portia walked arm in arm with her mother as they slowly crossed the field. Ahead of them, the thick hedge of brambles and pine told her that they were nearing the cliffs. The smell of wild flowers and cut grass was in the air, though she wished the sun would break through once before they went in to dinner. It didn't matter, she thought. This was the most time the two of them had spent alone together in days. As they walked farther away from the castle, they eventually came to a path through the thick brambles and brush. The sound of the flowing water promised a view of the cliffs and the river, if the rising fog was not too thick yet.

"You never told me what you and Lady Primrose talked about."

"The obvious," Helena replied. "The one person we both dote on."

"Bonnie Prince Charlie?"

"No, you goose." Helena laughed softly. "I had a hundred questions about your growing up and your temperament and the things you did as a child. I wanted to hear all those stories that mothers savor in their memories."

"Now, why should you want to know those things?"

"So I can remind you of them and tease you whenever your children do the same things." Helena smiled. "And you must promise to give me plenty of them. Grandchildren, I mean."

Portia felt her stomach flip at the mere mention of it. She hadn't thought about it much since Pierce had brought it up the first time. But it was very possible that she was with child right now. Her body was certainly acting differently than it ever had before. She was tender in places where she had never been. And there was the question of her monthly.

"Have you two decided on a date for your wedding?"

Portia felt herself grow warm. "He would like us to marry very soon. In fact, as soon as his mother arrives from Hertfordshire. That would be fine with me since, other than you, I cannot think of anyone else."

"Lady Primrose told me she will be in Edinburgh for a month, and she was hoping to be asked."

Portia was touched by that. "Of course. She has been a good friend to us."

The path turned and suddenly they were standing on a bluff overlooking the river. The mists were drifting and swirling in thick clouds, though, only giving her brief glimpses of the river far below.

"Would you like to start back?" she asked. "This path along the cliff follows the river for some distance from the castle."

"Let's walk a ways further," Helena replied. "I'm enjoying this."

They walked in silence for a while, listening to the birds and the rush of the water below. Portia took the outside, for the path often passed right along the edge

of the cliffs. She knew that these were the cliffs where Lyon's first wife had fallen to her death . . . where Pierce had discovered both his brother and Emma.

The mist was growing thicker, obscuring sections of the path ahead. They had walked farther than she had intended.

"I think we should go back, Mother."

"As you wish, dear."

They turned around, and Portia decided they had made the right choice. She could not see two dozen paces ahead of them. Still, she didn't want to worry her mother.

"It would be lovely to have the wedding in the summer, don't you th—"

The word became a sharp cry as she felt herself jerked backward by her hair, the blade of a knife pressing against her throat. She turned ever slightly and caught a glimpse of her assailant.

Turner.

Wrapped up in the safety of her husband's arms, Millicent was still upset about the unexpected visit. Lyon and Pierce and Truscott, riding up the road from the village, had not seen the red-coated soldiers as they marched away from Baronsford.

"Now I understand why he mentions one day in his correspondence, but shows up the day before," Lyon said.

"These letters must be intercepted all the time," Pierce agreed.

"I'm very glad you knew, Lyon," Millicent noted. "Otherwise, I would have been quite taken by surprise when the prince arrived."

"That is why Lady Primrose preceded him, my love."

"Lucky for all of us, though, these soldiers did not know," Millicent asserted.

"Tell me everything that was said," Lyon told her. "I want to hear every detail of my brave wife's defense of the castle."

Pierce, keen to hear all the details as well, became concerned when she related the part about the second officer, the one who was put in his place by the young lieutenant.

"Do you recall the other officer's name?" he asked, breaking into her narrative.

"Indeed I do. Captain Turner."

Pierce felt his heart stop beating.

"Where are Portia and Helena?"

The path became narrower as they moved away from Baronsford. Thick briars, boulders, and stunted pines formed an impassible hedge on one side, at times crowding them dangerously close to the edge of the cliff. Below them, the river sometimes became visible through the fog. Occasionally, Portia caught glimpses of jagged rocks protruding from the moving water and at the base of the cliff. At other times, all she could see was the swirling mist and the roots of trees reaching out like tentacles from the cliff face.

Even with Turner's fist clutching her hair, Portia hugged Helena tightly to her side, keeping her away from the edge.

"Push her in front of you," he said, jabbing the point of the knife into her back. "At this rate, we will still be on this ledge when the sun goes down."

Turner jerked Portia's head forward, causing her to slip on some loose gravel. She grabbed for a branch, though, regaining her footing.

"She cannot see to lead the way." She held tight to her mother's arm. "At least, let me go in front."

"So you can run away? You think I don't know you and your tricks?"

She winced as he jerked her hair again. He was a fool, though. He didn't know her at all. If he did, then he would know that his most valuable weapon was Helena herself. Portia would not run anywhere so long as her mother was in his clutches.

"Do as I say. Push her ahead of you."

Still holding on to her mother's hand, Portia guided her to the front, trying to keep her away from the edge. If anything, they went slower now, as Helena had to feel with her hand along the branches and rock.

Portia didn't know where this path led, but she assumed Turner must have left a horse in a clearing somewhere. At some point they had to come to an opening that would lead them to it. How he had found them out here, though, she had no idea. They were far from the castle now, and she doubted anyone knew they were in trouble. She wondered how much time would pass before anyone even realized they were missing.

Suddenly her mother stopped and turned back toward them. "And just who do you think you are, Captain, to steal us away like this?"

Portia was surprised to hear the fearlessness in her mother's tone.

Turner shoved Portia hard into her mother, though, and the older woman grabbed for a branch as she stumbled backward.

"Keep moving, you Jacobite whore."

"Shut your mouth, Turner," Portia spat out, earning another vicious jerk of her head.

"Keep moving, both of you."

"And just where do you think you are taking us?" Helena's voice rose. "How far do you think you can go before they catch up to us?"

"Tell her to be quiet," he said fiercely to Portia.

She stumbled over a branch and glanced over the edge. There was a stony beach below. They were still quite high. Just ahead, there was a bend in the river. They passed occasional breaks in the foliage now, though Portia could see no passage through. If there were even a small clearing, she thought, she would try to tear her hair free of his grip, push Helena into the clearing, and then face Turner herself, no matter what the consequences. That knife be damned, she'd drag him off the cliff with her if she had to.

The path took several more sharp turns, but Helena, still ahead of them, managed to keep moving.

"If you think there will be a prize for returning me to my father, then you are a greater fool than I thought." Helena stopped and looked over her shoulder at him again. "But he said a number of times you had no more wit than a footman."

She moved forward a little without waiting for an answer. The path widened slightly and then narrowed sharply. Just holding on to her hand, Portia could feel the confidence growing in her mother.

"I hope you know that in the Admiral's estimation," she started again, "you ranked even below his horses. Below his dogs even."

Portia could hear the river moving over rocks below them, and the fog enshrouding the cliffs was heavier here. Briars and boulders formed a solid barrier now, and Portia could barely see ahead of her mother at all. Suddenly, Helena stopped dead beside a boulder. The path was so narrow here that Portia's foot was only inches from the edge.

"But I think I know why my father kept you around, Captain." Helena turned around. "And you say *I'm* the whore!"

Portia felt the knife again at her throat. Turner's breath was in her ear.

"I have been waiting for an excuse to give your daughter what she has coming. One more word from you and I'll cut her—"

"And a coward, too. Just as the Admiral used to say." Helena squeezed Portia's hand and took a step back. "But wouldn't your master be upset if you went back empty-handed?"

Helena took another step back and then, to Portia's astonishment, she turned and disappeared behind the boulder.

It took Turner less than a second to realize what had happened. He jerked Portia hard toward the cliff and

pushed by her. She reached out, clutching at anything she could as she teetered on the edge.

By sheer luck, her fingers closed on his sword scabbard as he went by, and she held tight, stopping him abruptly. Then, with a snap, the cord holding the sword gave way and she was again falling, scratching and clawing at the crumbling face of the cliff. With dirt and rocks showering her, she caught hold of a thin root.

Above her, Turner fell backward as if shot from a bow, careened off the boulder, and stumbled toward the edge. She only saw his flailing arms and legs as he fell, and his scream ended with a sickening thud somewhere below her.

The root snapped as Portia's fingers reached for another. Each branch she caught held for only a moment and then broke, sending her sliding another few inches. Her strength was giving out, and her hands were slippery with blood.

And then he caught hold of her wrist.

Pierce pulled Portia up onto the ledge and sat back against the boulder, holding her tightly in his arms. He didn't know which one of them was shuddering more violently.

The panic that had gripped him when he'd heard Turner was at Baronsford had nearly crushed him. Racing through the castle, he ran into Helena's attendant Bess, who told him that she'd seen them heading toward the river path.

As Pierce ran out of the house, Lyon shouted to him from atop one of the towers. From there parts of the path along the cliffs were visible, and he thought he could see three people walking there.

Pierce sprinted across the fields with Truscott following. Threading their way through the groves of pine and briar, they headed for a point where they would be ahead of the two women and their abductor. At one point, they came close enough that Pierce could hear them. Turner

had gone mad, he thought. From the voices, they knew that Helena was in the front and the captain was in the rear.

Even having Truscott with him, Pierce could not risk a face to face confrontation on the cliff. He would not take the chance of Portia going over the edge. The image of Lyon's and Emma's broken bodies on those rocks was still too vivid.

Finally, they reached a point where they knew a boulder shielded an entry onto the path. The fog was thick, and Pierce decided that this would be his best opportunity to surprise Turner as they passed. The two men waited until Helena reached the opening. Truscott reached for the older woman, and everything happened too quickly from there.

Pierce held Portia in his arms and thanked God that she was safe.

"Where is my mother?" she cried out in panic.

"She is safe. Walter Truscott has her."

"Turner went over."

"I know. I saw him go. We'll send someone down there, but I doubt he survived the fall."

She held him again. "I don't know what he thought he could accomplish by taking us. Helena, for one, would have fought every step of the journey back to Boston."

"I think this was a final act of desperation to walk away with something," Pierce said.

Helping her to her feet, he guided her toward the small opening beside the boulder. She stopped and looked over the edge of the cliff where Turner had fallen. There was only the mist, and the sound of water rushing over rocks.

A few moments later, Portia was holding Helena in her arms as the two men looked on. When they were feeling more composed, Pierce told them quickly about the attempt to apprehend Charles Edward.

"All this happened this afternoon?"

"While you and your mother must have been in the gardens. Turner must have seen you and then separated

himself from the company. From what Millicent says, the lieutenant in charge probably wasn't sorry to see him go." Pierce could see that Helena was looking a little pale. He turned to Truscott.

"Take them back, Walter. I need to go down to the river."

His cousin shook his head. "Not you. I'll take a couple of men and search the river's edge." Truscott clapped Pierce on the shoulder and motioned with his head toward Portia. "Forget about these cliffs and go to her. That's where the future lies."

Chapter 28

A bright August sun was shining in a pale, blue sky as the early crowds began to gather by the steps of the small stone kirk in the village. All were dressed in their finest clothes, and the sound of pipes filled the air. At Baronsford, the rooms had been decorated and the entire household seemed to be holding its breath in anticipation. For the wedding celebration that would follow the ceremony, a thousand daisies and roses had been gathered and arranged throughout the castle, and the smells of meat and cakes wafted from the kitchens.

Lady Primrose had returned from Edinburgh. The Dowager Countess Aytoun arrived the week before the wedding, as well, accompanied by her companion Ohenewaa and Sir Richard Maitland, the family lawyer. Family and friends had been flocking to Baronsford, filling the castle's rooms and adding to the festive atmosphere. There were even a few unexpected guests—members of Bonnie Prince Charlie's tight-knit community of followers among the Scottish aristocracy—who wanted to see Portia and pay their respects.

Three days before the wedding, a courier had arrived bearing gifts from an unnamed admirer who, Lady Primrose said, was quite unhappy that he was unable to attend. For the groom, there was a gold snuffbox encrusted with diamonds. There were whispers that the value of the gift easily exceeded ten thousand pounds.

For the bride, there were two items. The first was the outlawed Stewart tartan, to be worn like a sash over her wedding dress. The second was a gold chain bearing an intricately jeweled locket. In it, Portia found the side by side miniatures of two lovers. She cried as she stared at the likenesses of Helena and Charles as they had once been.

Portia had just donned the gifts over her wedding gown when Helena came to fetch her. Through the open window, she could hear the entourage that would escort her to the church gathering in the courtyard.

"I am sorry that you were robbed of this happiness," Portia said softly to her mother, showing her the keepsake.

"Nonsense." Helena smiled and placed a soft kiss on her daughter's brow. "I've been robbed of nothing. I've found my child again. Today brings me more happiness than I could have ever dreamed possible. No, my angel, I shall never again dwell in the past. Now and tomorrow are all we shall live for."

The light blue gown fit Helena to perfection. The fashionable arrangement of her powdered golden hair made her look much younger. But Portia also saw in her mother's face a deep sense of well-being that made Helena glow.

"I understand you sent a letter to Boston with Lord Aytoun's."

Helena could not hide her smile. "Indeed I did, my own. I had a few things to convey to your grandfather."

After Turner's death, Lord Aytoun had sent off a number of letters concerning the incident. One of them had gone to Admiral Middleton, apprising him of the erratic behavior of his officer prior to the accident that claimed the man's life.

"I wanted to let him know about your upcoming marriage to Pierce." The pleased smile spread even wider, lighting up her face. "And I told him that if he wanted to preserve his precious reputation, he would need to

make the necessary announcement of your nuptials in every newspaper from London to Edinburgh . . . and to make the same declaration in Boston, where you are to be acknowledged as his granddaughter."

Portia clutched the locket. "That will not be easy for him."

"Perhaps, but it means a great deal to me." Helena took her daughter's hand. "In acknowledging you, he relinquishes his hold over me. I can remain here in England . . . where I wish to be for now. And if I decide to go back to the colonies, I shall do so because 'tis what I choose."

Portia embraced her mother. The letter was a declaration of Helena's independence. She could only imagine the threats that must had been woven into the text. And this was perfectly fine with Portia. The threat of exposure had caused her mother to live in captivity for too many years. The same threat would now be the hammer to break those chains forever.

A soft knock on the door drew them apart. Everyone was waiting for them.

" 'Tis time," Helena whispered wiping the tears off Portia's cheeks. "Your future awaits, my love."

To the hauntingly beautiful music of the bagpipes, Portia was led from Baronsford to the tiny church in the village. Around her, little girls dressed all in white danced gaily the entire way, waving their ribbons in the dazzling sunlight. Her mother held her hand and smiled happily as they walked. The village itself had been decked out with garlands of flowers and banners flying at every window.

As Portia was escorted through the festive crowd, she considered the loneliness that had been her constant companion just a few months earlier. She thought of all the trouble she had caused Pierce in the pursuit of rescuing her mother. And all along, she had never dared to

think that he would become the center of her dreams—her very own prince.

At the sight of the large crowd gathered outside the church, Portia's throat grew tight with emotion. By the church door, she saw the Lord and Lady Aytoun, the dowager countess, and all the faces that had become so dear to her over this past month. She was no longer alone. She now had a family.

Portia's gaze fell on Pierce as he stepped from the church. After that, she saw no one else.

From now on, the two of them would form a new family, and their dreams would belong to both of them. It was already happening, for Portia knew she was expecting. It had not required much discussion to decide that they would remain in Scotland until next spring when their own child would be born.

After that, Pierce dreamed of all of them going back to America. Together, they would raise their new family in what he believed would be a better land. And this was Portia's dream, too, for she had been there and felt the stirrings of freedom.

Helena stopped her, kissing both of her daughter's cheeks and sighing contentedly. Portia turned to her future husband, and Pierce's loving gaze warmed her as he took her hand.

"I feel like a thief," she whispered to him as they walked down the aisle of the kirk. "Not in a thousand dreams would I have imagined a moment like this."

"You *are* a thief, my love." He entwined their fingers affectionately. "You've stolen my heart."

Authors' Note

We hope you enjoyed this second book in our Scottish Dreams trilogy. In *Borrowed Dreams,* you met Lyon and Millicent and had a brief introduction to Emma's murder. In the final book of the trilogy, the youngest brother David will return to Baronsford against his will. There, he will face the mystery of Emma's murder, which has yet to be solved. In this next book, you will also follow the lives of Walter Truscott, the close cousin of the brothers, and Violet, the young woman who disappeared from Melbury Hall at the end of *Borrowed Dreams.*

As with all of our novels, in this book we have tried to bring a little history to life. The burning of the *Gaspee* was an actual event that took place pretty much as we portrayed it in the book. We also tried to capture a little of the historical flavor of Boston in those rebellious 1770s. And across the Atlantic, Lady Primrose's "orphanage" for the children of Jacobite exiles can still be seen in the Welsh village of Wrexham.

Portia Edwards, however, is a figment of our overactive imaginations, though she is certainly representative of a number of children produced by the ever romantic Bonnie Prince Charlie. For those purists out there, however, please forgive our use of poetic license.

As always, we love to hear from our readers.

May McGoldrick
P.O. Box 665
Watertown, CT 06795

McGoldMay@aol.com
www.MayMcGoldrick.com

Read on for a preview
of May McGoldrick's

Dreams of Destiny

Coming from Signet in June 2004

Baronsford, Scotland
August 1771

The cold breezes of the spring morning brushed across his naked shoulder where the blanket had slipped down. Still more asleep than awake, he snuggled closer to the warm back that had fit itself to the contours of his abdomen.

He was not entirely conscious of the leg that was lying between his own, nor of his own arms that had encircled her body. Her head lay on his arm, and her back was pressed against his chest. The shirt that she wore had ridden up, and the skin of her legs lay warmly against his own.

The Highlander's hand was resting on her breast, and when he moved, she responded to his tightening embrace by pushing her body even tighter against his.

As she did, his hand brushed lightly across the sensitive—

"Gwyneth Douglas!"

At the sound of the deep voice, Gwyneth started, the tip of her Keswick pencil breaking and skidding across the paper. In her rush to shut the notebook, two letters inside slipped out and fluttered a moment in the air before diving toward the ledge. She jumped to her feet

from the stone bench beside the cliff walk and shoved her writings under one arm, grabbing in panic for the letters before they sailed off the ledge and out over the river Tweed below. The first one proved an easy mark, and she quickly stuffed it deep in the pocket of her skirt. She whirled around and dove for the second, but as she did, Gwyneth was mortified to see the black boot descend upon it. She looked up at the officer's uniform, and her heart leapt.

"David!" she cried and then tried to control her excitement. "I mean, Captain Pennington . . . so you are back in Scotland."

"Could I miss my mother's bloody birthday celebration? But what's meaning of all this formality between two old friends?"

Gwyneth gasped as the tall officer swept her into his embrace and lifted her off the ground, whirling her around. She closed her eyes, her arms wrapping uncontrollably around his neck. For those few seconds, she imagined the gesture was more than just the friendly affection toward a neighbor that he had not seen in over a year. Her head was spinning slightly when he finally put her back down.

"I cannot believe it. You've grown so since I saw you last."

Gwyneth realized she was still holding on to him, her body pressed against his tall and powerful frame. He must have realized the same thing, and her face caught fire when David took her hands from around his neck. He held them, though, as he stepped back to look at her at arm's length.

"Definitely taller. And your hair is more fiery red than I remember. But I'm happy to say those freckles on the bridge of your nose have not disappeared."

Gwyneth freed her hands and took a step back, frowning up into the deep blue eyes that were so dear to her. She had fallen in love with David Pennington the summer she had turned nine years old, the same summer

that she had been left an orphan. The same summer she had been sent to the Borders to live with the family of her uncle, Lord Cavers, in his country house at Greenbrae Hall. The nearest neighbors to the east of Baronsford, she had grown up trailing after her cousin Emma and David through the hills and forests between the two estates.

"I would suggest you keep all your compliments to yourself, Captain, if you cannot think of anything *nice* to say."

"You are even thinner than I remember, too," he continued in the same tone. "Do they feed you nothing at Greenbrae Hall?"

"I am well fed, I assure you." She spotted her notebook lying open at her feet and quickly snatched it up. David picked up the letter he had trapped before with his boot. Gwyneth could see it had been ground into the dirt. She extended her hand toward him. "That is mine, I believe."

He gave it a cursory glance. "This had better not be a love letter from some secret admirer."

" 'Tis no such thing!" She snatched it out of his hand and shoved it into her pocket with the other letter. With her secret safely tucked away again, she felt a bit of confidence return. "But on the slim chance that 'twas a note from some gentleman, I cannot see why you should object, Captain Pennington."

"I believe I have every right to object to a child receiving that kind of attention from some rogue."

"*Child,* did you say?" she cried, trying to sound indignant, but fighting back her smile. "I'll have you know I am seventeen . . . on the verge of turning eighteen. And just because you no longer come around to Baronsford or Greenbrae Hall, that doesn't mean that life has ceased to move ahead. People do age, Captain . . . and mature . . . and make their own lives."

The sun was sinking steadily in the western sky, and Baronsford—its walls and towers a picture of gleaming

gold and shadow—sat majestically high on the hill behind him. David looked like a hero from one of her stories. He stood tall and straight. His jacket of crimson was brilliant in the setting sun, the color set off by the gold trim, the white breeches, and the black boots. He had a face more handsome than any she could ever invent or describe. His hair was so dark it was nearly black, tied back in a long queue with a black ribbon. He studied her closely, and Gwyneth felt her blush return, scorching her skin.

"I can see that a few things have indeed changed." He sat down on the stone bench overlooking the river and pulled her down beside him. "So tell me, my fiery-headed nymph. Who is the scoundrel?"

She laughed and shook her head. "There is no one."

"You cannot fool me." He tugged not so gently on a wayward curl, making her yelp. "There are over a hundred guests milling about Baronsford. At least a dozen lasses your age are gliding arm in arm through the gardens, acting as if they're promenading along the Grand Walk at Vauxhall. Still, you leave all that excitement and come all the way down here to the river. And why? To read some villain's letter."

All Gwyneth could do was to shake her head. Their shoulders bumped together, and he leaned over to look at her. Gwyneth's breath caught in her chest as his blue eyes stared into her.

"Not just reading . . . you were answering him, were you not?" he whispered.

A delicious tingle ran down her spine. Gwyneth wrapped her arms around the notebook, hugging it tightly against her chest. "I was only writing in my journal."

"Oh, of course. That fascinating chronicle of pirates and Highlanders and bloody battles you used to read to me." He looped an arm around Gwyneth's shoulders and smiled into her face. "I'm glad to know you are still

writing your tales. I always thought you had a gift for storytelling."

Hidden in her pocket, the two letters that had nearly fallen down the cliff into the river reaffirmed whatever gift she had, Gwyneth thought. At least, in the opinion of Mr. Thomas Ruddiman of High Street, Edinburgh. The first had been accompanied by twelve pounds. The second, received two months later, had contained fifteen pounds. A momentary lapse made her almost blurt out her news that Mr. Ruddiman planned to print and distribute her long tales in serial form. Gwyneth contained herself, however. She didn't think it would be wise to share any of that with David now—considering the fact that these tales were scandalous enough that the publisher intended to print them anonymously.

"Would you read me what you were writing?"

She bit her lip and shook her had, looking away.

He took hold of her chin and drew her face back to his. "What have you done with my talkative and spirited Gwyneth? The young lass who could not wait to tell me everything she'd dreamed, or read, or written in her notebooks? What is the reason for this sudden shyness?"

Instead of searching for an excuse, she found herself studying every feature of David's face. His eyes a shade of blue that she'd never been able to describe in her stories. His lashes were dark and long, curling slightly at the tips. He had changed much this past year, too. There was a weariness about him, creases at the corners of the eyes and a furrow in his brow that Gwyneth had not seen when he had stopped at Greenbrae Hall for a single afternoon thirteen months ago. David was no longer the tireless young man who rode between the two estates with Emma beside him.

The thought made her shiver and tear her gaze away from his face. Her cousin was the one David had always loved.

Gwyneth knew the blade had cut deep when Emma

married David's oldest brother two summers ago to become the Countess of Aytoun. That was when he'd begun to stay away from Baronsford for long stretches of time—just like a tragic hero in her stories.

"Well, 'tis all the same to me," he said breaking into her thoughts. "We can just sit here and enjoy the—"

"So this is where you have been hiding!"

Gwyneth's chin sank at the sound of Emma's voice coming down the hill behind them. David's hands dropped away, and she carefully hid the notebook beneath her skirt on the bench. When he stood to greet the other woman, Gwyneth turned slightly to look at her.

The world around them suddenly paled at the appearance of Emma. The sun spread only its most radiant light on her. The breeze seemed to sweep the grasses clean for Emma's feet. Her golden curls, stylishly arranged, shone in the afternoon sun. Her white and gold brocade dress fit her slim body to perfection, and the low neckline was perfect for drawing a man's attention. Her skin was flawless. Her lips were red and turned up in corners. She looked as regal as a young queen, more beautiful than the moon and stars—and she knew it.

And now, Emma's blue eyes were on David.

And his face . . .

Gwyneth's heart ached as she noted the pain in his expression. He watched her every step. His gaze paid homage to her, from the tips of her silk slippers up to the feathers adorning her hair. She watched, though, as one large hand fisted once and opened. He did not walk toward her, but stood waiting for her. Always waiting.

One did not have to be an expert in knowing people to recognize that he still loved her, and how tormented he was by her. Gwyneth turned her gaze back to the cliffs and the river below, unable to bear witness to his pain.

"I am very disappointed with you, David Pennington. I had to hear the news from that old dragon Mrs. MacAlister, that you had arrived. Why did you not come looking for me?"

Gwyneth guessed her cousin was only a dozen paces from the bench. She grabbed her notebook and rose to her feet, deciding to walk quietly away, giving them the privacy they sought. David's hand on her arm made her look up, surprised. He wanted her to stay.

"I thought I would come see this one first. I cannot believe she's had another birthday while I was gone."

Gwyneth had no option but to remain where she was, and Emma's gaze never wavered from David. She swept up against him, pressing a kiss to his cheek. Gwyneth noticed that he did not return the kiss as he quickly backed away a step. The obvious reserve in him brought a tint of red to Emma's cheeks. Her eyes turned hard when they flicked toward Gwyneth.

"Oh, indeed. Our little heiress. Always buried in her books and never having time to pay attention to how she looks or to the displays she makes of herself. And never a thought about the fortune she has coming to her. Mother keeps telling her that in another year, every wolf from London to Edinburgh will be knocking at the gate at Greenbrae Hall, hoping to steal her away."

As was her habit, Emma shifted her attention to another topic without taking a breath.

"But didn't Augusta tell you that there would be many distinguished guests here at Baronsford for my party? I hope you are not planning to dine in that dress."

"I am not staying for dinner," Gwyneth replied quietly. "Nor staying for the party."

"Oh, nonsense. Your scribbling can wait," Emma scolded. With a pretty shake of her head, she cast aside her annoyance. "I have gone to a great deal of difficulty making the arrangements for this party, and I shall not allow you to miss a moment of it. You might surprise yourself and actually have fun."

Emma looped an arm through Gwyneth's, and the other through David's, turning them back up toward the house.

"Come, you two, you cannot hide yourselves away

down here. I shall have Truscott arrange to have Augusta's carriage take Gwyneth over to Greenbrae Hall and wait until you change into something appropriate. Wear that deep green gown I helped you pick in London last month, the one with the satin sash. The color matches your eyes. Also, bring back the yellow dress for tomorrow."

"I really do not think—"

"Do not argue," Emma ordered as they continued on across the fields toward Baronsford. "But if you must have a reason to come, then think of it as doing me a favor. I know that if you are not here, Augusta is going to fret over you, never mind threatening to leave every time she loses a hand at whist."

At the age of fifteen, Gwyneth had lost yet another person she cared for, her Uncle Charles. Since then, she had been under the direct control of his wife. At the time, Emma had just married Lyon Pennington, and Lady Cavers had been quite amenable to Gwyneth's remaining her companion until she married and came into her inheritance.

Having Emma marry well—which meant finding a husband with a fine income and a title besides—had been a priority in Augusta's life. She saw it as a reflection on herself, and she made it known to them both on many occasions. Gwyneth always sensed, though, that there were storm clouds ahead, for in her own mind she believed that Emma was destined for David, and Augusta would never allow her daughter to marry any third son, no matter what his income might be.

When Emma had married Lyon instead, and had become the Countess of Aytoun, Augusta had fairly crowed at her success, and Gwyneth had won a couple of years reprieve. This year, however, the subject of marriage was becoming a continuous source of contention between her and her aunt. Augusta wanted to place her on an a marital auction block and take offers from potential suitors before the young woman had even experienced her first

Season in London. Gwyneth rebelled at the mere idea of it.

She was happy with her life as it was. She cherished her writing. Without anyone knowing, she was even beginning to draw a modest income from it. She had no need for a husband in her life. Like the heroines in the novels she wrote, there was only one man in Gwyneth's life—one love.

Emma let go of her, but Gwyneth noticed how her cousin's arm remained linked with David's. The three of them continued to walk up the long hill toward the house. Emma was telling some story about entering their townhouse on Hanover Square in London last month, only to be told that her husband Lyon had left that same morning, even though he had been informed that she would be arriving.

Gwyneth took a step away from them, not wishing to hear any of this. Complaining about her marriage to anyone who would listen had become a favorite game for Emma. They were coming up to the formal terrace gardens, where numerous guests were enjoying the late afternoon sun.

David broke in on Emma's story. "You know very well that one quality . . . or flaw . . . that Lyon and Pierce and I all share is our fondness for routines."

As Gwyneth began to veer off toward the gardens, David came around and took her by the arm, keeping her with them.

"After two years of marriage, Emma, you should be an expert at knowing how long my brother likes to stay in London or at Baronsford, and when he likes to travel."

"Indeed I do know, all too well, about his precious routines and schedules. But what I am finding out is that he is even changing those to avoid me." Emma lowered her voice. "This might sound ridiculous, but 'tis the truth. I need to make an appointment through his manservant Gibbs to have a private moment with him."

"I am certain if you really needed to see Lyon, he would be available. You are making too much of a single incident."

"I am not," she said dramatically. "I haven't even told you about his outbursts of temper."

"Lyon's temper has always been foul, but we all know how to handle him. He shows a lot of teeth, but he rarely bites."

"That was the brother you once knew. But you have been away so much." She took David's other arm, leaning against him as they walked. "Lyon has changed. There is not a month that goes by that I do not hear of some duel he's fought with some unsuspecting victim. He cannot control his temper. He overreacts to any innuendo or gossip, with no regard to how false it might be. He listens to no reasonable explanations—especially if they come from me. I am starting to fear for his safety, David . . . and for my own."

Gwyneth wanted to shut her ears. She didn't want to hear this drivel. Several times in the past two years, she'd been forced to overhear arguments between Lyon and Emma. Each time, she'd heard the provocation that generally involved the rumor of some indiscretion . . . or worse . . . that Emma had committed. She'd heard her cousin lie openly, too, all the while pushing Lyon as far as she could. No matter how explosive their arguments had been, though, Lyon had stormed off each time. She'd never thought to fear for Emma's safety.

"I do not know what is happening to us—to our marriage." Emma continued in a whisper. "More than ever before, I need your support now. I need you to intervene on my behalf and make Lyon realize the error of his ways."

"I cannot," David said, his voice thick. "This is something between the two of you, Emma."

"Not anymore. I cannot go on alone . . . feeling so helpless." She slowed down. "With you away, I have

taken only a few of my troubles to Pierce. But he already wearies of it all. He is tired of fighting with Lyon. You are my last hope, David. If you will not help me, I do not know where I can turn. I am desperate."

Gwyneth pulled her arm free and stepped back. David turned to her. Emma stopped, too.

"I shall go and find Walter Truscott." Gwyneth turned and fled toward the stables before David could say another word. She could not listen to one more lie.

She and Emma were almost six years apart. Coming to Greenbrae Hall as a child, Gwyneth had doted on Emma. She had followed her cousin, admired her beauty, her spirit, tried to imitate the older girl as much as her age had permitted. The fact that they both carried a torch for the same young man couldn't even diminish how much she idolized her cousin. Emma was the heroine in every romantic story she read. She was the model for every tale she weaved in her imagination. There was more to her than physical beauty. Emma was outrageous, daring, exciting. No man could resist her allure.

At the stables, Gwyneth asked a groom for a horse. One was brought to her, and in a few moments she was racing toward Greenbrae Hall. Even the feel of the wind in her face and hair couldn't cool her anger. It was like a fever burning inside of her.

The first blow to Gwyneth's adoration came when Emma openly shifted her attentions to David's oldest brother, Lyon. Their father had recently died, and Lyon had become the fourth Earl of Aytoun. He had returned to Baronsford after his years of military service. It did not matter to Emma that ten years separated them—that for all the years of growing up, David was the one who she had been closest to. Once she made up her mind to marry the earl, Lyon had no change. They were wed that same summer.

The temple of devotion Gwyneth had built around her cousin began to crumble rapidly after that. And her

growing disillusionment had nothing to do with the wrong that Emma had done to David. It was in London that the walls had come crashing down.

Emma's mother always spent the spring in London, and Gwyneth was required to go. It was there that she realized the dangerous extent of the games Emma was playing with her marriage. The constant arguments with Lyon were a very small part of it. A side of Emma she'd never really seen emerged. Vanity, selfishness, cruelty. Emma lied to get her way. She accused others unjustly, and was unkind to many. But what was most shocking, Emma had affairs.

Gwyneth had been stunned when she'd walked in on her cousin and a strange man in Lady Cavers's town-house in London. She had left behind her notebook after writing a letter that morning in the library. It was early in the afternoon when Gwyneth returned to fetch it. She'd hurried into the room, hardly suspecting that anyone would be inside. She could still see them so vividly . . . Emma straddling the man as he sat on a sofa. His breeches were down around his ankles, and her skirts were up around her hips. His mouth was suckling one exposed breast, and she was writhing on his lap and making noises Gwyneth had never heard. Neither of them had even noticed her presence, and she'd fled.

Later, Gwyneth had confronted Emma about it. At first, she had just laughed. Then, she had threatened Gwyneth to keep her secret. She had little choice. Who was she go to? How could she stop her from such brazen infidelity? Augusta, still elated over her daughter's advantageous marriage, would hardly be receptive to such a report . . . if she believed Gwyneth at all.

She skirted the wooded deer park along the river. Golden rays from the descending sun looked like streaks of fire across the sky overhead. It was so much easier to live one's life within the pages of a book. To read or to create lives in which passion was shared between a man and a woman who were truly in love . . . where marriage

was forever. Gwyneth was not ashamed of the intimacy she weaved into her tales. Her characters were true to each other. They were honest. They loved each other. Lies and deceit belonged to villains, and they were punished in the end. Goodness and love always triumphed—at least in fiction.

Gwyneth's admiration had vanished, and Emma knew it. But they remained outwardly civil. They even managed to display moments of friendliness for the sake of Augusta and others. Gwyneth decided finally that it was not her place to make a judgment about her cousin's life. As David said, this was between Lyon and Emma.

Still though, she could not stomach it when her cousin played the two younger Pennington brothers against Lyon. Emma was tearing their family apart, but they were at fault, too, Gwyneth realized. Both Pierce and David allowed themselves to be blind when it came to Emma and her lies. As far as they each were concerned, she had no flaws. They trusted her.

She rode up the hill to the stables behind Greenbrae Hall and swung down easily from the panting steed. A groom took the reins from her and she started up the path toward the house. The sound of another rider caused her to look back. It was David. He dismounted and walked up.

"You ride like a madwoman. Did you not hear me calling you?"

She shook her head. "What are you doing here?"

"You left so abruptly, without taking a carriage. I wanted to be sure you were not unwell."

"I am quite well, thank you," she said, unable to mask the sarcasm in her tone. "And you?"

"Quite well. Why shouldn't I be?" Whatever cheerfulness he'd displayed when she saw him first by the cliffs at Baronsford had disappeared. There was a fierceness in his face now.

She shrugged, tucking her notebook under her arm and started up the path.

He fell in step with her. "Why are you acting like this?"

"I don't know what you mean. I was eager to get back to Greenbrae Hall." She did not look at him. "So how did your talk go with Emma?"

"You were there for most of it. She is very glad I am back. She has problems, and she needs help. Lyon is being very difficult. 'Tis nothing new. I promised her that I would talk to him when he arrives." He let out a deep breath. "She has gone through all this work—planning this affair for the dowager. Two hundred guests, half of them already arrived, and he decided to wait until the last moment to make his entrance. I do not understand why he is treating her so badly. She does not deserve this, to my thinking."

Gwyneth hurried up the path. She needed to get away from him. David grabbed her arm, though, and he forced her to stop. She stood looking at the ground, her arms clutching her notebook to her chest.

"What is going on?"

"Nothing! Nothing is going on with me."

"What are you running away from?"

"I am not running away. I just do not care to be at Baronsford right now. That should not be too difficult for you to understand."

"As a matter of fact, I don't understand your behavior at all. But 'tis obvious something is bothering you." His tone became confidential. "Are you in any kind of trouble, Gwyneth?"

She stared at him, trying to keep her composure. She failed.

"I am in no trouble. And no, I was not rushing back here for a secret rendezvous with my lover. And no, I am not carrying anyone's child. Nor I am afraid that time is running out on me and unless I do something drastic, one more secret will be exposed."

"You are speaking nonsense."

"Am I?" she challenged before turning up the path again.

His grip on her arm was hard when he turned her around. "What is this all about? Why these bloody riddles, Gwyneth? You were behaving normally one moment and then, as soon as Emma arrived, you turned into this enigmatic brat. What has she done to you?"

"Nothing." She tried to wrench her arm free. "Let me go."

"Who is having secret rendezvous? Who is carrying a child?"

"Why not ask Emma?" she snapped angrily. "Open your eyes, David. Why do you think she wants all these people around her? Why, suddenly, does she need so many protectors? Try to see your brother's side, as well. He is your own flesh and blood. For once, try to understand his suffering."

David stared at her, obviously shocked by her outburst. But Gwyneth knew it would be no use. He was under Emma's spell. He always had been. His large hands clamped onto her shoulders when she tried to turn away.

"I know, Gwyneth, that you must be going through a difficult time. Lady Cavers has never been much of a mother. Not to Emma, and I'm certain she must be doing even less for you. I'm sure it must be hard to watch Emma get so much attention." He leaned down and looked into her face, speaking to her as if she were a child. "But this does not mean you should be so openly hostile to the one person who's been like a sister to you. 'Tis understandable that you would be jealous of her, but I have never known you to be so disparaging of her. Emma truly cares for you. She does not deserve to be treated like this. Not by you and not by Lyon."

Tears rushed into Gwyneth's eyes. He was blind to it. He didn't want to see the truth.

"I will wait for you to change your dress, and then we

shall go back to Baronsford. Emma never needs to know the things you told me. She—"

"No." She shook her head and stepped back. "I am not going back. Tell them what you wish, but I am not going back."

Gwyneth turned and ran up the path as fast as her legs would take her. The tears turned to sobs, but as she entered the house, she couldn't decide for whom she was shedding them.

Perhaps for herself. She'd been made to sound like a jealous and foolish child for speaking the truth.

Perhaps for Lyon. His wife had churned up his life, making it a bloody mess, turning his own family against him.

Or perhaps she was crying for David, so blinded by love that he was incapable of seeing or hearing the truth.

Perhaps, Gwyneth thought, her tears might even be for Emma. She was a woman who didn't know how to be happy, didn't know what was enough. But how could she shed tears for a woman who didn't even know how miserable her schemes were making those who cared for her? Lyon. Pierce. And most important, David.

No, Gwyneth realized, she could not cry for Emma. Not for the woman she hated.

Not long after sunset, the storm rolled in from the west, and a fierce rain pelted her windows through the night. Gwyneth tossed and turned every time the thunder rolled across the valley, every time the wind buffeted the walls of Greenbrae. A feeling of doom infused her dreams, lying like a shroud over her, suffocating her. She wished she had gone back to Baronsford. She feared being alone. She was horrified by the visions her imagination invoked on nights like this.

Dawn brought an end to the storm, but a light rain continued to fall and the skies remained low and gray and heavy. Gwyneth found no relief in the soft whir of activity that she could hear as the servants readied them-

selves for the day. It was midmorning when she finally forced herself to dress and leave her bedchamber. Coming down the steps, she heard shouts and the sound of horses clattering up to the front door.

At the top of the landing, Gwyneth clutched the banister as the door was thrown open and the steward rushed back in. He looked up at her.

" 'Tis horrible, miss," he cried, wringing his hat in his hands.

"Emma," she whispered, sitting down n the steps.

"Aye, miss. She's . . . she's *dead*! They say Lord Aytoun threw her from the cliffs with his own hands . . . and then went over himself!"

SIGNET
Published by New American Library, a division of
Penguin Group (USA) Inc., 375 Hudson Street,
New York, New York 10014, U.S.A.
Penguin Books Ltd, 80 Strand,
London WC2R 0RL, England
Penguin Books Australia Ltd, 250 Camberwell Road,
Camberwell, Victoria 3124, Australia
Penguin Books Canada Ltd, 10 Alcorn Avenue,
Toronto, Ontario, Canada M4V 3B2
Penguin Books (N.Z.) Ltd, Cnr Rosedale and Airborne Roads,
Albany, Auckland 1310, New Zealand

Penguin Books Ltd, Registered Offices:
80 Strand, London WC2R 0RL, England

First published by Signet, an imprint of New American Library,
a division of Penguin Group (USA) Inc.

First Printing, December 2003
10 9 8 7 6 5 4 3 2 1

PUBLISHER'S NOTE
This is a work of fiction. Names, characters, places, and incidents either are the product of the author's imagination or are used fictitiously, and any resemblance to actual persons, living or dead, business establishments, events, or locales is entirely coincidental.

BOOKS ARE AVAILABLE AT QUANTITY DISCOUNTS WHEN USED TO PROMOTE PRODUCTS OR SERVICES. FOR INFORMATION PLEASE WRITE TO PREMIUM MARKETING DIVISION, PENGUIN GROUP (USA) INC., 375 HUDSON STREET, NEW YORK, NEW YORK 10014.

Captured
Dreams

May McGoldrick

A SIGNET BOOK

Previous books by May McGoldrick

BORROWED DREAMS

THE REBEL
THE PROMISE

Highland Treasure Trilogy
THE FIREBRAND
THE ENCHANTRESS
THE DREAMER

FLAME
THE INTENDED
THE BEAUTY OF THE MIST
HEART OF GOLD
ANGEL OF SKYE
THE THISTLE AND THE ROSE

"No one captu............................ of the
British Isles like May McGoldrick."
—Miranda Jarrett

Praise for *The Promise*

"Filled with warmth and emotion . . . *The Promise* is a
wonderful book for any lover of historical fiction. . . .
Cuddle up in a chair and simply enjoy. . . . Don't miss
it."
—*New York Times* bestselling author Heather Graham

"This vibrant Georgian historical is perfect for readers
who like a nice mix of history and passion." —*Booklist*

"If you like passionate stories about people you can care
deeply about, that take you on an emotional ride, that
tell of battles between good and evil, I promise you will
love *The Promise*." —Romance Reviews Today

"Readers will strike gold with this fabulous historical
romance." —BookBrowser

continued . . .